# THE RISE OF SHEM

Sequel to *Perished: The World That Was*

by R. Frederick Riddle

*Andi Tubbs,*

*R. Frederick Riddle*

PublishAmerica
Baltimore

Softcover 9781462678594
PUBLISHED BY PUBLISHAMERICA, LLLP
www.publishamerica.com
Baltimore

Printed in the United States of America

DEDICATION PAGE
OF
*RISE OF SHEM*

DEDICATED TO
FRANK (RANDY) JENKINS
WHOSE FAITHFULNESS
AS A CHRISTIAN,
UNFAILING FRIENDSHIP,
AND ENTHUSIASTIC FAN
BOTH ENCOURAGED
AND INSPIRED ME.

*R. Frederick Riddle*

*Special Thanks to...*

*My wife, Teresa, who critiqued this book and offered helpful insight and/or observations. I also am grateful for her loving patience and understanding as I spend many hours writing, editing, and preparing my novels for publication. She is the perfect 'help-mate'.*

*I would also like to thank Dr. Neal Weaver, President of Louisiana Baptist University, who praised my first novel about Genesis and who's encouragement was both timely and genuine. I valued the help and advice from Mrs. Sherryl Richey. Her suggestions and insights have been and continue to be invaluable.*

*Most of all I would like to thank God for all that He has done to and through me. Whether it is my salvation, service or scribing, the Lord Jesus has been the source of all blessings. As you read this novel, I pray you will extract not only the pleasure of reading, which is every author's goal, but I pray that you will get specific blessings that God has in store for you. If you desire more information about me or about how you can know the Redeemer (Jesus Christ), go to my website at http://www.rfrederickriddle.com.*

*R. Frederick Riddle*

# PROLOGUE

## THE FLOOD

**2351 BC -** *DAY ONE OF FLOOD* (pop. 8 on Ark)

The rain came suddenly without warning. Except for the stiff winds, there hadn't been the slightest hint of rain before the heavens opened up and the rain poured down in sheets like a waterfall. The winds also increased more than they had ever been in the history of man.

God's promised judgment had fallen upon a sinful world. It began with eruptions that continued unabated and spewed volcanic ash upward, piercing the water vapor encircling the earth. Meanwhile, rivers all over the world overflowed their channels flooding the earth as the cisterns below were broken up.

Noah wasn't certain about the time it started. Although an aura of light enveloped the ship, he couldn't use a sundial. He guessed it was the twelfth hour (6 pm) when the first pelts of rain were heard. Soon the windswept rain forced him to close the remaining shutter.

Ordering the ship inspected for leaks, Noah was pleased when the report came back that there was no leakage. It was also reported that the animals showed no sign of panic, but continued sleeping. God, appearing in a dream, had assured him that henceforth animals would need to hibernate. Noah didn't understand what hibernation meant, but he trusted God's Word and left it in His hands.

People stopped what they were doing and, looking to the dark sky, held up their hands in joy. Their spirits were high, immorality higher.

Outside of the Ark the mockers grew in number. Several hundred men, women and children surrounded the silent vessel singing, "This is the flood spoken of by old man Noah and promised by Kar. This is the water of life that shall renew the earth. Shall we run in fear? Shall we hide? No, No, No! We shall drink of this water; we shall celebrate in it joyfully."

Before closing the shutter, Noah saw what was happening. He grimaced in disgust. Neither he nor any member of his family needed to see such wickedness! He closed the shutter; effectively sparing them further pain and grief.

Soon the people around the Ark lost any vestiges of morality they had left. In drunken depravity they continued their sin, rejoicing in the rain. Indeed, instead of fear they welcomed the rain!

&&&

*DAY TWO OF FLOOD*

A few of the revelers in Uruk remembered Noah's prophecy with startling clarity. Many of these men, with their families, now headed toward Noah's Ark. As fear clawed at their chests, they remembered his warnings and urgent pleas for them to join him. With water swirling at their ankles, they loaded their belongings in carts and headed out. The horses were fearful, some refusing to move, thereby forcing their owner to release them and take their place.

The Ark was now bathed in a light, making it stand out for all to see. Inside the Ark, Noah opened the window to look out. His eyes were immediately attracted to Majestic Mountain, which was also bathed in light.

In that light he could make out movement on the mountain's side. *That must be people heading for the supposed safety of the caves. What a tragedy!*

Closing the shutter, he turned to Naamah, his wife.

"The truth of my words has finally become apparent. I could see a long line of people coming from the direction of Uruk. But they are too late. Soon their doom will make itself known to them. And those who once danced and sang will cry for mercy."

"And it will be too late?"

"Yes. Their fate is sealed. God is not a man that He should repent. He gave them 120 years, but they would not listen. Now they suffer the consequences of their own actions."

They descended the ladder and walked back to the Great Hall, a large compartment in the middle of the third floor. Here, in space ample enough to house many of the people of Uruk if they had responded to his pleas, they joined the rest of the family for a light meal.

The rest of the day he spent visiting the various cells. Pausing at the larger cells, he marveled at the sleeping animals. They had not awakened even in the noise of pelting rain. *Hibernate? Sleep? What does sleep have to do with the animals? Surely they already know how to sleep. This is of God. So whether I understand or not, His plan will come to pass. At least the women won't have any difficulty caring for them. And we will certainly have more than enough grain and other foodstuff to take care of the other animals.*

While inspecting the ship, he also observed his family. In one way or another, each was losing loved ones and friends. It was a terrible sense of loss bearing down on them, but each seemed to be handling it well.

&&&

*DAY THREE OF FLOOD*

Noah gathered his family together in the 'hall' where they knelt on the floor, assuming a prostrate position. Noah paused, looking over the small group consisting of his wife, Naamah, his son Japheth and his wife Hagaba, Shem and his wife Achsah, and Ham and his wife Bithiah.

Noah prayed.

"O God, my God. From the beginning of time You have loved us. With great love You created us out of the dust of the earth. Lovingly, You breathed into us the spirit of life and man began walking upon the face of the earth.

"With great care You prepared a garden for Adam and Eve. There they had perfect fellowship with You daily. It was no small thing to bask in Your love. But sin came into the Garden and they fell. For man's sake, they were removed from that Garden, but You never left them. You guided them as they traveled in this world. You watched over them and provided their daily needs.

"Children were born and raised in the nurture of Thy love. Yet Cain slew Abel in hatred and rebellion. Ever since, man has continually shown contempt for Your love and Your will. We have slain Your servants, destroyed Your altars and trampled upon Your worship!

"You warned us of coming judgment. You gave us many opportunities to repent, to turn back to You, but most would not. You directed the building of this Ark so that many people could be saved. You invited all to come in and find refuge in Your love, but the people would not.

"Now, even now, we, the few who obeyed Your call, can hear their screams. The water is rising, the judgment is upon them and now they demand You open the door. But though there be loved members of my family and friends among them, I do not ask for Your mercy. You have been merciful and they mocked You. Even my good friend Hiram, who oversaw the building of this Ark, did not believe You. Instead, he turned to the false god that Jareb, my nephew, serves. A god that pretends to be You, but is not.

"Today they are in the presumed safety of the Majestic Mountains. I do not hate Jareb. He meant well, but never truly turned to You. Now he will die. I do not enjoy this thought, but rather grieve that it must be so. All that I and my family ask is that…"

Something caused him to pause. Opening his eyes he saw standing before him a man. No, an angel!

"Fear not, Noah. I am Gabriel that stands in the presence of God. I am sent to encourage you. God is with you and will see you through the flood."

Noah glanced at his family. In the past, they had never seen the One Who called him by name nor the appearance of any angel. But this time it was different as all eyes were riveted upon the celestial being.

"Is it permitted to know how long this will last?"

"Forty days and forty nights of which two are past and one is now. Be at peace for God is with you."

The angel disappeared.

"O God, I accept Your word," Noah resumed. "We are in Your care. I pray that we will trust You always and never depart from obeying and serving You."

Overcome with grief, he fell silent.

&&&

DAY THIRTY-ONE OF FLOOD

The sudden movement caught everyone by surprise even though they had been expecting it. But the surprise was not due to the sudden movement itself, but by its' lack of violence. The Ark was free!

But that gentle shudder lasted only a moment. Immediately afterward the ship seemed to buck as a wave caught it and lifted the bow upwards. Noah wondered if the ship was going to capsize.

"Hold on everyone," he hollered.

That command was unnecessary, as everyone was already gripping the window frame tightly. As the bow pointed skyward, rain entered the window drenching everyone. Then the ship suddenly righted itself.

Still holding firmly to the window, Noah reached over and took Naamah's hand. She smiled at him and took Shem's hand. Each one followed suit until all were linked together. Noah bowed his head and prayed.

"O God, thank You for Your great salvation. Today, we witness a great miracle. It saddens me that so many must die. But they chose death over You.

"My Lord, my heart goes out to those poor souls who have trusted in a mountain for their salvation. They are doomed, as is the man who led them there. I love Jareb. But he never truly loved or trusted You. I know that death awaits him and all who followed him. I want to pray for mercy, but I cannot."

He paused again, looking out. The man had disappeared inside. All he could see were the poor souls struggling up the mountainside, not knowing they were doomed.

"Dear Lord," he continued, "we thank You for Your protection. We commit ourselves into Your hands. Amen."

&&&

*DAY FORTY OF FLOOD*

Noah awoke.

Quietly getting up and leaving his bed, he climbed to the viewing deck and opened the shutter enough to see out. Even so, he was immediately drenched. Looking out he found an eerie scene. All around was water, but in the midst of it all was Majestic Mountain, its peak still above the water. All about it was light though not the same light as before. That light was gone and now a light shone upon it as though God Himself was holding the lamp.

In that moment the mountain exploded. It seemed to leap into the air and fall back into the seas. Then it was gone. *It is over!* He closed the window and bowed his head in grief. Slowly he returned to his bed, mildly surprised that the explosion had not awakened anyone, although he realized instantly that the storm's noise had drowned the explosion.

Kneeling beside his bed, Noah whispered a prayer.

"Dear God. It is over. Jareb is gone. Too late he found the futility of his caverns. O, I wonder if I could have done more?"

For a moment, his grief overcame his thoughts and he just listened to the raging storm outside. He could tell by the ship's motion that the waters were not quite as violent as before.

He lay down and closed his eyes.

&&&

Later that night, Shem arose and slipped out of bed. Like Noah, he had a separate room for study, prayer, and writing. Each one of the sons maintained records, although Shem's were now considered the primary family record.

He sat down at the table and began etching on a tablet. He had been writing for several minutes when he paused, picked up a fresh tablet and began writing more.

"…and it came to pass after seven days, that the waters of the flood were upon the earth. In the six hundredth year of Noah's life, in the second month, the seventeenth day of the month, the same day were all the fountains of the great deep broken up, and the windows of heaven were opened."

He stared at what he had just written. *Fountains of the great deep? Windows of heaven? This cannot be right. I had better cross it out and rewrite it.*

He reached for a tool to scrape the tablet clean.

*Leave it be.*

Shem looked around. He was alone.

He took the tablet and prepared to remove the etchings.

*Leave it be! It is not for you to know.*

Shem nodded in understanding. His father had told him that God often spoke in the quiet of his mind. But Shem was surprised that God had spoken to him.

"Why have you chosen me to write this and not father?"

*I choose whom I choose.*

The young man sighed, reread his journal and stored it away. For the first time he noticed that the storm outside had quieted and the ship was gently rocking. Returning to his chamber, he lay down and went to sleep.

&&&

*DAY FORTY-ONE*
*Noah!*

Noah awoke with a start. He sat up and rubbed the sleep from his eyes.

*Noah!*

He looked up in recognition. Slipping to the floor and laying prostrate, he answered.

"Yes, Lord. I am here."

*Open the window. The rain has ceased.*

Noah got up and hurried to the viewing deck. Opening the shutter, he looked out.

Sunlight streamed into the Ark. But more amazing was the calmer sea, now barren of rotting bodies. Suddenly he couldn't contain himself.

"Shem! Japheth! Ham!" he shouted. "Open the shutters! Let the sunlight in!"

Awakened by the shouting, Naamah soon joined him.

"The Lord is good, Naamah. He kept His promise! The storm is over."

"What about Jareb and his mountain?"

"The mountain blew apart during the night. I actually saw it happen, Naamah. It was perhaps the saddest moment of my life. Jareb was so close to the truth, yet never accepted it. He led a whole multitude to their deaths."

"Will you write Jareb's story so that people will see the danger of not listening to God?"

"Yes. While Shem has been busy with writing the family record of these days, I have written down all about Methuselah, Lamech, and Jareb. I have even chronicled the building of the Ark under Hiram."

"Will man ever again face judgment?"

"I hope not! But God has not promised me that; in fact, Enoch prophesied another judgment, and man's record is not too encouraging."

"But," Naamah continued, her face full of confusion, "if man has your records to read and remember, surely he would not tempt God again?"

"I do not know the future, Naamah. But I know men. They may have all the knowledge this Ark contains and still they would be prone to sin. I only know this: God is merciful and slow to anger. He will preserve His Word and provide a Redeemer. That is our hope, Naamah and the hope of mankind!"

# ONE

## ON THE ARK

2350BC (pop. 8)

Beneath the raging seas the world was changing. Where once a single continent contained all of civilization, it was now being ripped apart to eventually become seven continents. The earth shuddered from these catastrophic events unseen by human eye.

On day forty one, Noah and his family had seen a calm sea, but that had changed with a suddenness that was both unexpected and violent! Like a man shivering from the cold the entire earth trembled. Entire mountain ranges had disappeared below the seas, while being replaced elsewhere with new mountain ranges. But all this was under the turbulent seas, not to be seen until the waters receded.

The storm passed, but the turbulent seas continued to roil though not quite as much. The entire globe was still covered with water. Looking out the window, Noah and his family could see what remained of the former civilization, that had existed for hundreds of years, now floating on the surface. Still much more was buried beneath the sea.

The bright sun, shining unimpeded upon the ocean surface, revealed this terrible destruction and judgment of God. The sight caused such tremendous grief that he ordered the shutters closed once again.

The Ark, having been subject to the powerful forces of nature, had completely survived. Its critics, now dead, would have been astonished with its sea worthiness. It would be another 4000 years before ships of comparable size traveled the ocean.

As the cataclysmic events under the sea continued, the ocean currents reacted with violence causing the Ark to ride the waves much as a man rides a raging bull. The ship was lifted up upon giant waves, only to be dropped with a sickening drop into a deep valley.

Soon afterward another wave would lift the ship, which strained and groaned against such mistreatment. But it held together.

Inside, the human passengers found life on board to be terrifying and sickening. Although the ocean seemed gentle in comparison to the initial violence of the Flood, the ship was still like a cork upon the sea. Every one of them experienced the ship's twisting movements. It seems that with each rise and fall, not to mention the rolling from side to side, their stomachs had an equally severe churning with bile rising to their throats. It drove them to their knees, sometimes ending with violent and terrifying heaves. Unfortunately, after awhile, there was no more food to throw up since no one had the strength to go down to the storage cells and bring more food up or to go to the "garden." The mere thought of food made them feel worse.

Thus, began their first experience with dry heaves. Color left their cheeks, sweat bathed their faces, and they felt weak all over. During those first few days upon the angry sea, they felt this nausea repeatedly. It was the kind of sickness that the sea can cause for even the most experienced seafarers.

But, fortunately, this lasted only for a few days. Except for Hagaba, everyone's stomach settled down and they began to eat once again. The three women would go each morning to the "garden" and gather vegetables.

This "garden" existed because of the command of God ("and take thou unto thee of all food that is eaten") and the insistence of Naamah. Hiram had built the framework, Noah had filled it with fertile loam and planted small shrubs, and the sons had tilled it. All in the stern of the ship. Now it was the ladies work to reap the harvest.

Hagaba finally did eat and ceased to have the dry heaves, but she still had trouble keeping the food down. However, the rest of them showed definite signs of improvement as they began to get their sea legs.

Even so, the rough seas made it difficult to take care of the animals, most of which had slept through the storm. Although some turbulence would continue throughout the Flood, it did show signs of lessening with the gigantic waves shrinking and the violence easing.

Meanwhile, the Ark bobbed upon the still powerful currents, but not with the former violence. Still, the ship protested the violence and creaked with each twisting turn. Moreover, its constant rocking from side to side forced the family to grab any post or permanently secured structure to keep from falling.

This constant lurching caused them to stagger about like drunken men. But in the midst of this violence came laughter as one or another would sometimes end up in hilarious positions. Even so, it was with great relief that the turbulence finally settled down and everything returned to a semblance of order.

As the ship continued moving toward an unknown destination, a sense of peace crept over the family. These eight humans found a renewed sense of calmness and faith, although the recent turbulence had proved too much for Japheth's wife Hagaba. She now lay sick upon her bed with Achsah, Shem's wife, spending time comforting and cleaning up after her.

Achsah searched for and found a clean bucket, which she placed beside her sister-in-law's bed. Hagaba lay there, her face dotted with drops of sweat and Achsah, sitting in a chair next to the bed, gently took Hagaba's hand.

"Just lean over and throw up into it," she instructed, trying to maintain a cheerful tone.

Tired and depressed by the overpowering smell, she eventually left Hagaba and found her husband in his private chamber recording the day's events in the Writings. She softly knocked on the bulwark just outside his "writing" room.

"Yes, Achsah. Is something wrong?"

"No, my lord. I am just weary. Will you be much longer?

"I don't think so. By the way, how is Hagaba doing?"

"She's feeling a little better," responded Achsah. "As long as she lays down, her stomach seems to be fine."

"It sounds like what the sailors used to call sea sickness," suggested Shem. "I've heard many stories of how that sickness felled even the strongest of men. That's why so few entered that life and fewer yet that stayed in it."

"Perhaps. I should probably get back to her."

Shem quietly stood and walked over to his wife, placing his hands upon her shoulders. Gently, his lips brushed her forehead.

"Achsah, you are a blessing to father and mother. I heard Naamah tell father that she didn't know what she would do without your strength. I am very proud of you."

She smiled sheepishly.

"Thanks. I guess I was feeling unappreciated."

"Don't do that," he responded. "You and mother are the glue that holds this family together. But don't tell anyone I said that."

She laughed as she embraced him. He tilted her head and kissed her on the nose before his lips finally locked onto hers. For several moments, the two lingered in this embrace.

&&&

During the night, Achsah slipped out of bed, put on her robe, and headed down the ramps to the first deck. Stopping by the lions cage, she watched as the lion and his mate slept peacefully. *Such peace in the midst of a storm. Dear Lord, grant us such peace in our spirits.*

Resuming her walk, she headed aft to a small storage chamber. Occasionally she would stop and watch as the large animals slept. It didn't matter whether it was a lion, an elephant, a giraffe, or any other large animal. They were all asleep.

"Noah says you are hibernating. I don't know what that really means other than you are asleep, but he says that is what God calls it."

Continuing on, she finally reached the stern of the ship. Before her was a small enclosure that the men had set aside for storage. Parting the simple curtain that acted as a door, she entered. Carefully setting her lamp down, she looked around. From floor to ceiling were stacks of food and provender for the animals. Stepping into the middle of the room, she knelt and prostrated herself.

"Dear Father God," she whispered, "I wish I had the faith of my husband or of Noah, but You know I am afraid. Hagaba is sick, Naamah doesn't feel well, and while Bithiah is fine, she looks to me for leadership.

"Dear God, I feel so inadequate. I will do whatever You want, but I need Your constant presence."

She paused a moment before adding "amen." Then she lay there listening, hearing only her heart beat.

Suddenly she felt a hand upon her shoulder. Startled, she looked up, expecting to see Shem's or Noah's face, surprised they had found her so quickly. Instead, she found herself looking into the face of an angel!

"Fear not, Achsah. Your righteousness is known of God and He, the Almighty, has sent me, Gabriel, in response to your prayer. He loves you and will strengthen and guide you throughout your life. Indeed, others shall look to you for leadership, and Your God shall supply all your need. Only be thou faithful and not doubting."

Tears flowing from her eyes, she looked at the angel.

"But what does God want of me?"

"He desires your heart and mind. Give yourself to Him and let Him take care of your fears. He has called you to be a strength to others. You shall know heart-ache, but He shall sustain and guide you.

"God is preparing your husband to serve Him. If he is faithful, he will live a long life and shall be a blessing to others. But he will need you by his side. Be strong and of good cheer; support your husband in all that he does."

"I do; I will," she said with rising conviction.

Just as suddenly as he had appeared, the angel was gone. Achsah got up, feeling a strength and a confidence she had not previously known.

&&&

A few days later, Hagaba recovered. Although weak from her agonizing sickness, she tried to get up and return to work. But she was thwarted as everyone insisted she take it easy for a couple more days. Reluctantly, she gave in.

Everything soon returned to normal; at least as normal as shipboard life can be. It soon became apparent that Achsah had become Naamah's most reliable helper. The two women were often seen together, while Hagaba and Bithiah usually worked alone. Achsah enjoyed listening to Naamah's conversation and her stories about the ancient world.

The two women were responsible for the care and feeding of the animals in the bow of the ship. Actually, Naamah was responsible for the most forward area of the bottom deck, while Achsah took care of the deck above. For years they had shared duties around Noah's Vineyard, so it was quite natural for the two of them to work together on the ship.

"The animals are still sleeping," Achsah commented. "It seems so wasteful to throw out their uneaten food."

"Yes," agreed Naamah. "I asked Noah about that and he doesn't want to take any chances of disease. But at least we don't have to put out much. He thinks they will sleep right on through the voyage."

"So we just put out a little?"

"Yes. From now on we will just put out a handful of feed. Noah says he will inform the others."

"How long do you think the voyage will be?" Achsah asked.

"At least one hundred and fifty days. That's what Methuselah wrote. But Noah says it could be longer."

"What do you think it will be like?"

"What?"

"The world. When we finally leave the ship, what will we find?"

"I don't know, Achsah. Nor does Noah. I have asked him and he just says we will have to trust the Lord."

Achsah opened a cage door and gingerly stepped inside. Lying only a few feet away was a sleeping lion and a lioness. She carefully moved closer until only inches away. Pausing, her heart pounding, she watched for any movement. But the two beasts slept on, oblivious to her presence.

Using her broom, she began sweeping the floor, allowing the debris to fall through the slots in the floor, which led directly to the small waste compartment below. Meanwhile, Naamah emptied the food bowls before replenishing them.

Although the work was boring and hard on their backs, the time passed quickly as they talked and reminisced. Sometimes they were interrupted as one of the men would stop by and inspect the ship for leakage. Other times the men would come with buckets and shovels to clean out the waste compartments.

The women were also responsible for preparing foods and washing clothes. In other words, life had returned to normal for the women.

But for the men it wasn't normal at all. All were farmers not used to shipboard life. They couldn't farm land since it was under water, or engage in commerce. Fortunately none were seasick and had quickly developed a degree of "sea legs," at least enough that they could move about the ship confidently.

But Noah, realizing how much out of their element his sons were, decreed that every day he and his sons would explore the ship and check for any leakage. They would descend to the first deck and slowly inspect for any sign of moisture. Whenever they encountered joints from the supporting beams, they would place their hands on the wood, feeling for moisture. This was time consuming, as they would carefully inspect the entire ship.

It was also their responsibility to make sure everything was secure. Like the women, they divided the ship into sections, four to be exact. Each day they would work a section, usually from its forward position and work aft. Because it required painstaking and minute inspections, it took the four men four weeks to do a full inspection. Even when they teamed up, it still took a month. But Noah felt the constant inspections were too important and they continued for several months before he was satisfied with their safety.

Combining waste pickup with inspections proved to be a wise decision. Although hibernating, the animals still managed to relieve themselves. The larger animals would do so every few days, while the smaller ones did so daily. The amazing thing was that some did this without waking up. Those that did wake up would move to a favorite spot, relieve themselves, and return to their straw beds.

Periodically, with bucket and shovel in hand, the men would visit each cell and clean the small compartments beneath the floors. They would then clean out these cells and dump the waste into leather buckets, which would then be carried outside and dumped.

This last chore was difficult, because the only door to the Ark was sealed shut and the window was only 1½ feet high. This meant that one of the men had to slip through the opening, have the small buckets passed through to him, and then dump the waste over the side. Unfortunately for Noah, he was the smallest of the men, so even his position as patriarch didn't prevent him from this unsavory job.

# TWO

## THE OCEAN

2350BC (continued)

Noah quickly found that his slight build had actually provided him with an extraordinary view. Out on the deck, he could see the vastness of the ocean. Looking in any direction he could see the ocean as it met the horizon in the distance. *This is amazing! I thought the Gihon was wide, but there is no land at all. It is like the circle of the earth is nothing but water!*

Fascinated, he stood there watching the waves crashing against the ship. Unlike the first days of the Flood, the waves simply moved the ship forward. Looking over the side, he could see the gentle, but steady movement. *We have no sails or oars, but we are moving. But where to?*

Straightening, he looked out again, but there was no way to tell whether they were heading north, south, east, or west. *Wait! The sun. Which way is it moving. It is on my right and it is still morning. The sun is rising from the east, my right, which means we are heading north, maybe northeast.* He sighed. *But if there is no land, what difference does it make. We can circle the entire planet and not touch land. It is certainly true that we are in Your hands, Lord. Wherever You want to take us is fine with me.*

This breathtaking view caused him to pause every time before going to the side and lowering the buckets by rope to the water. It was during these trips outside that he discovered a new phenomenon: clouds.

Staring up at them, he was fascinated by the many sizes and shapes. Sometimes he saw shapes that looked like a man's head, other times he saw animals. Still other shapes resembled buildings, and, at least once, a ship.

It usually required extra effort to pull his mind back to the task at hand. Dropping a bucket over the side, he would pull on a second rope and dump the waste into the ocean. He would then use the ropes to dip the bucket repeatedly so that the ocean washed it out. Retrieving his bucket, he would lower another loaded bucket and repeat the procedure. He would usually have seven buckets to empty, so the chore took a while.

One advantage of this job quickly became apparent. Many a day he would watch in wonder as pods of whales cavorted before his eyes. It was as if they were putting a show on just for him. He soon discovered that the ocean was full of other mammals and fish.

"God spared much of the creatures of the ocean," he later explained to his family. "I'm sure many died, but many have survived."

"What about the fresh water fish?" Japheth asked.

"I'm no expert, son. But God has assured me that some of them will survive. Something to do with the saltiness of the ocean being diluted by all the fresh rainwater. Then, of course, some fish can adapt.

"One thing I know for sure is that if God can create a world and provide all manner of living organisms, He will have no trouble preserving a few fish."

&&&

One day he saw a school of dolphins, which swam up close to the ship, raised themselves out of the water and then did an amazing thing! They began moving backwards on their tails! Noah watched in mounting glee as they entertained him with their antics. Sometimes they would stay close to the ship and look straight up at him. He found their method of communicating by sounds and whistles, emitting from their blowholes, to be very intriguing.

"They are such intelligent looking creatures," he mused. "It is like they are trying to tell me something."

He sat down on the deck and watched as they played. He was fascinated with how such large mammals (approximately 10 feet long and 500 lbs.) could so easily swim and leap out of the water. He also noticed that these huge, gray mammals had sharp eyesight. After his initial sighting of them, he began carrying food out with him. He would toss the food in the air and they would leap out of the ocean and snare it before it ever touched water.

The most entertaining moments were their frequent playing with each other. He quickly identified one of their favorite games as the Chase. One dolphin would nudge another and a moment later the chase was on. Noah would sit and laugh at the games they played.

Some days they would suddenly vanish, leaving only a wake where they had been only moments before. Looking around, the cause was usually quickly seen as a very different dorsal fin showed up!

"Shark!" he would yell leaping to his feet. In fascination, he would watch as the sharks slowly circled the ship. After a while, they would get bored and swim away.

&&&

His privileged status of watching as the creatures of the sea played turned out to be short lived. About a week after his first excursion outside and on the same day he first saw the dolphins, he re-entered the ship and called everyone to the Great Hall. Once everyone was seated, he spoke.

"Today, when I was dumping the waste, I saw a wonderful sight. I saw dolphins!"

"Dolphins?" The question came from everyone, though not in unison.

"Yes. I've told you before of whales, but these were dolphins. I also saw sharks. I'm telling you this because I want each of you to know that we are not alone. It is true that we are the only humans, but there other creatures other than the animals on board the Ark. There is life out there, and plenty of it!"

"Did you see anything else, father?" asked Japheth.

"Yes. Something entirely new. I call them clouds."

"What's a cloud?" asked Shem.

Noah could see the same question was on everyone's mind.

"It is a strange looking thing in the sky. I spotted several of them today scurrying across the sky. I don't know their purpose or how they are formed, but they are beautiful to watch."

Seeing their still questioning looks, he made a decision.

"You all have questions. So I am going to let you ask me whatever is on your mind. But I may not know the answers. Naamah, you go first."

All eyes now turned toward her.

She cleared her throat before speaking.

"Noah, I've been thinking about us being cooped up in this ship. Speaking as a mother, I have noticed that we are all getting on each others nerves. Unless we do something soon, we won't survive the Ark no matter how well-built it is."

Noah and the rest of the family nodded in agreement.

"What do you propose?" he asked.

"I didn't have any idea at all until just now. Ever since you have been going outside, you have been seeing these dolphins, whales, and sharks. When you are out there and seeing all of that, how does that make you feel?"

"That's easy," he smiled. "First, I am always impressed with God's handiwork. His creation is amazing! But I must confess that it also relaxes me and make me laugh."

"That's what I thought. Is there any way that all of us could go out on the deck and share this experience?"

"Afraid not, mother," responded Japheth. "The window is too small. Only father and you would be able to squeeze through. The rest of us are too big."

"Unless," interrupted Shem.

"Unless what?" demanded Japheth.

"Couldn't we enlarge the window or remove a portion for a door? Then we could all have access to the deck."

"That's a thought," replied Noah. "Let me think on that for awhile and see what we can do."

Everyone agreed and the meeting broke up. Noah went to his study room and entered. Pulling the curtain closed, he knelt upon the floor and sought God's wisdom.

&&&

A few days later, after hours of praying, Noah gave permission to enlarge one of the window openings. He and Shem worked on one of the openings and increased its size three-fold. Afterward, they built steps that they placed inside and outside the opening.

&&&

The ship had been floating on the broad sea for a couple weeks with no land in sight. While on his bucket duty, Noah watched as the currents carried the Ark along. Without rudder, sails, or oars, the ship was completely at the mercy of the sea. Studying the ripples in the water, he had a sudden thought, *These currents can carry us for hundreds of miles and we have no idea where we are going! Yet it is God Who is in control of the ocean. He moves us according to His will and not ours.*

Shaking his head in wonder, he finished cleaning the buckets and headed back inside. As he stepped through the window, he saw Shem standing sheepishly nearby.

"You look a little worried, son," Noah remarked. "What is it?"

Shem hesitated before answering, "Something I don't understand, father."

"Then tell me about it," his father responded as he settled upon the deck and leaned against the bulkhead, stretching his legs out.

Shem took a spot next to his father before speaking. He remained quiet for a short time and then chose his next words carefully.

"It's about God's call to record the events of the Flood. He told me to record everything, including family life."

"You think it should have been me called instead of yourself?"

"There is that, but I was thinking of Japheth. He is the oldest."

"Good point. But God chooses whom He chooses. I perceive that your concern is not so much whether Japheth is chosen or not, but whether you are up to the job. Is that correct?"

Shem shook his head, "God expects me to record all the events and to organized them into logical sections. I can do that."

He paused, sighing.

"But Japheth is the oldest. If you were not around, we would naturally look to him for direction. I know that God wants me to do the recording and I will do it. But it just seems that Japheth being the oldest should have the honor. I don't want him to get upset with me."

"That sounds just like you, son. Always aware of the other person's feelings. But, in this case, your concern is groundless. Japheth is the nearest thing we have to a captain. I'm in charge, but I know nothing of sea travel. Your brother has his hands full seeing that we are kept safe and the ship is kept sea-worthy. Besides, he doesn't like to write."

"You're right, of course. Then you think I need to devote myself to this calling no matter what?"

"Yes, I do. Just obey God and leave the rest up to Him. He doesn't require you to understand His will, but to just obey it. Obey God, even if His will seems unreasonable. He knows what He is doing.

"And don't forget that we'll be on this ship for a long time. Son, God is obviously selecting you for something far greater than simply recording events. I sense He is grooming you for a special purpose. You'll be wise to follow Him faithfully."

"I will, father."

&&&

Shortly after creating the small opening for everyone to go out upon the deck, a new problem arose. Instead of doing their chores as before, both the men and the women began frequenting the deck to watch the dolphins, whales, and whatever other creature might appear. Work and discipline suffered.

The women had discovered an exciting world beckoning them. At first afraid, they soon delighted in the whales, dolphins, and even the sharks. Their squeals of delight brought a smile to Noah's face. But when he noticed their visits outside were increasing in frequency, he became alarmed.

To the sons' consternation, one day Noah told the women they could spend an hour each day together on the deck, while his sons were restricted to once every other day without their wives. A fact that even the women protested.

"My decision stands. Prove to me that you can obey me in this matter and I may reconsider it later," he responded.

In spite of these new restrictions, he noticed that the affect of these excursions continued to lift their spirits. His sons were not happy, but they obeyed. Thereafter, the men took turns dumping the waste and enjoying the antics of the whales and dolphins. In spite of themselves, they found the new arrangement working.

Noah let this arrangement exist for about a month. Satisfied that they could be trusted, he relented and let everyone come out once a month in the evening to enjoy the soft breeze. These evening gatherings soon took on other aspects as the women taught the men several songs from the past. Songs they had forgotten, but which brought joy to their hearts. Many of these songs spoke of the Redeemer. Their voices blended and were carried over the ocean for miles in every direction.

Another aspect of the evening get-together was sundown. They would watch in amazement as the bright sun would sink below the skyline. They had seen such sights on land, but this was different with the sun seeming to dip below the waves.

The unending waves stretching as far as the eye could see presented an eerie beauty all its own. It was during their brief visits to the outer deck that all got an appreciation for the sailor's love of the sea.

&&&

*She's amazing!*

Shem sat on the edge of the bed and watched his wife's bedtime preparations. Though they had been married many years, Achsah still was the most beautiful woman he had ever seen. *And she's definitely the most beautiful woman in the world!*

For a moment his mind went back to their first meeting. Achsah had been only a young teenage girl when she was betrothed to him. Noah had chosen her because her parents were believers, as was she. They had been among the few that had responded to Noah's early preaching. A flashback of their untimely deaths only weeks before the Flood caused a momentary sense of sorrow.

Finally finished, she came over and gently kissed him. He reached up and pulled her down into his embrace. Laying back on the bed, his arms wrapped around her, he gently kissed the top of her head, while she listened to his heartbeat.

"Shem?"

"Yes?"

"Do you think our children will turn out better than the people who perished?"

He shot upright and looked down at her.

"Are you with child?"

Achsah burst out laughing.

"You should see yourself. Are you afraid of children? Of being a father?"

"No. I look forward to many children. But you didn't answer my question. Are you with child?"

"No," she smiled. "We women were just discussing the idea of raising children in the new world. Now that God has judged the people, will we get it right this time?"

He gently caressed her hair and bent over to kiss her nose.

"I pray so, my sweet wife. But father says that we don't have a very good record so far. The only thing I know for sure is that we will do our best to raise our children to praise Him. Ultimately, the choice is theirs, not ours."

Silence settled over the room and he lay back down. Soon there was only the sound of their soft breathing.

# THREE

## LAND!

2350BC (continued)

As the day began, the family gathered in the "Great Room," located in the midsection of the ship. Although originally constructed with numerous cells, they were all torn down by Noah and his sons shortly after the Flood began. Turning the area into one large meeting room, it effectively divided the 3rd deck, separating the forward (Noah and Naomi's living quarters) from the aft (living quarters for the sons and their families). The large table sitting in the middle and rescued from Noah's home before the Flood, served as a dining table as well as a work table.

The women placed bowls of fruit on the table that amazingly were still fresh, a reminder of God's providential promise: "And take thou unto thee of all food that is eaten, and thou shalt gather it to thee; and it shall be for food for thee, and for them." As an added treat, they had prepared small bowls of nuts, which the men loved. The helpings were generous, since whatever was leftover would be taken to the smaller animals not hibernating.

Once finished, the day's tasks began with the women first feeding and later cleaning up after the animals, while the men continued their inspection of the ship. In late afternoon, the men collected the waste and passed the buckets to Noah.

After dumping the waste, Noah finished cleaning the buckets. Strangely, there were no dolphins or sharks around, so he re-entered the ship. Once inside, he pulled his knife out and marked 150 on the wall. He paused, looking over the etched numbers.

*It is the seventh month, the seventeenth day of the month. The Flood has been one hundred and fifty days on the earth! The end will be soon.*

He stooped to pick up the buckets. Suddenly the ship lurched causing Noah to be thrown violently against the bulkhead. He managed to break his fall with his hands, but still the pain was felt throughout. As he lay on the deck, he could feel the whole ship vibrating. He lay still until it settled down.

Rising, he looked around. Everything seemed all right. His first thought was of Naamah, so he rushed for the ladder, but as he was about to descend, he saw Japheth and Shem coming to check on him.

"I'm OK, sons. How are the women?"

"They are fine, father. Ham is with them. What happened?" Japheth asked.

"I think I know," offered Shem when Noah didn't immediately respond.

"What do you think it was?" Noah inquired.

"Well, as you know, God has been directing me to write about the Flood and our journey to a new land. Every night I record the day's events. Well, last night was different. When I finished recording the day's activities, He instructed me to write, 'And the ark rested in the seventh month, on the seventeenth day of the month, upon the mountains of Ararat.' Today's the seventeenth day of the month."

"So we have landed on the top of a mountain range called Ararat," mused Noah.

"What are we to do?" asked Japheth.

"For now, we shall wait," Noah replied.

&&&

"Sons, we need to have a meeting," announced Noah later that day.

A few minutes later the four men sat around the table in the Great Hall. Once they were all settled, Noah reached for a handful of nuts, before speaking.

"With today's landing upon the mountains of Ararat, we can safely assume that in due time we will be disembarking from this ship. We will be finding ourselves in a world that may be markedly different from what we knew. Mountains that we once knew no longer will exist. And new mountains, like these called Ararat, have risen. The rivers, cities, and landmarks of the past will all be gone.

"But that is not all. Since at least the 41$^{st}$ day, we have been moving, driven by the currents. These Ararat Mountains may be hundreds, even thousands of miles from what we called home.

"What this means is that we will find everything different. Perhaps even the climate. And, since we are on the top of a mountain, we will have to find a way to the land below. "Which is why I called this meeting.

"God spoke to me and has said from now on only I will be permitted to step outside and only to dump waste. He wants us to stay inside."

"But why, father?" asked Ham. "After all these months, surely it is safe. We survived the great Flood itself and the periodic storms this past year. Why?"

"God didn't explain that to me. He expects us to obey," he answered with a firm look at Ham. "I suspect that there may be some dangers we are unaware of out there. In any case, we will obey.

"Once we have disembarked and established a temporary home, which may be the Ark or perhaps a mountain cave, you will set about establishing a passable trail to the bottom. We will need a trail wide enough for sleds to safely maneuver. Once you've completed that task, you will return and guide us down. Now, let me hear your ideas on preparing and conducting this task."

For the next three hours the men discussed tools needed, safety procedures, and anything else that they could think of that would govern their trail blazing.

&&&

The very next day a vicious wind storm hit, churning the water in a manner not seen since the Flood began. Imprisoned upon the top of Mt. Ararat, the ship took the full brunt of the angry waves. This was followed by loud thunder, lightning and heavy downpours.

One day they watched as the waves, full of foam, struck the stranded ship so hard that the entire structure shuttered. Everyone grabbed something to steady themselves. The ship groaned much like it did when the Flood waters first lifted it off the dry-dock. But it remained where it had been lodged.

Throughout this latest storm, the waters continued to recede. Slowed by the storm, it still was definitely going down. But it wasn't until the first day of the tenth month that they saw the mountain peaks appearing. The whole family gathered in the Great Hall and celebrated. The women prepared a special meal for the occasion.

The storm ceased. Then day after day for the next 40 days the ocean level continued to decrease with the mountains drying and showing their barren sides. Noah looked in vain for any sign of foliage, but there was none.

On the fortieth day, Noah once again returned from dumping the waste, marked the day '264' on the wall, and prepared to descend the ladder.

"Father, may I make a suggestion?"

He looked down at his middle son, who was climbing toward him.

"What is it, Shem?"

"We have been on this mountain now for forty days. It occurred to me that we could send one of the birds out and see if it is safe to disembark."

Noah thought about that for a moment before responding.

"I am not sure, my son. God told us when to enter and it was God that shut the door and sealed it. Perhaps we should trust Him."

"I do trust Him, father. But doesn't He expect us to be aware? It seems to me that trusting God requires action. Sending forth a bird indicates we believe God's promise and are acting on it."

Noah scratched his jaw. *It certainly makes sense.*

"What bird do you want to send?" he asked.

"One of the ravens. They're pretty smart."

"OK, bring me a raven."

Shem quickly descended, carefully retrieved a raven from its cage, and returned to the platform. Noah took the bird, which sat calmly upon his right hand, and walked out upon the deck. Extending his arm, Noah watched the bird. At first, it just sat there, but after a couple of moments the raven flew away.

For the next six days they watched eagerly for the raven's return, but to no avail. On the seventh day, Noah decided to try again. But this time, he chose a dove.

Watching it fly away, he prayed for its well being and return. Later that day, the dove reappeared with nothing that suggested land, so

Noah decided to wait another week. The following week, day 278, he sent forth the dove once again.

That night the entire family was together for the evening meal when the dove flew through the window and lit upon Noah's shoulder. Noah reacted in such surprise that everyone, including Noah, laughed.

Looking down at the bird, Noah noticed that she was holding an olive leaf in her mouth. He gently removed it and held it up for all to see.

"It is beautiful father," remarked Shem. "Does this mean we are to leave?"

Noah looked around at the hopeful faces. Even Naamah showed her eagerness to disembark.

"Not yet, my son. God will tell us when. We shall wait another week and send the dove out again."

He groaned as he saw the disappointed looks cross their faces.

"I'm sorry, but I have waited on God for six hundred years. I will not change now."

The following week the dove was sent out again, but did not return. This got a "Very soon!" response from Noah when asked when they would leave. By this time, every one was growing antsy and a few times there arose small spats between the humans. But these were quickly settled by the stern, yet gentle authority of Noah.

On the 314th day of the Flood, God spoke to Noah.

"Remove thou the covering so that all may view the dry earth."

Eagerly, Noah and his sons set about removing the roof. It was hard work, but their enthusiasm made it go by quickly. Even the women joined in the work, bringing tools and whatever else the men needed. By nightfall it was finished. But because it was night, they had to wait until the morning.

&&&

On the morning of the 286th day, they all climbed the ladder and, for the first time, viewed their new home. It was both exciting and discouraging at the same time. They all remembered the Majestic Mountains they had left behind. Its beauty far surpassed what they now saw before them. It was, for all appearances, a desolate wilderness. Even the air seemed stiff and cooler than what they had been used to experiencing.

It would be another 57 days before they disembarked.

# FOUR

## NEW BEGINNINGS

2350BC (continued)

"Naamah, they are moving!"

Turning, Naamah looked in the direction Bithiah was pointing, immediately noticing that the elephants were stirring. As she watched, the animals raised their heads, looking at their keepers. One reached out with his trunk to explore his surroundings.

Grinning, Achsah raced up the platform only to return a few moments later carrying a basket. Withdrawing an apple, she threw it through through the bars and it landed near the closest elephant. The elephant's trunk immediately reached out and picked it up. Satisfied with its examination, the elephant placed the apple in its mouth and began eating.

"Ladies, I believe we have work to do. Hibernation has ended!" Naamah declared as the other animals began showing signs of life.

&&&

Noah stepped upon the platform and looked out the window. He paused, etching a mark upon the ship's wall, sighing. *This is the fifty-seventh day since God instructed us to remove the covering. When will it be time to leave this ship?*

He looked back at his family. There was his faithful wife, Naamah, coming up from feeding the animals below. Behind her were his daughters-in-law: Hagaba, Achsah, and Bithiah. Along with his three sons, they numbered a mere eight people.

After such a long time of shipboard life on the seas, Noah and the whole family were anxious to leave the Ark. More than a year ago, they had entered and watched as God closed the door. Now as Noah peered out the window, he found himself wondering what awaited them in this newly cleansed world. *These mountains look rugged and barren. It'll be hard on the women at first, but hopefully we will find a more agreeable place to live soon.*

"Noah!"

He instinctively looked back at his family. But they, like him, knew that Voice. Immediately everyone fell prostrate upon the floor.

"I am listening, my Lord," he responded.

"Go forth of the ark, thou, and thy wife, and thy sons, and son's wives with thee.

"Bring forth with thee every living thing that is with thee, of all flesh, both of fowl, and of cattle, and of every creeping thing that creepeth upon the earth; that they may breed abundantly in the earth, and be fruitful and multiply upon the earth."

Silence returned. Realizing God had finished, Noah stood and issued instructions.

"Japheth! You and your brothers open the door and lower the ramp. Naamah! You and the women get the animals ready. It is time to leave!"

The knowledge that they were finally leaving the ship inspired everyone. Enthusiastically they arose and went about their tasks as Noah watched with an approving eye. Although his assistance wasn't really needed, he stepped up and helped his sons break the seal that God had applied. Holding the ropes firmly, they lowered the ramp until it rested on earth once again.

As their leader, he was the first down the ramp and the first to set foot upon the new verdant earth. He knelt and stretched himself out upon the ground, tears streaming down his face. *Thank You, Lord!*

Rising, he inspected the ramp to make sure it was secure. Once assured, he re-entered the Ark just in time to see Naamah leading the smaller animals (rabbits, mice, and other rodents) to the door. Stepping aside, he watched an amazing scene that would be repeated throughout the day.

The animals stopped at the doorway with noses twitching and their ears attentive, seemingly unsure of themselves. Suddenly, they dashed down the ramp and unto the plateau where they scampered here and there until finally coming to a stop in the middle of the plateau. To Noah's amazement, it seemed like they were waiting for the others to join them.

He heard a noise behind him and looked to see Achsah leading two elephants up the ramp to the door. She stopped, turned, and affectionately patted the male elephant's trunk.

"Time for you to leave," she said as she stepped away.

The elephant's trunk reached toward her, but she smilingly moved aside. Turning his attention toward the doorway and the ramp leading down, he edged forward, his mate following behind.

As Achsah left to get others, Bithiah moved forward, leading two lions. She also paused, caressed the lion's mane, and stepped away. The lion looked sadly at her before turning his attention to the open door. The powerful scent of fresh air seemed to brighten his eyes and energize him. With his mate eagerly following, he raced down the ramp and soon joined the growing circle.

Throughout the day the women led the animals to their freedom. While each animal reacted in his or her own way, they all joined the circle until all were off the ship.

Curious as to what would happen next, Noah and his family watched from the doorway as the circle of animals growled, beeped, roared, and clucked. A small smile played on Noah's face. *It is as if they are saying goodbye to each other.* The very idea brought a chuckle to his lips.

The circle began moving slowly with a line of animals breaking from the circle and heading for a nearby opening that Noah had not previously noticed. Two by two they moved down through that opening until all were gone except the sheep, goats, donkeys, and cattle. When all had left, a very noticeable trail was left behind, a trail that Noah instinctively knew they would follow.

# FIVE

## THE PROMISE

2350BC (continued)

On the following day, Noah arose as the sun peaked over the mountains. Moments later, he was joined by his family eager to get started.

"Before we unload, we need to explore. You ladies stay here and get ready to start unpacking, while we look for a suitable place to live."

"Not so, Noah."

He looked at his wife in surprise.

"What?"

"If you think we are going to stay on board this ship while the four of you have fun, you can think again. You need a woman's view, as well as a man's view, when choosing a place to live. However temporary it may be, it is a place that all of us need to see for ourselves."

"You're right Naamah. We'll explore together. But this is a new world. If any of us men sense any danger, you will be ordered back to the ship. Is that understood?"

"Yes," she replied, confident that no such danger would arise.

The eight of them walked down the ramp and headed for the eastern wall of the mountain. It didn't take long for them to discover two large caves next to one another. Entering the larger one, they found that it had "rooms" off to the sides. Lighting candles, most of which they mounted on nearby ledges, they proceeded deeper.

"This is ideal, father," spoke up Japheth. "We can all live in this cave with our own rooms, while the other cave can be used for supplies."

"I agree," Noah replied as he turned toward Naamah. "What do you ladies think?"

"After more than a year on that ship," laughed Naamah, "it looks wonderful!"

"Let's get started," spoke up Achsah.

"Hold on a moment," ordered Noah. "Why don't you women stay here. We'll unload and bring the furniture, clothing, and the Writings. You can sort them out, but don't do anything with them until we are done.

The men hurried back to the ship to unload. Noah decided to gather the Writings first. He wanted to be very careful with the Writings, which contained the history of all mankind and the dealings of God with His people. He and his sons unwrapped each tablet, examining, re-wrapping, and carrying them off the ship. Some of the tablets had broken during the Flood despite their diligent care. Such losses were tragic, since he could not replace them, therefore, he was determined that no more would be destroyed.

After unloading the Writings, they turned to the furniture, clothing and tablets. These they carefully carried over to the caves, depositing them where the women indicated. By noon, they had completed the unloading of essentials.

"That's it for now. We need to stop and give God thanks for our new home. But before that, we need to build an alter," Noah stated.

With the help of his sons, he gathered large, heavy rocks that required two men to carry them. Not having any mortar available, he instructed his sons to place them side by side and one on top of another as snugly as possible. Using a mental picture of the altar built by Adam at Eden Falls and memorized by Noah, he had the altar built four feet high, two feet wide, and three feet long. When finished, he purposely tried to knock it over, to the alarm of his sons. But it passed the test.

Next, he had Achsah bring a lamb to him, which he examined carefully. The lamb must be without blemish. Satisfied, he lifted the lamb up and placed it upon the altar. While Japheth held the lamb down, Noah took the sacrificial knife from Ham, who presented it to him in an oil cloth, and slit the throat. Shem was standing by with a bowl ready to receive the blood. Taking the blood filled bowl from Shem, Noah sprinkled the blood upon the altar.

Turning to his family, he said: "The blood of this lamb cannot cleanse us of sin, but with this sacrifice we look forward to the Promise of God, which is the Redeemer. When He comes, then shall our sins be cleansed; our hearts shall be without blot or blemish. And He shall gather us to Himself."

Everyone bowed their heads and solemnly worshiped.

Into this silence came the Voice.

"Noah, I have smelled the sweet savor of your offerings. You have found favor with Me. Be fruitful and multiply, and replenish the earth. And the fear of you and the dread of you shall be upon every beast of the earth…"

Noah's heart was thrilled at hearing God's Voice. Listening carefully, he was astonished at the words God now spoke!

"…Whoso sheddeth man's blood, by man shall his blood be shed: for in the image of God made He man."

Sudden realization struck Noah. *From this day on, God holds man individually and as a people responsible for their actions. Each of us will answer to a holy God, but He will also hold us responsible for others. If someone slays another, I must also take his life. That means I must not only take responsibility for them, but I must also exercise authority over them.*

These thoughts and their implications staggered Noah. But God was still talking.

"And I, behold, I establish My covenant with you, and with your seed after you; and with every living creature that is with you, of the fowl, of the cattle, and of every beast of the earth with you; from all that go out of the ark, to every beast of the earth. And I will establish my covenant with you; neither shall all flesh be cut off any more by the waters of a flood; neither shall there any more be a flood to destroy the earth.

"This is the token of the covenant which I make between me and you and every living creature that is with you, for perpetual generations: I do set my bow in the cloud, and it shall be for a token of a covenant between me and the earth."

Noah gripped Shem's shoulder and steadied himself. *God is covenanting with us!* With difficulty, he subdued his wild thoughts and listened.

"And it shall come to pass, when I bring a cloud over the earth, that the bow shall be seen in the cloud: And I will remember my covenant, which is between me and you and every living creature of all flesh; and the waters shall no more become a flood to destroy all flesh. And the bow shall be in the cloud; and I will look upon it, that I may remember the everlasting covenant between God and every living creature of all flesh that is upon the earth.

"This is the token of the covenant, which I have established between me and all flesh that is upon the earth."

The Voice ceased and silence hung in the air.

Noah bowed his head and began to pray within himself. *O God, Thy love is so great and Thy wisdom so vast that I cannot comprehend it all. Thy...*

"Father!"

His thoughts broken, Noah struggled to regain his focus. Ignoring his son, he continued praying.

"Father!"

Angrily, Noah hissed, "Quiet, Japheth! I am praying."

"But father, look!"

Noah sighed. *I must talk to Japheth about interrupting me during prayer.*

Opening his eyes, he followed his eldest son's eyes and looked toward the sky. Startled, he beheld a multicolored bow arcing across the sky. *It is beautiful! How many colors are there? I see red, orange, and yellow. And there is green, blue, and purple. Six colors in all. I have never seen anything so beautiful before!*

"What is it?" all three sons asked in unison.

"It is the covenant token God spoke of just now. It is a bow. Whenever it rains, He will place that bow in the sky as a remembrance that never again will He destroy all with a flood. There will still be rains and local floods, but nothing that will encircle the earth again."

"Every time?" asked Shem.

"Yes."

"I suppose we could call it a 'rain bow'," mused Japheth.

"I suppose so," Noah agreed, smiling.

# SIX

## NOAH THE CARPENTER

2350BC (continued)

During the next ten days, they lived in the cave while resuming the unloading. On the first day they had unloaded only the essentials, but now everything of value was unloaded. The women busied themselves by cleaning the individual rooms and arranging the furniture. But, following Noah's orders, only items necessary for living were unpacked. The rest was stored for when they found permanent living quarters.

Once he was satisfied with the unloading, Noah decided it was time for his sons to become trailblazers.

"Japheth, you are in charge. Is everything packed and ready to go?"

"Yes, father. Each of us has a roll of tools necessary for everything from cutting brush to chopping trees to moving boulders."

"What about food?"

"Mother insisted we pack food, but we think it is important to eat off the land. This way we will learn first hand what food there is and what prospects exist for farming."

"Good. Take some seed with you. Once you find a suitable place at the base of this mountain, cast them forth that they may be fruitful and spread."

"We have already thought of that. We have seed with us to plant. We will also see if any wild fruits exist. We will bring back samples."

"I guess that's it, then. God go with you," Noah replied.

The men embraced Noah and headed down the same trail the animals had taken eleven days earlier. Noah returned to the cave and grabbed his tools.

"Are you going, also?" asked Naamah.

"No. When they get back, I want to be ready to move out. We'll need sleds to carry our supplies and the Writings. I have a lot of work to do."

He left the cave and crossed over to the Ark. Boarding, he took the ramp to the second floor, making his way aft to the storage chamber. Here, he found the wood he would need. Hearing a step, he turned. All three women had followed him.

"You aren't planning to carry all that wood off by yourself, are you?" asked Naamah.

He smiled. *I should have known they would want to help.*

"Well, now that you mention it, I do think I could use some help. Naamah and Achsah will carry a load, Hagaba and Bithiah will carry a load, and I will follow with a load. We'll take them to just outside the cave entrance.

"I think Achsah and Bithiah should lead. You two are the strongest. You will have to move backwards going down the ramps, so be careful."

Supervising them, he had the women line up in a single file with Achsah at its head. She and Naamah stepped forward. Putting Achsah in front facing the rear and Naamah in the rear facing front, Noah loaded them with three two by four boards. Achsah began moving backward with Naamah walking toward her. As they left, Bithiah and Hagaba stepped forward for their load.

Once he had sent them off, he grabbed five boards and hefted them upon his right shoulder. With barely a grunt, he walked back to the door and down the ramp. Pausing to adjust the boards, he continued on, carrying them to the pile that the women had made.

Looking at their pile he was secretly pleased that they had stacked them rather than just dropping them to the ground.

"Father Noah! That's five!" exclaimed Hagaba.

"Yes it is. If it was your husband, he would probably have six or more. Don't worry, I can handle it."

With the ladies help, unloading the wood took only a couple of hours. After the last of the wood was brought and stacked, he immediately set to work building the sleds. First he gathered his tools, which had last been used building the Ark and began the tasks of sawing, planing, and fitting the boards until the first sled was finished.

The women gathered around with excited curiosity. Naamah studied it with a critical eye.

"It appears, my lord, that you have learned how to build things."

"Hiram was a great teacher," he laughed, then grew serious as he remembered his friend lost in the Flood.

"How many will you build?"

"I think three. But the last will be special. It will carry the Writings, therefore it will need to be stronger and better than the others. That is why it will be last. Hopefully by that time I will have mastered the craftsmanship needed.

"That won't be enough for all our possessions, so at least one additional trip will have to be made."

The new sled was nothing like the playthings that people in later years would use for snowy slopes. This and the other two sleds were actually similar to the oxen drawn sleds from the past – tough and durable.

But with only a limited supply of oxen, he chose two mules and two cows to pull the sleds. It seemed even the sheep would be used, not to pull but to carry supplies on their backs. Even so, there were still supplies to be carried on the backs of his wife, his children, and himself.

&&&

Sixty days later, his three sons returned from their explorations raving about the beautiful lake at the base of the mountain. Lake Ararat, as they called it, elicited their enthusiastic report on its possibilities.

"There is plenty of land to plant, fish in the lakes, and young trees for building homes in the future," Japheth stated emphatically. "Father, it will serve us for years!"

"Trees. Are they big enough for our uses?"

"There are a few trees we can use immediately, but most are young. In time all the trees will be available."

"And what about a route?" Noah asked.

"We've found a good route also, father," Shem volunteered. "The animals trod a trail that we were able to follow all the way to the bottom. It can be steep at times and it seems to curve constantly, but if we take it slow, it will be safe."

"Shem should know," laughed Ham. "He tried going too fast and fell into a mud hole. Had to strip and clean his clothes. You should have seen him standing there naked and all. It was hilarious!"

Embarrassed, Shem saw the obvious displeasure in his father's eyes and changed the subject.

"Father, we built an altar where your house will be. We found the best location for the house and placed the altar right in front. It is built of stone and is the same size as this one. All it needs for proper worship is a sacrificial lamb for sanctification."

"Excellent. Whose idea was that?"

"Shem's," Japheth spoke up. "He even thought to collect brush for the fire. By the time we return it will be all dried up and ready to use."

"Then our only concern is safely making the journey down the mountain," remarked Noah.

"Father, I am sure we can make it safely," said Shem. "We may have to travel slow, but we can make it. I see you've been busy building sleds. They are perfect for the journey."

"I agree," Japheth nodded.

"Good," Noah replied. "Tomorrow, we will finish loading the sleds and putting the packs on our backs. By early afternoon, we will start down the mountain."

&&&

The following morning's activities went so well that all the sleds were packed by mid-morning. By noon both the men and the women had packs strapped to their backs ready to move out. With Japheth leading the way, they headed downhill.

Not far away, Satan and his lieutenants stood watching.

"What do we do now?" asked one of the demons.

"We wait," responded Satan. "We forced God to destroy the world with all its refinements. Now man has to start all over. I have already spotted a weakness in Noah's family that I will exploit. Soon it will be I that Noah worships and not his God."

"What weakness?"

Satan sighed. It was so obvious, it surprised him that no one else saw it.

"The one called Ham. Did you not notice before the Flood how he could not take his eyes off the naked men and women? And did you not notice just now his preoccupation with Shem's nakedness?

"I shall attack him through his lust for the flesh. It will be his undoing and the undoing of the entire family!"

"How?"

"As I said, we wait. The opportunity will come. I will destroy him and Noah."

"But Noah is so strong in his faith?"

"True, but take away that which he loves the most and he shall curse God to His face."

Satan laughed out loud as he contemplated God's collapse.

# SEVEN

## THE MOUNTAIN TRAIL

2350BC (continued)

The small caravan slowly made its way down the mountain. Shem had been correct in his description of the winding path that they had prepared. Several times the sleds broke down under their weight as they traveled the rocky trail. Aside from Noah's sons, no man had ever traversed these mountains before, accounting for the roughness of the way. It seemed like every step they encountered rocks, loose shale, or small crevices.

Noah had Naamah stay beside the sled carrying his precious tablets, the Writings. Sometimes, Noah would look back and think to himself, *All the writings of God and all the wisdom of man are in that sled. It must not perish.*

Fortunately it was the other sleds which kept breaking down. Not as strong or sturdy as the 'sled of Writings,' they were more susceptible to the pathway's perils. Each time one of the sleds broke down, the caravan stopped and repaired them. This took valuable time and kept them from making great progress. After only three days of travel, they could look back up the mountain and still see a portion of the Ark.

Suddenly, Noah turned to his sons.

"I am going back to the Ark. I must speak with God!"

With that cryptic comment, he turned and headed back the way they had come. Japheth took charge and ordered everyone to make camp.

"We shall wait father's return."

Carrying only his backpack, Noah was able to climb upward rapidly until he reached the plateau. By late afternoon, he stood on a hill and studied the magnificent ship. After awhile, he shifted his gaze to the altar, which he approached. Kneeling before it, he bowed his head to the ground, praying:

"Dear God, we are on a strange mountain and have already experienced difficulties. I know You want us to move and establish our home by the lake. But the way is difficult and dangerous. I am afraid of losing the Writings.

"The way is difficult for the women although they keep silent about it. Only Achsah appears strong enough to make the trip. Perhaps I have burdened them too much.

"Have I been careless Lord? Have I endangered my wife and our daughter-in-laws? Was I presumptuous and not following Your lead?

"I pray, dear Lord, that thou wilt give me guidance. Do we return to the Ark and await a more fortuitous day? O Lord, I pray that if it is Thy will, that Thou would go before us and clear the way. Keep us safe and preserve Your Word.

"I am Your humble servant, Lord. I only desire Thy perfect will.

"Amen."

He remained in a prone position, listening. But only the stillness of the evening was there. An hour went by with no sound except a discernible wind.

Rising, he headed for the cave that had so recently been their home. He had no sooner reached it than a drenching storm struck. Once safely inside, he looked out and watched as sheets of rain poured from the heavens accompanied by thunderous roars and bright lightning. These new sights and sounds made the storm seem worse that it really was to Noah. He felt a shiver of fear before retreating further into the cave.

&&&

Shem was the first to notice the darkening sky.

"Storm clouds!" he yelled. "Hurry, head for the caves to your left. They're coming fast!"

As the women obeyed and turned the sleds toward the nearby caves, the men began herding the cattle and sheep behind them. It was only with minutes to spare that everyone and everything was safely within the shelter of the caves.

Japheth turned to Shem.

"It is a good thing you have a sharp eye. If this storm had hit while we were out there, we could have all died."

"What about father?"

"He has the cave near the Ark. He will be safe there."

"Hey," Ham interrupted them, "lets all strip and dance like they did before the Flood."

"Ham!" the women all cried.

Japheth glared at his brother.

"I don't know what is wrong with you, but you had better change your ways. Father will be sore displeased with you."

"I was just having fun," he protested.

With that, he turned and went deeper into the cave. Japheth and Shem watched sadly.

"Ever since he saw that orgy outside the Ark during the Feast of Rain, he has not been the same," commented Shem. "He is heading for trouble."

Japheth nodded in agreement.

The two men turned and gazed at the turbulence, watching the spectacle of thunder and lightning. At first nervous, they became entranced by the dancing light and the angry roar.

&&&

The next day Noah reappeared just as a brilliant rainbow arched across the sunlit sky. It was obvious to all that he was energized and ready to move again.

The day started out with them making good time. The sleds slid over the rocky terrain without any trouble until they tried to cross a naturally narrow bridge that spanned a deep crevice. As they crossed, Naamah's sled suddenly tipped over and Noah watched in horror as tablets were seen plunging downward.

He hurried back to the sled with mounting alarm. Naamah was no longer in sight. It was with a sigh of relief when he found her on her knees beside the sled.

"Naamah, are you all right?"

"Yes, my lord," she sobbed.

"Then why are you crying?"

"Because I have lost the Writings," she cried.

Noah placed his arms around her shoulders and held her tenderly.

"My precious Naamah. Even if that were true, we still have God's Word in our hearts. Your life is far more important than a few tablets. And it was only a few. Let's get the sled across and then we will find out how serious it is."

Everybody gathered around and managed to right the sled and get it across. It was then that they unloaded it. While some tablets were missing, only the Book of Enoch of the prophetic writings was among them.

Noah went to a nearby rocky place and knelt as though before an altar. There he prayed seeking wisdom. Later he arose and returned.

"This trail is too steep and the way too rough to continue as we have. Shem, I want you to stay with the sleds. Naamah, I am putting him in charge; no arguments. Shem, your brothers and I will go ahead. If we find anything too dangerous, we will do whatever necessary to change it. But it will be up to you, as you move down the mountain, to determine the safest route."

"Will we see you tonight?" Naamah asked.

"No. We will start right away. One of us will return in three days to check on you. But Shem, safety of the women, as well as the Writings, comes first."

With that, he turned and headed down the narrow path with Japheth and Ham behind him. Naamah turned toward Shem.

"Don't worry son. We will do as you say. I am glad he put you in charge."

"Thanks mother. My first order is for us to make camp here for the night. We will resume the journey tomorrow."

&&&

The next morning, the three women and solitary man began their downward journey. It quickly became obvious that Shem took his father's instructions seriously. From his position beside the 'sled of Writings,' as Noah called it, he had a clear view of the women and their sheep. As they moved downward, he carefully watched, paying special attention to their body language. He soon developed a plan where every two hours he would order them to stop and rest, which the women secretly approved. This gave them a chance to rest weary legs and to relieve themselves as nature demanded.

After a rest that ranged from a few minutes to a half-hour, they would resume the journey. While this strategy slowed them down, it succeeded in preventing further accidents.

&&&

Noah, Japheth, and Ham headed down the mountain. Led by Japheth, the three men easily reached bottom by early afternoon. As they left the trail and stepped upon level ground, Noah stopped.

Before him lay the beautiful Lake Ararat, surrounded by grassy land with forest not far away. Drinking in the beauty, he spotted the lonely altar overlooking the lake. He nodded in approval as he joined in sons. *We may have time to build a shelter.*

&&&

Eight days later, Shem and the women reached the bottom to find that Noah and his sons had built a large, rectangular, log hut for their safety. It reminded everyone of the much larger Ark.

That night, after everyone enjoyed their first real dinner since leaving the plateau, they settled down and shared stories of their week's adventure. But it wasn't long before they all started yawning and headed for bed. They were so exhausted that all but Shem slept right through the storm that passed through during the night.

Hearing the winds and the rain striking the walls, he quietly got up and looked out. In the moonlight, he could see the storm clouds and the lightning. It was fascinating to watch a lightning bolt, followed a couple seconds later, sometimes instantly, by a thunderclap.

Closing the door, he looked about the interior. *Everyone is fast asleep. I am glad we got this place built. It is taking the storm in stride. But we are going to need separate homes soon.*

&&&

Several months later, Noah and his sons completed the building of four stout structures, one for each family. Each home featured a wood-burning fireplace patterned after the ovens built for the wealthiest homes prior to the Flood. Although it created a temporary problem with smoke dispersal, the heated interiors were welcomed by all. With the air increasingly getting cold, the families gratefully moved into their new lodgings.

The large hut would continue to be used as the meeting place for meals and other social gatherings. A new fireplace was built for it and the women discovered that they could use it just like the oven it resembled.

One morning shortly afterward, Noah awoke and rolled out of bed. He shivered as the cold immediately penetrated his meager clothing. Going to the fireplace, he discovered it had burned itself out. *I will need to get more wood.*

Pulling a cloak about himself, he went to the door and pulled it open. To his amazement, a gust of cold air blew a cold, white, and wet substance against his face. He wiped it off and stepped outside.

His feet suddenly left the ground and he was momentarily in the air. An instant later, he fell to the ground, landing on his back. Sitting up, he looked around. The three homes of his sons were all covered with the white substance.

He reached out and tried to pick some up, but it melted in his hands. Slipping his hand beneath some more, he quietly examined it. *I shall call this snow.* He picked up some more snow and soon learned how to pack it together into something firmer. As he packed it together, he was able to fashion it into a ball. He smiled as a mischievous thought crossed his mind.

He tried to get up, but the ground was slippery. Feeling around, he realized it was water. *It is hard water! It is frozen.*

After several attempts, he managed to stand. He moved over until he found firmer footing, and then he began fashioning more balls of snow. At first, he was alone with the snow and hard water, but as the sun slowly rose, he could hear his sons moving about. He smiled with patient glee.

Shem was the first unfortunate victim. He stepped out of his home and almost fell. Grabbing hold of the door, he managed to steady himself just as the first snowball hit. Startled, he looked down and saw the white substance clinging to his cloak. At that moment, Japheth and Ham stepped out of their homes and were promptly struck.

It took a moment for the young men to realize what was happening, but once they did they began fashioning their own snowballs and the fight was on. The women were awakened by the sounds of laughter and shouting. Going to their respective doors, they found their husbands engaged in the first ever snowball fight.

The women watched in amusement until a snowball hit Achsah in the shoulder. Laughing, she gingerly stepped out and stooped to pick up a snowball. As she straightened up, she was hit again and lost her balance. A moment later, she was sprawled on her back in the snow. But she would not be deterred as she got back up and joined the fight. Soon the other women joined in.

&&&

Later as spring made its first arrival, Noah planted a new vineyard not far from their home. With his sons' help, he found a nearby plot of land that was open to the sun. Immediately they set about removing the top layer of soil including the weeds and roots. Afterward, they fashioned a tiller and tilled the ground until it was workable. Only then did they plant the shoots they had brought over during the Flood.

Every day, he would go forth to care for the young vines, knowing that it would take at least two years or longer for the vines to mature and bear grapes. But in his mind he could see the day when it would be time to harvest.

# EIGHT

## TRAGEDY

2296BC (pop. 176)

A childish shout brought Noah back from his memories. The older boys were racing horses across the field with his grandson Nimrod in the lead. *That boy knows no fear.* He shook his head. *Nimrod will only be twelve this year, yet he seems to already have the qualities of a leader. If only he had faith in God.*

He looked around for Nimrod's father, but Cush was nowhere in sight. Again Noah shook his head. *He still blames me for the curse.*

He allowed his mind to drift back over the years to the small village they had built after descending Mount Ararat. Located alongside Lake Ararat, it had naturally been named Ararat. It was only 18 years after the Flood and they were expecting another grandchild. Ham's wife was only days away from giving birth to her fourth child. Into this happy scene tragedy struck!

Satan had been watching for an opportunity to strike. Focusing on Noah, he put his plan in action and soon thereafter Naamah, Noah's beloved wife, took violently sick. Hagaba and Achsah immediately came to her aid, finding her on her knees and vomiting. Hagaba paled and looked apologetically at Achsah.

"Achsah, you are more experienced in matters like this. You're in charge."

"But you're Japheth's wife. You should be in charge."

"Perhaps. But when we were on the Ark, it was you that kept everyone healthy, especially me. Even Naamah commented how good you are with the sick. I think you should be the one in charge. Besides, Bithiah is close to giving birth. If the baby comes early, I will be needed there."

Achsah reluctantly agreed before turning her full attention to Naamah. Placing her arm around Naamah's shoulder, she helped her stand. For a moment Naamah just leaned against her, but she finally gathered enough strength and walked into her house. Once inside, Achsah put Naamah to bed. Both Hagaba and Achsah helped their mother-in-law undress. The clothing was soaked and their mother-in-law was sweating profusely. Achsah placed her right hand upon Naamah's forehead.

"She's burning up. We need to get her temperature down. Have the men bring plenty of water."

Hagaba nodded and left. Achsah looked with concern upon Naamah. *Whatever is ailing you mother, I don't know what it is. But we've got to get your temperature down.*

Outside the men hurried to the lake, filled their buckets with water, and returned. Noah kept looking back at the house, but he knew he could do more by helping with the water. Soon they had ten full buckets ready and sitting outside the house.

Meanwhile, Achsah hurried to her own home. Entering, she found her only other dress, her favorite, hanging on a peg. Her plan was simple. Rip the dress in strips and use them as cold compresses to fight Naamah's fever. Looking at the dress, she momentarily considered changing to the good dress and using the older one. Rejecting that idea, she grabbed the dress and rushed back to Naamah's side.

Ripping the dress into shreds, she grabbed a strip and dunked it in a bucket of water. Wringing some of the water out, she placed it upon Naamah's head. Once that was in place, she reached for another strip, which she promptly dipped into the water. Wringing only slightly, she proceeded to bathe her mother-in-law. By this time, Hagaba returned to help. For the next two hours the women fought to get the temperature down. When they ran out of strips, Hagaba went and got her dress, which soon lay in a pile of strips.

But the fever kept rising until Naamah took a turn for the worse and began shivering violently.

"She's freezing!" exclaimed Achsah.

Immediately, the two women gathered additional blankets and began wrapping her in them. But Naamah still continued to shake uncontrollably. Achsah got up and went to the fireplace. She piled on more wood and quickly had a roaring fire going. For her and Hagaba the heat was unbearable, but Naamah continued shivering.

Suddenly their mother-in-law convulsed, sitting up wide-eyed. Turning, she looked directly at Achsah.

"Where's Noah?"

"He's outside, Naamah," Achsah said trying to push her down.

Naamah's eyes seemed to clear as she recognized Achsah.

"Take care of him and tell him I love him," she said as she fell backwards one last time.

Achsah leaned forward, checking for breath, but Naamah lay still. She was gone!

The suddenness of her loss stunned everyone. Hearing the women weeping, Noah rushed in and moved quickly to his wife's bedside. The sight of his beloved Naamah lying still upon the bed brought on a grief so powerful and overwhelming that Noah almost broke down. But he managed to hold himself together.

Later that day, the rest of the family came inside to pay their respects. Noah stood next to the bed and thanked everyone for their help.

&&&

Sadness enveloped the small community, which had known the firm, gentle hand of Naamah for eighteen years. Noah was the patriarch, but it was Naamah who had quietly kept the family unity and traditions. Now that calm strength was gone and Noah seemed at a loss as to what to do.

This lack of leadership was noticeable in the matter of her burial. Noah didn't want to deal with it and, in fact, just wanted a simple burial, but Shem objected.

"Father, we are in a new world. Mother's death is tragic, but it is also important. How we bury mother will set a standard for all who follow. We must do this right."

Noah, slowly settling in his chair, nodded quietly.

"Do what you think best," he replied, his voice full of sadness and despair.

As his father slumped in his chair, Shem turned to his brothers. "Any ideas?"

"Not really," responded Japheth. "But you must have one or you wouldn't have spoken so forcefully."

"I do. We don't have the means of a proper burial in the ground like they did on the other side of the Flood. Besides, mother is - was the mother of us all. Her burial should be special.

"I suggest that we take her back to the Ark. There was a small chamber in the cave we called home that she considered her own. She didn't live there long, but while she lived there and during her visits back to the Ark, that chamber was where she retired to be alone. We could bury her there and close the chamber off so that no wild animals would disturb her body."

"I like it," responded Japheth. "And we should wrap her body in linen cloth like they did in the past. Wrap her body first, then wrap her head with a small cloth to keep her mouth shut. I've seen it done before."

Noah lifted his head and looked at them.

"Her body should be prepared with spices first. Achsah would know how."

Shem nodded in agreement, while Japheth resumed his directions.

"Father is right. First we will have the women prepare the body with spices and wrap her in linen. Then we shall carry her up to the Ark and place her body in the chamber. If father is willing, he should speak and commit her to God's care. Afterward, we will close it up with rock and mortar."

With everyone agreeing to this simple but logical plan, the women immediately set about their task. Gently removing the blanket covering Naamah, they began preparing her. First they removed her jewelery, which they placed in her jewelery box. Next, they carefully bathed her, making sure that all the dirt, body fluids and anything else was removed and her body cleaned.

Shem suggested the next step, which was to the purifying of the body. He had seen it done on the other side of the Flood and was able to construct a container, which was filled with water. Her body was then immersed for several minutes. Afterward, she was lifted out and they began the wrapping.

Finding her nightgown, they slipped it over her. Then they gathered as much linen that they could find and cut it into long strips. Beginning at her feet, they began wrapping the strips around her feet and legs and over the nightgown. After each initial layer of strips was wound, they would stop and apply spices. They continued this until she was covered from her feet to her neck. The final act was when Achsah took a long strip and bound the face to keep the mouth shut.

After the women were done with the preparations, the men came in and carried the body out to the sled that had previously carried the Writings. After tenderly securing her to the slid, they began their sorrowful journey.

Going slowly, it took them three days to reach the cave. By that time the body had started smelling in spite of the spices.

Stopping the cart in front of the cave, the men carefully lifted her out and placed her on the ground. Stepping back, they watched as the women finished the preparations, which included additional spices. Once that was accomplished, they stepped forward and picked her up. With Japheth in the lead and Shem and Ham on either side, they solemnly carried her into the inner chamber.

Behind them came the women weeping, while Noah trailed behind in somber silence. The procession made the short journey into the inner cave and stopped. At that moment the men laid her body on a small ledge jutting from the rocky wall. Stepping back, they waited for Noah to speak.

Noah stood, staring at the inert body, with tears working their way down his cheeks. For a moment it looked like he couldn't go on, but he took a deep breath and opened his mouth.

"O holy Father, we come to Thee at a sorrowful time. We have laid my Naamah here to rest. My heart breaks as I think of her. She was a joy to my heart and a loyal wife. She followed me, but it was You she truly loved.

"I know she can never return to me, but I shall be with her someday. Take her to Thy bosom Lord and nourish her soul. Let her rest in Thy love and be comforted in Thy care.

"No man has ever been blessed with as loving, loyal, and devoted wife as I have been. She has truly been my 'help-meet.'"

He stopped, not able to continue. His sons placed their hands on his shoulders. All three sons, beginning with Japheth and ending with Ham, took the opportunity to commit her soul to God. When Ham finished, everyone simply stood there in quiet contemplation, praying within themselves.

After allowing a few moments of such reflection, Japheth ordered the chamber closed. Noah and his sons began gathering stones and laying them one on top of another. They would mortar each layer before adding another. It took most of the day, but the chamber was finally closed completely.

Once this task was finished, Noah went to the altar to commune with God. He stayed there for a couple of hours before rising and signaling it was time to leave. Shem, noticing his silent grieving, moved to Noah's side. Soon the group was heading back down the trail to their homes below.

# NINE

## THE CURSE

2296BC (continued)

After their return home, the force of Noah's grief struck him harder than anything he had ever known. In all their years of marriage, he had always assumed he would be the first to go. The sudden, mystifying loss proved too much for him!

Going to his storage shed, he set about collecting wine bottles. Finally, with arms full of bottles, he returned to his home. Grabbing a cup, he calmly poured liquid into it, tilted his head back and poured the entire contents into his mouth. Refilling his cup with more wine, he drained it as well. Later he lay down and fell asleep.

The next day, he resumed his drinking.

Japheth met with his brothers at his house.

"Father has never drank more than a couple of cups of wine in all the years that I have known him. I am open to suggestions as to what to do."

"We'll follow your lead, Japheth," replied Shem. "You are the eldest and would be the head of the family after Noah."

"I agree," said Ham. "Whatever you say."

"In that case, I think we will watch over him. As long as he does not injure himself, we will not interfere. He's lost his wife, our mother. I don't know what I would do in similar circumstances."

"Will we keep someone with him?" Shem asked.

"Yes and no. Father would not stand for one of us staying with him. What we will do is take turns outside his house. Four hour watches. If anything happens, the person watching will make sure the rest of us knows.

"That way, we can watch him without his knowledge, yet be ready to intercede if something bad happens."

Both Shem and Ham nodded in agreement to this plan.

"One thing, Ham," Japheth said. "Bithiah is expecting a baby. If the baby comes while father is grieving, we'll take your place so you can be with your family."

Ham shook his head.

"I appreciate your concern," he said. "But that wouldn't be right. I won't be needed until the baby is born, so I'll take my part."

"Very well," Japheth remarked with an approving smile. "Then I will take the first watch, Shem the second, and Ham, you will take the third."

With that issue settled, the three men broke up. Japheth went to Noah's house and began his watch.

&&&

For several days Noah sat alone in the middle of his house, drinking continuously. It quickly became a growing concern to everyone, especially the women. When they tried to get him to eat, he refused.

Hagaba grew exasperated. She made some of his favorite foods, using recipes that Naamah had used. Still he refused to eat. Frustrated, she turned to Achsah for help.

"It is not good that he doesn't eat. He is growing weak and the wine is affecting his speech."

"I agree, but we can't force him to eat. Will he listen to Japheth?"

"No. He has shut us all out."

The two women shook their head in despair. In the midst of this tragedy, Bithiah went into labor. Hagaba and Achsah now focused on her needs and tended her as she gave birth to a baby boy. But even that normally joyous occasion did little to brighten the atmosphere.

&&&

Prior to the Flood, skin color had been pretty uniform, although some people were of different skin tones. Ham had been distinguished by a much blacker skin tone, thus his name. His children were all dark and his latest son was no different. But Ham didn't focus on his coloring, which to him was normal, but upon his facial appearance. Looking at his young son triggered memories.

"He shall be called Canaan."

Everyone protested, as there was no one in the family with such a name. But he was adamant.

"Look at his face. Does it not remind you of the trader Canaan that we saw in Abel. He was quite wise, capable and a believer. Up to the day he died, he was friend to father and to us. I think it is fitting."

Both Japheth and Shem thought back to their business trips to Abel. Prior to the Flood, Noah had sent them into the great city on several occasions. Sometimes to see Methuselah, but other times to deal with Canaan the Trader. *Ham is right*, thought Shem. *He was probably one of the wisest traders we ever dealt with, although not well known. He certainly believed in the Ark. Only his death kept him from joining us in it.*

Although hesitant about such a name, Japheth and Shem knew only Noah could overrule the proud father and he was in no condition for such a decision. So they backed off and accepted the name.

Ham lifted the baby up and cradled him in his arms. Smiling, he took the new born to Noah. His father was still able to hold the baby, but Ham watched carefully.

"His name is Canaan, father."

"Canaan," Noah's tongue slurred the name.

"Yes."

"A good name, son."

As Noah's attention drifted away, Ham retrieved the baby and quietly left.

&&&

Noah's drinking got worse. What had started out as an all day affair now had become all day and all night. His speech became more incoherent with each passing day. After three more days of steady drinking and no food, he was quite drunk. He would sit there in silence staring straight ahead, although he occasionally would break out in song.

The day came when he arose at noontime on unsteady legs, singing in a loud voice. Ham, who was in the second hour of standing guard outside the door, couldn't make out a single word, although he thought he recognized the tune.

Noah began a little dance circling the room. Ham peeked in the window and saw him doing what amounted to a jig. As he danced, Noah continued singing and raising his voice. He dipped, he bowed; he spun completely around. Feeling a bit dizzy, he grabbed the center column supporting the roof and held on. Recovering himself, he returned to his dancing and singing.

The combination of wine and exertion made him feel warm. Unfastening his garment, he removed it and tossed it aside. Now dressed only in a tunic, he continued dancing and singing, breaking into a sweat. Faster and faster he moved around the room in an ever-tightening circle. Now drenched, he started pulling and tearing at his tunic until the tattered garment lay on the floor, leaving him entirely naked. But that hardly fazed him. He just continued dancing.

Suddenly the room began spinning as he lost his balance and collapsed to the floor. Falling upon his back, he found himself looking upward at the peak of the roof. *Why is it moving?* A moment later, he lapsed into unconsciousness.

&&&

Standing off in the corner of the room, Satan smiled. He turned to a demon standing beside him.

"Watch and learn. I told you I had a plan."

The demon was suitably impressed. At that moment any doubts he may have had about Satan's ability to wage war were cast aside.

&&&

Outside, Ham was listening intently. He remembered Japheth's command to inform the others if anything happened. But when Noah fell to the floor with a thud, curiosity won over duty. Opening the door, he went inside where he found his father lying unconscious in the middle of the room.

*He is naked!* His first reaction was that of alarm. *I'd better tell the others!*

But instead of retreating, he stayed and looked. Fascinated, his eyes explored his father's naked body. He remembered the orgies that had taken place outside the Ark while the people waited for the rain. They had shed their clothes in wanton abandon. He broke into a sweat as he remembered the feelings of lust he had felt then toward the young maidens and the young men. A lust he felt now more powerful than ever before!

In the grip of sin, he stood there unable to do what his conscience demanded. Over and over he heard his brother's command to tell them. But his feet were rooted to the floor and heart was racing.

Several minutes passed before he once again remembered the command to inform his brothers of anything new. Feeling weak and sweating profusely, he stepped outside into the cool air. Regaining control, he hurried to Shem's home.

Once Shem was awake, Ham began describing in graphic detail their father's condition.

"Ham! Stop it! You should not be speaking of father like that. Go home. Japheth and I will take care of him. And you might consider praying and asking for God's forgiveness!"

Stunned and shamed, Ham departed. Quickly, Shem went to Japheth's home where he found his brother already up because of the noise. Shem told him what had happened and the two of them hurried to their father's house.

"If we go in and behold father's nakedness, won't we be as guilty as Ham?" Shem asked.

"No, because we will go in backwards and cover him with something."

Shem nodded in understanding. The two of them entered the one room house and purposely turned their backs to Noah. Carefully, they stepped backward. Japheth removed his own cloak and, with Shem's help, covered their father with it. Shem took some of Noah's tattered clothes and, folding them together, placed them under his father's head. Satisfied, the two men quietly slipped out.

&&&

Several days later, Noah was sober enough to remember his sin. Rising, he dressed and made his way to his altar. Refusing all help from his family, he prepared an offering and knelt before the altar.

"O God, I have sinned before You. I allowed my grief to turn me against You and to get drunk before my family. It is with shame that I come before Thee now. O Father God, forgive Thy servant!"

A quiet peace overcame him and seemed to spread throughout his body.

It was later in the day when Japheth and Shem told him of Ham's sin. It brought instant anger and additional grief. But this time, he returned to his altar and talked to God about the grief, as well as the anger. God comforted him as a Father would comfort a son. Over time the grief went away, but Ham's actions were never forgotten.

Still later, Noah prophesied concerning all three sons. It was at this time that the consequences of Ham's sin became apparent. God appeared to Noah during the night. At first Noah thought it was a dream.

"Thou dreamest not, Noah. I have come to tell thee what thou shalt prophesy to thy sons."

The brilliant light seemed to penetrate his skull, even though he wasn't looking at Him. Eyes closed, he pressed his face against the floor.

The next day Noah spoke them to his sons and told them of his Heavenly Visitor.

"He came in the middle of the night and gave me what I now tell you. Cursed be Canaan; a servant of servants shall he be unto his brethren. Blessed be the LORD God of Shem; and Canaan shall be his servant. God shall enlarge Japheth, and he shall dwell in the tents of Shem; and Canaan shall be his servant."

# TEN

## A STORY TO TELL

2296BC (continued)

Years had come and gone since the prophecy, but Cush, the eldest son of Ham, still resented it, as did his brothers Phut and Canaan when they were older. He understood the curse to be on Ham's entire family and that Canaan was named to emphasize the full extent of it. Perhaps they felt that Noah was being unfair. Or maybe they envied the blessings showered upon their uncles, which they were denied.

In any case, this resentment grew daily. Cush, when he grew to manhood, passed this resentment onto his own children. This was particularly evident whenever he talked about Noah and the worship of God.

"I will not tell you not to worship the God of Noah, but you need to know why I don't," he said on one occasion.

"Remember, sons, whenever your grandfather visits, you are to treat him with the utmost respect and listen to his sermons on God. He is your grandfather. But don't forget it is he and his God that placed the curse on this family. All because of one man's sin. A sin, by the way, that I'm not even sure actually took place.

"I want you to spend time with him now, because when you turn twelve, your duties will bring an end to playtime. Listen to his stories, show respect, but always remember that it was he, not Ham, who got drunk and got naked. It was he who placed Ham in an awkward situation.

"It is for that reason that I do not spend time with him. It is also for that reason that I do not worship God after his example. A God Who will forgive drunkenness, but will not forgive sin caused by that drunkenness, is not a God I can worship."

It was his youngest son, Nimrod, whom he found to be a ready listener. All the boys loved Noah, their great grandfather, and loved his story telling. But the poison of rebellion planted by Cush was already being demonstrated in their lives, usually in the form of independence.

The various families slowly moved apart, even as they traveled from Mount Ararat. Shem, along with his family, stayed with Noah in the town of Ararat, which grew on the slopes of the famous mountain.

For Japheth it was an agonizing decision. On the one hand, there was his love and admiration for his father and his close relationship with Shem; on the other hand, his entire family wanted to move south and get away from the mountains. As the tug on his heart to move south grew, he went aside to seek God's will.

"Oh, God. You know I love my father, but my heart yearns to be with my children. Surely this is your will."

With no audible response from God in answer to his prayer, he arose with determination to travel south. The following day, he and his wife said their goodbyes to Noah, Shem and Achsah before heading south to soon join the rest of his family.

Later, on looking back, Japheth wrote, "It was a mistake. I should have stayed. It is true that I have always maintained contact with both father and Shem, but I should have stayed."

&&&

Japheth's and Ham's families traveled in tandem. Their journey took several turns as they followed the rivers and the terrain. Sometimes they traveled south, sometimes east, and sometimes west. At least once it looked like they were heading north.

Noah would frequently mount a donkey, not his favorite activity, and visit all the families. But every day they grew farther apart. Even Japheth's and Ham's families seemed to spread over larger areas as they grew in number.

Still Noah would visit each camp at least once a year. In this way, he hoped to keep the growing family close. Today, as on every occasion of Noah's visit, Cush managed to be absent, a fact which Noah sadly observed.

*Still, I have been greatly blessed. It has been fifty-four years since the Ark landed. Look how we have prospered. There are now one hundred and fifty-three souls counting myself. Thank You, Lord.*

&&&

In spite of Cush's absence and anger, Noah smiled. It was a delight to his eyes to watch his grandchildren at play, especially Nimrod.

*He is such a handsome lad with both intelligence and a natural inquisitiveness. But that is not all. He possesses a natural ability to lead others. They follow him without question, even those older than him. On top of that he excels in all forms of hunting, such as archery, knives, spears, and horseback riding. There seems to be no limit to his capabilities.*

Noah often found himself comparing the young man to Jareb, his once famous nephew. A comparison he increasingly found disturbing.

Noah was deeply aware of Cush's resentment, but had been unable to assuage these feelings. He could not change God's Word, which is exactly what Cush wanted him to do. Noah prayed that Cush would change, but the bitterness and resentment continued to increase with each passing day. With Noah's influence over the children waning, he feared they would turn against God.

Today, Cush and his older sons were out hunting. All the boys, younger than twelve, were left behind. Normally, they would have chores to do. But right now, Nimrod was racing his horse against any that dared and, as usual, winning. After several races, he rode up to his great grandfather and dismounted. *Soon he will be twelve and out hunting with his father.* It was a thought that both pleased and bothered Noah.

"Did you see me ride, Grandfather?"

"Yes," Noah said, smiling. "I did. I know of no one who could beat you, except maybe Jareb."

"O, you mean The Avenger?"

"Yes. I see you have been told of him. And what do you know about The Avenger?"

"Not much, except that he was a mighty man before the Lord."

"He was a great man," Noah replied sadly. "You are, I am afraid, much like him."

"Why are you afraid, Grandfather?"

"Because you are too independent, just like him. And like him, you do not put God first in all you do. It will lead you to a tragic end, just like it did to Jareb."

"What was he really like?" asked Nimrod, not wanting to get into religion. "Was he tall? Could he thro…"

"Stop!" Noah laughed. "You will weary me with all these questions. Gather your friends around me and I will tell you the story of Jareb the Avenger."

Nimrod ran and invited his friends to come hear about the great Jareb. Choosing listening to a story told by Noah rather than doing chores, all the boys were soon gathered in a semicircle, sitting cross-legged on the ground. Their faces shone with excitement as Noah stood before them.

*O God, what an opportunity!*

Clearing his throat, he looked down at the boys.

"I will now tell you of Jareb the Avenger, perhaps the greatest soldier that ever lived in the Old World before the Flood, and of his wife Naomi, who possessed greater faith and courage than most men."

Pausing, he looked the boys over again: "Before I begin my sons, it is important that you understand the world that existed before the Flood.

"Today's world is much more ordered than it was in those days. Here I am the Patriarch. God has established government where I am not only the head of the family, but the ruler over all. I don't rule by means of a great army, I have none. Neither do I rule because my sons and grandsons respect me. Unfortunately, there is precious little respect these days. But I rule by God's command and God's grace. It was not always so!"

The boys squirmed in anticipation.

"The Old World was filled with violence. There were murders, rapes, and all forms of evil. Men enslaved one another. Kings and Queens existed, as I am sure they will again. But they didn't run their kingdoms by rule of law. It was by might. Whosoever was the strongest, he was the king. What he said, that was the law. In the future, God intends us to have laws and governments, but back then the king was the only law. If you displeased him, he could have you executed on the spot.

"Furthermore, most of these kings were ungodly. Rather than obey and serve God, they rebelled against His worship and followed their own ways; their own conscience. Their wickedness was one of the causes of the Flood.

"A few kings stayed true to God. The greatest of these and indeed the greatest king ever, was Methuselah, king of Abel. He ruled from Abel, a city which had been founded by Adam and named after his murdered son.

"My story takes place a hundred miles west of Abel in a city called Uruk. It was located on the Nile River, which was a branch of the great Gihon. Rather than emptying into the Gihon, it actually branched off of the great river at Abel and angled southwest.

"Uruk was a medium sized city that served as the last outpost of civilization before reaching the great wilderness. It was only a few miles east of the Majestic Mountains.

"I will begin my story twenty years after I received God's command to build the Ark."

Once again he paused. All talking had ceased. It was so silent that Noah was certain that he could hear his own heart beating. *O Lord, help me to tell this story so that they will see Your love, compassion and patience. Not only that, but that they may see how important it is to trust and obey You!*

Taking a big breath, he opened his mouth to speak and the boys leaned forward, their imaginations already alive. Using his hands for emphasis, Noah soon had the boys entranced.

Although Noah went to great pains to show that Jareb was a failure, Nimrod found himself identifying with the Great Avenger. And though Noah emphasized Jareb's lack of faith and tragic death, Nimrod sympathized with Jareb's anger and defiance.

*Someday I will be great like Jareb and I will defy God's curse on my family!*

# ELEVEN

## A NEW EVIL

2285BC (pop. 308)

Mizraim saw his younger brother coming toward him with something in his hands. *What's that he's carrying? It's a new bow! It sure looks different than his other one.*

Intrigued by the bow, he couldn't take his eyes off it as Phut approached. The two men met and started walking together.

"Where are you going?" Mizraim asked.

"Yonder," he replied as he pointed to a cluster of trees. "Need to practice with my new bow."

"What's wrong with your old bow?"

"Nothing. This one is just better."

"Mind if I look at it?"

Phut answered by handing the bow to Mizraim.

Mizraim immediately noticed a difference in weight and feel. *I like this!*

"How good with it are you?" he asked.

"Pretty good. Watch," responded Phut as he took the bow back.

Pulling an arrow out of his side pouch, he fitted it into his bow.

"See that tree over yonder with the twisted limb. I will hit it right where it connects to the tree's trunk."

Taking aim, he pulled the arrow back almost to his chin and let the arrow fly. Moments later it struck the tree, lodging in the exact center of the node.

"Wow! That was great!" shouted Mizraim, running up to the tree. "I don't know of anyone, not even Nimrod, who could do better than that. Maybe you could teach me and my sons to shoot like that."

"Sure. I've been working with my sons lately, I'll just include yours. As for you, we can start now. The first lesson will be making your own bow."

"I have a bow."

"Yes, I know. But the bow makes all the difference. That bow was made for you. You need to make your own bow so that it is an extension of yourself."

"Extension," Mizraim laughed. "Is that a play on your name?"

"Well, I'm not sure why they named me Phut, but good weapons are an extension whether they are knives, spears, or arrows. I prefer the bow and arrow. Now let's find the proper wood. I prefer oak."

&&&

Nimrod patted his horse. He looked down at the bags sitting on the ground. Grabbing the two bags which were connected by a rope, he lifted them over the horse's back. He turned just as Noah approached.

"You have enough food there for a small army," Noah laughed.

"Oh grandfather! It's a long journey home and I get hungry easily."

"In that case, you can have more if you want."

"No, this will be fine."

The two men embraced before Nimrod leaped upon the horse's bare back.

"You always were agile with a horse," Noah remarked.

"Father says he thinks I was born on a horse. To be honest, I love riding. Speaking of which, I better get moving."

Saluting his grandfather, he urged his horse forward and headed for the forest. He didn't look back until he was sure he was out of sight. Halting, he took a quick glance back and could barely make out the small village.

Reaching down into one of the bags, he pulled out a clay tablet. As he studied it, he realized that the tablet contained the directions for constructing a multistory building. Included was a sketch of such a building. *Excellent! Grandfather almost discovered me taking this and it contains important information. If he knew that I've been stealing his precious tablets, he would have a fit. Perhaps place a curse on me like he did Canaan. But these and the others I've collected will someday make me very powerful.*

Urging his horse forward, he continued along the trail that would lead to his father's house. But after an hour of travel along the well used trail, something shiny attracted his attention off to the right. Curious, he halted and considered whether to investigate. Curiosity won over and he left the trail and, being forced by the heavily wooded forest to slow down, he headed in the direction of the unusual sight.

About a half hour later, he came upon a stream that was clear and flowing rapidly. *I'm thirsty!*

Dismounting, he led his horse to the stream and knelt beside it. As he bent over to get a drink, he heard a soft step.

"Shall the mighty Nimrod drink as a dog?"

Surprised, he jumped to his feet while simultaneously pulling his sword from his girdle. Looking around, his eyes lit upon a man standing a few feet away clothed in shiny armor. The man's sword was stuck in the ground, while he rested on its hilt. Nimrod detected a smirk on the man's face.

"Who are you?"

"The only one who can exalt your name above all other names and remove the curse!"

"You can remove the curse?"

The man smiled. Straightening, he pulled the sword out of the ground and slid it into the girdle. Still smiling, he moved closer. Nimrod noticed that the man was taller and more powerfully built than himself.

"Do you wish it removed?" asked the stranger, the smirk never leaving his face.

"Yes! It is unjust. Why should a whole family be cursed for one man's sin?"

"The God of Noah placed that curse upon your family. How can you call it unjust?"

"Because it is!"

"Thou has well said. The God of Noah is a capricious god and can be quite annoying. But I can remove that curse, if you are willing to bow before me."

"Who are you? How can I trust you?"

The man raised his hand and Nimrod was immediately lifted off his feet. Looking down, he was dumbfounded as he realized that he was hanging helplessly at least a foot above the ground. Then before his startled eyes the stranger rose up until he was level with Nimrod. For a moment the handsome man looked Nimrod in the eyes and said nothing. It was as if the man was letting Nimrod consider his awesome power.

"My name is Lucifer," he finally spoke, his voice deep and powerful like a roaring mountain stream. "I was brought up with the one you call God. You can trust me because I am greater than He."

Suddenly the power that held Nimrod off the ground was gone and he fell back to earth. Slowly getting up and brushing off the dirt, he straightened and watched as Lucifer gracefully settled back on earth. Nimrod, his heart beating nervously, stepped closer to the angel and managed to look Lucifer in the eye.

"I was always taught you were a fallen angel and was banished from heaven for your disobedience."

"Banished? I go there regularly to watch the rest of the angels submit to this God of yours. Do I look fallen?"

"No. But how can you say you are greater than Him?"

"Who do you think it was that tricked Him into destroying almost all of mankind. It was I! Who do you think forced Him to destroy His Garden of Eden? It was I."

Nimrod studied the angel, remembering all that he'd heard of Satan's rebellion and banishment from the councils of God. Then he remembered something Satan had said to him.

"You called me mighty. Why?"

"Has any other man but you slain a dinosaur? Or a mammoth? You are a mighty hunter before the Lord. But if you choose, I can make you a mighty ruler over all the people? And a god!"

Nimrod thought back a few months, remembering the battle with the dinosaur. It had been exciting and dangerous. His arm ribs still ached from the dragon's tail thrashing him against a tree. It had looked bad for him, but his growing skill with the sword had won the day. Slaying the mammoth had required great flexibility and determination. *Yes, I am a mighty hunter!*

Recalling what Satan said about making him a ruler, a thought occurred to him.

"Including over the Shemites and the Japhethites?"

"Yes."

"And all I have to do is submit to you. How can this be since I am merely 23 and my father rules?"

"In the eyes of your people you are already a great man. Listen to the stories they are telling about you. But I can make you greater than their stories. Worship me as your true god and I will give you all your heart's desire. You shall be greater than any man, including your grandfather Noah."

Nimrod studied Satan for a moment. *Greater than Noah! What a prospect. I could rule the world.*

"What do you mean by me submitting to you? I am my own man," he said with pride.

"True, and those tablets you have stolen will make you greater than anyone else."

Nimrod raised his eyes in surprise.

"You know about the tablets?"

"Of course I do. As I said, they will make you great. But only if you understand them. I can give you understanding and I can show you how to use them."

Nimrod considered this statement very carefully. Although he had many tablets and the ability to read them, he lacked the training to understand them. *But if he can teach me the meaning of them and how to unlock their secrets, I would have immense power.*

"I admit that they can be hard to understand. But does submitting to you mean I have to do your bidding?"

"Yes and no. Yes, if you want what I can give you. No, if you don't want it."

Nimrod pursed his lips as he contemplated all that he had heard. Finally, he nodded his head.

"What must I do?"

"First, you must acknowledge me as your god and swear your allegiance."

Nimrod heaved a sigh. Giving up his independence to anyone was hard for him, but for the key to power he would do it. He knelt before Lucifer and clutched his fist over his heart.

"Then I shall worship and serve you throughout my life."

Satan grinned as the warrior looked up to him.

"Arise, Nimrod. Follow and obey me and thou shalt surely rule this people. But you must do one thing for me before I shall grant your desires."

"What must I do?"

"You must sacrifice unto me a newborn baby boy."

Nimrod's mind immediately recalled the recent birth of new baby boy.

"I know of one. But how do I convince the parents?"

"You take the baby and bring it to me. They shall weep, but they shall not oppose you. Now go. Bring me the baby and I shall make thee a ruler and a god."

&&&

Noah sat upon a rock with a clay tablet upon his lap. He had been reading the latest journal entries by Shem.

His middle son had become his most reliable child. Not only had Shem stayed with him, but he maintained the written records and sometimes rode with Noah on his infrequent trips. The latest entries recorded new births in each of the growing tribes.

*Three hundred and eight people! In only 65 years! How God has blessed us. Let me see, Shem's family numbers thirty-five and Japheth's fifty-three. That means Ham's is the largest at sixty-five. And they continue to grow!*

He looked up at the nearby mountain where the Ark rested.

*I need to visit the Ark and the altar. It's been almost six months since my last visit. And I always feel closer to God when there.*

&&&

Nimrod rode up to the mother as she cradled the baby in her arms, dismounted and ripped the boy from her. Weeping, she grasped the baby and tried to pull him away, but Nimrod shoved her away. His face hardened and his eyes glowing, he spoke harshly to her.

"I have greater need for your son than you do. Fight me and I shall kill you and, if necessary, your husband. Now leave!"

She fell prostrate before him, grabbing his feet.

"Please Nimrod. He is mine only son. Take me and let the baby live."

Contemptuously he kicked her away.

"The sacrifice must be a baby boy and yours is the newest and most innocent."

Mounting his horse, he rode away. Even as he distanced himself from her home, he could hear her wailing. For a moment he felt what passed for compassion, but straightening his shoulders he rode on.

Spurring his horse forward, he soon arrived at the creek where he last saw the angel. As he approached, he saw Satan sitting on a log waiting for him. He rode up, dismounted, and started to hand the baby to Satan. But Satan held up his hand signifying to stop.

"This must be done by you and only you.

"Now lay the boy down on the ground and build an altar. When it is done, ye shall remove the baby's clothing before tying him down. Next, you shall take the clothing and cast it aside. Finally, thou shalt take up your knife and slay him as you would a lamb for the slaughter.'

Nimrod quickly set about building the altar. When satisfied that it was complete, he turned to the baby boy, who was crying. Kneeling down, he removed the blanket and cloth, ripping the blanket into strips, while he tossed the remaining clothes into a nearby bush. He then lifted him up and placed him upon the altar. Pulling out his knife, he tilted the boy's head back and made a quick incisive cut across the throat. He stepped back and watched as the boy's blood dripped into the altar.

"Make a fire under the altar."

Obediently, Nimrod knelt and started a fire. A skilled woodsman, it only took a few moments for him to get a fire started. He fanned the fire until it was burning strongly.

A few minutes later the altar was roaring and the baby's body was consumed. When this was accomplished, Nimrod knelt once again before the angel.

"Your name is Nimrod, the valiant one. Henceforth thou art Nimrod, the ruler. You shall rule with iron. No longer will you or the people follow Noah or Japheth or Ham, but they shall follow you. I shall guide you and lead you, and you shall build me a tower that shall protect you from God's wrath and give you a name higher than any name. It shall be higher than any flood can reach unto."

"How shall I rule? I am but one man."

"Gather about yourself others like unto yourself. Men who shall follow you wherever you lead them. Teach them to hunt as you hunt. Allow no man to stand in defiance before you. As you took the baby from its mother's arms, so shall you rule over men."

"Shall I teach them to worship you?"

"No! Thou shalt teach them to worship the heavenly host. I will instruct you how they are to worship. Only you shall know of me and worship me."

Nimrod looked up when the angel stopped speaking, but Satan was gone. Standing, he looked around with firm and determined grimace.

*I shall begin gathering my men today.*

# TWELVE

## A NEW GOD?

2285 BC (*continued*)

Shem kissed Achsah passionately.

"Shem! You're impossible. What if someone sees us?"

"You are my wife and the star of my life. Besides, how many times did we see Noah kiss Naamah when she was alive?"

"But that is just what I mean. It's always private."

"How can it be private if we saw it?"

"Shem!"

He laughed and embraced her.

"I love you, Achsah. And I want everyone to know it."

"You're impossible," she repeated as she turned away just before she smiled.

Shem noticed a rider racing into camp and went out to meet him.

"What's the hurry, lad?"

"I have an important message for Noah!"

"Noah is not here right now. I'm his son, Shem. Tell me."

The boy's message was a rush of words, but Shem's face paled, as he understood the meaning. Mounting his donkey, he immediately rode without stopping until he heard wailing. A few minutes later, he found a man doubled over in helpless rage and a woman in great anguish.

Dismounting, he hurried over to them. They looked at him with tear stained pleading eyes.

"Nimrod took our baby!" the father cried. "And I wasn't here to stop him!"

Shem felt rage building within him. Silently he fought and brought it under control. Reaching out, he placed his hand upon the man's shoulder. The man's grief and anger was so great that he shook all over. Shem waited until the man brought himself under control.

"There is not much you could have done. Do you know where he took your son?"

"He rode toward those trees," the mother sobbed, pointing to the east.

Then grasping his arm, she squeezed it so tightly that Shem flinched.

"Please bring my baby home. Please!"

"I'll do what I can," he responded. Gripping her by the shoulders, he looked into her eyes.

"Do you know why he took him?"

"He said to sacrifice," she sobbed.

Shem gently disengaged himself from her, remounted his donkey and rode toward the trees. As he rode, he studied the forest. *Wait. I was here just last week. As I recall, there's a river flowing down from the mountain just beyond those trees. Perhaps he is camped along its banks.*

Urging his donkey forward, it took another quarter hour before he reached the trees and entered the forest. It was then that he saw a horseman riding toward him.

*That must be Nimrod!*

As the rider neared, Shem's suspicion was verified as Nimrod was riding straight toward him. Stopping the mule, he waited. A few minutes later, Nimrod rode up to him, shifting uneasily before speaking to Shem.

"Shem, I salute you."

"And I you, Nimrod. I have come to retrieve the baby you stole. Where is it?"

Nimrod straightened, his eyes hardening. But Shem noted a bead of sweat suddenly appearing on his forehead.

"I do not answer to you, Shem."

"True," Shem smiled as he purposely looked him over. "But do you really believe Ham would approve of what you have done?"

"What have I done?"

"You know. You took an innocent baby from its mother."

"I don't deny that. I had use of him."

"And you killed him, didn't you?"

"He served my purpose."

"Then you are no better than Cain."

"Maybe so. But I am not afraid of you, Shem."

With that, Nimrod turned his horse and rode off in the direction of his home. Shem watched with a mixture of anger and sadness. Turning, he continued on, following the trail he had left.

Riding slowly, it took about three hours before he came upon the charred and smoldering remains of an altar. Dismounting, he examined the altar, but found no evidence of the baby. *All burned up. O Lord, have we come to this already?*

As he turned away something caught his eye. Walking over to a nearby bush and kneeling down, he parted the leaves and sighed at the sight before him. Lying amongst the wild grass was the swaddling cloth the baby had worn. Stained and emitting a strong order, it was the only thing left of the newborn. Quietly he picked it up and folded it. *This is all that remains, but this cloth will at least be something of his she can keep.*

&&&

A loud snap broke the sad silence. Shem froze. Slowly turning around, he found a male lion facing him and licking his lips. The lion seemed to be in anticipation of an early meal. His yellow eyes appeared fully focused upon him.

Shem slowly edged closer to his mule, all the while watching the lion. For his part, the lion turned parallel and kept pace with his movements. Shem felt a little trickle of sweat sliding down the middle of his back. He felt for his knife and eased it out of its sheath.

"You don't want me for dinner," Shem spoke quietly. "I'm too tough."

The lion stopped, looking directly at him, and yawned. Shem, moving in slow motion, bent over to pick up a broken branch. About 30 inches long, he hefted it in his hand. *This could be a very short fight.*

The lion took a step forward, sniffing the air. Shem calmly waited. The lion took another step, then another. Shem could hear his heart beating and was certain he could smell the lion's breath. Glancing down at the stick he held, he knew his chances of survival were extremely low.

Stopping, the lion crouched and tensed. With a burst of energy the lion sprang into action, covering the distance between them in a flash.

Suddenly a light from heaven shone upon the lion as it was in midstride!

To Shem, it seemed like the lion was frozen in time while he was free to move. Looking around and seeing nothing but the light, he edged back to a nearby tree. He looked down at his weapons, which consisted of a branch in his left hand and a knife in his right. Straightening, he stared at the lion and waited.

Just as suddenly as the light appeared, it was gone! The lion tumbled, but immediately regained his feet. Now that it was free, Shem fully expected it to resume its attack. But instead of leaping upon its next meal, the lion relaxed.

To Shem's surprise, the lion made no further move toward him. It was as if he had lost all interest in the human. For a moment it looked like the lion was confused. He pawed the ground and, pausing at the stream, took a deep drink. Once again he turned and looked directly at Shem.

After a moment which seemed like an eternity, the lion bounded away into the forest and quickly disappeared from sight.

Shem fell to his knees.

"Thank You, my Lord God. I am not afraid of dying for I know that if anything happens I will be with You. But I am not in a hurry to leave this world. Thank You."

Remounting his mule, he retraced his route back to the grieving couple. This time he maintained a quiet vigil, being alert to any sound or movement indicating the possibility of a wild animal lurking nearby.

&&&

Approximately 200 miles southwest of Ararat are the Taurus Mountains and in the midst of that range is a small mountain lake, which is the source of a river flowing southeast. As it winds its way down the mountains it is fed by a number of small tributaries, gaining mass and power as it continues southward for hundreds of miles before reaching the plains.

Sometimes running between sheer cliffs, it is surrounded by marshes, swamps, and freshwater lakes providing fertile land. It leaves the mountains and enters the plains. The further south it goes the more apparent is the change in scenery. Instead of mountains, it found itself rushing along a land barren of rocks, but rich in trees and wild wheat.

It was only a few months after the sacrifice of the baby that a small caravan arrived upon this scene. They had been following a smaller river (Khosr River), but they now found themselves at the juncture of these two rivers. Camping along the larger river's eastern shoreline, the travelers could still see the mountains to the north.

At the head of the caravan and riding upon a black horse was Nimrod. The horse was beautiful to behold, one of the reasons Nimrod had chosen it for himself. Sitting astride the stead, Nimrod appeared as a mighty warrior. Many of the travelers looked upon him with a mixture of fear and awe.

As they made camp at the junction of the two rivers, he remembered the stories told by Noah about the world that perished and decided to call the swiftly flowing river the Tigris. Although the river was flowing southeast, whereas he had been traveling southwest, he decided to follow it for awhile.

Nimrod was impressed with the area. Situated on level plains in a triangular plat that bordered the Tigris and Khosr Rivers, it held much promise. *Someday I will return here and build a city. But Satan wants me to travel further south. So for now, I will follow the Tigris. Apparently it will eventually flow more to the east. Whatever his reasons, I will obey and lead my people south where we shall settle and build a great city.*

&&&

Not far away, Shem busied himself making his own camp. But the agitation of his mule caused him to look up to the heaven. He was startled when he saw heavy clouds moving overhead.

*Rain! I must find shelter!*

Jumping up, he put out the fire and looked around. The only thing remotely looking like shelter was a hill with a cluster of trees in the midst. Grabbing the mule's reins, he headed toward it.

&&&

With night already coming upon the land, dark, menacing clouds moved overhead. But the weary travelers had quickly made camp and pitched their tents. The unsuspecting campers easily fell asleep, completely unaware of the impending storm.

With the clouds came the wind. At first it was only a gentle breeze, but it soon changed into a mighty wind. As the last rays of dusk disappeared over the horizon, the rain began in earnest, coming down in a torrential downpour!

The now powerful winds almost stampeded the horses. It was only with sheer effort that the few guards were able to prevent such a catastrophe from taking place. But such triumphs were rare.

Sweeping through the encampment the storm showed no mercy as it ripped tents apart, overturned carts, and wrecked havoc throughout the encampment. Jarred from their sleep, the travelers soon found themselves drenched and endangered. Suddenly the cattle stampeded, racing southward. Having been grazing just north of the camp, they now raced right through the encampment itself, smashing earthen jars, overturning carts not already turned by the storm, trampled over tents, and knocked over anyone who got too close!

But the worst of the storm was the panic that struck the people. This was the most violent storm they had ever experienced and they didn't know how to react. The thunderous roar mixed with crackling lightning sent fear through their consciences.

In the midst of this storm, a little girl frightened by the thunder, escaped from her mother's arm and ran toward her father, who was trying to secure his horse. Halfway to him, lightning struck and killed the little girl. Panic spread wildly.

The rampaging cattle also took their toll of human lives. Some people were trampled in their tents before they ever had a chance to flee. Still others were unfortunate enough to be in the way and got trampled. One man was gored by a bull.

While the people were fearful and confused, Nimrod took action. Alarmed by reports of panic, he was determined that his people would not perish. Fighting against the wind and rain, he went from family to family reassuring and calming them. In some cases, he found more than one family huddled together.

Throughout the night, he visited the people, encouraging and helping them cope. More than once, Nimrod helped secure their tents against the onslaught. Once certain of their safety, he would move on to the next tent.

Word of his courage and compassion spread throughout the encampment faster than he was able to move. By the dawn of a new day the people were singing his praises!

Then, as suddenly as it appeared, the rain was gone and a bright rainbow arched through the sky. The people emerged from their tents and a mighty cheer was lifted up. The one name mentioned above all others was the name, Nimrod!

Nimrod headed back toward his tent, but the people came to him and fell upon their faces before him. Sensing an opportunity to push his religious ideas, he went from person to person mentioning his prayers to God and His angels. When he finally reached his tent, he had a large crowd of men, women, and children behind him. He turned and, facing them, raised his hand for silence.

"I am so thankful that God sent His angels to watch over us. I think we should all take time to offer Him our thanks. Also, be thankful for His angels who held back this storm and preserved our lives. They have interceded upon our behalf and preserved our lives this day. Therefore, I, Nimrod, proclaim this day to be a day of thanksgiving and prayer.

"Take time to pray. We shall not travel this day, but shall rest. Gather yourselves together, search for loved ones, and mourn for those who died. Meanwhile, remember whatever repairs are needed and or cattle found, my men will assist you."

The people responded as he anticipated. Soon the name of Nimrod was on the lips of the people in worship and praise. More than one considered Nimrod godlike! From that day forward mothers sought to name their newborn sons Nimrod.

# THIRTEEN

## THE CALL OF SHEM

2285 (*continued*)

Two months later, Shem rode into Ararat, dismounted and wearily joined his father, who was sitting outside his home facing the mountain.

"Where are they now?" Noah asked.

"They have reached a large river, which they named the Tigris. I believe they plan on following it southward," responded Shem.

"And what of Cush? What are his plans?"

"Actually, father, I don't think Cush is in charge anymore. It appears that his son Nimrod now rules."

"Nimrod? He is still a young man. Why would he rule and Cush not?"

"I have only heard rumors?"

"About what?"

"That Nimrod has gathered about him a great number of youths his own age and some men older. He is now their leader and has taken over the rule of the families. It appears the people practically worship him."

Noah bowed his head. Pinching his nose with his right hand, it appeared like his head was actually resting upon his hand. It was a pose that Shem was increasingly seeing.

"What is it, father?"

"It has begun again. Mans' rebellion against God. Mark my word, son, Nimrod will wax stronger and stronger and will someday lead the people away from God."

"But every report I have received says that he encourages the people to worship. He even refrains from traveling on the seventh day."

"Appearances are not always what they seem, my son. I hope I am wrong, Shem. But I think not. I have not told you before, but someone stole several of the tablets."

Shem looked at him in alarm.

"None of my children, surely!"

"No. I suspect it was Nimrod. He spent time with me a few years ago, and has visited often since then. I don't like to speak ill of anyone, but he had the opportunity and may have taken them during those visits. I trusted him and had no reason to check on the tablets until recently. It was only then I discovered some were missing."

"Do you known what was taken?"

"Not completely, but I know some of them concerned how to make bricks and construct tall buildings, including temples. There were some tablets that spoke of fortifications and warfare, possibly more."

"I understand the warfare as he is certainly a mighty hunter and warrior, but why construction?"

"I am not sure, but I have an idea. He was always fascinated with my stories of the past, especially of the great cities and temples. Now that he has the rule, he eventually will want to build cities of his own. And if they are moving south, your own report has indicated they are heading toward the plains where rocks are scarce. He will need knowledge of brick making."

Shem didn't want to believe that such a thing could be happening, but the facts all supported his father's theory. He reached out and gripped his father's shoulder. The two men settled into silence as they contemplated the future.

&&&

Nimrod sat on his horse watching the encampment. All the Hamites, numbering about sixty-five people, had chosen to follow him. That included his uncles Mizraim and Phut. Their famous proficiency with bow and arrow had already attracted his attention. Although he didn't anticipate any trouble, he had given them the task of providing perimeter defense.

The resentment toward God that was felt by his father Cush now embodied him. He still remembered the story of Jareb the Avenger, who had died in the Flood. He could still close his eyes and picture the famous warrior who had so revolutionized warfare. It was Jareb who had introduced the world to the cavalry.

Noah had related the thrilling story with a terrible end, but Nimrod's imagination had been inspired. Not only by the cavalry, but Jareb's courage and skill in fighting. But the thing that impressed him the most was that Jareb had stood up to Noah.

In his mind, the rejection by God of Jareb was similar to the rejection of Ham, both having been cursed by God. Intervening years had not lessened that feeling, but had magnified it.

Now he was the leader in defiance of God. *And I shall not fail! Jareb failed because he trusted in a mountain, but I trust Satan. He is my god!*

He glanced at a small cart being guarded by a stout soldier. In it were the precious clay tablets that he had stolen from his grandfather Noah. *I wonder if he knows they are missing yet.*

He smiled, remembering the many trips he had made to visit his "favorite" grandfather. Each time he had visited, he had managed to steal at least one tablet. And once he had taken several.

*With this knowledge I shall be able to build cities and walls and towers that shall be the envy of the world!*

&&&

Shem turned and watched his son Arpachshad climb the hill toward him. Now a man of 58 with a wife, Arpachshad was Shem's favorite although not the firstborn.

"Father, I have news from the twins."

Shem's attention was immediately heightened at the mention of his two oldest boys. Born only a year after the Flood both Elam and Asshur had proven to be disappointments. Elam especially, since he was born first.

"What are they doing now?"

"They have joined with Nimrod's people."

"Are they taking their families with them?"

"Yes. Also, some of the younger men are joining Nimrod's army. Is there anything we can do about it?"

"I am afraid not, son. They have chosen their path. But what about you and the rest?"

"I will follow you, father. And Lud and Aram have said so also."

"Well, for now that means we stay here with Noah. Let your brethren know that we will stay put until God directs otherwise."

Watching Arpachshad retrace his steps, Shem moved over to his favorite tree. He often thought of it as his praying spot.

Stretching himself upon the ground, he began praying.

"O God, our memories are so short. It seems but yesterday that You sent the Flood and destroyed all but eight of us. Now our sons and daughters are again leaving You. It is only a matter of time before they erect idols and worship them instead of You. Is there nothing we can do?"

The silence was so profound that he felt his prayer would not be answered, then suddenly God's voice, so soft he had to strain to hear it, came to him: "I have heard thy prayer and the prayers of thy father. To him I have promised that I will not again destroy man by water, but I have called you to serve Me.

"Henceforth, thou shalt have power with men. They shall fear thee. Thy father shall send thee forth and thou shalt be his messenger to them and a messenger of their doings to him. Rise and go to thy father."

&&&

In the same hour, Noah knelt before his altar in the vineyard. Stretching himself upon the ground, he agonized in prayer. Minutes slipped, the heavens seeming like brass. Then as he supposed that God would not answer, the Lord appeared unto him.

"Noah."

"Yes, my Lord?"

"I have heard thy prayers and the prayers of thy son, Shem. Therefore, I have chosen him and he shall serve Me. Thou shalt instruct him in the Writings and he shall be an ambassador unto Me."

"I have instructed him in the Writings since his youth, My Lord."

"Yea, and thou shalt instruct him the more.

"And he shall visit the tribes and preach the Writings to them. He shall warn them of judgment if they persist in their present course.

Moreover, he shall by and by bring you a report of their doings that you might strengthen and guide him."

"I shall do as Thou commandeth, Lord."

"Rise, for thy son cometh."

Standing, Noah could see his son approaching.

# FOURTEEN

## ASSHUR

2283BC (pop. 320)

At twice Nimrod's age, the 66 year-old Asshur was an accomplished hunter in his own right. He was quite accurate with bow and arrow, with only Phut and his sons being better archers.

But his real strength lay in his inventive mind. Early on, he asked Nimrod if he could study the tablets. Having grown up as Noah's grandson, he had seen them as a youth and been taught by Noah of their significance.

As he searched the tablets in Nimrod's possession, he discovered that among them were tablets describing different weapons. The one that caught his eye described the various chariots used by the ancients. Using this stolen tablet, he was able to re-invent the small ox-drawn chariot that appeared more like a battle wagon than a fast chariot. Drawn by four oxen and constructed of wicker and leather it could mount both a driver and a warrior. They looked slow and clumsy, but still could be used to intimidate others and they certainly impressed Nimrod. Looking at them, the ruler saw their potential for both military and royal purposes.

Asshur and Elam quickly rose to become Nimrod's top lieutenants. Recognizing his expertise, Nimrod appointed Asshur the duty to build a mobile force centered around the new chariots. Although the chariots were small in number, they none-the-less quickly proved effective as a tool of intimating power.

Although no enemies were yet existing, Asshur developed a military strategy that employed the two-man chariot as an advance offensive force. Each chariot would lead a contingent of foot soldiers into battle. Later, as the number of wagons or chariots multiplied, he designed armed units that consisted entirely of the chariots. Again, these proved to be highly effective, serving to dissuade any potential rivals to Nimrod's power.

A very proud man, Asshur did not like the growing power of Nimrod. As the son of Shem and the grandson of Noah, he felt he held a privileged position. That fact alone should have made him better than almost anyone else. He felt superior to Nimrod and the rightful leader of the people, but he kept silent biding his time.

With each passing day, he grew more and more restive. His small chariot force gave him influence far exceeding its size. He felt caged, as the pace of the caravan was slow and tedious with delays and other distractions. Frustration gnawed at him and found voice in the incident at Calneh.

&&&

Nimrod had watched as the people camped 18 miles south of where they originally came upon the river. Located in a triangular area bounded by the Tigris and a smaller river, it was fertile land that held much promise for an industrious farmer.

Nimrod dismounted and was looking across the river when Jamin rode up, dismounted, and joined him.

Nimrod turned to Jamin.

"We'll cross the river here while the water is calm. Who knows what tomorrow will bring."

Jamin nodded before answering. "Before we do, there is a problem you must resolve. Mahli says he is too sick to continue any further. He wants to settle here along with his family."

"Sick again? He is aptly named," Nimrod sighed.

He mounted his horse and rode back to where Mahli was resting. Dismounting, he approached the older man.

"You wish to stay here?"

"Yes, Nimrod. I am too sick to travel. I will only slow you down. I would like to stay here and start my own village, which I would call Calneh. It is a good plan don't you agree?"

"Yes, it is. It is just you and your family?"

"My brother wishes to stay with us."

"OK, Calneh it shall be. But once we move south you will be on your own. It may be a while before we send anyone to check on your needs. This is still a wild, untamed land with wild animals. Are you sure?"

"Yes I am and I do understand, my lord. But my health is poor and my family refuses to leave me."

*Lord?* Nimrod was shocked. It was the first time anyone had addressed him as "my lord." *But I could get used to such a title!*

When Asshur learned of these developments, he looked with contempt upon Mahli. His excuse that he was sick and couldn't travel further simply branded him a coward in Asshur's eyes. For Nimrod to allow such cowardice was almost too much! Mounting his horse, he sought out the ruler.

He found Nimrod back at the river where the people would cross to the other side. His contempt exploded.

"If you keep letting these cowards depart, you will have no one to build your city! All our sacrifices will have been in vain."

Nimrod slowly turned and stared into Asshur's face. He could feel anger rising. *Not now. This is not the time to show anger to anyone, let alone this fool.*

"Asshur, I understand your concern. But I have only lost two families here, totaling 23 people. Yet we have grown to over 72 people and we are still growing. I will get my city built. Besides, Calneh shall be mine as well!"

"But if we lose another family, we will end up with fewer people than only two years ago. Where will it stop?"

"True. We shall need to clamp down. You and your chariots can see to that little matter. Is that sufficient assurance?"

Asshur nodded as he contemplated that aspect, but then his face took on an even more serious look.

"Yes, I suppose. But I do have another concern."

Nimrod looked at him, smiling thinly. As if his earlier comment wasn't bad enough, Asshur's tone of voice had now noticeably lost its respect, something Nimrod was not about to abide for very long.

"I have heard talk that you no longer worship God."

Nimrod calmly studied Asshur although there was nothing calm in his stomach. *Be careful. He could be dangerous.*

"That is silly, Asshur. Of course I worship God. I not only worship Him, but I worship all His creation."

"What does that mean?"

"You know the Writings. In the beginning God created the whole world and He gave us a multitude of stars for a reason. Merely to look at? I think not. God has placed the stars of heaven there for our benefit. We must learn why?"

Asshur stared at him, trying to understand the logic.

"Then you still worship God?"

"Yes, of course I do. I worship Him and His whole world. And I intend to honor Him further when we build our city. Perhaps a tower. Look Asshur, we cannot make the same mistake our forefathers made.

"They ignored God and His creation at their own peril. They worshiped strange gods and defied His laws. They had ample time to learn of Him and of His creation, but they chose not to know Him. They paid for this arrogance with their lives.

"Asshur, it is our sacred duty to learn all we can about God, including the meaning of these stars. We have some of the truth in the Writings that Noah guards. But there are more truths that we must discover or we shall suffer God's righteous judgment the same as our forefathers."

Somewhat mollified, Asshur left. As he did so, Jamin moved closer to Nimrod.

"He could prove a problem."

"Perhaps. We will keep a watch on him."

&&&

Asshur paced about his tent, the words of Nimrod turning over in his mind. *He is right about our forefathers. They had the writings and the preaching of Noah, yet they perished! But is Nimrod greater than Noah? Is he a god that we should worship?*

Finally he could stand it no longer. Leaving his tent, he found Elam sitting at meal with his family. After quick greetings, he managed to take him aside.

"We need to watch Nimrod carefully," he told his brother.

"Why?"

"He is departing from the faith of our father."

"But so have we, haven't we? I mean, departed from the faith."

"No Elam, we still worship God; just not like father or Noah does. But Nimrod, I fear, is doing something altogether different. He claims he still worships God, but I fear that he is making himself a god. His talk is smooth and convincing. He speaks as though he worships God, yet he also speaks as one with superior knowledge. It is almost as though he is trying to become a god himself? I fear that if he continues, he will bring God's wrath upon us once again!"

Elam raised his eyebrows in surprise.

"So you think we must stop him?"

"No. I am not sure that would be possible. I'm not even sure about the existence of God. But one thing I do know for sure: I have no intention of worshiping Nimrod!"

Elam nodded knowingly.

"If you are right, it would mean our complete and permanent separation from Nimrod. Which means that since we don't believe in the God of our father, then we will be all alone."

"Yes, you are correct. So we must attract our own followers, but quietly. We don't want Nimrod to get suspicious."

Elam thought about this for a moment.

"I have an idea."

"What?"

"We stay and help Nimrod build his city. Sooner or later, he will find where he wants to build. When that happens, we will serve him and help build it. But we will send out scouts to explore the land to the south of it just in case. Then, when the separation does come, we will have a place where we can go."

"I like that," agreed Asshur, "except we will need to keep this quiet. The fewer people who know of such a contingency the better. Why don't you do the exploring?"

"I suppose I could slip out on occasion. When I do, I will need you to cover for me. I don't want Nimrod suspicious."

"Don't worry. He'll not hear it from me," responded Asshur with a smile.

# FIFTEEN

## A NEW RIVER

Shem knelt before the altar, sighing, and looking to the heavens. *O, God. I feel the weight of responsibility on my shoulders. Father is leaning more and more upon me, even as Thou has commanded. Achsah also looks to me for leadership.*

*But Nimrod is leading the people astray from following You. Two of my own sons follow him closely and will probably stray from the truths I have taught them. How can I keep people from following him?*

The silence seemed intolerably long. He bowed his head to the earth.

"Shem. Remove thy shoes for this is holy ground."

Quickly he removed his sandals and resumed his position.

"Thy servant listens, Lord."

"I choose whom I choose. I have chosen thee to lead the people. Nimrod serves Satan and follows his directions. I shall bless you and give you long life. I shall guide you and give you strength. Be of good cheer, I am your strength."

Suddenly the voice ceased and Shem was alone. He lay there contemplating what God had said. *Be of good cheer, I am your strength! O thank You, my Lord God. I shall serve You in Thy strength and worship You with all my soul. I shall daily seek Thy face and worship Thee wherever I go.*

As he arose, his face beamed!

&&&

Nimrod arose quietly during the night and slipped past the guards as he left the camp. Once sure he was at a safe distance, he knelt by a lonely tree.

"Your servant is here."

A moment later, Satan appeared.

"Why do you seek me?" he asked.

"O Lucifer, I have done as you have commanded. I have gathered men about me. They are a hard lot, but they trust me and are following me. We are moving south just as you commanded. But I have a man who may cause problems."

"You speak of Asshur," Satan responded. "I know him. Do not fear him. I shall make him great, but you shall be greater."

"Then I have no reason to fear?"

"Obey me. Fear me. I shall direct thy paths. But be careful of the one called Shem."

"Shem? The son of Noah? He does not travel with us. He stays with his father. Why should I fear him."

"He follows you at a distance and reports your activities back to Noah. Be careful for he is a tool of the Elohim."

"Will he try to stop us with force?"

"I shall protect you from any force, but you must not let him turn the people back. He will use words to sway them, you must use greater words and your own armed men to keep the people from turning back. Listen to Jamin, he is wise and serves me. Now return unto your camp and, in the morning, lead the people to the plains of Shiner."

"The plains of Shiner?"

"Yes. It lies several days further south of here and alongside another river west of the Tigris. There you shall find a choice place to build your city. There you shall build a tower unto the heavens according to the directions I shall give and you shall worship the host of heaven."

This was the second time that Satan had mentioned building a tower on the other side of the Tigris. Nimrod thought back several days ago when he had first seen the Tigris. Satan had appeared and told him of these plans. But now the instructions were more detailed.

Alone again, Nimrod arose and returned to camp. In the morning, he decided to walk among the people. Since the taking of the baby boy and sacrificing him, the people now feared him. But Jamin had advised him to show mercy so that the people would both fear and honor him.

The advice worked. Now, as he walked among them, the people would look at him with fear in their eyes. But he also saw gratitude as he spoke kindly to them and, in the case of one woman, promised help.

&&&

Later that same day, Nimrod began preparing the people to cross the Tigris. Mounting his horse, he rode among them and stopped to encourage the men. Using a mixture of praise and care, as instructed by Jamin, he urged them forward. Fortunately, the tide was low enough they were able to cross without incident.

Once across the river, he rode apart from the camp and sat on his horse looking west. Eventually, he returned and gave temporary command to Jamin with orders to set up camp. Turning his horse west, he rode off at a steady pace. *I shall find this river Lucifer speaks of!*

For three days, he maintained a steady but quick pace, stopping occasionally for food and rest. At night he would find a hilltop and stop. There he would make a small camp, and feed his horse before settling down.

Once satisfied that all was well, he would eat and get a restful sleep before rising at the break of dawn. In this manner, he was able to cover about 50 miles a day.

It was at the end of the third day, tired and looking for a place to camp that he noticed signs of wildlife and fertile ground. *I must be near water. I will continue on.*

It was another hour and a half before he came upon the river that snaked its way toward the south.

Flowing SE, just as the Tigris, but more sluggish, it was an impressive sight. So much so that he imagined it compared to the Euphrates River of the old world! *Except that the Euphrates was far more violent. Still, I like the name.*

"That is what I shall call it. The Euphrates River!"

Making camp, he settled down to eat and consider what Satan wanted him to do. *This is a large land between the two rivers. Lucifer has picked well. He has chosen me to establish his kingdom. I shall not fail him!*

As he closed his eyes, he decided to spend a few more days exploring along its shore before returning to the main camp.

&&&

Shem sat astride his mule watching as Nimrod rode out of the encampment and traveled west.

*Now where is he going? And should I follow?*

With Nimrod riding a horse and he a mule, the choice became quickly apparent. He turned and rode back to his own camp. *I shall wait for his return. Whatever he is up to will have to remain a mystery for the present time. He probably left Jamin in charge, so I shall keep an eye on him. I shall also keep a watch over the people, and when he returns, I shall continue following him. I wonder what he is planning?*

&&&

Asshur and Elam huddled together inside their tent.

"Maybe we should rebel now," Elam suggested, "while he is gone. Jamin can't stop us."

"Perhaps," agreed Asshur, "but the people won't follow us. They fear Nimrod, yes. But they also believe he is almost a god. Right now they will follow him anywhere. No, we must wait for a better time."

"How long?"

"Until we are strong enough to defeat him. Believe me, Elam, when I say that the day will come when I shall rule. I know more about military strategy than Nimrod will ever know. Be assured, it will happen!"

"And I will be by your side!"

# SIXTEEN

## DEPARTURE FROM GOD

2275BC (pop. 488)

"Long live Nimrod! Long live Nimrod!

The chant echoed along the plains of Shinar, which was already being called the Land of Nimrod. Up on a hill overlooking the encampment, Nimrod sat upon his shiny black stallion. The crowds below cheered lustily, some waving at him excitedly. Although a few families remained in their tents, most of the people were loudly acknowledging Nimrod as their ruler. Some even dared to call him a god.

Absent from this adoring crowd were Noah and his son Shem. But Japheth and Ham both were there, Japheth having recently moved into the encampment. However, Japheth was not enamored with Nimrod and refused to participate in this celebration. Instead he stayed in his tent determined to remain free of Nimrod's entanglements.

Most of Shem's family still resided in the mountains with Noah, but Nimrod's influence was so great that a good number of Shem's family had also joined him. This brought Nimrod's followers to 137 men, women and children. This was a small group of people, but they were growing rapidly due to a bountiful birth rate.

Nimrod had reason to be proud, since such numbers meant only about 34 people were in the mountains of Ararat with Noah. This fact further meant that he was the undisputed leader of the world!

Sitting upon his magnificent horse, Nimrod was dressed in his newest finery. With a sword sheathed by his side and the sun behind him, he looked like the world leader that the crowd was cheering. It was at this moment that he chose to turn his horse toward the people and slowly, majestically ride toward them.

As the cheering grew louder and louder, his own pride grew. *I'm only 33 and I now rule the world! Not bad!*

As he rode forward, the crowd parted making a path for him to pass through. Some of them were daring enough to edge closer to him; some close enough to touch him and his horse. Grinning from ear to ear, he rode the entire length of the camp before turning around and retracing his route. He continued this activity for several minutes until he decided to stop and get busy.

Riding to his tent, he dismounted with a flourish. Turning the horse over to a servant, he turned back facing the people. He stood there waving at the people as they continued to cheer him.

After a few moments of basking in their adulation, he walked over to his tent. There he stood at the doorway and waited while several of his closest friends and counselors gathered about him. Except for the brothers, Asshur and Elam, who were conspicuously absent. A fact that pleased him rather than angering him. He didn't need their negative attitude.

"Men, the plains of Shinar lay before us. A little further south is the land that I have decided we shall dwell in, build our cities, and worship the gods of heaven.

"In the past we have worshiped the God of Noah. But this is the same God that cursed my grandfather! Belief in Him is a poison that must be removed. And the only way that can be accomplished involves doing two things. As ruler, I shall have dominion over this land and all the people. You have heard their shouts of praise. They will follow me anywhere!

"Secondly, let us build us a city and a tower, whose top may reach unto heaven; and let us make us a name, lest we be scattered abroad upon the face of the whole earth. Since there are no rocks available, we shall make bricks and use slime as mortar. If it was good enough for the Ark, it is good enough for the tower. When it is built, the tower will pull the people unto itself."

"Won't the people object?"

"No! You heard them. I am a god to them. Besides, they won't know what is happening. We shall teach them that the host of heaven,

God's own created angels, represent His power. And the stars of heaven represent them. Later they shall be taught that the angels are gods that they can pray to and get answers."

"Then it is your plan that this will be gradual and not right away?" asked Jamin, his right hand man.

"Yes. It will take time, but eventually the people will turn from God."

"What about Asshur? He has resisted you all along on anything that splits with the past, especially the worship of other gods. Neither he nor his brother honored you just now."

"True, he is a problem. But I may include him as one of the gods to be worshiped. However, don't let him fool you. He wants to be a ruler. Religion is no more important to him than it is to me."

"That's even more reason to consider him a danger! Especially if he wants to rule in your place."

"I do not fear Asshur. He is a fine warrior and has an inventive mind. But he does not have the vision needed on the battlefield. In time of war, that will be his undoing. But I see your concern. What do you suggest?"

"If he becomes too great a problem, you will have to expel him or remove him permanently."

"Perhaps that is true. If the time comes to deal with him, we will do what you suggest. But for now, his inventive mind is more valuable than any possible threat that he can muster. His inventions strengthen us as well as himself. So we shall continue to use him as long as that is true."

"And what about Noah?"

"We need not fear him. Noah is far to the north in Ararat. He and Shem chose to stay there near their precious Ark. We are too far south for them to exert any influence here. Besides, if they were to cause any problems, we are the ones with weapons! Plus, I am not afraid to use them."

&&&

Shelah laughed as he watched his son Eber pick up his younger brother Ahban. Only nine, Eber was quite active and inquisitive, but his brother was his true joy. And Ahban followed Eber around everywhere.

"Enjoying fatherhood, Shelah?"

He looked up with a grin at his father.

"Yes. Ahban is well named. He is only three and is already showing his intelligence."

He stood and joined his father as they walked a little away from the tent.

"I want you to be careful, son," solemnly spoke Arpachshad.

"Is there trouble?"

"Yes, I have heard that you plan to follow Nimrod."

"If you mean follow them to the plains, then you are correct. We will leave in the next few days. But only because I have heard the ground is fertile and there is much water."

"I don't oppose that my son," responded Arpachshad. "But I fear if you follow him, he will turn you against Noah. And worse, against God!"

"You needn't fear on that matter, father. Noah is the greatest man alive! Who else but he has the ear of God?"

"Well, your grandfather Shem seems to know Him quite well."

"Oh, I didn't mean to say he doesn't know God. But wouldn't even he point to Noah?"

"Yes, of course. But I am really concerned. Some of Nimrod's men and methods are very rough. They may try to force you to follow their ways."

"Then they will have a problem. I only plan to live amongst them, not worship their gods. If they try to force me to do otherwise, I will protect my family with my life if I have to!"

"Good. If you are certain to move to the plains, I would request your eyes and ears."

"I don't understand."

"Your grandfather Shem is keeping an eye on them as a directive from God. He still records the history of all mankind, so I suspect this directive is part of that. He travels a lot, following the caravan. But they are growing in number and he cannot be everywhere. It would be most helpful if you could keep him informed of all that transpires."

"I would be delighted, father."

&&&

"No. I will not accept that!" Asshur shouted, his face flushing. "God destroyed the world once before because of unbelief. I will not be a part of this!"

"Asshur, no one said anything about not worshiping God," Nimrod replied calmly. "We are simply honoring His own creation. As I have explained before, God is the Creator. He created all things, including the stars.

"Surely you can see that the worship of God as Noah practices it, is not good for us. His ways are outdated. God has revealed more truth than just what Noah preaches. It is time to move past Noah and embrace the greater truth."

"I don't object to not following Noah. Noah is a great man, but he doesn't speak for me. But you don't fool me, Nimrod, for a minute; what you are talking about is worshiping new gods!"

"No Asshur, I am merely talking about worshiping the very angels that God created. Noah calls them stars, but God has revealed to me that they are angels He created for our benefit. They have names and they are there as our friends.

"They are there to guide us and keep us from making the same mistakes of the past. Back then, on the other side of the Flood, the people ignorantly worshiped the gods of their imagination. This led them to all sorts of immorality. That is wrong and it led to the destruction of the whole world.

"As I said before, Asshur, we must guard against the wicked practices of the past, else God will destroy our world again. If that comes to pass, God may never give us another chance to get it right. The only way we can be assured of His protection is to worship God entirely.

"He not only created the earth, but the stars of heaven as well. God speaks to us through the Writings, yes. But He also speaks to us through His own creation. It would be a fatal mistake to ignore what He created.

"I am not seeking the worship of men, Asshur. I would rather not be worshiped, but if God sees fit to exalt me in such a fashion, who am I to object?"

"You may fool others, but not me."

Asshur turned, striding away in anger.

"Well, that went well."

"Yes, Jamin, it did. But we will still keep an eye on him. He will stay and will not be much trouble to us for the time being. But he is a capable soldier and could cause problems later."

"I could arrange an accident.'

Nimrod looked at Jamin.

"No, not now. But the day may come."

&&&

Later that day, a short distance away, Phut and Mizraim were gathered with their families. Though the two families were small in number, they had complete loyalty in Phut and would resist Nimrod if that was Phut's desire.

One of the men stood and directed his words at the leaders.

"Phut, have you heard the rumors?"

"What rumors?"

"Nimrod and Asshur had a falling out. It had something to do with gods."

"Gods? What do you mean?" asked Phut.

"Not sure, but maybe Nimrod wants us to worship him now? I heard this tower he wants to build will have his image on it."

"Haven't heard that one," remarked Phut, "but I did hear they had an argument. Where did you hear that rumor?"

"I heard it from one of Asshur's servants. What should we do?"

"About the rumor, nothing. We will let them fight it out. If they are occupied with one another, that is good for us. If they have a falling out, we will be put in a position of strength.

"In the meantime, we are growing in number and in skill. If either Nimrod or Asshur tries to intimidate us, we can protect ourselves. We already have a skilled force that is man-for-man better than anything either Nimrod or Asshur can mount."

"Do we continue following Nimrod?"

"For now, yes. But we must stay alert!"

&&&

Shem dismounted from his donkey and started a small campfire. Roasting a hart, he quietly mused over what he had observed. Earlier in the day, he received word from Shelah describing the celebrations. But the most intriguing information concerned the argument between Nimrod and Asshur, suggesting that problems were already cropping up amidst the people.

*Right now they are all united in their rebellion, but in time they will break up. Perhaps God will use that event to bring them back to His worship. What a day that would be, when the people return to Him!*

Climbing a nearby hill, he walked over to a single, twisted tree and knelt to pray. He felt an overwhelming sense of foreboding engulf him and his voice cracked as he spoke.

"O God, every day they drift further and further from You. They create new gods and idols that neither speak or have any life. They are nothing but lifeless idols!

"O that they would return and worship You as before when the Ark first landed on Ararat. My heart breaks for them. I fear what they are doing. Every day they grow in number, power, and arrogance. They look at those of us who believe in You and in Your Word as though we are ignorant and foolish. They laugh and their hearts are filled with scorn.

"O Lord, when You send me; when I go amidst them, grant that Thy servant will speak Thy Word in power."

He paused, waiting for an answer but only silence surrounded him. He strained that he might hear that quiet voice, but nothing came. He remained in that position for a good amount of time.

Finally realizing that he wasn't going to get a response until later, he stood. With a heavy heart, he returned unto the campfire and sat before its warmth. As the night darkened, he stifled a yawn. Stretching out on the hard earth, he drifted off to sleep.

&&&

Asshur stuck his head into Elam's tent.

"It is time!"

Elam was startled by the interruption and the saying. Rising, he stepped outside to speak with his brother.

"What do you mean it is time? Are we now to rebel?"

"No. It is time for you to search to the south. If anyone notices your absence, have your wife tell them you are sick and cannot come forth. I will support whatever she says."

"When do you want me to go?"

"I believe Nimrod is going to call a meeting soon to discuss his plans. As soon as that has taken place, we will put this plan into action. But you should not be gone for very long."

"How about two weeks. Surely I can learn enough in two weeks."

"Sounds good," Asshur said.

# SEVENTEEN

## A NEW CITY

2270BC (pop. 732)

Shem dismounted as he watched the scene a few miles away. Under the dominant rule of Nimrod, the people had moved into the land of Shinar and started building his first city along the western shore of the wide, but calm Euphrates River. The fertile land along the river's banks was mostly flat, with occasional hills.

To Shem the plains were a poor comparison to the forested land of his youth. If he closed his eyes, he could still picture the city of Uruk and the surrounding Majestic Forest. He remembered the famous vineyards of Noah, the gigantic trees, and the luscious foliage of the forest.

But that wasn't all. He remembered the colorful and beautiful Majestic Mountains rising to the west. In his mind he could still picture the mountains in all their glory, whereas the Mountains of Ararat were plain in comparison. Just as the Ararat Mountains failed in comparison to the Majestic Mountains, so too did the comparison of Shinar to the Majestic Forest.

"For that matter," he mused aloud, "it doesn't compare to the rolling hills of Abel."

He looked at the small hilltop he had chosen for his campsite. Several miles north of Nimrod's camp, it provided a broad vision of the overall area. Facing south, he could see the Euphrates River and the encampment on its western shore. On the eastern side of the river he could see distant mountains.

"If they need wood, they'll have quite a ways to go to get it. It will be interesting to see how they resolve this problem."

&&&

Meanwhile, Nimrod settled the people a little north of where he planned to build his new city. He already had a name for it: Babel, which meant the Gate of God. Little did he know that the God he defied would change the meaning.

The absence of mountains in the immediate area meant there would be no rocks to be used as building material. Upon discovering this fact, Nimrod quickly realized he needed something else to build his city. Fortunately, he knew where to look. Reading the stolen tablets, he discovered the ancient art of making bricks.

As he studied the tablets, he learned that the bricks would need to be baked in the sun and tested for lasting endurance. According to the ancient documents, sun-dried bricks were excellent substitutes for stone. Moreover, as he looked over the land, he realized the soil was highly desirable for brick making.

*With such a short supply of men available, I think that this can be the work of the boys between twelve and twenty. The older men can make the tools, but the boys can do the actual work. We'll have them work right near the river so they will have plenty of water. The women can gather the wild straw.*

The tablets mentioned the use of tar, but he didn't know of any tar in the area. He took his problem to Jamin.

"If we have no tar to use, what can we use?"

"Why not use animal dung. There is plenty of it around. Chop the straw and mix it with the dung, maybe that will work."

Nimrod liked the idea and decided to use it.

&&&

As part of his building plan, he realized that he would need an efficient way of governing the new city and overseeing the construction itself. Remembering the stories of the ancient world and its cities, especially the city of Abel, he marveled at the broad avenues and boulevards as well as the well-laid out city.

The more he thought about it, the more determined he was to build such a city again. It was with this thought in mind that he sent for the elders of the families.

Gathering them together outside his tent, he took a stick and drew a circle on the ground.

"Men, I have been thinking about this for some time now. To build a city that will last, we need to go about it in the right way. This circle I have drawn represents the new city of Babel, the Gate of God. When finished, it will be the greatest city ever built, but it will take your cooperation to see such a result.

"So I have decided that we will divide this city into three parts; a part for the family of Japheth, a part for the family of Ham, and a part for Shem's descendants' Asshur and Elam."

"Why?" asked Phut.

"To keep the families together and to have an efficient way of administering the construction and the city itself. For example, Phut, I would put you in charge of the families of Ham. You, in turn, would further divide your portion of the city so that you could rule it effectively."

Heads bobbed in agreement as the elders realized the wisdom of such an arrangement.

"One more thing," resumed Nimrod. "Because we are on the plains and not in the mountains, there are no rocks to be used for building. Therefore, much brick will need to be made by the people. Within each of the three families there should be female laborers to gather straw, boy laborers to make bricks, and adult male laborers to mortar the bricks into place."

With that final instruction, the meeting broke up into several conversations as each of the elders considered what the new rules would entail. Nimrod listened politely, happy to see their enthusiasm. After several minutes of such talk the elders left his tent and headed to their respective families.

Upon reaching their tents, each elder immediately called a meeting of their family heads, namely all the men aged twelve and up, to discuss the new arrangements. Some meetings lasted well into the night, while others were quite brief. The end result, however, was the same: enthusiastic agreement!

The next day was very exciting to the people. Arising at dawn, they set about loading their carts or strapping supplies to their backs and began moving toward their assigned portions. Although they stirred up a lot of dust, the people cheerfully followed their leaders, some even breaking out in song.

To Shem, watching from the distance, it all appeared as a confusing mass of people.

"They are moving again? I was sure this was where Nimrod planned to build."

But through the dust, he began to see that instead of continuing southward, the people were actually moving in a circle. Moreover, it was quite well organized. He watched as the slow moving process took place. It was like watching an army moving into position just before battle.

&&&

Three days later, with the dust settling and each family was camping just outside their assigned position, Nimrod's plan was working. He made a point of visiting the various families and congratulating them on the success of their move.

Soon the family leaders were assigning work, first by family and then individually. A sense of excitement raced through the encampment. Throughout the day everyone thought about what they would be doing. Nimrod had promised that they would be able to learn even as they worked.

On the following day, the work began in earnest. Teenage boys raced to the river to begin making bricks, while both teenage and adult women went into the wild fields of straw. The older men began making the tools they would need.

As the sun rose in the sky, the women busily went about gathering the straw, which grew naturally throughout the area. At first the women were confused about how to harvest the straw, but Nimrod, as promised, sent overseers out to instruct them. This proved beneficial as the women quickly caught on and were bringing in abundant shafts of straw within a few days.

The craftsmen started learning their new trade. Overseers were sent among them to teach the men how to construct wooden molds. This proved a simple task. After only one day of training, they were constructing a great quantity of wooden molds. Within days, the molds were ready to start making bricks. Nimrod issued instructions for brick making based on the tablets.

"Water shall be drawn from the Euphrates and used to turn the clay into mud. Then the mud shall be put by hand into the molds and shall be mixed with straw and dung. Each brick will be allowed a full day to dry in the sun, two if necessary. Once dried, they are to be stacked one upon another and left for several days.

"After this time the brick shall be examined for cracks or crumbling. Any bricks failing this test must be removed. All other bricks shall be transported to where the construction is taking place."

The boys were frustrated at first because they had to wait for the molds. But once the molds were ready, the work began. It took a few days to actually get everyone working together and following Nimrod's instructions, but it soon began to show results. Nimrod had anticipated 100 bricks a day, but the boys were soon turning out thousands of bricks every day!

&&&

Taking only a servant and several days provisions with him, Elam slipped away and headed south. With the two of them riding horses and trailing a pack horse behind, they made rapid time. Once out of sight of the camp, they urged their horses forward at a comfortable trot that found them quickly putting miles between the city and themselves.

During the next three days, they traveled night and day with only an occasional stop. Even night time found them traveling. Elam wasn't interested in the land as he passed through it. He didn't even start looking until the fourth day!

It was then that he made his decision.

"We shall turn east," he told his servant. "We shall see if the Tigris continues this far downstream and if it is passable. If so, we will cross to the other side."

&&&

Nimrod had thought long and hard on how to get the most out of the people. His attempt to turn the people from the worship of the one true God was working. By substituting the various angels for God, he was able to see a definite shift in the people's religious fervor. It was only a first step, but he was pleased.

Moreover, his popularity was rising. Gathering the people into one place, he stood before them and spoke of his plan for building the city. It immediately pleased the people. Some wanted to name the city after him, but he demurred. This attitude strengthened his position with the populace.

His next step was to call upon Amzi (*Robust*) to take charge of the construction. Amzi easily lived up to his name, as he was short, strong, and a good worker. Jamin spotted him early on and told Nimrod of his capabilities.

"The only drawback is that he still worships the Elohim. Nor does he demonstrate any belief in your divinity."

"Is he loyal?"

"Yes, as long as you don't ask him to violate his beliefs. Up to that point, he will do whatever you ask."

"Good. He will do."

A short time later, Nimrod appointed Amzi to take command of the project. He immediately set about getting the men busy laying brick. Using mud plaster as mortar, they would place the bricks one upon the other. Once satisfied that the brick was mortared below and on each end, they would put another brick on, adjoining the previous brick. They would continue this until a section was completed, then they would start on the next tier.

These single story buildings were to house Nimrod's army, providing them with the necessary shelter from the frequent rains. When finished, each building could hold up to ten men with simple mats for sleeping. Later these buildings would be upgraded with furniture, including cots.

Amzi did such a masterful job, that he was given the title Brick Master and awarded the first private home built, which consisted of two rooms with a door and small window. But to Amzi, the house, when compared to a tent, was a palace! Although not in the original plans, he added a second window in the rear, although primarily for ventilation. This was to please his wife, as she had difficulty breathing in closed places.

Once he had moved his wife Abigail and daughter Chloe into their new home, he moved to the next site and began building another home. In each one, he added the ventilation window. This was repeated continually over a span of many months.

The result however was instantaneous: the loyalty of both the army and the people to Nimrod!

&&&

Two weeks after he left the camp, Elam and his servant returned. His absence had largely been undetected by Nimrod and his men. The story that was circulated, saying he was sick and could not see anyone, had kept his absence a secret.

He actually arrived during the daytime. Although tired, hungry, and eager to see his family, he thought it wise not to be seen by Nimrod or his men. Remaining a distance away on a hill south of the city, they didn't enter until darkness had fallen. It was then that they mounted their horses and slipped into the encampment.

They made their way through the now sleeping camp and dismounted at Elam's tent. Sending the servant to his own family, Elam unpacked. After greeting his wife and family, he made his way to Asshur's tent.

After warm greetings, the two men walked a safe distance from the tents to where they could speak confidentially.

"What have you found, my brother?" asked Asshur, barely containing his eagerness.

"I have found a land to the southeast that is very inviting. It is on the other side of the Tigris and shall be a place easily defended. I searched to the east of the river and discovered another river whereby we can build our own city."

"That is wonderful. We shall await our opportunity."

&&&

While the citizens saw the work as a product of his benevolence, the real reason was much more practical. It was practice for the more important projects: the construction of Nimrod's palace and the temple.

Amongst the stolen clay tablets, he found descriptions of Methuselah's house in Abel before the Flood. He used that design as a basis for his own design although he eliminated the Little Eden room. Once completed, it towered three stories high with stairs on the inside ascending to the second floor. Meanwhile, the outside stairs led to the roof or third floor where the baths were located. This third floor was open to the air, with neither walls nor ceiling; the belief being that an open-air bath was healthier than an enclosed bath.

The entrance to the house was a massive double door swinging easily on hinges. The wood used for its construction and indeed used throughout the house was transported from the forested hills to the east. This required the use of horse-drawn wagons, plus many men to cut and bring the trees to the plains. For that reason the palace took over a year to build.

Three months after beginning the project, the actual construction began with the laying of the foundation. This consisted primarily of using bulls pulling a long wooden plow behind them. This served to level the ground. After this, they began laying bricks for the outer wall. It was only after the walls were in place that the actual foundation for the floor was laid. The easy part had been completed, now it got harder.

Up to now, floors had consisted of beaten earth, so the floor for the palace had never been done before. Using only the basic tools available, they struggled to get the ground completely level. This delayed the work a couple of weeks, but eventually they succeeded.

Next, they started working on the second floor. Using scaffolds, the workers built the first floor walls to a height of ten feet. They also erected inside walls to support the second floor. Then came the tricky part. Using 12' beams, they laid them across the tops of the walls side by side.

It was while doing this that a tragic accident occurred. One of the more experienced men got careless while walking upon the still loose beams. He was halfway across when the beam moved. Normally, he would have paused and caught his balance before continuing on. But whether he was distracted or simply overconfident, he failed to react properly. Suddenly his feet slipped as the beam moved again and he fell to his death. Nimrod was determined not to let this mishap stop his construction. Ordering the work to continue, he personally picked up the dead body and carried it outside the city. There it was tossed into a pile of waste products and left to rot.

Nimrod waited until evening to visit the man's home and inform his wife of his death. Nimrod told her she could have the following day off to grieve, but she would be needed afterward.

"Thank you, my lord. But I cannot accept your graciousness. The other women need me. With your permission, I shall return to the field tomorrow.

"Granted."

&&&

When all three stories were finished, Nimrod took a tour of the new building.

Entering through a large, single door, he paused to close the door behind him. He then placed two beams through rings attached to the doors, which served to secure the door. He turned and entered a well-lit room and proceeded through to a dimly lit hallway, with adjoining rooms on either side. Both rooms had couches where diners could relax, and oaken tables big enough for feasts. Visitors would be escorted through another door leading into a large throne-room.

This room was entirely of Nimrod's imagination. Upon entering, a visitor would see a raised platform at the far end where Nimrod's throne rested. The visitor would thus be required to cross the room and mount a series of three steps leading from the floor to the platform where he would stand or kneel before the throne. But to climb those stairs uninvited would risk certain death!

At first the floor was beaten earth just like the poorer homes, but later it was covered with tile and in the throne room with a multicolored carpet.. Meanwhile, the walls were decorated with tapestries that the women of the city offered in praise. Strategically located along the walls were torches that illuminated the entire room.

The second floor was basically the same, but was to be used primarily for servant quarters. Meanwhile, the third floor was to be exclusively for Nimrod and his family. Here they added a balcony overlooking the city.

Once completed, Nimrod turned his attention to building a tower that would reach to the heavens!

# EIGHTEEN

## TOWER OF BABEL

2272BC (pop. 770)

About two days journey to the north, on a hill situated along the Euphrates River's western bank, a small fire glowed in the evening sky. A lone bird, attracted by the light, flew overhead. Looking down, the bird spotted the campsite of a lone man lying next to the fire and enjoying its heat. A few feet away was the man's mule. His curiosity satisfied, the bird resumed its westward flight.

Shem lay upon the ground with his hands acting as a pillow for his head. Staring up at the twinkling stars, he thought of Achsah. *O, the comfort of her lap and her fingers massaging my temple!*

He had been on the road for some time now. During the course of the last month he had visited Babel twice and explored, at God's direction, the Euphrates River. His body ached from the constant riding.

Withdrawing his hands, his heavy eyes closed as sleep overtook him. Moments later an angel visited him in a dream.

"Arise, thou sleepy head. Arise and hear thou the Word of thy Lord. Tomorrow thou shalt mount up and get thee to Babel. For the Lord God has a word for the rebellious in heart, a warning to the people of this city."

Shem bolted up, staring at the angel. Seeing the angel's brilliance caused an immediate fear. But this initial feeling of fear was erased the moment the angel spoke. Now, as he tried to understand what the angel was saying, he waited. In the quiet of the night, the angel delivered his message and left.

&&&

The next morning Shem arose, saddled his mule and rode south. During the next three days of riding, he meditated upon the message given by the angel. He was mildly surprised that the angel did not reappear.

On the third day he rode into the now beautiful city of Babel. Seeing his sons, Elam and Asshur, should have been a time of rejoicing, but Shem avoided them completely. Instead, he rode along the main street, which ran north/south.

Riding through the North Gate, which was wide enough to allow four men walking abreast and tall enough that a man on horseback or mule, such as himself, would not need to duck, he paused to watch the women as they shopped.

Nearby were several men working on a building that when finished would adjoin the northern wall. Observing the ongoing work and the wide thoroughfare, he was immediately impressed with the progress since his last visit. *This thoroughfare is primarily for merchants. It is amazing how many there are!*

Continuing southward, he remained in awe as he could hear the women haggling over produce. He smiled as he remembered the many times he had observed Achsah do the same.

Shem arrived at the primary cross street, which ran east/west, and turned toward the east. As he turned the corner, he brought his mule to a complete stop.

Although still on the west side of the city, he had a clear view of the king's palace, which was located over the bridge and on the east side. *It is clearly the largest building in all the city; indeed, in all the world!*

As he rode toward the bridge straddling the Euphrates, he became acutely aware of a significant divide. The homes he was passing were small well-built houses for the poor and the smaller merchants. But, even as he drew near the bridge, he could see other homes on the opposite side that even from a distance were beautiful to behold. *The bridge is more than a physical divide. It is a division between the poor and the rich!*

At this moment, a strong fish smell struck his nose. Almost at the same moment, he saw fishermen below the bridge and on the north side mending their nets. He nodded as he remembered that the best time for fishing was at night, while daylight was needed for mending nets. But even the sight and smell of fish added to the overall separation between rich and poor. The entire Fish Market was here on the western bank of the Euphrates!

As if to emphasize this observation, the palace came into view again. It was at this time that he noticed that the palace was at least three times larger than any of the homes he could see in the vicinity. Urging his mount forward, some of the large two story homes surrounding the palace came into better view. Although large and magnificent, they only added to the overall dominance of the regal house. A short distance away he could see an entire acre of barren land already cleared and ready for construction. *This is where the temple will be built,* he thought.

&&&

Crossing over the bridge, he immediately became aware of an influx of men, women and children entering the street. Most were heading the same direction as he was traveling. Moving along slowly in the crowd, he had a clear view of the barren land that lay in contrast to the nearby palace. He paused and turned his gaze on the palace, which had a certain elegance and power to it. Looking it over in admiration, he found himself comparing it to his home back in the mountains. He had to force himself to look back at the temple site.

Continuing on, he headed straight for the outskirts of the temple area where he finally stopped. Noting the markings on the ground, he understood that he was looking at the outside border of the temple. Not a single brick had been laid yet, although he could see a nearby stack of bricks being added to by a worker.

"Impressive isn't it?"

Shem turned to see Nimrod.

"Yes, it is a very large area."

"That's because it will reach unto the heavens. Such height requires a large base. It will be 300 feet wide, 300 feet long, and 110 feet high."

"Just the base?" Shem asked in surprise.

"Yes. The second tier will be 260 by 260 by 60 feet. After that, each succeeding tier will be 20 feet high, except the seventh and final tier. It will be 70 by 80 by 50 feet. Of course, each tier between the second and seventh is smaller than the one under it, thus allowing for structural strength."

"Where did you get such wisdom?"

"From above," Nimrod smiled slyly.

"Or perhaps from tablets stolen from Noah."

Nimrod's face darkened at the accusation, but Shem simply turned his back on him. Seeing a prominent spot nearby, he dismounted and walked over to it, taking up a position. Immediately, he started preaching to any that would listen.

"O citizens of Babel, do you build this tower unto God? Will you worship God here? Or is this tower of Nimrod's built in defiance of the One Who destroyed the world for its idolatry?"

While Nimrod watched in disgust, several nearby workers, as well as women, gathered around him to listen. Shem directed his gaze upon them as he continued.

"Beware, for if you build this tower in defiance of the living God, thou shalt suffer the consequences. God has not told me what He will do, but He is dismayed with your disobedience. Your sin shall be your undoing!"

&&&

Shelah took Eber, now thirteen, aside to instruct him in carpentry.

"Father, if they are using bricks, what do they need carpenters for?"

"Son, carpenters are extremely important. You can use bricks to build walls and in some cases ceilings, but you need carpenters to furnish the interiors."

"You mean tables and chairs?"

"That and much more. Ours' is an honored trade, my son. You have never traveled north, but if you did, you would find that the homes where Noah, Shem, and others live are all made of wood. Thus, requiring carpenters. And I might add that the day will come when they will want ships to travel the rivers. That also is our work."

"What about Ahban? Will he be a carpenter also?"

"When he is old enough. But for now, he must stay with his mother."

Putting his arm around his son's shoulders, Shelah took Eber to work at Nimrod's palace, where they were working on a library to contain the many tablets and future writings.

Living on the west side, they had to cross the bridge, then make their way to the palace. Eber liked walking with his father, but he loved the view of the palace. The closer they got, the more impressive it became.

Arriving at the palace, Shelah took Eber over to a large table where many tools lay ready to be used. Eber listened carefully as Shelah pointed out each tool and described its purpose. Eber saw and handled saws, chisels, hammers, braces, nails, and glue. Today he was introduced to the tools, but tomorrow would begin his education.

&&&

Phut liked the work arrangements. It allowed him full control over his people and over his portion of the temple construction. Showing deference to Nimrod was therefore much easier.

Mizraim came to him one night and the two moved away from the others so that their voices would not be heard.

"Are we really going to build this tower for Nimrod?" Mizraim asked.

"Yes. It means nothing to me. But I shall do what it takes to keep him happy and out of my affairs. Perhaps later I will know what to do. But for now we follow him."

Mizraim nodded. "But some day, we must rebel. And lead our people elsewhere."

"True. But where would you lead them?"

Mizraim had no answer.

&&&

Later that year, actual construction of the temple began as the bricklayers began working on the foundation. The entire first floor was to be bricked with only a small interior room. The rest consisted of almost solid brick, since each succeeding floor would be sitting upon the structure below.

Using the stolen tablets as a guide, the temple was to be built in receding tiers upon a platform with a flat top. Sun-baked bricks would be used for the core of the ziggurat while facings of fired bricks, a new technology, were on the outside.

Nimrod commissioned artists to glaze the bricks in different colors with each succeeding floor representing astrological deities, while each tier's tops would be painted in indigo. He also ordered that his name be engraved on these glazed bricks. The entire height was to be seven tiers with a spiral ramp beginning at the base and continuing until reaching the top. There a shrine was to be built upon the flat top. The total height was 300 feet and the area would be 90,000 square feet.

Jamin, looking over the plans, noticed something.

"I don't see any rooms big enough to allow worshipers."

"This is not a temple that you go inside to worship. It will be the dwelling places for the gods. Each god will have a special small room set aside for a statue to reside within."

"And the shrine on top is for Ishtar, the goddess of love and war?"

"Yes. I would have preferred Marduk, but you may have Ishtar. Did you notice the three ramps?"

"Yes. But two only reach halfway up."

"That's correct. They are temporary to allow workers to easily get up to the higher heights. This third one leads to the shrine. Once done, the first two will be destroyed.

Jamin was impressed.

"This will be the greatest temple ever built!"

While others didn't have the same opportunity to see the sketches, the rising ziggurat evinced almost immediate pride and praise. Each succeeding tier drew more praise as the temple slowly rose.

&&&

"Judgment must come, son," Noah remarked after Shem finished his report. "God will not allow them to build this tower unto heaven without suffering the consequences."

"I agree, father," acknowledged Shem. "But I daily pray that my sons will be spared."

"They are all my descendants and judgment will cause anguish to my heart," responded Noah. "But it is certain to come. There are two things I am certain of: one, the judgment of God will come and secondly, it won't be a flood. Beyond that I do not know."

Father and son lapsed into silence as they considered the impending judgment.

# NINETEEN

## SEMIRAMIS

2265BC (pop. 873)

The sickness came suddenly taking Nimrod's wife in a single night. The whole palace was awake, yet not a sound was heard as the slaves moved about quietly afraid to disturb the king.

The king sat quietly upon the bed looking at his wife's dead body. Her sudden death had struck him deeply. *Has the God of Noah taken revenge upon me? Is this the judgment spoken of by Shem?*

His thoughts were interrupted as the priest Jamin entered.

"It is time to remove her body," Jamin said calmly.

Nimrod stood, nodded, and left the room.

&&&

Two months later, Jamin took two of Nimrod's servants aside.

"I want you to do something for your king," he began. "Search the city and find three virgins. You have thirty days to bring them to me. Failure will mean death for you and your families."

The men paled, and one asked, "But where shall we look and what shall we look for?"

Jamin studied the men, his harsh eyes seeming to pierce their inner beings.

"Search the city; search the alleyways; search the marketplace. I don't care whether they are poor, rich, or slaves. I don't care where they are, you find them. As for what to look for, that is easy. You are to find virgins that are eighteen, beautiful, and strong. You have thirty days. Now, be gone!"

The men scurried away with trembling hearts and immediately began their search for the virgins. One of the servants decided to visit the homes of wealthier families. His plan was simple: look first among the elite families and, if that fails, to look among the working families.

The other servant decided to search the palace slave quarters, which were located behind the palace and enclosed. Only recently, Nimrod had begun the practice of enslaving people who owed him great debt. He would enslave an entire family and they would labor in the palace. As such, the families would have no say and could not resist if one of their daughters was selected.

The servant felt like holding his nose at the foul odor that seemed to pervade the quarter. He stopped and looked around. The quarter was really one large rectangular area that was divided into simple living quarters for the families.

*It is going to be difficult finding a virgin here. Maybe this is a mistake.*

He paused and mulled over the problem.

*Still, I have seen some rather attractive maidens working in the palace. I will just need to be alert. Don't take anything for granted. Whoa, who is this walking toward me?*

He had just seen an attractive woman walking toward him. Her beauty was stunning! With intense interest he watched as she approached. Although carrying a large jar of water upon her shoulder, she moved easily. Such ease suggested supple strength.

When she drew even with him, he singled for her to stop. Halting, she stood with her free hand resting on her hip. Her deep black eyes seemed to swallow him. The servant's mouth seemed dry as he spoke.

"What is your name?"

"Semiramis, master."

"I am not your master, but I serve him. How old are you?"

"Eighteen."

"Come with me."

"But I must bring the water to the house or I shall be punished."

"Then do so and return here. If you do not return, your punishment will be far greater."

He watched as she hurried off. *The priest will be pleased with her. I have never seen anyone with such a great combination of beauty and strength.*

A few minutes later, the girl returned and he took her to the priest.

"Leave us," Jamin commanded.

After the servant departed, Jamin turned his attention to the girl before him.

"Remove your clothes."

Semiramis gulped. But to disobey would bring punishment for her and maybe her family. She removed her dress and stood naked before him.

For his part, Jamin had never seen a maiden so beautiful. *If the king rejects her, I shall take her for myself!*

"Have you been with a man?"

"No, sire. I have not."

"Well, I must examine you. If you are a virgin as you say, then you must be prepared for the king."

"For the king?" her lips trembled as the words came out.

"Yes, you undoubtedly have heard his wife has died. He needs a woman or women who can make him forget her loss. It will be your job to please him."

*To please the king! To be his wife!*

A feeling of pride infused her. It made the humiliation of his examination much easier to bear.

&&&

Three months after his wife's death, Nimrod was sitting on the balcony watching as the moon rose above his city. Not normally a sensitive man, nonetheless, her death had greatly affected him. A sense of loneliness had overcome him then and had not departed. *I wonder if I will ever be happy again. If this is the punishment threatened by Shem's God, it is truly cruel.*

He was surprised when Jamin entered the chamber, followed by three females dressed in very revealing clothes. He felt an immediate attraction. All thoughts about loneliness disappeared in an instant!

"Your highness, do not be angry," Jamin began. "But I have decided that you need someone to replace your wife. You have mourned her death appropriately. But now I beg that thou observe the women as they dance before you.

"They are eighteen and have never known a man. They desire to serve you and please you."

Jamin clapped his hands and the girls immediately began dancing before Nimrod. He was fascinated as the girls moved about the room with a combination of grace and sexuality.

"Your highness. I had the city thoroughly searched. These women have been chosen for their great beauty and their ability to please thee. All three are virgins. I examined each one personally and can attest to that fact.

"As you can see, they have been cleaned and prepared for your pleasure. The choice is yours. You may have one or all three."

Nimrod's attention had settled upon the tallest of the three. He motioned her to step forward.

"What is your name?"

"Semiramis, your highness."

"And who are your parents?"

"My father is Agee and my mother is Agar. They could not pay their debt and are your slaves here in the palace."

He nodded and motioned her to step back. He then inquired of the second girl and finally the third. He turned to Jamin.

"I choose all three. Their bodies suggest much pleasure for me. But the girl called Semiramis, she shall be my wife."

Jamin smiled as he backed out of the room. *Now Nimrod can get back to building his city and the tower.*

Semiramis remained standing while the other girls were led away. The king motioned her forward and she approached his throne confidently. Kneeling before him, she waited, smiling inwardly. *I shall be his queen. But no man shall control me! He shall be mine to control! I can see it in his eyes.*

The king arose and led his queen to his chambers.

# TWENTY

## MESSAGE FROM GOD

2250BC (pop. 1296)

God nodded His approval as Gabriel entered the throne room of heaven and approached the Father. Stopping before the throne, he waited for the Father to speak. God's visage was grim as He looked at the angel.

"Gabriel, thou shalt go unto Shem and give him My Words that he shall deliver to the people of Babel. He shall speak my words and leave; he shall not turn to the right nor to the left, but shall leave as he entered. And there shall be mourning and gnashing of teeth."

Gabriel bowed in acknowledgment and left the room.

&&&

Shem entered Babel and rode straight for the temple. Refusing to even look at it or consider its grandeur, he dismounted and turned his back to the gigantic structure. Two weeks ago the angel Gabriel had appeared unto him in a dream, given him God's terse message and left.

The next morning, he arose, kissed Achsah goodbye, mounted his mule and headed for Babel. No one other than his wife knew of his mission, not even Noah. Every day after leaving, he spent time riding and meditating in prayer. The closer he got to Babel, the heavier his heart became. When the great city came into sight, he reined his mule to a stop. In spite of his heavy heart, he was enthralled by the beauty of this city that rose majestically in the plains.

Straddling the Euphrates River, Babel was now a breathtaking city that was surrounded by a high wall encircling the city like a snake. As he watched from the height of a nearby hill, he noted its internal sprawl with its broad boulevards and intersecting side streets. One of the unique features of the city was that it was on both sides of the river, connected by a bridge high enough to allow small boats to pass under.

It was the eastern half of the city that always caught Shem's attention and held it. Nimrod's completed palace covered an entire block with massive doors and crafted lions on either side of the steps. Although he had never been inside, he had heard that Nimrod had installed carpets, sturdy furniture, and costly furnishings. Rumors told of lavish meals and immoral activity.

But as bold and powerful in appearance as the palace was, it didn't dominate the skyline as it once did. Rather, the towering nearby ziggurat demanded attention from miles around. While the palace was four stories high, the tower extended considerably higher. Though still a fair distance away, Shem could see that the top of the tower was unfinished. He knew from previous visits that a shrine to Ishtar was supposed to be built there.

He sighed. *It shall not be. Soon shall come God's judgment.*

Remembering God's command, he pulled his eyes away and focused his attention on the barely discernible North Gate. The minutes slipped by as he slowly rode toward it.

Stopping just outside the gate, he took a deep breath. *Dear God, help Thy servant deliver Thy message. Grant me the courage to deliver it with power. Grant me the strength to shut out the sights and sounds of this godless city.*

Urging his mule forward, he entered the gate and started down the broad avenue. Neither looking to the left or to the right, he made his way inward until he reached the main or central avenue. Turning east, he found it almost impossible to ignore the magnificent tower rising in the center of the city, but he did. Even so, he could not keep it entirely out of his consciousness. Built of such magnitude there was virtually nowhere in Babel that you could not see it! It filled your vision so much that you could feel its power.

Keeping his eyes averted, he rode up to the building, dismounted and walked over to the same spot he had preached from on previous occasions. Turning, he saw men and women running towards him. At first he felt a sense of immediate fear, but he heard a still, small voice whisper, "Fear not. I am with thee."

"Citizens of Babel, hear ye me. The Lord Himself created this earth and planted it with seed and herb. When finished, He pronounced it "very good." Out of the dust he created man, male and female He created them. He put them in a Garden where they basked in His presence. Again He declared it "very good."

"But the day came when they sinned before Him and ate of the forbidden fruit. In righteous wrath, He cast them out, barring them from ever re-entering the Garden again.

"Even then He cared for them. He watched over them like a hen watches her young. He guided and comforted them. He gave them men of God to speak on His behalf to man. He blessed their actions abundantly.

"They built a great society. They founded cities, built ships, established commerce, and erected temples unto the only God, the Elohim.

"But they turned from Him and committed murders, rapes, and despicable things. They fought wars and slew one another. Giants arose and slew many men. But God did not destroy them for their murders, rapes, and wars. He didn't bring the Flood because of the giants. God destroyed the world because man worshiped idols instead of him. All the evil that took place happened because of man's unbelief.

"Look about you. Does this city, with its great buildings and tower, look secure to you? Is this a place where God's name is honored? You have taken 20 years to build this temple and for what purpose? To worship the Creator God of Heaven and Earth? I think not! You have turned from God to idols. You worship the host of heaven, which are angels created by God to be your servants. You worship nature instead of the One Who created nature.

"This city is called Babel meaning 'Gate of God.' But God shall bring judgment and it shall be Babel, 'the city of confusion.'

"I have spoken. Let it begin even as God has declared!"

Stopping, he looked around. A few moments later, he rode out of the city to a nearby hill just north of the city. Dismounting, he set up camp and sat upon the hill facing the city. *Now we shall see what it is that God is about to do.*

# TWENTY ONE

## GOD'S PROTECTION

2250BC *(continued)*

Nimrod watched with anger as Shem rode out of the city. Jamin, standing beside him, could sense the rage.

"Why not eliminate him?"

Turning, Nimrod simply stared at him, obviously trying to control his emotions and comprehend what Jamin was saying.

"I know some men who will gladly cut short this man's life."

"How many and how much will it cost?" Nimrod asked.

"I figure ten men and we only need promise a talent of gold to each one."

"Ten talents?"

"I know it is a lot, but would it not be worth it?"

By this time Nimrod had settled down and the idea of being rid of Shem intrigued him. *With him gone, I will have no problem getting the ten talents back. I will have absolute power! No one shall stop me!*

"Do it!"

Jamin grinned in anticipation as he hurried to the barracks to find the men. By the time he arrived, he had already decided which soldiers he would seek.

Spotting a soldier exiting the building, he stopped him.

"Is Captain Jalon yet inside?"

"Yes, sir. He and his men are eating their noon meal. Would you like me to announce you?"

"No. I'll announce myself."

Brushing past the surprised soldier, he entered the barracks. Spotting the captain, he walked up to him. The captain looked up, wondering why he was being interrupted.

"Captain Jalon, I assume?"

The captain sprang to attention as it downed on him just who this man was.

"At your service, your eminence."

"Captain, how would you like to get a talent of gold? One for you and one each for your men."

The captain studied him, wondering if he was serious. Having heard the word gold, his men gathered around.

"A talent of gold?" the captain asked. "What would we have to do? Kill someone?"

"All you need do is seize Shem and bring him back to the king. Whether he dies or lives is of no concern to us."

The captain glanced back at his men, who were all grinning.

"That would be fine with us, sir. Where would we find him?"

Jamin smiled and immediately told him where he would find him.

&&&

An hour later ten men marched out of the city singing lustily as they went. Led by Captain Jalon, the soldiers marched until they reached the base of the hill where Shem resided.

"Art thou Shem, the one who threatens our city?"

"My name is Shem, but it is Nimrod which brings God's wrath by his disobedience and turning to other gods."

"Thou art to come down from there and be taken to his majesty. This is by order of his majesty, King Nimrod."

"I will not come down."

"Then we shall take you by force."

"I am the servant of God. Thou has erred in that you have taken it upon yourself to arrest the servant of God. If He does not slay you where you stand, I shall surely come with you."

His men looking nervously at him, Captain Jalon felt fear gnaw at his innards. Swallowing hard, he straightened and pushed out his chest. Simultaneously pulling out his sword, he made as to mount the hill. In that moment, fire came down from heaven. In a twinkling of an eye, all but one were turned into ashes.

The lone survivor looked around and saw the remains of his friends. Fear gripping his heart, he fell before Shem. Fearful of even looking at the man, he simply pleaded for mercy. His face was sprinkled with beads of sweat.

Shem looked down at the ashes that once were men. Ignoring the survivor's pleas, he lifted up his hands toward heaven.

"O Lord God, why does not man fear You?"

In the silence that followed, he looked down at the soldier who was still pleading for mercy.

"Rise. Go and tell your king what has happened."

Immediately the soldier jumped up and ran toward the city. Shem watched until he disappeared from view, then lifted his eyes to heaven.

"Surely word of this shall get back to Nimrod and he will repent of his evil."

The long silence that followed seemed overpowering. Finally, Shem could not stand it any longer.

"According to Thy will, O Lord. Be it even as You have said."

&&&

The temple was almost finished. Standing seven tiers tall, the immense temple could be seen for miles around. On a sunny day it literally glittered hurting the eyes of anyone so daring as to look directly at it!

On the top tier, the finishing touches were being applied to Ishtar's shrine. Nimrod stepped out unto his balcony to view the tower. While the palace rose higher than all the other homes, the nearby temple towered over it making the palace seem quite small. To view it from his balcony, he had to actually lean back and look almost straight up.

A sense of pride swept over him, being reflected not only in his smile but also his entire face. *It is the greatest achievement of man. Ever!*

Not even the failed attempt to kill Shem could diminish his pride. His pleasure was interrupted by Jamin.

"I've sent for the engineers and the carpenters," he said as he stepped upon the balcony. "They should be here shortly."

"Excellent. I want to make plans for the dedication of the temple. I want to make sure it will be completed either tomorrow or the next day."

Jamin nodded.

"I have already issued directions to the family heads to gather around the temple at the time designated by you, sire. They will have the people ready. You just have to say when."

"Excellent. Do you have the festivities planned?"

"Yes. It will begin with a procession with you at the head. The people should see you in front and know that you are both king and high priest to Ishtar. I will, of course, follow after you. Then behind me will come all the priests.

"As we climb upward, a priest will stop off at each succeeding tier and worship one of the gods at the small altar built into the tower. When we arrive at the top, I will enter Ishtar's shrine and offer newborn babies, a boy and a girl, to sanctify her altar. When I have sanctified it, I will come back out and the celebration shall begin."

"I approve!" exclaimed Nimrod.

Just then the engineers arrived.

&&&

Unknown to Nimrod, a heavenly visitor had previously visited Babel and viewed the cause for such pride. Later in the council of heaven God said, "Behold, the people is one, and they have all one language; and this they begin to do: and now nothing will be restrained from them, which they have imagined to do.

"Go to, let us go down, and there confound their language, that they may not understand each others speech."

But before They did, God once again sent Gabriel to visit Shem, who had been sitting on the hill for six days, and inform him of what was about to come to pass.

When the angel finished delivering his message and departed, Shem fell prostrate and wept.

"O my Lord, Thou art righteous. Thou hast patiently waited for their repentance, but they would not! Be it even as Thou hast proclaimed."

# TWENTY TWO

## CONFUSION!

2250BC (*continued*)

In the house of Amzi, his daughter Chloe first knew something was wrong when she saw the look of alarm on her mother's face.

"Mother, what is it?"

Her mother was standing and looking out the window. What she was seeing was something she had never witnessed before. Mobs!

"I don't know, dear, but don't go outside. It is too dangerous."

Chloe joined her mother at the window and watched the mob. Suddenly the mob stormed a nearby home and, moments later, dragged a woman and her two young sons out. Chloe covered her face in horror as the family was murdered there in the street. But her mother watched, frozen in place.

Chloe opened her eyes and saw that her mother wasn't moving but was standing still, her face pale and drawn. Looking out the window, Chloe could see other families being beaten to death.

"Mother, what are we to do?"

No answer came as her mother remained paralyzed.

"Mother!" Chloe yelled, shaking her mother.

It seemed to work. Her mother turned and looked at her with terror-filled eyes.

"Hide Chloe. Hide!"

As Chloe turned to obey, her mother simply sat down at the table.

"Mother, come with me!"

"No, Chloe. Hide in the back and pray. I will stay here and pray. Perhaps God will have mercy upon us. Now go!"

Chloe had been an obedient girl for as long as she could remember, but she was tempted to disobey now. But the stern look from her mother quelled such thoughts and she fled to the rear room and hid behind a large basket of clothes. Her mother simply bowed her head and prayed.

"Dear God, the mob will soon be here. How could these men, my neighbors, do such terrible things to people they know? What is happening? O God, I fear my husband is dead and I shall soon join him. Protect my daughter. And grant that I remain faithful as I face death."

She had barely finished her prayer when the door was kicked open with such violence that it splintered. Moments later, several men stormed inside speaking in unintelligible words. (Chloe, listening from her hiding place, was surprised that she couldn't understand a single word.) Rushing the table, one of the men struck her mother so hard that she fell out of the chair and unto the floor. Instinctively she tried to back away. But the men grabbed her by the legs, pulling her out the doorway and into the street where they began pounding and kicking her.

Hands reached down and ripped her clothes off. Shame and terror filled her heart as she tried to hide her nakedness. Closing her eyes, she never saw the knife that suddenly pierced her heart. As the men continued to rain clubs and swords upon her, life was rapidly leaving.

*O Lord, protect my Chloe!*

Chloe remained hidden in the back of the house, too terrified to look out and see what was happening.

&&&

The angry men looked down at the woman they had once called neighbor and friend. But no compassion filled their hearts. Instead, one of the men produced a torch and headed for her house. Smiles spreading on their faces, the other men followed.

Re-entering the house, they smashed the table and chairs, turning them into small shards of wood. As the men began piling them into a stack in the middle of the room, one of them saw the large basket of clothes, behind which a terrified Chloe hid. But even as the thought crossed his mind, one of his fellows torched the stack. His attention reverted to the pile of burning wood.

As the fire rapidly spread, the men laughed and left, only to gather outside to watch the burning house. One of the men saw the dead woman lying on the street and walked over. Kicking her hard, he was disappointed that no sign of life remained. He rejoined the others.

In her hiding place, Chloe smelled the smoke. Peaking over the basket, she saw flames engulfing the front of the house. Jumping up, she realized that the clothes were also now burning. Like a trapped animal, she looked around wildly for a way of escape.

*Use the window.* The sudden thought stopped her. *Window?* At first all she thought about was the front window, but it was blocked by fire. *The back window! The one for ventilation.* As the thought crossed her mind, she looked toward the back. *Yes! Hurry!*

Like most houses built in Babel, her house had only one door. But her father, the Brick Master, had foreseen the need for ventilation and had placed windows in both the front and the back. One difficulty remained. The back window was both small and high above her head as it was meant only for ventilation rather than viewing the outside world. How was she to get out?

The roaring flames were getting closer, sweat was soaking her clothes, and breathing was getting harder. Pulling a chest over against the wall and directly below the window, she stood upon it. But she was too small. Her fingers could not reach the ledge. Looking back at the approaching fire, she gambled.

As a child growing up she had always been agile. Playing with other girls, when their mothers were not watching, she had shown the ability to both run and jump. Now she desperately needed that jumping ability. Crouching, she looked up at the ledge and sprang upward. A moment later her fingers grasped the ledge!

Pulling herself up, she saw the window only inches away. Lowering herself, she hung there trying to think of what next to do.

Hanging from the ledge, her arms already aching and fingers throbbing, she knew she had to do something soon. Taking a deep breath, she managed to pull herself up until she was able to get the rest of her arms upon the ledge. Fortunately, the window was large enough for her to squeeze through, or so she thought. Suddenly it looked awfully small!

Still hanging there, she stared at the opening. Small or not, she had to get through it to safety. It still looked awfully small to her, but she could already feel the heat of the fire below her.

*It's now or die! Help me, Lord!*

She reached through the window, pulling herself forward. Poking her head through, she used the outside wall to pull herself further through the window. But she suddenly found herself stuck at the hips!

*O no, I can't move. O Lord, what can I do?*

As she hung half-in and half-out, the fire reached her sandals. Feeling the sudden burning, she started shaking her legs violently trying to get rid of her burning sandals. The violence of her actions worked. Not only freeing her of the sandals, but also freeing her from the extremely tight window. Suddenly she fell to the ground, painfully landing on her back. She was momentarily stunned as her head grazed the side of the house.

Lying there confused and scared with a throbbing head, she quietly prayed to God. In her mind, she replayed the awful scenes she had witnessed, the strange language of the attackers (her neighbors), and the stinging smoke. Her mind clearing, she suddenly knew she had to get away. Jumping up, she ran!

&&&

Eber was confused. Moments earlier, he had been listening to Nimrod and others discussing the tower and the plans for the dedication. He had perfectly understood their conversation and Nimrod's words. But then an engineer had spoken up and in mid-sentence, his words suddenly were very confusing.

*Something's wrong!*

Turning to a fellow carpenter, he whispered, "Something's wrong. I can no longer understand what is being said."

His friend's face went from blank confusion to anger in almost an instant. Eber quickly retreated. As he did so, he remembered the fiery message by Shem only days before. Looking around the room, he saw faces of confusion. Turning toward Nimrod, he saw fear and confusion in his face as well!

"Is this the judgment he spoke of? Whatever is happening is causing people to get very angry. I better go home."

He turned and headed out the door and down the stairway. A feeling of caution, and maybe fear, caused him to avoid others. Once out the palace door, he ran toward home, all the time wondering what he would find.

&&&

Up in Heaven there was no cheering. Angels trod the streets of gold with gloom and sorrow much like previous occasions. Some may even have remembered the Fall of man into sin and the subsequent ejection of Adam and Eve. Others may have remembered the Flood, not so distant, when judgment had destroyed the world that had existed for centuries.

In the Sanctuary of Heaven, where God abode and where the thrones were situated, God the Father, God the Son, and God the Holy Spirit sat.

They watched with sadness the confusion that had been caused by the people's rebellion. If the people had obeyed God, this would not have been necessary. All Three wiped tears from Their eyes.

# TWENTY THREE

## RIOTING

2250BC (*continued*)

"You're not making sense!" Nimrod shouted angrily at the engineer.
"What did you say -"

Nimrod stopped in mid-sentence. Some of his audience had stopped listening to him, while some of his carpenters were leaving. He turned to his priest, but apparently Jamin had also noticed.

"It's as if they don't understand what you're saying."

"Yes," responded Nimrod. Feeling a sense of rage building within, he fought to maintain control. Only then did he turn back to his men and, forcing calmness, speak.

"Any that understand me raise your hands."

Of the remaining ten men, only two raised their hands.

Before Nimrod could comment on this, the men suddenly started fighting amongst themselves. At least one dagger suddenly appeared and moments later blood was spilled. Observing this and hearing a large racket from the street below, Jamin stepped further out on the balcony. Leaning over the rampart, he had a better view of the city. Leaning further, he looked down.

To his startled eyes there appeared multiple scenes of rioting mobs. The people were fighting, some already lying in the streets amidst pools of blood. And in some neighborhoods, he could see smoke.

&&&

Racing over the bridge, Eber headed for his home. One thought kept going through his mind. *I've got to get home. Mother and Ahban may be in danger!*

Rushing past a building, Eber collided with a young woman and they fell in a heap on the ground.

"Are you OK?" he asked as he stood.

"Yes."

Their eyes grew large in surprise.

"I understand you," they both exclaimed.

"My name is Eber," he said as he helped her up. "What is yours?"

"Chloe." She said, shivering.

"What's wrong, Chloe?"

"They killed my mother and burned our house. I don't know where my father is."

Suddenly a shout pierced the air.

"Chloe!"

They both turned to see a man staggering toward them.

"Father!" she yelled as she ran to him.

He collapsed in her arms and they fell to the ground. Recognizing the Brick Master Amzi, Eber hurried over and saw a pool of blood growing under the man.

"Chloe," her father said weakly, "Go get your mother and leave. Save her."

At that moment, he stopped breathing. Chloe panicked and looked up at Eber.

"Help him, please! He's hurt."

Eber knelt down and placed his ear near the man's nose. He heard nothing. Placing his ear on the man's chest, he listened for a heartbeat. Hearing nothing, he sadly raised his head and looked at his new friend.

"I'm sorry, Chloe. Your father is gone."

Chloe broke down and sobbed. Eber gently broke her away from her father.

"I heard your father tell you to go to your mother. Didn't you say she is dead?"

"Yes, she's dead, murdered," she cried.

Eber shook his head, thinking. *She's got no place to go. I guess that makes me responsible for her.*

"Look, we don't know one another, but I can't leave you here. Come with me and we will decide what to do. But we must hurry!"

"I c-can't leave father here."

"You have no choice. We stay here and we will die also. We must leave now!"

She nodded soberly as they stood. Eber looked around for any further danger. Satisfied, he turned to leave.

As he hurried toward his house, she tried to keep up, but the combination of pain and grief seemed to take a toll on her body. Suddenly realizing he had left her behind, Eber stopped and waited for her to catch up. Taking her by the hand, he resumed his route, but now at a slightly slower pace.

Several minutes later they arrived at his house. Fortunately there were no mobs around. In fact, there was no one! He hurried up to the door and went inside dreading what he might find. As he stepped in, he saw a note lying on the table.

In spite of her grief, Chloe noted that it was a modest home and unusually clean considering that Eber was apparently single.

"What now?" she asked as she watched him gather a few belongings together and stuff them in a goatskin bag.

"We must leave the city. It is too dangerous to stay here. It looks like my parents are gone. They left a note on my the table that says to meet them and my brother outside the city."

"Outside the city? But there are mobs between here and the gates."

"You are right. And I don't know which gate they took. Probably the West Gate since it is closer, but the way out that gate looked to be blocked. We'll try to leave by the South Gate, then make our way to the West Gate."

Chloe fought back the tears that welled up in her eyes. Eber noticed and gently wrapped her in his arms.

"Go ahead and cry, Chloe. We're losing everything we hold dear today. It is OK to weep."

She buried her face in his shoulder and let the tears flow. After a while, he stroked her hair. *It is so soft and smells so good.*

"We must go now, Chloe. God will take care of us."

She nodded. Releasing her, he picked up his bag and stepped outside. Chloe followed closely behind him. As they stepped out, Eber noticed a burly man approaching. Recognizing him as one of the bricklayers he had seen at the tower, Eber started to say something. Then he saw hatred in the man's eyes and the large mallet in his hands.

"Stay back, Chloe," he ordered gently pushing her behind him and dropping his bag at the same time.

Before he could say anything more, the bricklayer lunged at Eber with his mallet aimed straight for his head. Eber quickly sidestepped, allowing the attacker to lose his balance as he swung at nothing but air. Before the man could recover his balance, Eber landed a hard right into his gut. As the bricklayer staggered and bent over, Eber moved closer and struck with a two fist-ed pounding upon his back, dropping the man like one of his bricks.

Eber quickly retrieved his bag and hollered, "Quick, follow me."

&&&

Shem stood upon the hilltop watching the unfolding tragedy. He could hear the shrieks of terror, the roar of the mobs, the sounds of fighting and the terrible sounds of collapsing buildings. This was followed by the fires. At first he only smelled the acrid odor of burning wood and clothing, but soon he saw rising billows of smoke as fires seemed to be breaking out all over the city.

Tears streamed unbidden down his cheeks as he realized that among these terrified people were his own sons and their families. Disappointed in them as he was, they were still family. His mind went back to the bygone days when they were all one happy family nourished by the abundance that God had provided. Now they faced ruin!

&&&

Nimrod immediately took charge of the situation. Not only were his engineers fighting among themselves, but servants had joined the fray. Disgusted, he turned to his royal guards.

"Guards, slay these infidels! If they cannot speak in your tongue, then kill them and dispose of their bodies outside the city."

Even as he spoke, he wasn't sure if they understood. But moments later several of his royal guards did rush upon the engineers. Eight out of the ten engineers were quickly slain along with several of the servants; in some cases the guards killed two men at the same time.

This was possible because the men were grappling together and one thrust penetrated both.

But even the guards were affected by this strange malady, turning upon one another and spilling blood. While Nimrod and the others watched in horror two of the guards turned toward the king.

"Khak-too-saret!" yelled one guard, meaning 'The grave of your death,' a particularly harsh statement considering he was yelling to Nimrod.

Their daggers dripping with blood, these powerful men advanced with hatred in their eyes. At that precise moment three more elite guards appeared. Immediately seeing the danger to their king, all three hurled their daggers at the two attackers!

The daggers, expertly thrown, were right on target. As the attackers fell mortally wounded, the three drew their short swords and placed themselves between the royal party and the fighting. Nimrod, Jamin, and his officers quickly gathered their families together and left the palace with the three closely behind.

As Nimrod exited the palace and made as if to head toward the Eastern Gate, a soldier quickly approached him, stopped before getting too close. He was well aware that getting to close to the king without the king's permission could cost him his life.

"Your highness, the Eastern Gate is unsafe! The people are in the midst thereof and have made it quite unsafe."

"Then we shall cross the bridge and leave at the Northern Gate. If anyone gets in our way, slay them," Nimrod ordered.

Soon the royal procession began its march across the bridge with the four (the three plus the newest soldier) leading the way. Brandishing their swords, they forced the masses to part and allow them to proceed. Those unlucky enough to not get out of the way were slain on the spot. The sight of the soldiers and their blood covered swords cast fear into the people. Immediately the warring factions moved aside to let the king pass. But they resumed their fighting once the royal entourage was out of sight.

Once across the bridge, the procession turned north at the main intersection and headed for the North Gate. Several times the four would advance to forcibly remove someone so filled with hate that they no longer felt fear. The four would quickly resolve the situation with quick thrusts, usually resulting in instant death.

&&&

Once outside, the royal party sought higher ground. Upon reaching the top of a small hill, the four immediately set up camp.

"What do we do now?" asked Jamin.

Nimrod looked back at the city where the sounds of battle were still being heard. He noticed smoke coming from the direction of the temple. Meanwhile, people were streaming out of the North Gate. But it was obvious to his trained eye that they had no leader and were milling about in a confused manner.

"I do not know," he replied with a sigh.

"I do."

Turning, they saw Queen Semiramis standing there. Smiling, she moved forward. Nimrod caught his breath. Her dress was virtually transparent and her every movement seemed to suggest sexual power. Jamin, standing beside him, could not help but also stare at her.

She smiled, knowing the effect she was having on these two powerful leaders.

Nimrod was the first to speak.

"You know what to do?" he asked, his voice husky with sudden desire.

"Yes, post your guards near the gate. They will seek people they can understand. These will be sent to us and we will gather them together. By morning we should be strong enough for you to once again assert your power.

"Also, later we will send servants back into the city after the mobs have left. They will go back to the palace and start bringing out the valuables. This event need not deter your plans. We will simply move to another location."

Nimrod's spirit soared. Straightening his back, he once again appeared the confident leader. He nodded approval of her plan. Still smiling, she turned and left.

In spite of himself, Jamin pulled his eyes away from the queen and turned toward a lone man standing atop another hill looking in their direction. Noticing Jamin's questioning look, Nimrod turned to see what he was looking at.

"That's Shem, Jamin. He's been there for seven days."

"I know," Jamin spat out. "It is like he knew this would happen!"

"Perhaps. But I am not concerned with him."

"What do you think happened?"

"I'm not sure. One thing is obvious; where once we all spoke one language, now there are many languages. I just don't know why. But if his God is responsible, it is His mistake. We can use this to keep the people from turning back to Him."

"But how, if they don't understand us?"

"Some will understand our words, others will understand at the point of a sword."

&&&

Unknown to the king and queen, events were taking place that would thwart at least some of their plans. Shortly after they left the palace it was invaded by a mob of men. Nimrod had left a few servants to protect the palace and its furnishings, but they were easily overcome by the rampaging mob.

Many of them went racing through the palace looking for women, others looked for treasures. They did find valuables, but no women. One man found expensive tapestries, another found a jewel box left behind by the queen, and still others found furniture and other furnishings. If it was portable, they took it.

Once satisfied, they started to leave. But one of the leaders grabbed a torch from a wall and started a fire. Excited, the others followed suit as they scurried into the rooms and set on fire anything they could find. When finished, they exited and retrieved their treasures, which they had wisely placed outside. Some raced off with their valuables, but others stayed to watch as the palace was consumed in roaring flames.

&&&

Some of the men now turned their attention to the tower. But they reckoned not with the wisdom of Jamin. Before leaving, he had sent a servant to the Temple Guards that guarded its entrance. While few in number, they were loyal to Jamin.

Only a few were affected by the language problem, probably because most of the guards came from one family. Those affected were quickly slain.

When the servant delivered the message to the Captain of the Guard, the captain immediately organized his men. From his vantage point he could see what the rampaging mob was doing to the palace. In anticipation of Jamin's order, he had already placed the guards in strategic positions.

When the mob turned its attention upon the temple, the guards soon demonstrated their skill with the sword. The only way up the temple were the two temporary ramps, constructed of wood, and the permanent ramp of brick and mortar. The captain ordered the two wooden ramps set on fire.

This action forced the mob to concentrate their efforts at the main ramp, thus providing the guards with an easily defensible position. The mob, on the other hand, was no match and soon many lay dying on the street.

# TWENTY FOUR

## DISPERSED!

2250BC *(continued)*

Asshur hurried through the streets toward his home. *I must find out how my family is doing! All this confusion and fighting makes me tremble at what I'll find.*

Accompanied by two strong guards, their powerful legs pounding the street, they rushed forward with determination. Seeing this onrushing force of three men with drawn swords was a formidable sight for anyone standing in their way. Rioters momentarily cowered and scattered as they raced through the city blocks looking neither to the left nor the right.

As they neared the house, he could see nearby homes on fire. The smoke was so thick that they had to slow down. Finally the house came into sight and they quickened their pace. Arriving at his home, Asshur found his family armed and already engaged in fending off intruders. Joining the fray, they attacked the mob and it promptly scattered.

Once the mob was gone, Asshur entered his courtyard where he found his brother Elam and his family. The two men rushed forward and embraced.

"Elam, it is so good to see you."

Elam pulled away, his face full of shock. Then a look of sadness as a tear coursed its way down his cheek.

Without another word spoken, Asshur knew the horrible truth. They no longer spoke the same language! But suddenly Elam grinned. Kneeling, he drew a circle upon the ground. Understanding came to Asshur; his brother was using the silent language they had developed as children to prevent their parents from hearing.

He watched as Elam drew symbols on the ground obviously questioning what was happening.

Kneeling down, he erased Elam's symbols and replaced them with his own.

"You saw what was happening here," he said as he drew his symbols. "Well, it is happening all over the city. The smoke you see here is all over the city. Mobs are setting fires throughout. I have never seen anything like it before. Normally hardworking obedient men have been transformed into gangs bent on murder, rape, and destruction."

Elam thoughtfully considered this information before he reached down and erased the symbols. Then he drew one symbol.

"Where will you go?" Asshur read.

"The North Gate," he wrote.

Elam's sadness was now quite apparent as he responded.

"Then we will have to split up," he wrote. "I have decided to leave through the South Gate and travel to the land I discovered to the southeast."

Asshur looked sadly at his brother. The sudden realization struck him that he may never see Elam or his family again.

The two men arose and entered the house together. It was obvious that the women had discovered the same lack of communication and were sitting on opposite sides.

While the noise of rioting could be heard outside, everyone inside the house grew quiet.

Asshur ordered his wife to get ready to leave.

"Take only that which you can carry. Be quick. There will be more of these mobs coming soon!"

As the women scurried in obedience, Asshur organized the men he had available. A short while later, he and his family emerged from the house and turned north, while Elam and his family turned south.

With a precision born of his militaristic training, Asshur marched his family forward heading toward the North Gate. He would have preferred a faster pace, but having women and children in tow slowed them down. Moving as rapidly as possible, they hurried through the streets.

While they were not large in number, they were well armed and forced the milling mobs to flee to other areas of the city. As they rushed out of the North Gate, Asshur spotted Nimrod's encampment and rushed to join them. As the two groups merged, Nimrod had Asshur place his guards at the gate to look for more people that spoke the same tongue.

Meanwhile, Elam and his family worked their way south. Several times they had to stop and battle angry mobs. At one point they had to detour around a raging fire. This resulted in a longer, more dangerous trip. In the midst of their hurried march, several women fell and were injured. A little boy fell under an onrushing wagon.

Even as Elam's group was exiting the South Gate, Phut was leading another contingent through the Western Gate. With mobs blocking the way, he sent his sword wielding soldiers to clear them out. They were met by men either too brave or too crazed. The soldiers attacked swinging their swords. Several minutes later there were bodies strewn around the Gateway in pools of blood.

"Clear those bodies away, men. We're coming through!"

Obediently his men cleared away the bodies of dead and dying so that Phut's people could move forward. Within minutes, both carts pulled by mules and others by men were moving through the gate. Phut stood to the side and watched as his people poured through the gate. It wasn't until the last of his family had passed through that he and his personal guards fell in behind.

Racing to the front of the column, Phut shouted for them to continue marching toward a distant orchard he knew was due west. Although it was too far away to be seen, he knew its exact location and was determined to reach it before nightfall.

While they marched, a young man ran up to him.

"There are people following us!"

Phut headed for the rear. As he approached, he could see the large group behind them rapidly closing the gap. Watching, his face broke into a knowing smile as he realized it was Mizraim and his family. He quickly sent an invitation to join him at the grove.

&&&

Still others left through the South and Eastern Gates. By day's end the once unified people speaking one common tongue had been divided into numerous tribes speaking in languages strange and harsh to other ears. As the anger subsided, confusion took its place. In some cases entire families were preserved, while in others the families were torn apart.

As nightfall took its place, a new unsettling world took shape.

# TWENTY FIVE

## JOY AND SADNESS

2250BC *(continued)*

Satan stood near the base of the temple watching the temple and the guards defending it. Few of the rioters remained and they were quickly racing away in defeat. All around were the results of the turmoil and bloodshed. He smiled.

"God has defeated you, Lucifer," observed an angel, who was standing beside him. "Why are you smiling?"

Satan's grin widened.

"To you it may seem that God has won this battle, but to me I see that He has failed once again. Sure, the temple is unfinished and will probably never serve its intended use to draw men from Him, and the city looks like it is to be abandoned. But look at what I have accomplished this time.

"Man no longer speaks in one tongue. From now on, man will no longer be able to obey God's commands as a people. They are divided. But such division shall not last forever. I shall bring them together in a time and in a place that I choose."

His grin turned into a broad smile as he spun the facts to suit his purpose. What was even more pleasing was the fact his spin was convincing even to himself.

"God has done me a great service. I can use this confusion of tongues to both divide and conquer the people. It shall be much easier to sway the loyalties of a divided people than one united. When the time comes, I shall raise up a man of my own choosing, one who shall lead mankind in open rebellion against God. One that I will control and use howsoever I choose."

"You mean Nimrod?"

"Perhaps him or, perhaps, I will choose Phut. Now there's a natural leader. On the other hand, I may use Mizraim, a man who is cunning in the ways of war. Then again, I may raise up someone else. Or perhaps I shall use all of them.

"It doesn't matter who I choose; they are all tools for me to use. God wants man to spread out and master this world on His behalf. Well, we shall work to bring this expansion about. But instead of worshiping God, they shall worship the gods of heaven and ultimately me! I shall use God's own plans to defeat Him!"

Satan continued smiling as he looked to his future and, indeed, the future of the world. He saw nothing to defeat him.

&&&

In heaven there was much sadness pervading the holy city. The angels slowly moved about with their minds flooding with confusing thoughts. Why had this happened? What could have been done to prevent it? How strong is Satan?

However, God would allow no such thoughts to last long in the city. He called Gabriel into His Presence and instructed him to deliver a message to all the angels of the city. It was a message that clearly demonstrated His control and ultimate victory.

As Gabriel exited the Great Throne Room to deliver the message, he met Michael who had just arrived.

"Any news, Gabriel?" Michael asked.

"Yes. I believe that God has an assignment for you and He has given me a message to deliver to the city."

"What message?"

"Though Satan may claim victory, this action was foreseen and planned for by God. He wants all the angels to be alert and to be patient. God's timing is not as man's. With Him a thousand years is but one."

Michael nodded somberly.

"Any idea what my assignment is?"

"No. But He is waiting for you."

"I had better go then."

The two angels parted.

Michael paused before the door, then opened it and stepped into the room. A few feet away God sat waiting for him. Approaching the holy throne, he knelt to one knee.

"You wish to see me, Father God."

"Yes. You have been dealing with Shem for awhile now. I have been pleased with your work. Shem shall serve me faithfully. Furthermore, you shall continue to work with him.

"But beginning now, you will also take upon yourself young Eber, and his descendants. Through them I shall raise up a people from which shall come the Redeemer! And Eber himself shall play an important role."

"Where shall I find this Eber?"

"Even now he is leaving Babel with the young maiden Chloe. You shall guide him to a land south of Babel. Be with him, protect and guide him, for I have great plans for him."

"As you command, Father God."

# TWENTY SIX

## LOVE IN THE MIDST OF TROUBLE

2250BC *(continued)*

Eber gently yet firmly held Chloe against him. Lying amidst refuse that bore a horrible scent, he listened to her soft crying and thought of the day's events and their present circumstances.

The city of Babel was built with a surrounding wall of approximately twelve miles in length. Within the city, the streets had a straight and grid-like layout. Some of the wealthier homes were two stories high.

The city actually straddled the Euphrates with a bridge connecting the two halves. Both the palace and the temple occupied the eastern half, while the poorer sections were located on the western half of the city. Both the homes of Eber and Chloe were located there.

In-between the streets were narrow alleys running behind the homes. It was in one such alley that Eber and Chloe had found a shelter to hide them from malicious eyes and now were spending a sleepless night together. As the first rays of sunlight appeared, the two of them rose. Eber took her hands in his.

"I am sorry Chloe. We must continue on. Do you trust me?

"Yes."

"Then follow me."

Moments later, they were racing down the alley, scattering cats and dogs that had found refuge in its narrow confines. Coming to a cross street, they stopped. Eber edged closer to the street and looked out.

Satisfied that the way was clear, he took Chloe's hand and quickly led her across the wide boulevard into another alley. Pausing, he looked back to see if anyone had noticed, but the scene was quiet with no one in sight.

"Let's go!"

The two continued to run until they got to another cross street. Once again they stopped and Eber looked out. This time he saw people milling about, their faces contorted in anger. Watching them, an idea formed in his brain.

"Chloe, we have to cross this street. If we run across, it will attract everyone's attention. If we walk across calmly, they may not notice. But it is risky."

"If you go, I will go also," she averred firmly.

They stepped out and calmly strolled across the street with only a few eyes turning their way. Fortunately, none took a serious interest in them and they made it across safely. They repeated this scenario several times as they passed several crowded streets and covered several city blocks. Although they ran along the alley ways, the actual progress was slow because of their zigzag route.

He finally stopped and turned to her.

"We're safer now, Chloe. We will slow down and stay off the main street. If you do as I do, we will both be safe. We're going to get out of the city. I promise you!"

She nodded as she took advantage of the moment to catch her breath.

Continuing on, carefully avoiding the main street, and following the narrow meandering alleys behind the shops and homes, they kept to the shadows. Trying to avoid contact with anyone else, Eber figured the shadows would effectively hide them from piercing eyes. Still, they periodically stopped to check for unwanted visitors. This slowed their progress considerably. Several times he spotted someone coming and they would immediately hide until the danger was over.

It took three hours to travel what normally took fifteen minutes. Finally arriving at the southern gate, they found several people wandering around the gate, apparently unsure of what to do. The street showed the results of the previous day's riots. Bodies were strewn everywhere, but the violence seemed to have dissipated, leaving the people simply confused.

"What do we do now?" asked Chloe.

Eber studied the scene. The gate was open and unattended. The milling people walked about in a daze. An idea began taking shape.

"Chloe, do you trust me?"

"Yes."

"Then I have a plan. We'll walk out of here and head toward the gate just like we have before when crossing streets. Act normal, don't look at anyone and if any speak to you, ignore them. Keep up with me and do whatever I tell you."

Chloe nodded. Her confidence in Eber had risen with each passing moment.

They walked out of the alley, walking toward the gate. Eber walked as one in charge. With his shoulders back, he strode forward staring straight ahead with Chloe right behind him. The people immediately sensed that he was a man of authority and moved aside, allowing them to pass unhindered.

They walked this way in total silence with the distance to the gate rapidly closing. One man yelled something unintelligible, but they ignored him and continued on. Reaching the open gate, Eber stopped and sent a withering glare at those who had been brave enough to follow them. Immediately the group of men backed off.

Eber smiled and motioned for Chloe. Together they passed through the gateway where they stopped again before exiting. Scanning the area, he searched for a place of safety. Suddenly, he spotted a hill to the southwest. Estimating the distance to be about an hour's walk away, he turned to Chloe.

"See that hill," he said pointing. "We will go there and set up a small camp. Then we will decide what to do."

The hill Eber had chosen was a good walk from the city, which was one of the reasons he had chosen it. There were closer hills that would have been in easy reach and attractive to others still in the city. He sighed. *Chloe and I would certainly be no match for any gang or group wanting our plot of land. That hill should provide a degree of safety until we figure out where to go.*

From the gate he had estimated a hour's walk, but it turned out to be two hours. Partly because he misjudged the distance, and partly because Chloe kept stopping. The first time that happened, he wasn't sure what to say.

"Chloe, we can't stay here. It's unsafe!"

"What does it matter? My parents are dead. People I once called friends hate me. They even speak a different language. What does it matter?"

"It matters a lot, Chloe. It matters to me! Come on, trust me. Together we will make it."

She looked up at him through tear-stained eyes. Allowing him to pull her to her feet, she held tightly to his hand as they moved forward.

This scene repeated itself several times, but eventually they reached the hill and climbed to the top. He led her to one of the few trees in the area. Sitting against it, she looked up at him. He knelt before her and gently wiped tears from her face.

"Wait here, while I make camp."

Standing, he studied the tree. While it provided a little shade, it wasn't really adequate. Looking up at the sky, he was glad there were no clouds. Nonetheless, he removed his cloak and spread it among the limbs providing additional shade.

Then he opened the bag he'd carried on his shoulders. Unrolling a small blanket, he combined it with the cloak to make a small tent.

Satisfied, he came over and knelt once again before her. Chloe rose to her knees and embraced him, burying her head on his shoulder. For a moment he was stunned. *Dear Lord, what do I do? What do I say?*

For several moments he just held her as she sobbed. Finally, he gently pushed her away and looked into her red-rimmed eyes. Once again, he wiped the tears away.

"Listen Chloe. We have not known each other for very long, but I think I know one thing about you. You love God, right?"

"Y-Yes."

"So do I. I don't understand all that has happened, but I think God has judged all of us. Father always warned me that I must stay away from the city's idolatry. We had to live there, but we didn't have to worship false gods like everyone else. He said that God would have to judge.

"But he also told me that if I loved and obeyed God that He would take care of me. Well, that is still true. Why don't we pray, asking for God's help?"

She nodded. He took her hands and held them in his as he prayed: "Dear Lord, Your judgment has befallen mankind. You have divided one from another. Where once we all spoke with one tongue, now we are divided by different tongues. Moreover I have been separated from my parents and don't know if I will ever be with them again.

"It is particularly hard on Chloe as her parents have died horrible deaths. It is devastating. She has no one, except me."

He paused as the truth of that statement penetrated his soul.

"Dear Lord, we need; no, we urgently desire Thy help. O Lord, grant us the wisdom to know what to do and the courage to do it. Moreover Lord, we desire your protection. We have no weapons and are only two in number. Put Thy hedge around us, protect us from danger. And we will give You all the praise, Amen."

Chloe looked at him as she wiped away the last of her tears.

"That was beautiful. You talk like you know Him."

"Father raised me to trust God and follow His tenets. He has always taught me to reverence God and to pray regularly. I guess it is part of me."

Chloe nodded in understanding. Her mother had been a woman of prayer.

"What do we do now?" she asked.

Eber took a deep breath. At sixteen, Chloe was quite pretty. A fact that Eber, single and thirty-three, had already noticed. Now that the initial shock and the resulting dangers were past, he had time to appreciate such things.

As he contemplated their situation, he realized that she was now completely dependent upon him. For some reason God had separated her from her family. *I am all the family she has! I am responsible for her now!*

The fact that he had fallen in love at first sight made things easier, assuming she shared the same feelings.

"Chloe, I know this is sudden and I am being presumptive, but I fell in love with you the moment you ran into me. I desire to take you as my wife.

"Normally I would ask your parents and then my father would negotiate with your father. But you are now without family and it is uncertain whether I will ever find my own parents. So a traditional ceremony is not possible. If you want to search for the rest of your family, we can. I don't want to raise your hopes. But know this, I love you and feel like we are already one."

"I do also," she replied softly.

"Then do you agree to be my wife?"

"Yes."

"We have an additional problem," he said. "We are here alone. A single man alone with a young woman. We have already spent one night together. When things settle down, people will talk. We can wait until later and endure the talk, or we can get married now."

She looked at him, then around the hill, before setting her gaze once again upon him.

"But I see no priest."

He smiled and gripped her shoulders.

"You are correct. But we have the witness of God and the angels. So I declare us to be man and wife. Perhaps later we can find a man of God to bless us and perform a more acceptable marriage."

They knelt down and prayed, seeking God's blessing. When finished, they crawled inside the tent and sank to the ground oblivious to all the noise about them. And, as night settled, they enjoyed the pleasures of a husband and wife!

# TWENTY SEVEN

## PICKING UP THE PIECES

2250BC (pop. 982) *(continued)*

Shem mounted his donkey and headed into the village of Ararat resting near the base of the mountain. Though his house was small when compared to the rest of the world, it was home to him. After almost two weeks of constant traveling, he was tired and looking forward to seeing his wife.

Riding up to his house, he dismounted. But Achsah, having seen him coming, was already outside and waiting for his arrival. As soon as he dismounted, she was in his arms. Wrapping his arms around her, he guided her inside, away from prying eyes. Shutting the door, he turned to her with a big grin on his face. A moment later their lips met as they simultaneously embraced.

Knowing of his desire to see his father, Achsah pushed him back out the door.

"Go. You see Noah and share all your news. He can have you the rest of the day, but I have you all to myself afterward!"

Still feeling the warm glow of her embrace and the touch of her lips, he turned and headed across the street to his father's house. Walking up to the house, he saw that the door was open. Glancing inside, he saw what he expected – nothing. Moving on, he rounded the house and he found his father in the back, staring up at the mountain. As Shem walked up to his father, Noah turned and looked at him.

"Something has happened. Am I right?"

"Yes. God has judged Nimrod and confused the language of the people. Henceforth, man shall not be as one, but shall be divided by tongue."

"It is as I feared. God could not sit back and allow such rebellion. But nothing like that occurred here."

"Probably because you have not turned away from God. Plus, it appears to be somewhat divided along family lines."

"You are probably right. I imagine you are recording all this so that our descendents will know why this all happened."

"Yes, and I noticed something else, father."

"What is that?"

"On my way here, I came across two men who were fighting because they could not understand each other. It took a few moments for me to break up the fight. Once I got them apart, I quizzed them about why they were fighting. It was because they couldn't understand each other.

"But, father, I was talking to both of them! I understood them and they understood me. While it greatly helped me in bringing peace, it wasn't until later that I realized that I was conversing with both of them in their own tongues."

"Then the Lord has given you the ability to understand the different languages. He must have great plans for you, which explains His visit to me."

"What do you mean?" asked Shem.

"He appeared to me about two weeks ago as I was performing my evening prayers. Suddenly there was a great light and I fell prostrate in fear.

"'Thy prayers have come before Me,' He said and then added, 'judgment has fallen upon Babel.' He did not tell me what the judgment was, but He did tell me of your new role."

Shem studied his father, patiently waiting.

"The Lord has said that you will continue serving Him as before. But because of the judgment, the people will be scattered abroad. It will mean a great deal of travel. You being gone for long periods of time. But it is important for you to record the movements and the events of the people. Not for my knowledge, but for our descendents who shall follow us. God has a plan, but He has not shared it with me."

"Then it is good that my children have all grown and left. I shall take my wife and we shall travel as the Lord leads us. Has He told you where I will be traveling? Or am I to wait for His directions?"

"Afraid you will have to wait on Him, my son. But with the families now separated by language, I suspect they will be moving away from the area."

"Then I better get busy. Achsah will have much to do to prepare for our travels."

"Good, my son. I shall miss your companionship, but I know you will be serving our Lord."

&&&

Meanwhile, Elam and his family traveled further south and prepared to cross the Tigris. Sitting upon his horse, he watched as his people began wading into the river. Because at this point the water was swift, he insisted that they tie ropes to each other and cross single file. The few wagons that they had among themselves entered first. Unfortunately one of the wagons got stuck and it took several men to free it and get it across. Although the currents were strong and a powerful wind assailed them, they managed to get all the wagons across safely.

Once the last of the emigrants stepped ashore, he gathered the people and declared it to be their new home.

"We shall call it the Land of Elam. The people shall be known as Elamites. Here we shall establish our kingdom. Here we shall build a city and shall be a people free from Nimrod and his tyranny!"

"Will we build here?" asked one of his soldiers.

Elam looked around and shook his head.

"No. We shall move inland. During my exploration I discovered a river I have named Karun. There we shall build."

&&&

Several months after the Confusion of Tongues, the city of Babel lay in partial ruins and almost completely abandoned. Homes were burned to the ground, the palace had been ransacked and burned, and the temple stood as a reminder of all that had transpired.

Shortly after the Dispersion, Nimrod invited Asshur to his tent. As Asshur entered, Nimrod motioned for him to take a seat at the table. As his guest took his seat, Nimrod smiled and asked his opening question.

"All well with your people?"

"Yes," replied Asshur, wondering what this was all about.

"You are probably wondering why I asked you to come here. Well, it's really quite simple. You see, while you and I have had our differences, we have always been able to get things done. We actually worked well together. I believe that together we can rebuild."

"Rebuild Babel?"

"No. Perhaps someday we shall return, but I have decided to move north."

"North? Where?"

"To a place along the Tigris River. When we first moved south from the mountains of Ararat, we passed through land that was ideal for a city. But, at the time, I had my eyes fixed on moving further south, eventually settling in Babel. In any case, I plan to move there and build a new city, and I need your help to do that."

"My help? Why? Surely you have engineers left who can build."

"Most are dead or have left. The few remaining do not have your intellect. Asshur, I need you and to show you how much I value your help, I will name the new city Assur in your honor. Will you join me?"

"This is strange," responded Asshur. "A few weeks ago I would have said no because of your departure from God. But now I find that I no longer believe in Him. Oh, He is a powerful god, but I lost loved ones due to His latest judgment. So, yes, I will follow you and help you build Assur."

The two men stood and embraced. Shortly afterward, Asshur left to get his people ready. Within two weeks the combined families, along with others who joined them, crossed the Euphrates and headed northeast. Moving slowly, it took them another week to arrive at the site for Nimrod's new capital.

&&&

In the meantime, Eber and Chloe found others of like tongue, although only a few. As they all moved south, he went about searching for relatives with no success. Meanwhile the refugees continued to move southward.

Eber wanted to put a good distance between himself and Babel, so he led his people south. Their progress was slowed by storms that crisscrossed their route for several weeks. Even so they were able to travel 100 miles south of Babel. On the last day of stormy weather, as the sun came out, they came upon a plain along the Euphrates that was large enough to not only support them, but their descendants.

As soon as he saw it, he knew this was where he would settle. Through the remainder of the day, the people erected makeshift tents and settled down for the night. Once he was satisfied that all were settled, he returned to his own tent where a hot meal awaited him.

Chloe waited until Eber finished the evening meal before making her announcement.

"I am with child."

The statement was so matter-of-fact that Eber almost missed it. But he paused and looked at her.

"What did you say?"

"I am with child?"

"So soon?"

"It only takes a moment," she laughed. "I figure I am about three months along. I have been suspicious for a while, but not sure until now."

"But you are sure?"

"Yes, my lord, I am sure. God is going to bless us with a son."

"A son? Is it possible?"

"I believe so. Yes. It could be a girl, but I am praying it will be a boy."

"Then I shall name him Peleg, because God has divided us."

He reached out and took her hands.

&&&

A few days later Shem rode into camp. As he dismounted, Eber approached him.

"Shem, it is so good to see you."

"Same here, Eber."

"Have you heard anything from my father?"

"Shelah and his family are fine. They speak the same language as you. He worries about you and wants you to travel to meet him further north at a new city Nimrod is building called Assur."

"Assur? Does that mean that Asshur and Nimrod are still together?"

"More than ever," responded Shem.

"Well, that is interesting. But I am fine here. We have a small group of people and have established our own community right here. We plan on living here beside the Euphrates."

"Your father will be disappointed, but I am sure he will understand. What are you calling the village?"

"I thought we might call it Ur?"

"Light? Interesting. Any particular reason?"

"As a matter of fact, yes. There were two reasons. The first is that when we first arrived here the sky was dark with storm clouds and it had been raining hard for several days. But on that very first day the clouds parted and sunlight poured through upon the river and this land! It was in that light that we first saw its beauty."

"And the second reason?"

"No one had a better name," Eber smiled ruefully.

"Well, it is a good name. I shall record that Eber founded the city of Ur. Who is the young lady I see yonder?"

"That is my wife, Chloe. She is carrying our first child."

"That is good news, because there have been no births since the Confusion, but a lot of deaths. We must get back to expanding our population as God commanded Adam and Eve and my parents, Noah and Naamah."

"How many people are there in the world now?" Eber asked.

"It is difficult to say because so many people have moved in so many directions. It is very hard to keep up-to-date records, which is why I am making this trip. But there were almost thirteen hundred at the time of the Confusion, so I think it is about one thousand now."

"Three hundred have died?"

"Sadly, yes. Many people died during the Babel riots, but since then murders have increased dramatically. It has taken awhile, but Nimrod is re-establishing his control, so that should slow down such violence, if not stop it altogether. But there are also deaths simply because people have been scattered to the four winds and don't have access to proper care. Disease is taking a big toll.

"But enough of that. I would like you to show me around. When my wife arrives, she will insist that you introduce us to your lovely wife."

"I will do that. Chloe and I are married. I took her as my wife the day after the Confusion, but we never had a proper marriage ceremony."

"I would be honored to perform it," Shem smiled.

&&&

Shortly after arriving at Assur, Nimrod and Asshur explored the land and began making plans. For several days they roamed the site deciding on where the palace would be located as well as other structures.

Using similar plans as those followed in constructing Babel, they soon had the people clearing the land and making bricks. The biggest difference between Babel and Assur was that the new city would not straddle a river, but would be completely upon the western shore.

Week after week, month after month the construction continued. As with Babel, the first buildings to go up were the smaller, one room homes for the workers and the barracks for the soldiers. Then came the larger homes, and finally the palace. At this time, no ziggurat was planned, although a small temple for Ishtar would be built.

During this time, Nimrod focused on rebuilding his army. He began by ordering that all able-bodied men carry weapons and begin training immediately. This took precious time from the construction, but he was determined that both would go forward.

With this focus, he was able to begin the re-establishing of his kingdom. By the end of two years, he was once again in complete charge. But not as before. Elam had moved south and established his own kingdom east of the Tigris. This created a concern for Nimrod.

But the growing restiveness of Asshur was also a problem and Nimrod could ill afford a rebellion at this time.

It was with that in mind that Nimrod presented a new plan to Asshur.

"I know you don't agree with me on a few matters, but you have been a loyal soldier. I have decided to move south to counter the threat of Elam. I am leaving some of my people behind to help you build, but you I am placing in charge. You will be like a king."

"Why me?"

"Because you have the leadership and the men to rule this city and all of the land north of Babel. You are also ambitious, which I don't mind as long as you remember that I am the king and you are under my hand."

"Not a problem. How far south will you be going?"

"There is land a day's journey south of Babel. There I will build a new city that will be greater than Babel. There I will rule. But you shall rule the north. No man shall be greater than you except myself.."

"Well, don't worry about us. We will rule the north for you and send much goods to you. What about Babel?"

"Babel will be rebuilt in time, but not now."

With that settled, Nimrod and his officers mounted their horses and left the city with the army marching behind. Standing in his palace balcony, Asshur watched as the army slowly disappeared. *King! Now I am King Asshur and my people shall be known as the Asshurites. The beginning of my rule shall be here in Assur and the end shall be the far corners of the world!*

# TWENTY EIGHT

## GROWTH & EXPANSION

2248BC (pop. 1009)

The year following the birth of Eber's firstborn, Peleg, was an exciting year for the young family. Eber, a carpenter by trade, was busy building new homes and establishing the new city of Ur. As the founder, he easily became its ruler. Some would have made him king, but with Nimrod's city of Erech only a couple days ride away, he decided prudence dictated a more humble title. So he became Ur's first mayor.

But the first matter he had to confront was not an enemy, but the townspeople. When he named his firstborn child Peleg, the people wondered at the boy's name and would ask about it.

"That is easy," Eber smiled. "He is the first born since the Confusion of Tongues. Therefore, because he was conceived when the Lord our God divided our tongues and scattered our people, he shall be named Peleg."

Everyone nodded in agreement. The name Peleg was appropriate.

That had been a year ago and now Peleg was crawling around on all fours with Chloe chasing after him. Eber delighted in the child and found it refreshing to come home after a long day and watch his son's antics.

*&&&*

Shortly after founding his new capital city of Erech, Nimrod took a band of men to explore the land to the east and to see what Elam was doing. He left Jamin in charge with instructions to immediately begin construction of the new city.

As soon as Nimrod was gone, Jamin turned with relish to his new task. Soon the ground was being cleared and the women were sent

174 R. Frederick Riddle

into the wild fields to seed the ground. He hoped to be able to start making bricks within a couple months.

One night while lying upon his bed, Jamin heard a knock upon his tent door. *Who can that be at this late hour?*

Slipping a robe on, he walked over and opened the flap only to find Queen Semiramis standing there. He swallowed hard as the moonlight lent her an alluring beauty.

"Your highness! What are you doing here?"

"The king has gone on a journey and I find his bed lonely," she said peering into his tent. "Your bed, on the other hand, looks inviting."

Jamin took a deep breath. For fifteen years he had desired her, but no one knew. Yet she acted like she knew. *If she tells the king, I am dead.*

"Are you going to invite me in?" she inquired.

He stepped back as she entered. She walked over to the bed.

"You have been staring at me for fifteen years, Jamin. It is time for you to show me that you can do more."

"But the king. He will kill me."

She laughed softly.

"Do you think that you are the first man I have had outside of the marriage bed? I have slept with others and the king does not know. How can he know? All the servants are loyal to me and won't breathe a word. So come and let us enjoy the night."

Jamin made up his mind.

&&&

Nimrod and his band of men had been camped for several days overlooking the Tigris River. From their vantage point they could see the land on the other side, but the city of Susa, the capital of Elam, was yet another 155 miles to the east, hidden by distance and intervening hills.

Searching among his men, he found two trustworthy and able men whom he sent acroos the river. Their mission? Spy out the city and report back to him.

&&&

Northwest of Babel was another encampment. Here Phut and Mizraim had gathered their people. The fighting in Babel and the later pestilence that had plagued them since those days of Confusion had left them with less than fifty people.

But Phut moved quickly. Although he only had a small force at his disposal, it was well trained. With them, he was able to quickly re-establish and enforce strict rules. Where before he had ruled by right of age, he now asserted his growing authority through sheer power. Most of the men were trained soldiers, willing to die for him and, if necessary, kill for him!

His brother Mizraim led his own people, numbering about 23 out of the 50. Phut decided it was better to let their forces remain divided into two camps. From the start, it was Phut and his people in the lead with Mizraim and his people following.

At first, travel was mainly on foot, which was painful and slow. The quick exit from Babel had not allowed for large wagons, thus forcing the people to carry much of their belongings on their backs.

In addition, there were almost daily storms causing many delays and, when they were able to travel, the muddy trails made movement extremely difficult. After several such delays, Mizraim visited Phut.

"Phut," began Mizraim after they entered Phut's tent and found a dry place to sit, "these constant delays are causing further discouragement and, in some cases, my people are getting sick. We haven't made much progress and the Euphrates is still nearby. I think we should stop here for awhile."

"Have you considered that Nimrod is not far away?"

"Actually, I have heard a rumor that he is moving east," replied Mizraim. "But, even if he stays in the area, he is not strong enough to cause us harm. My concern is for the health of my people. Why not stay here until we are stronger?"

"To be honest, I think you are right. But we will have to be vigilant. It is true that Nimrod is not as strong as before, but we are few in number. How long do you think we should stay here?"

"At least two years. We can use the time to build larger, stronger wagons and increase our supplies, as well as mend the tents. It will also allow us time to increase our cattle. By then we shall be completely independent and able to move wherever we desire."

Phut scratched his beard as he considered the possibilities. The more he thought about it, the more convinced he was that such an action not only had merit, but was practical as well.

"You make much sense, my brother. We will stay here in our two camps, multiply our people and be ready to move south. We can also use this time to train our solders. I want them to be the best solders in the world!

That meeting, shortly after the Confusion of Tongues, proved a wise decision. During the ensuing two years they had seen their cattle and supplies increase. But it was the rising morale of the people that really made the long encampment worthwhile.

# TWENTY NINE

## A REPORT AND A VISION

2248BC (*continued*)
The priest Jamin proudly entered the newly built temple. He had insisted that the very first building to be built in the new city of Erech had to be the temple to Ishtar.

Nimrod had thought about that for a moment.

"OK. But this new temple must also have representations of the stars of heaven. The people were turning to the worship of the host of heaven, and I don't want to lose that. Let Ishtar be the primary god, if you want, but surround her with all the other gods. Perhaps each god can represent a time of year or a particular need. The sooner they become a part of the people's daily life, the sooner they depart completely from this God of Noah's!"

"I agree."

Thus had been their conversation three months before and now a simple temple stood on what had been barren ground. Stepping inside, Jamin looked around. In the middle of the temple stood the statue of Ishtar facing the entrance.

The idol stood almost six feet tall, wearing a dress extending to her ankles in repeating folds. The hair of her head was similarly layered ending in a point at the top, while perhaps her most striking feature was the candle she held in her left hand. This candle was kept lighted at all times.

At her feet was a sacrificial pit that he intended to use both for worship and as a method of removing Nimrod's enemies.

"This temple does not suit you like the one at Babel, but it will do," he murmured.

&&&

Several weeks later a weary Shem and Achsah drove their wagon into Ararat. Not finding his father at home, Shem realized Noah must have gone up the mountain, where he liked to spend time at the Ark in prayer to God.

Leaving Achsah behind, he unhitched a mule and rode up the trail. Darkness came quickly forcing him to spend the night about midway up the mountain. Though years had passed since first he had descended the mountain, he easily found the cave where he and the rest of the family had stayed. Entering, he found almost no evidence of their earlier stay. Spying a broken piece of clay, Shem went over and picked it up.

"I remember this. It is a piece of one of the Writings that broke on the very first day of our descent," he said, as the recollections of that day became crystal clear.

"We almost lost Naamah as well as the tablets. But God was gracious and only a few tablets fell out of the cart. Later we stayed here while a great storm passed through."

He exited the cave and began gathering broken branches laying on the ground. Because some were too long, he broke them in half. Re-entering the cave, he soon had a small fire started and he settled down for the night.

Early the next morning, he was on his way again and arrived at the Ark in early afternoon. He spotted his father kneeling before the altar.

Dismounting, he walked over and knelt behind his father and waited for him to finish his prayer.

Many minutes went by before he felt his father's hand upon his shoulder. Looking up, he smiled and stood. The two men warmly embraced. Afterward, Noah walked over to his favorite spot. Shem noted that it was the cave adjoining Naamah's burial place. Inside, Noah had a blanket, a small fire going, and a cooking pot nearby.

As they sat upon the ground, Noah studied Shem with the appraising eye of a knowing father.

"You look tired, my son."

"I am, father. Since the Confusion, Achsah and I have been traveling about trying to understand all that is happening. It has been a journey of despair as we have seen much death. But I also have good news."

"What good news?"

"My great grandson Eber has married and they have a new born son. I believe he is the first born since the Confusion took place. They named him Peleg because he was conceived at the time of the dividing of tongues."

"That is fitting."

"Yes, and they have joined with other families and founded the city of Ur. Some other people, Hamites, have lodged there as well. Already there are buildings rising.

"Meanwhile, Nimrod has regained his authority and is stronger than ever. He now rules from Erech, which is between Babel and Ur; actually about 50 miles north of Ur. My son Asshur now rules the city of Assur under the authority of Nimrod, although I sense a restive spirit in him. It is only a matter of time before he rebels. My son Elam has moved further to the south across the Tigris and has established the kingdom of Elam.

"I have also noted that many other families have had children since Peleg's birth. Plus, more are about to have new births. So the population is growing again. At least in that they obey God."

"That is good."

"Yes, but Nimrod has successfully started a new religion. It began in Babel, but now involves the whole host of heaven with the primary god being Ishtar, who is actually female. She is the goddess of love and war, while some say she is also the goddess of fertility."

Noah shook his head.

"Tell me more of this host of heaven."

"They worship all the stars and planets. I think Ishtar represents one of the planets, just as the other gods represent planets. This worship of the host of heaven was particularly evident with the temple at Babel. I think each rising tier represented another god or goddess.

"Nimrod's priest, a man by the name of Jamin, teaches that God created these gods and we are to worship them. In that way we honor God. He is very persuasive."

"Humph!" exclaimed Noah. "And in time that will be dropped. So Nimrod has been able to deceive the people and give them new gods. Nothing good will come of that!"

"I agree."

"And what of your wife. Did she come with you?"

"She is at your place. We'll be traveling as soon as I get back, so she has some washings and other womanly preparations to do. And don't be surprised if she straightens up your home in the process."

"Then perhaps we should stay up here longer," Noah laughed.

&&&

Phut issued a call to all his people to gather about his tent. He watched as they came together and settled in a semi-circle in front of his tent door. Everyone, except the Mizraimites, whom he hadn't called, arrived. He waited until all were settled and their attention directed toward himself.

"At 93 years of age, I am still a young man," he began. "I have seen much in this world. Like you, I followed my cousin Nimrod. He showed us that we didn't need the God of Noah. With his wisdom, we were organized as a people. We built his city and a glorious temple. Like him, we suffered when the Judgment of Tongues fell upon us.

"But where is Nimrod now? His kingdom is broken, his temple vacant, and his city lies deserted. The last I heard, he has moved north and left us to ourselves.

"But I have had a vision."

The men and their wives leaned forward in anticipation. He could see he had their rapt attention.

"In this vision, I saw a great river flowing north and a great land that was fed of this river. It is uninhabited, waiting for us. The river is like a mother to the land and is beautiful. I have decided that this land shall be divided between my sons.

"But that is not where my vision ends. Far to the west of this river lays an even more beautiful land beside a great sea. I and my house shall migrate to this land. There I shall raise up a mighty kingdom that the world shall not forget. Its beginning shall be there beside the Great Sea, but it shall extend without end.

"This is where we shall go. The rest of you shall choose to stay with my sons, or follow me."

This announcement had the immediate effect of electrifying everyone. Simultaneously, people started asking questions, wanting to know more about his dream, but Phut declined. Smiling to himself, he thought, *It is true about the great river and the great sea, but it wasn't really a vision.*

He remembered the incident that happened only days before as he watered his horse. It was only a day's ride away from the camp, but both animal and human were thirsty.

"Thou shalt find greater waters than these for your horses."

Phut turned so abruptly that he almost fell into the river. He immediately unsheathed his sword.

"Who are you?"

"I am he that is worshiped by Nimrod, the mighty hunter before God."

"What is Nimrod to me? We are dispersed from Babel and I know not where he has gone. Moreover, he has forgotten us and may not even speak our language."

"What I have done for him, I can do for you."

Phut considered that statement. *Nimrod became a mighty ruler and even now after the catastrophe in Babel, he is still poweerful.*

He relaxed a little and studied the warrior standing before him. Garbed in armor with a sword at his side, the unknown man appeared quite capable of using his sword, which remained sheathed. But how could this man have helped Nimrod or, for that matter, help him?

"Tell me your name that I can tell others."

"My name is Lucifer, but thou shalt not call me that. Thou shalt call me Horus and thou shalt make an idol unto me that is of a hawk."

"Lucifer, the one called Satan."

"I do not like that name. You are fortunate that I like you or I would slay you where you stand."

For the first time that he could remember, Phut felt sweat coursing down his back. Short and stocky, he had known many a fight and usually won. Rarely was he scared. But the very sound of the name of Satan, though from his own lips, had sent shivers down his back.

"Why do you speak to me, Lucifer? I am but a man with the care of a few families as we seek to survive the catastrophe at Babel. A catastrophe brought about by your leading Nimrod into rebellion."

Lucifer's eyes took on an evil and unsettling glare.

"Your words have no effect upon me. If I wish, I could slay you where you stand.

"I have chosen you because I know you. I know how much you desire to rule and how you detest Nimrod. I know that you do not worship the God of Noah nor the goddess Ishtar."

"I worship no god," Phut said with rising voice.

Phut suddenly felt a constriction upon his throat as breath was denied him. He sank to his knees, his eyes pleading for mercy.

"True," responded Lucifer. "But, as you can see and feel, I am a god truly worthy of your worship. Worship me, for I have the power to bring all your dreams to pass."

Suddenly the constriction was gone and Phut felt his strength restored. He felt both anger and fear.

"You know nothing of my dreams!"

Lucifer crossed his arms and smiled at Phut.

"That is untrue. You dream of greatness. You dream of being a ruler. You have dreams of great wealth. Need I go on?"

"OK, you know my dreams. But what happens if I worship you?"

"To begin with, you shall do as I say and shall be more respectful. I would hate to make an example of you to your family."

Phut swallowed hard before answering.

"I shall obey."

"Much better. Now listen carefully.

"You will take these families to lands that I shall tell you of. There is a great river to the south that you shall call Ar. It flows contrary to the way of rivers as it flows northward into the Great Sea. It waters a vast land and shall be a place which you may give to others to dwell. But I shall guide you to a great land to the west. It is a land that borders upon the Great Sea, a land wherein you shall put your name."

"But why would the people follow me. Especially if I cannot tell them your name."

"They would be too fearful to follow the name of Lucifer. Consider yourself, how fearful you became at the sound of my name. But give them a new name that they have never heard, and they shall follow. Tell them this god is called Horus and they shall worship."

Phut stared at Lucifer in surprise. *How did he know I was* fearful. Lucifer smiled back.

"You thought perhaps that your thoughts were hidden from me, but I have powers you have no idea exist. Fear me, yes. Doubt me, no!"

"OK. If you can truly make me a great man, I will worship you. I certainly cannot worship the God of Noah. What next?"

"Gather your people together and tell them of a vision concerning a great river and a great sea. By and by you can reveal the name of the river. It too shall be a god. Then thou shalt set off tomorrow for this land."

"Mizraim and his people are with me. Do I speak to them as well?"

"No. Thou shalt separate thyself from Mizraim. I have plans for him as well. He shall follow you, but you and your people shall be separate."

"I will do as you say."

As soon as Phut made his declaration, Lucifer/Horus disappeared.

Now, only hours after that fateful meeting, as the men eagerly questioned him, Phut announced their new god.

"Listen to me. Before you were born, indeed before I was born there was a great Flood and God brought Noah and his family through it. Noah is my grandfather and a great man is he. But he, speaking on behalf of his God, placed a great curse upon my father. That curse is to be a servant of servants.

"It is a curse that must not stand. There is one who has the power to lift that curse and his name is Horus. It was Horus who taught Nimrod how to make war and to build cities. It was Horus who gave me this vision of a well watered land. It is Horus I shall worship."

Immediately everyone grew quiet. Phut stood there observing them. Then with a smile on his face, he calmly declared unto them: "If you agree to make Horus your god and to follow me, then tomorrow we leave."

He turned and left, knowing that none would sleep this night.

# THIRTY

## RISE OF ASSHUR

2247BC (pop. 1203)

Asshur watched as his sons and their slaves labored erecting the storage building. He smiled as he watched the slaves. It had been his idea to raid some of the nearby camps and villages, seizing their young men and women. Although they spoke a different language, they could be taught enough to understand commands.

His sons claimed several of the young maidens as their wives, while others were sold.

The raids had been more successful than he had anticipated. So much so, that he was determined to make additional raids, thus increasing Assur's population and ability to defend itself from others.

*I shall build a kingdom and free myself of the yoke of Nimrod. I shall raise an army and conquer the world. I shall rule!*

&&&

Many months later, Asshur was standing on his balcony overlooking the city named after him, when he heard the sound of a step behind him. Turning, he saw coming through the throne room two men, his captain of the guard and a young soldier. They came up to the door leading to the balcony and stopped. The captain saluted.

"Your highness, I have a soldier here that has some important information for you."

"Speak," Asshur commanded.

With obvious nervousness, the soldier began describing a land about 62 miles north of Assur. It was with growing excitement that Asshur listened to the young soldier describing the perfect place. His memory was excited as the soldier told of the triangular land situated between the Tigris and Khosr Rivers. *I remember that land. We passed through there years ago as we moved south from the mountains of Ararat. It is about 18 miles north of Calah.*

The soldier continued and told of the fertile land which proved very attractive. In addition, it was noted that the rivers bounded with fish, plus it was easily accessible from several directions.

Asshur smiled.

"How did you learn of this land?"

"I and others were sent to explore the land for your highness."

Asshur nodded as he remembered the order. It had been an afterthought that he had promptly forgotten.

"I remember that land. You are right. We shall build a great city right there, perhaps on both sides of the Khosr."

"What shall you call it?" asked the captain.

"Nineveh, the fish town," he declared. "I remember the river. It is teeming with fish. We shall be able to feed a multitude there."

&&&

Nimrod stood tall and proud in his chariot. Seeing the town of Ur in the distance, he ordered the driver to turn toward it, although it was a little out of the way. As the chariot turned toward the town, there followed a band of twenty soldiers marching behind. About thirty minutes later the chariot entered the town and stopped in the center.

Eber, who had watched with other elders as the band of soldiers approached, hurried forward and bowed before the monarch.

"Are you Eber?"

"Yes, sire. How may I assist you?"

"I have come to claim this city for myself. You call it Ur?"

"Yes, sire."

"That shall remain. If you are loyal to me, I shall leave you in charge."

"You have my loyalty, your majesty."

"Are you prepared to prove that?"

"What do you mean?"

"To prove your loyalty?"

"Yes, sire."

"Are there any maidens here of marrying age?"

"There are two, your highness."

"Bring them to me."

Eber paled.

"Sire?"

"I said bring them to me. I have need of young maidens."

"But sire, they are all that their parents have."

"Bring them."

Eber looked at Nimrod and then at the troops behind him. The hard, lustful looks on their faces testified to what was in store for the maidens. To resist might mean death, but to surrender would cost the girls their freedom and perhaps their lives.

"I am your servant, Nimrod. But I cannot do what you ask."

"I am not asking. Bring the girls to me or I shall destroy this village and everyone in it."

Eber took a breath and straightened his shoulders.

"I cannot do that, sire."

Nimrod's rage was immediate. His hand closed upon the sword at his side, but then something startling happened.

In that instant, there suddenly appeared a multitude of angels surrounding Eber and, indeed, the entire village!

Shaken, the king looked at Eber, who was unaware of this vision. But the sudden paleness of the king was readily apparent. Eber glanced at the soldiers who seemed frozen in place. *What is happening?*

As color slowly returned to the king's face, he knelt before Eber.

"I am sorry Eber. I beg of thy forgiveness for my rashness."

*Lord, what is going on?*

Suddenly, Eber's eyes were cleared. He now saw the army of angels camped about him, and understanding came.

"The power to forgive is the Lord's to give or hold back, Nimrod. As you can see, the Lord Himself fights my battles. You are a mighty warrior, but my God is greater.

"If thou truly desires forgiveness then thou shalt not harm me, my family, or this town. Thou shalt go your way peaceably or the wrath of God shall fall upon you."

Nimrod stood, all signs of rage gone. Still shaken, he managed to speak.

"I shall leave and not return. Neither my army nor I shall bring harm upon you or this village. You shall enjoy my protection as long as I live."

"Thank you."

Nimrod remounted his chariot and signaled his men to follow. Moments later, the troops marched out of Ur, heading north to Erech.

&&&

Once again Shem arrived at his father's house and lodged with him for a time. He had been busy gathering information about all the differing families and tribes. Now was the time to report.

"It is as we had originally surmised," he began. "It is still too soon to tell where all will end up, but I have come to some conclusions."

"Such as?" Noah asked.

"Well, beginning with your first born Japheth, he has seven sons. All except Madai are moving north or northwest. Madai is moving east.

"As for Ham, his people are moving toward the south and southwest."

"And yours?"

"Mostly south, those who are moving. Some are staying."

"It does appear that God's will for us to populate the world is coming to pass."

"Yes, father."

"Is it true that slavery has started up again?"

"Yes, father. My own son, Asshur, has turned even more wicked than before. He takes what he wants and will kill anyone who gets in his way. He has invented slavery and now enslaves both young men and women. Mostly they are from other tribes that have not yet moved out of his reach. Some, though, are his own people who no longer can pay his taxes.

"Though he still swears fealty to Nimrod, he is really independent. It is only a matter of time 'til he throws off Nimrod's yoke and there is war. It is a sad day."

"Yes," agreed Noah, "But it will get worse. Man has an insatiable desire to control other men. It was so before the Flood and is so now. So now we have two rulers?"

"Yes, Nimrod is the greater, but Asshur is gaining strength. As I said, it is only a matter of time before they go to war."

"And who would win?"

"Asshur, if you are talking strength of arms. But Nimrod, if you are talking cunning. But there are others."

"What do you mean?"

"Ham's sons Mizraim and Phut. They both have created small armies of archers and are moving south. Across the Tigris is Elam, who has established a kingdom at Susa. I am not sure what all that means."

"It is hard to believe that I was used of God to start all over and here the third generation has already departed from His will," Noah sighed.

"Yes, and my own son," responded Shem.

"But," he continued, "the very fact that He is using me to record events suggests that He has a plan and is patiently working toward it. We have much to consider."

The two men contemplated this sad state of affairs with wordless communion.

# THIRTY ONE

## PEACE

2247BC (*continued*)

"Eber, come here!" Chloe shouted.

Thinking something was wrong, Eber dashed inside only to be greeted by the sight of Peleg, his first-born son, walking toward him. The boy tottered from one step to another, struggling to reach his father. It lasted only for a few steps and down the boy went, but Eber gleefully lifted him high above his head.

"You can walk! Praise God. Chloe, he can walk!"

Chloe laughed and gently retrieved her son.

"I know you are already planning things for him, but right now he is still my baby boy."

Eber turned and left, going from house to house telling the people that his son could walk and hadn't even gotten to his second birthday yet!

For the next several days the whole town of Ur rejoiced with Eber. But amidst their joy they took practical actions. Ever since Nimrod had attempted to take the two girls, they kept their own daughters in hiding, especially those twelve and older. Nimrod's cruelty was reaching legendary status giving rise to stories, both true and untrue, of his exploits. Although he had promised to protect Ur, no one truly trusted him. Fear ruled not only Ur, but all the towns under his rule that were not enjoying such protection.

&&&

Nimrod sat upon his throne watching the young maidens dance before his guests. The banquet was going quite well. He glanced at Semiramis, seated in her throne beside him, and wondered. For some time he had suspected that she was unfaithful to him, but he had no proof.

He sighed, turning his attention back to the girls. *Why should I worry about her. Before this night is over, one of these maidens will be in my bed.* He smiled, but a moment later it was replaced with a frown. The very thought of someone else lying with his queen was disturbing.

"Are you pleased, your highness?"

Startled, Nimrod turned to Semiramis and nodded.

"I arranged for this entertainment for your pleasure. They are all virgins, ready for you," she said sweetly.

"And what do you expect in return?" he asked.

"Nothing, my lord. Your happiness is all that I want."

He relaxed. *To think I was suspicious of her. Don't be a fool Nimrod. She loves you. How could she not!*

&&&

Asshur arrived at Nineveh just as the sun was going down. As he stopped on a hill and looked down into the small city, he felt himself swell with pride. *This city shall be greater than Assur, even greater than Babel.*

Still in the early stages of building, the city was rising quickly. All the skills learned at Babel and Assur were now being applied here. One difference that had been suggested to Asshur, he'd forgotten by who, was that the wall surrounding the city would be quite wide. The width was as of yet unknown, but it would be at least wide enough for three chariots riding abreast. That much he was sure.

Another idea had occurred to him. It was well known that Ishtar was the favorite goddess of Jamin, Nimrod's priest. *It would be quite fitting if I were to dedicate the city to Ishtar, perhaps making Nineveh her city. That would surely make Jamin a bit upset.*

He chuckled. *Yes, that is what I will do.*

# THIRTY TWO

## REBELLION

2238BC (pop. 2500)

Phut sat upon his horse and watched as the waters of the Ar flowed northward. *What an amazing sight! Who would have guessed that a river could flow north? It is just as Horus said it would be.*

He turned on his horse and looked back at his people. On horseback, wagons, and foot they presented a strange sight. *But they are tough and they believe in me. How many miles have we traveled from Babel?*

His thoughts were broken as a soldier rode up to him.

"Report."

"I have searched north of here, O lord Phut and I found a place of crossing."

"Good. Tell the others. I have instructed you to call me Horus Hawk. Next time I will require your head. Understood?"

The soldier immediately saluted and left.

Phut watched him as he rode back to the camp. *It has only been forty-nine years and the people have completely accepted the idea of a god called Horus. How stupid and superstitious.*

&&&

Asshur stood on his balcony overlooking the main square of Assur. Standing in the square before him was his army consisting of 100 charioteers and another 100 foot-soldiers.

*Nimrod cannot match my army. My charioteers would run through his army as rapidly as the Tigris flows south.*

He held up his right hand in which he held his proclamation. The crowd quieted.

He took one last look over his army and the populace behind them.

"Citizens of Assur, soldiers and charioteers - hear me this day. For I hold in my hand a proclamation declaring our freedom from the rule of Nimrod. No more shall we feed his troops; no more shall we bow our knee to him! Henceforth, we are the Kingdom of Assur!

"Be prepared to battle for he shall surely come. But he cannot stand before our chariots. He cannot fight our army and expect to win. We will tear him apart, we shall devour him and spit him out!

"Great is the Kingdom of Assur!"

The square erupted into shouts of joy and both citizens and soldiers celebrated wildly.

&&&

Although he had warned the citizens of Nimrod's invasion, Asshur had other plans. The next morning his army secretly left the city. With Asshur at its head, the army, led by its chariots, turned south toward Erech.

Lurking in the shadows of the court, a man had watched the proceedings. The whole tenor of Asshur's speech was militaristic, rebellious. An agent of Nimrod's, he decided to wait through the night and see what happened.

As the sun began to rise in the east, he had observed troops silently moving into position. He watched as row upon row of chariots and soldiers, dressed for battle, stood outside the palace.

Not needing any further proof, he slipped out of the city. To avoid detection he rode north until out of sight of the city's watchmen. It was then that he made his discovery.

More troops and chariots were heading south toward Asshur.

"He's bringing his army from Nineveh, as well. I must hurry!"

Turning west, he traveled several miles before turning south. Traveling alone on a fast charger, he reached Babel at least a day ahead of Asshur's forces (They would be traveling slower and would have had to unite the two armies). Having out sped the army, he now struck out for Erech.

Racing his horse, he covered the 50 miles and reached Erech's North Gate before sunset. Saluting the watchman, he was quickly allowed inside. He rode through the street at a gallop and dismounted from his lathered horse before coming to a complete stop. Showing his identification (a letter signed by Nimrod) he was immediately escorted to Nimrod and Semiramis's presence.

"Report."

"Asshur has declared his independence from you and even now he marches toward this city."

"They're attacking us?"

"Yes, sire."

Nimrod smiled. He had hoped Asshur would make such a mistake.

"How many? Any reinforcements from Nineveh? How soon?"

"I estimate 600 men including chariots. That includes his army from Nineveh, which I saw. As for getting here, I made it in one day, but they have slow, heavy wagons. I would venture another two days, maybe three."

"Good. You're dismissed."

*Now to spring the trap!*

"You seem happy about the news, my lord," remarked the queen.

"Yes. You shall see that my prowess is not relegated to the bed."

At that moment, Jamin entered.

"What is it, my lord?" inquired Jamin.

"Asshur has rebelled and established his own kingdom!"

"Will you march on him?"

"No, he is marching against us. Unfortunately, most of our army is scattered abroad and cannot be recalled in time. He shall outnumber us. But we shall use his pride and arrogance against him."

"But what is that against so many?"

"A good question, Jamin. Therefore, you shalt go before Ishtar and seek her guidance. As for me, I shall prepare for Asshur's defeat."

&&&

Chloe placed a bowl of dried grasshoppers mixed with honey before Peleg. This was a much-loved treat for the eleven-year old boy. Chloe smiled as he gleefully plopped one into his mouth.

Hearing footsteps, she turned in time to see Eber walk inside.

"You're home early."

"Word has come that Asshur is going to attack Erech. We are going to hide our young men, just in case Nimrod wants more soldiers."

"Surely not Peleg or his brothers!"

"No, although Peleg will be of age next year. We must not assume anything; that would be a mistake. Don't forget the two maidens he almost stole to satisfy his lust! But for God, he would have taken them.

"I know he made promises, but time has a way of weakening promises. I will use every trick I can to prevent his taking our son."

"Do you really think we are in danger?"

"I'm not sure, so I'm not taking chances. If he defeats Asshur, we will feel his power more than ever. Gather your things, you leave tonight."

"Where are we going?"

"All our families will be moved further south until we know it is safe for their return."

"You won't be going with us?" asked Chloe, her voice showing alarm.

"No. The men will stay here to protect our homes. Don't worry, we know what we are doing."

Gathering the children up and placing them in a wagon along with several changes of garments and food supplies, Chloe and Peleg joined the others as the exodus from the city began. Chloe noticed that the normally happy, chatty women were unusually quiet and the men displayed a somberness she had rarely seen.

Eber had done a masterful job of organizing. From all over the city and from outlying farms came wagons, filled with women and children. Within hours the city was empty, except for a group of determined men.

Eber waited until the wagons, with their permanent escort, was gone before gathering the remaining men together. As they met, he heard the fear in their voices. *They are thinking if Nimrod wins, he will be worse than ever and will forget his promised protection. If Asshur wins, would he come and destroy Ur?*

It took several attempts before he could finally get the men quieted.

"Men of Ur, I call upon you this day to go to your homes and pray. If you have an altar, pray to God for our city's protection. Those of you who do not have an altar are welcome to use mine.

"Some of you want to fight, and fight we will if we must. But let me assure you of this: unless we have God on our side, we will not be able to defeat either Asshur or Nimrod. Both are too powerful for us. But God knows no such limitations.

"So I say again. Go to your homes, fall upon your knees and plead for God's intervention."

There was a stirring in the crowd and one young man shouted at Eber.

"How can we trust your God, Eber? Isn't He the same God that raised up Nimrod? Why should we trust Him?"

"Because," Eber responded firmly, "He has continually protected us. It was God Who stopped Nimrod when he would have struck me down and taken our young maidens from us. As for Nimrod, he worships the wicked one, not God. It is the wicked one who devours the lands and the people. But our God is mightier than him. You have seen His power before, be not afraid. He will protect us."

The crowd of men quieted. Most were not very religious and even fewer worshiped God, so Eber was not sure how much good their prayers would be. But it served one purpose; it calmed them down. He watched as they slowly dispersed with each man going to his home to pray. Eber sighed. Wiping beads of sweat from his forehead, he headed for his home.

Just outside his door was a small altar that he had built when he and Chloe first settled the land. Although he had enlarged his home several times, he had refrained from changing the altar. Sometimes he felt foolish, but the altar was special to him and he didn't want to change it. Kneeling before it now, he turned to God.

"My Lord, this is a dangerous time. The men of Ur are afraid and their faith in You is weak and with some non-existent. The best of us are but sinners. Even those of us who love You and desire Your will are but sinners. We don't deserve Your protection.

"Even so, I come to You asking that You place Your covering around this city. Protect us from the evil man and the wicked one. We are not worthy of Your protection or of Your love, but I know that You love us and desire us to know You, even as You know us. I pray for these men that their faith in You might be strengthened. Amen."

&&&

Nimrod had prepared for this day since the founding of Erech. Although the troops defending the city were small in number, they were well trained. The soldiers were well armed with battleaxes, thrusting spears and daggers. Every soldier wore studded leather cloaks and metal helmets. The studs were meant to protect against arrows and other sharp weapons. In addition, large shields were carried before them, which were capable of defending against the expected aerial attack launched by the archers.

The shields were quite impressive. Big enough for a full grown man to stand behind, light enough to be carried, and sturdy enough to withstand a fusillade of arrows. Nimrod had kept this defensive weapon a secret. Now it was time to unveil it!

With half his army elsewhere, much pressure would be place upon his battle wagons. His captains would ride in their own battle wagons, while he would lead them in his battle wagon. Each battle wagon was equipped with sheaves of javelins that the soldiers were trained to use as an effective weapon.

Jamin viewed the phalanx of soldiers with admiration.

"Asshur has a surprise waiting for him!"

"Perhaps, but he has more men and battle wagons than I do. If we are to defeat him, it will be with the chariots."

At that moment a dozen two-wheeled chariots came around the corner. Jamin turned to Nimrod in surprise and consternation.

"Surely you won't use those against the battle wagons! They're but flimsy toys!"

Nimrod laughed.

"Jamin, you have spent too much time with Ishtar. I have been secretly training these men to use their chariots as weapons. Sure they are flimsy when compared to the battle wagons, but they make up for that in speed! Combine that with surprise and we have a chance."

"What do you mean?"

"Just watch and you will understand as will Asshur, but it will be too late."

Semiramis was waiting as Nimrod descended the steps.

"My king, today shall be a great victory for us. Destroy them to the ground."

Nimrod smiled and the two kissed. As he left, he felt like a new man. *When I return from battle, I shall rejoice in her arms.*

The charioteers drove their chariots out the South Gate and waited. At a signal from Nimrod the North Gate was opened and he led his army out.

Semiramis took Jamin's hand.

"Come. While he is busy with Asshur, you can explore my delights."

&&&

Asshur turned in his battle wagon and looked back at his army as they assembled into two phalanxes, each consisting of 50 battle wagons and 50 foot soldiers. Turning his attention back to Erech, he couldn't help but smile. Nimrod had only twenty or thirty battle wagons and maybe 50 soldiers. He licked his lips in anticipation.

*Well, at least my erstwhile ruler has positioned himself on high ground. But they will not be able to hold it against my battle wagons!* Raising his hand, he signaled attack!

The two phalanxes drove at Nimrod's army. Even as they charged, they unleashed a barrage of arrows. But Asshur was astonished at what he next witnessed. The enemy soldiers each planted large shields in front of them. The first row simply knelt down with their shields touching, while the next row stood with their shields slightly tilted. Behind them were additional rows of shields raised above their heads. The net effect was an armored barrier that either bounced the arrows or absorbed them.

Even so, the barrage appeared effective. As his battle wagons slowly rolled forward and reached the base of the hill, the army of Nimrod began a grudging retreat. Asshur noticed that they didn't respond with their own arrows. *They either don't have any or they hope to use them later. Ha! That won't work.*

Urging his men on, Asshur ordered his driver into the midst of the enemy. Suddenly he spotted Nimrod. *What is this? He flees? The mighty Nimrod, hunter before God, flees from me?*

"That's Nimrod! After him," he shouted to his driver, who promptly turned the battle wagon toward the fleeing ruler.

Battle wagons are notoriously slow. But Asshur's wagon crept closer to Nimrod's fleeing battle wagon with each passing minute. Suddenly, Nimrod turned his battle wagon around until he was facing Asshur. It was obvious he intended to make a last stand.

Asshur smiled in triumph. *I've got him now!*

Asshur, looking back at his army, saw that most of his troops and battle wagons had broken through and were now approaching his position. Confidently he turned back toward Nimrod. What he saw froze him in place!

In that moment, a dozen small chariots were coming from behind the city and racing straight for him.

*What is this?*

But even as the question crossed his mind, he realized that these flimsy looking chariots were much faster than his battle wagon and would reach him before his army could rejoin him. He could see that Nimrod was now grinning. *It was a trap!*

"Turn around! Retreat," he ordered the driver. But before his command could be carried out, he felt an arrow strike his left arm. Gritting his teeth in pain, he looked down at the arrow and realized he would not be able to safely pull it out. Another arrow struck, this time hitting his right leg. Before he could react still other arrows found their mark. But it was a javelin thrown from one of the onrushing chariots that proved his undoing. Gripping the sides of the wagon, he looked down at the javelin protruding from his chest. *I'm dead!* Moments later he collapsed joining the driver in a pool of blood.

The soldiers from Assur watched this unfold before them even as they drew closer. Suddenly the chariots were among them and a great slaughter took place as the army of Erech stopped its retreat and counter-attacked. The few survivors fled toward Assur.

Nimrod re-entered Erech in triumph. The whole city seemed to erupt in cheers. He raised his right fist in a gesture of victory and the cheers grew louder. For several minutes, he basked in the adulation. Finally he entered his palace and saw a flushed Jamin rushing to meet him. *Even the dour Jamin rejoices over my triumph!*

Motioning Jamin and the generals to follow him, he burst through the doors to his throne room and took his seat. Settling comfortably, he looked with triumph upon his generals as Jamin came to his side.

"I am Nimrod and I rule the world! Henceforth, I shall rule with a fist of iron. Enemies will be dealt with quickly. All that bow their knee to me shall serve me and pay taxes to me. Only Ur shall remain free of my service and taxes."

From that day, the fear of Nimrod spread abroad. His army marched north and took Assur and all the cities beyond, including Nineveh. His rule was felt from the Tigris to west of the Euphrates.

As the years went by, he founded more cities, and brought order to his kingdom! As word of his victory and assurances spread, people returned to their homes, including the people of Ur. Later, to show his magnanimity, he built a great library at Ur and bestowed his precious tablets in its care.

# THIRTY THREE

## THE AR

2238BC (*continued*)

Far to the south, Shem watched from a distance as the people of Phut crossed the strange river. A few days ago, he had slipped up to the camp during the night and listened to the people talk. It was during this clandestine visit that he learned the name of the river was Ar and that it flowed north. Finding that bit of information doubtful, he decided to investigate further.

The following day he had traveled further south before venturing close to the now wide river. He paused and scanned the terrain. Assured that he could not be seen, he approached the river and dismounted. Walking up to its edge, he stood there in amazement as he watched the river flow northward.

*This is amazing!*

"Noah will certainly want to know about this. But I shall wait and see what Phut is planning."

That had been three days ago. Now he was back at his original vantage point and watching as the Phutites crossed the river. *Phut has chosen well. The river has narrowed and virtually stopped. He can cross easily.*

Although Shem was correct, the crossing took most of the day due to the heavy wagons. There was no problem at first. But from the moment the wagons entered the river problems began. Almost immediately a wagon got stuck in the riverbed.

Phut rode up and ordered the men to push the wagon forward. When it didn't respond to their efforts, he dismounted and stepped forward. Putting his weight into the effort along with the other men, they pushed hard. This time the wagon moved forward, only to roll back into place. Phut and the men gave another push, straining their muscles, and the wagon rolled free.

It seemed like one wagon would get freed and another would get stuck. One wagon tipped over and the women and children had to be rescued.

Shem was impressed with Phut's self-control. Once again on his horse, he rode up and down the line of wagons urging them onward. When the wagon tipped over, he leaped off his horse and helped carry a couple of children to safety. Then he returned to help right the wagon.

In spite of all the mishaps, everyone was across by nightfall. Phut quickly established a new camp and soon everything was back to normal. Shortly afterward, Shem crossed further downstream and found a place at a discreet distance to set up his own camp.

But the next morning, he stood and stared south. *Do I continue to follow or do I return north to report to father.* A few minutes later, his decision made, he rejoined his wife on the other side of Ar. He found her ready and soon they were heading north.

&&&

Nimrod paused, seeming to look at each person.

"Our army is the best in the world. But that is not enough. It is time to build a navy for trade and for war."

"A navy?" a general asked in surprise.

"Yes."

"You mean like the Ark?" Jamin asked.

"Not that big. But we can copy some of its features. But I had in mind the ships that plied the rivers of the ancient world."

"But how?" several of them asked in unison.

"My dear generals. You think only in terms of your army and of the now. You are masters of great armies. But I think in terms of the future. Just as naval power became important before, it can again. There is much knowledge and skill among our people that has not yet been realized."

Jamin rubbed his jaw.

"And how do we realize it?"

"Easy, Jamin. We have the account often spoken of by Noah and his sons. Plus, I have one of his precious tablets that details a sailing vessel's design. All we need are men, time, and a plan to combine our knowledge, skill, and the tablet's secrets into one coherent strategy."

"So what's your plan?" Jamin asked, speaking for all.

"First, we announce a great feast unto Ishtar. Perhaps a parade. We will gather the people together in festive celebration of her victories. We'll open the palace to the common people and let them share in the excitement.

"Then Jamin, you shall proclaim Ishtar's desire that we build a navy. You will tell them that Ishtar has spoken to you and she seeks men who can read, explain, and follow what the tablet says.

"Thus, we get the workers we need to build ships and, at the same time, isolate the people further from Noah's God."

"I like it!" Jamin exclaimed.

Nimrod smiled.

"I thought you would. Now excuse me while I go to my wife. She is waiting for me."

Watching him leave, Jamin smiled. *You shall find her ready!*

# THIRTY FOUR

## COMING OF AGE

2236BC (pop. 2730)

Peleg was excited! The whole city of Ur, now a prosperous center of trade, had turned out to celebrate his twelfth birthday. His heart was beating so strongly, he thought it would burst!

Earlier, his father had built a special altar for the occasion. Once used, it would be torn down. But now it stood ready for the sacrifice and his father stood before it ready to make the sacrifice.

"Citizens of Ur," he began, "Today is a great day. My eldest son is about to become a man and to take his place among us in our decisions and our labors. I am honored and pleased that you came to celebrate with us this important day.

"As custom dictates, Peleg, my first-born, has been cleaned, purified, and adorned with new clothing as befitting a young man. A lamb without blemish, chosen by him and inspected by me, has been prepared for his offering. But first tradition must be satisfied. Bring me the Writings."

One of the men brought a scroll of goatskin to him.

"This scroll is but a small copy of the real Writings that remain in Noah's care. But it has been diligently copied and is trustworthy."

He turned to his son.

"Peleg, my son, kneel before this altar and turn your eyes upon the God of Adam, the God of Noah, the God of Shem, and my God."

As the boy obeyed, his father began reading.

"In the beginning God created the heaven and the earth."

Peleg closed his eyes, trying to visualize the events as his father read from the Writings. He could hear God's voice, sounding much like his father, instructing Adam.

"Of every tree of the garden thou mayest freely eat: But of the tree of the knowledge of good and evil, thou shalt not eat of it: for in the day that thou eatest thereof thou shalt surely die."

Then in his mind's eye he watched as God brought all the animals before Adam, who promptly named them. He watched as Adam and Serpent explored the Garden and later as God formed Eve from his side. And the bond of marriage began!

But he shuddered as he watched Satan take possession of Serpent and use him to trick Eve.

"Now the serpent was more subtil than any beast of the field which the LORD God had made. And he said unto the woman, Yea, hath God said, Ye shall not eat of every tree of the garden?

"And the woman said unto the serpent, We may eat of the fruit of the trees of the garden: But of the fruit of the tree which is in the midst of the garden, God hath said, Ye shall not eat of it, neither shall ye touch it, lest ye die."

Eber paused and looked directly at his son.

"Peleg, tell me if there is anything wrong with Eve's statement."

"Yes, father. Eve said that God said they could not eat the fruit nor touch the tree, but He only said they could not eat of it."

"That is correct. And what does that teach us?'

"That we should speak only what God says and not add to it."

"Correct. Now let us resume.

"And the serpent said unto the woman, Ye shall not surely die: For God doth know that in the day ye eat thereof, then your eyes shall be opened, and ye shall be as gods, knowing good and evil.

"And when the woman saw that the tree was good for food, and that it was pleasant to the eyes, and a tree to be desired to make one wise, she took of the fruit thereof, and did eat, and gave also unto her husband with her; and he did eat.

"And the eyes of them both were opened, and they knew that they were naked; and they sewed fig leaves together, and made themselves aprons."

Once again Eber paused.

"Son, what was their sin?"

"They disobeyed God."

"That is correct. And that sin brought what upon all mankind?"

"Death."

Eber nodded in approval and continued reading. Peleg listened, picturing Adam and Eve trying to hide from God, their discovery, and judgment.

"And the LORD God said unto the serpent, Because thou hast done this, thou art cursed above all cattle, and above every beast of the field; upon they belly shalt thou go, and dust shalt thou eat all the days of thy life: And I will put enmity between thee and the woman, and between thy seed and her seed; it shall bruise thy head, and thou shalt bruise his heel."

Eber stopped and looked at Peleg.

"Son, what is the meaning of this?"

"That God will send a Redeemer from the seed of Eve to deliver us."

"Deliver us from what?"

"The penalty of death."

"Very good."

Eber resumed, telling of the judgment of God upon both Adam and Eve and their expulsion from the Garden.

"Son, God did something before He expelled Adam and Eve. What did He do and what does it mean.?"

"God slew a lamb and made coats of skin for them. It means that it is by the shedding of blood that our sins are covered."

"Whose blood?"

Peleg hesitated. For the first time during the entire ceremony his brain seemed to freeze.

"By whose blood are our sins covered?" his father asked again.

Suddenly Peleg knew!

"The Redeemer's."

"Correct. Arise son and take up the knife and slay your first lamb."

Standing, Peleg picked up the knife. As he approached the lamb, it looked at him and bleeped. Taking hold of the lamb's head, he quickly drew the knife across its throat. Then placing the knife down, he took a bowl to collect the blood.

As Peleg finished, Eber turned back to the people.

"This is my son Peleg. He is now a man and will sit in our councils. Let us pray."

As his father prayed for him, Peleg knew something was wrong. *Why do I feel sad?*

No one, including Eber, seemed to notice that he had stopped too soon. He had not challenged his son to trust and serve God, and to look for the Redeemer. If asked, he probably would have been sure he had done so. But in the end he would have been certain that Peleg knew the Lord and would serve him all his days. It was a mistake that Eber would regret for the rest of his life.

&&&

Two days later Shem and Achsah arrived. Shem apologized for his lateness.

"We got delayed by a severe storm and had to seek shelter. But now that we are here we want to express our congratulations to Peleg."

Eber smiled and embraced Shem.

"We knew you would be here if you could. And we wanted to wait, but there were others that came from far distances as well. But you are special to us and I know that Peleg would be delighted to see you."

"Where is the young man?"

"Come," Eber responded as he headed toward his house.

They found the young man squatting on the dirt floor and reading with the aid of the sunlight streaming through the window.

"You have a visitor, Peleg."

At the sound of his father's voice, the boy looked up and saw Shem. Leaping to his feet, he ran to the elderly man and hugged him. Shem grabbed a firm hold and held the lad up to where he was at eye level.

Eber watched in amazement. *Shem may be old, but he certainly isn't weak!*

"Hello Peleg," Shem said, his powerful voice reverberating through the house. "You have grown since I last saw you and now you are a man. Congratulations!"

"Thank you, Father Shem."

"Father Shem," Shem laughed. "It is true I have fathered many children and grandchildren, but the title Father belongs only to God. Just call me Shem."

"Yes, sir. I mean Shem."

"Now what are you doing?" Shem asked as he set Peleg down.

"I was learning to write. Father allowed me to use his ink and pen and some scraps of lambskin."

"What are you writing?"

"Father is teaching me to write receipts for the sale of goods."

"Excellent, but why not copy portions of the Writings?"

"The Writings?"

"Yes, I brought you a copy written by Noah. It is on sheepskin and is rolled in a scroll. I believe it includes the accounts of creation, the Garden, the expulsion, and all the way through the Flood. All of God's Word, copied by Noah and a gift to you."

"Thank you, Shem. I shall treasure it always."

"You do that, but better yet, use it to learn how to read and write. And to serve Him."

Peleg raised his eyes at that last comment. *Serve God? No, I don't want to be like you. Not having a life of your own.*

# THIRTY FIVE

## MIZRAIM

2228BC (pop. 3058)

Benah, king of Lower Egypt, greeted Phut upon his return from Upper Egypt, so-called because it was closer to the Ar River's beginnings, although further south. Lower Egypt, being in the north.

"Father, I am happy to see you back. How is my brother Adan?"

"He is fine," responded Phut. "But he is now Horus Scorpion even as you are Horus Crocodile. It is important that your people remember that you are gods."

"Sorry, I forgot that we are to refer to one another as gods. What news do you have from the south?"

"It's important that you call him Horus Scorpion and you insist on being called Horus Crocodile. Only then will the people consider you gods.

"As for Horus Scorpion, he grows in strength. I have left 12 good men to serve as a warrior army. Before I leave, I will do the same for you. Though few in number, they are strong and each is better than any three of Nimrod's."

"Before you leave?"

"Yes, this land is too confining for me and my future lies to the west. This was foretold me by Horus Hawk. Besides, I do not want to take sides when the two of you clash."

"Scorpion is my brother, why would we clash?"

"Because you both dream of ruling all of Egypt. I dare say the entire length of the Ar River. Either the two of you or your descendants will rule it all."

Benah thought about that for a minute.

"Where will you go?"

"West. The Great Sea extends westward and I will follow it and raise a new kingdom that I shall call Phut. But before I go, I must warn you."

"Warn me? You look very serious father."

"That is because there is a danger. We chose not to follow the God of Noah and have left his land for that reason. But his son Shem has taken it upon himself to visit all the tribes and to preach his God. If you allow him to do this, you may lose your people."

"When he comes I will be ready to smash him with my army."

"I hope it doesn't come to that. His God is powerful. But you must be firm. When he comes, and he will come, he will desire to preach. You cannot allow that."

"I understand. And if he tries to preach in spite of my insistence, I will kill him."

"Good. I have not heard of him causing any real trouble since the Dispersion, but we must be careful. I will spend the night here with you and in the morning I will leave."

&&&

Peleg stopped and simply stared at the young woman. *I have never seen any woman who was so beautiful. Who is she?*

Trying to be as discreet as possible, he began asking questions. He soon discovered that her name was Apphia and she, along with her family, had just moved into town. One look at her and he knew he wanted her!

Immediately, he began courting her. He would find a reason for visiting her house and would talk with her sometimes for hours. The relationship continued to grow to the extent that Apphia's parents contacted Eber and Chloe. Soon plans were being made for a wedding.

As the day approached, Peleg would often visit Apphia. One day he returned home early from a journey. Rushing over to her house, he entered without knocking and was immediately shocked. There in the middle of the room was Apphia and her parents worshiping and burning incense to an idol of Ishtar!

The family became aware of his presence and rushed to him as he appeared ready to faint. Apphia guided him to a chair and brought a bowl of fruit for him to refresh himself. After a while, his color returned and he was able to talk. But Apphia spoke first.

"I am sorry you saw that, Peleg. We are not believers like your family. I understand if you want to call off the wedding."

*Call off the wedding!* The mere thought made him feel weak all over. He gripped the chair and sat upright.

"No. I love you Apphia with all my heard. It is true that I worship God, but I am more tolerant than my father. If you wish to worship Ishtar or any other god, what is that to me?

"But please be more discreet. If my parents ever found out, they would forbid our marriage."

She gladly embraced him, promising to be more discreet.

&&&

Some ten years after their first visit, Shem and Achsah were once again setting up camp just north of the river of Ar. She quickly set about preparing their evening meal while he tethered the mules they used to pull the wagon. His own horse remained tethered to the rear of the wagon.

Gathering dried dung along with small sticks, she placed them in the small, stone-lined hole she had prepared and rubbed them together. When they erupted into flames, she used them to ignite and produce a fire. Once the fire was going, she placed the bread on the heated stones and waited while they baked. When done, she withdrew the thin, flat loaves that both she and Shem loved. She smiled as she remembered the stories of Noah, where shepherds would carry such tasty loaves with them as they led the sheep into the mountain ranges. Noah had often mentioned that the shepherds would fold the loaves for dipping, as well as carrying, while out with the flocks.

The savory aroma of the bread was upon the air and soon Shem was beside her.

"Are they ready?"

Grinning, she took one of the loaves, still a little on the hot side, and handed it to him. He held it close to his nose and enjoyed the aromatic smells. Sitting beside her, he bowed his head.

"Dear God. We are Your servants and take great delight in Thy provisions. We are simple people and this is a simple meal, yet it has such a delightful smell, only outdone by its taste. Thank You for this excellent meal.

"But more than that Lord, we thank You for Your daily provision and care. Every day You show us the way to go, and provide us all that we need. You are a great God, Who constantly protects and cares for us. Thank You and Amen."

The two of them began eating the bread along with delicious grapes. Neither spoke as this was Shem's habit: eat and meditate upon the goodness of God. But once they had finished eating their fill, Shem remained quiet. Achsah studied him.

"OK, out with it. I know you well enough to know you have something on your mind. Something you think I won't like."

He smiled sheepishly.

"You read me too well, woman. You are right. You are not going to like what I tell you."

"Then tell me now."

"I'm crossing over the river again."

"When?"

"Next month. I will be going alone."

"What!"

"I'm going alone. I have a sense of great danger."

"Shem, Shem," she said shaking her head. "We have traveled all over this land. I have endured the same trials as you, the same pestilence's, the same storms, and now you are worried about me? We agreed I would go wherever our Lord sends you. Nothing has changed since then.

"We go together," she added firmly.

"But there are no guarantees, Achsah. Phut, his sons, and Mizraim are living there. I no longer trust their good will toward us. Yet God has impressed upon my heart that I must make one last attempt to visit them and declare His love for them. If possible, to bring them back to Him."

"I understand all of what you are saying, Shem. Soon I will no longer be able to travel with you, but until that day comes, I intend to be your helpmeet as God intended. We go together!"

He studied her and could see that she was adamant. *O God, what a wonderful woman You have given me!*

&&&

Mizraim stood outside his tent and watched his people as they went about their daily chores. He sighed. *This land is a great land but it is a divided land. Phut has set up his sons in their own kingdoms, but if this land is to be great and prosperous, it must be as one kingdom. I shall wait and see how the sons rule. Phut has honored me by calling this land Egypt after me, therefore I will honor him and maintain peace. But if the brothers fail, I will step in.*

He smiled as he remembered the new name given him of Horus Aha. *Like a hawk I shall watch and, if necessary, I shall swoop down and devour them!*

At that moment, a young man ran up to him.

"Father Mizraim, your wife is near death!"

Alarmed, he arose, ran to his wife's room, and entered. The place was crowded with doctors and maidens, so he shooed everyone away. Finally alone, he went over and knelt beside her. But it was already too late as her breathing had stopped and her eyes had no life.

He let out a groan, and immediately a young maiden rushed inside. She came over and saw that her mistress was dead.

"I am sorry master. She was talking to me and suddenly collapsed. There was nothing I could do."

When Mizraim didn't respond, she retreated.

For the next several hours he remained by her bedside. He didn't weep or speak, but simply sat in silence. As the day lengthened, his people were finally able to get him to gather her up and take her outside the camp where she was promptly buried.

One of his men came to him afterward and spoke.

"She has been buried and now is with the gods. But she left behind three maidens. What are we to do with them?"

The question caught his attention. He immediately remembered the maiden's statement that "There was nothing I could do." Sudden anger seized him.

"Prepare three burial pits, one on each side of her and one at her feet. Then put each maiden in her own grave alive and bury them."

The man gasped, his face turning white.

"But nothing like that has ever been done before!"

"Then this shall be the first. Go, do as I command."

Immediately the man gathered other workers and dug three graves as he had instructed. Once that was finished, they seized the maidens and dragged them toward the pits. As one of the girls was thrust into a pit, another one broke away. Fleeing to Mizraim, she fell before him weeping and clutching his feet.

The guards rushed up to grab her just as he kicked her away. Grabbing her by the arms, they quickly took her back to the grave and threw her into it. Immediately, other servants began shoveling dirt upon her; the other two maidens already being half buried.

Mizraim ordered the burial to cease for an hour as the girls cried and begged for their lives. He stood there listening to them, a smile of satisfaction on his face. Finally, he signaled for the burial to be finished. It was still a few moments before the weeping ceased.

&&&

Thirty days later Mizraim traveled south, arriving at Adan's door where he was greeted warmly. Adan's wife prepared a feast for Mizraim and his entourage that was enjoyed by all.

When the feast was completed, Adan took Mizraim aside.

"I know of your grief, but the time has come for you to put your grief aside. What will you do now?"

"That is why I have come. You have a daughter. I wish to take her in marriage."

"But she has a husband."

"That is but a small matter. If she marries me, her sons shall inherit all that I have. What can this man offer her?"

Adan stood there and considered. *Mizraim has great wealth. Such wealth would make me greater than my brother. But our law does not allow multiple marriages.*

A slow grin spread across his face. *Tonight my daughter shall be a widow and in the morning she shall be married!*

"Give me till morning and she shall be yours."

"Agreed."

Calling over two of his warriors, he ordered them to fall upon his son-in-law. Only minutes later the young man was slain and his wife became a widow.

&&&

"Tomorrow we cross," Shem announced.

Achsah smiled. After all these years of observing her husband, she had known the time had come to cross before he had known it himself. Therefore, she had been ready since the sun had risen.

They arose in the morning, ate a good meal and crossed the Ar. Entering the land of Mizraim, the land of Egypt, Shem found himself wondering why the land was called the land of Mizraim. *Phut and his sons were here first. Perhaps it is Phut's way of honoring Mizraim.*

It was mid-morning when they came upon a small village, which they later discovered was named Buto. As they approached, they were met by a small band of warriors, whose black chests glistened in the sunlight.

As the riders neared, Shem recognized Benah, one of the sons of Phut. *Well Lord, we are about to find out just how bad it is here. I have heard of tensions, even fights between the brothers although they publicly espouse friendship.*

He stopped the wagon and waited. It wasn't long before the riders arrived and surrounded the wagon.

"Hello Benah. Is this the way you greet visitors?"

Benah nodded at his men and they put away their weapons and withdrew.

"We mean you no harm, Shem. You are a welcome visitor as long as you cause no trouble. We worship Horus here, not your God. You will not be allowed to preach to my people."

"Are you afraid of words, Benah?"

"No. But you cannot preach. If someone seeks you out, I will not stop them, but you may not enter the village."

With that Benah wheeled his horse about and rode back to the village followed by his companions.

As they watched the retreating riders, Achsah spoke up.

"If we cannot enter the village, where shall we stay?"

Shem was about to answer that when he saw more riders coming from the east. He waited, wondering who they were.

As the riders neared, he tried to make out the leader. It wasn't until they were almost upon him that he recognized Mizraim.

A moment later, they came to a stop and Mizraim raised his hand in a sign of peace.

"Shem, you are a long way from home. I imagine you are here to gather information about our people, to divine our futures perhaps. I imagine also that Benah did not give you a warm welcome."

"That is correct."

"That is unfortunate and not very polite. Let me apologize for the lack of manners he has displayed. May I invite you and your wife to stay at my humble home. My new wife and I would like to entertain you."

"New wife?"

"Yes, my first wife recently died rather suddenly. It was determined by others that I needed to choose another wife, so I chose her. We were just married this morning and are now heading home."

It was then that Shem realized one of the riders was a woman dressed in mourning. Turning back to Mizraim, he asked: "She appears to be in mourning."

"Yes, her previous husband died last night from an accident. As I fully understand the need to mourn, I have told her she can take up to three days for mourning. But after that we consummate the wedding."

*In other words, you had her husband murdered so you could take her as your wife!*

"Perhaps we would be an intrusion."

"Certainly not. She needs to learn her new responsibilities. It might as well be serving you and your wife."

"We would be honored to visit with you."

He turned the wagon around and followed Mizraim to his house. As they neared the home, he was pleasantly surprised at its size. But even more surprising was the beauty. Drawing nearer he observed several workers. *Slaves?*

He glanced at Achsah to see if she had noticed. Their eyes met in silent disapproval.

Pulling up to the front door, they got out of the wagon and entered. Meanwhile a slave got in the wagon and drove it to a more secure spot.

Mizraim's home was quite impressive. From the outside they could see it was built of large blocks of stone upon stone with small windows strategically placed. There was a strong masculine sense about the structure.

Stepping through the large wooden door, they found themselves in an entrance that could easily pass for a room. Achsah looked around with interest, noting the preponderance of animal skins, which acted as rugs and wall coverings.

For his part, Shem noticed that the right wall had a rack of spears, plus there was armor hanging nearby. *This place is a fortress. It could withstand a major siege.*

During the next few days Mizraim and his bride provided them with plenty of food and drink. But Mizraim always steered the conversation away from the worship of God. It became quite apparent that such a topic was taboo.

It was while they were visiting here that Mizraim talked to Shem about the nearby river.

"Phut and his sons call the big river the Ar. But it reminds me of the stories I've heard about the Nile before the Flood."

"Yes," agreed Shem. "In some ways it does resemble the Nile. What does Benah and Aden think?"

"Never discussed it with them. But I think the Nile is far more appropriate than Ar."

Shem nodded in agreement and from that moment he always referred to it as the Nile, rather than the Ar. It was the only positive thing he took from that visit. It was with a sigh of relief when the two travelers departed the next morning and headed south to the Upper Kingdom.

&&&

Later that year, Peleg and Apphia were married amidst great pomp. Her parents made sure it was a great wedding. By this time many traditions existed concerning what a marriage ceremony was like, and they followed it strictly.

The celebrations took several days, but eventually everyone left for home. Then Apphia brought out her idol and placed it in an honored place. She would begin every morning standing in front of the idol, bowing and whispering what sounded to Peleg as nothing but repeated and meaningless words.

Still, he was impressed. *I don't worship God as faithfully as she worships her god. Who am I to criticize?*

# THIRTY SIX

## LAND OF PHUT

2226BC (pop. 3200)

Phut leaned upon his spear as he viewed the vast green vegetation that extended as far as the eye could see. *It has been more than two years since we left Egypt and ten years since crossing the Ar. So much has happened in that time, but I have finally established my own kingdom.*

The Kingdom of Phut extended along the shore of the Great Sea. He envisioned the land filled with people, although it is doubtful he ever envisioned the millions that would someday dwell there. Nor did it enter his mind that the luscious greenery before his eyes would be replaced with arid land.

Now, as he stood staring out at the lush expanse, he felt a surge of pride. Phut, as he called the land, held much promise. Already his people had settled and started to grow. He could hear the happy chatter of children at play, and could see men and women in the fields. It was a peaceful scene that he thoroughly enjoyed.

But he had much greater reason to be proud. Not only was his kingdom growing, but its army's fame as a fighting force was rapidly expanding. He already had discovered that hiring his soldiers to other kingdoms was quite profitable. In fact, his grandsons Adan and Benah had received some of his soldiers to help establish both Upper and Lower Egypt. And now Mizraim was a rising force within Egypt.

Although Mizraim's rise in power caused Phut's sons some worry, Phut privately felt that Mizraim's influence was stabilizing.

His thoughts turned back to his army. He was particularly proud of the shield, which he had invented. The shield had come to be associated with, indeed was the symbol of, his warriors. A small shield with a staked end, it was as much a weapon of offense as of defense. Combined with their expert archers, the Phutites represented a formidable fighting force. It was what made them in such high demand!

Now Phut watched as in the distance a small caravan, if it could be called such, made its way along the shore of the Great Sea. He watched as they drew nearer and he could see the caravan was really only a single wagon. Studying the banner flying over it, he recognized it as Shem's.

Phut feared few men, but Shem was one he feared greatly. *So the great Shem has finally come to my land. When I refuse his request to preach, will it be peace or judgment from his God?*

Stepping inside his tent, he began putting on his armor. *Not that I need a lot of armor*, he chuckled to himself. Unlike the soldiers of the east, he refused to wear breastplates. Whenever going to battle, he (and his warriors) wore a helmet, a wide girdle about his loins, and his feet were shod with leather footwear. His shiny black breast was bare, emphasizing his muscular build. Though this left him vulnerable to sword as well as arrow, it presented an intimidating view.

Once dressed, Phut led his royal guards out to the campsite of Shem and his wife. Although dressed for war, Phut dreaded the God of Shem and chose not to attack. As they entered the campsite, Shem arose from the campfire and walked toward him.

"This is a beautiful land, Phut. I see why you settled here."

"Yes, it is beautiful. I and my people truly enjoy its beauty and its fertility. But the question, my lord, is why you are here?"

"It is simple, Phut. As you may recall, God has given to me the responsibility to record the movements of all our people. I keep a record for posterity's sake. Plus, you have departed from the worship of the true God and I desire to preach His Word that you and your people might return unto Him."

"You speak the truth, Shem. I no longer worship your God. My people think of me as a god and I find that is good. I must, therefore, forbid your preaching. We do not need your God."

Even as he said these words, Phut's stomach felt uneasy. Although his army was big, he feared what the God of Shem could do. But Shem only looked upon him sadly before speaking.

"You are right in that you say your people worship you as a god. But because you have turned your back on God, He turns His back on you. You will multiply and be great among men, but the day shall come when this land will no longer bear seed and show forth its glory. Your people will worship other gods more vile than you are. They will suffer greatly for your sins."

"Perhaps what you say will come to pass," Phut responded. "But we are already great in this land, in Egypt, and in Canaan. My soldiers are employed everywhere."

"That is true. And they are magnificent warriors, Phut. But without God they are weak."

"Talk like that is precisely why I won't let you preach."

Shem looked him in the eye.

"Phut, I have come in peace. But it is true that the Lord has commanded that I come to you. It is His desire that you repent and come back to Him. He loves you. But He will not force Himself upon you.

"If it is your attitude to resist His love and to turn your back upon Him, then we shall depart this land on the morrow. But even as we depart, know that God has also turned His back on you."

"So be it," declared Phut.

Remounting his horse, he left with his guards. Shem and Achsah quietly went a few paces away and knelt to pray.

"O God, You have heard Phut's rejection. Not only his, but his sons and all their people back in Egypt. They have turned away and embraced gods that will tickle their ears and fulfill their lusts. My heart breaks for them."

That night Shem and Achsah slept peacefully while Phut grew restive. Rising from his bed, he stepped outside. His attention was immediately drawn to just outside the village perimeter. He watched as two of his sentries marched toward each other with measured step. Coming to a complete stop, they saluted one another, spun on their heels, and marched the opposite direction. He nodded in approval.

It had taken time for him to train the men in patrolling. His soldiers were the only ones in the known world that marched while patrolling. It required discipline, which is one reason his soldiers were so much in demand.

Suddenly he was aware of someone behind him. Whirling and drawing his sword, he came face to face with Satan, who was standing with a drawn sword. Phut immediately bowed.

"What is this that thou art so afraid?" Satan asked with a sneer.

"Do you think that this Shem will quietly leave and do you no harm. Send thy men against him tonight while he sleeps."

"It is not Shem I fear, but his God."

"Have not I protected thee all these years. Send the men. Kill him if possible, but cause him to leave!"

Phut nodded in obedience, his stomach churning.

&&&

Two hours later, in the dark of night, twenty soldiers crept closer to Shem's camp. Looking up they could see the stars twinkling in the night sky. A soft breeze caressed their faces and gently moved the long grass.

Slowly they edged their way closer to the camp site. The leader licked his lips in anticipation as he could make out the man and woman asleep on the ground beside the fire. *This will be easy*, he thought.

The soldiers continued moving closer. The sleeping couple didn't stir. The animals slept, unaware of any danger. The men finally reached the camp's perimeter.

At the leader's signal the men sprang into action, racing into the camp and letting out a horrendous scream designed to create fear and paralysis in the intended victims. Their faces broke into delighted joy as the man and woman jumped up. As Shem raised a hand in protest, they surged toward him.

At that moment, Phut was on a nearby hill watching the battle unfold. He was proud of the manner in which his warriors executed his plans. Even so, he felt unease.

Suddenly a bolt of lightning came from heaven and struck the force he had sent! In an instant all twenty men disappeared! He gulped. His face, normally dark and proud, turned ashen. He turned toward Satan who was also watching the scene below.

"It is as I feared. His God is more powerful than even you."

Satan laughed harshly.

"You fool! Do you think that I could not have protected them? That was not my plan. In the morning, this Shem shall leave and your land shall be protected."

Meanwhile Shem and Achsah stood looking down at the burnt corpses.

"Why did they attack, Shem? You had already decided to leave. Why would they attack us?"

"Achsah, Phut is in the embrace of the evil one. There is no telling what he will do, but you have seen with your own eyes that God protects us. Now, let's get some sleep. We have a long trip before us."

&&&

Back in Upper Egypt, Aden paced in the banquet hall of his new palace. Not as large as some palaces, nevertheless it represented great power. Known as Scorpion to the people, he ruled firmly and dreamed of someday controlling all of Egypt.

But today he had another problem facing him. The most recent visit of Shem to his land, before traveling to Phut, had left behind a small family who worshiped the God of Shem rather than himself. It was a situation that called for immediate action.

He paused his pacing to watched as the family was dragged before him. He studied the family without pity before focusing on the father. He noted with approval that the man had already been severely beaten and bloodied.

"I give you one last chance for life. Deny this God and bow before me and I shall let you and your family live. Be aware that refusal means instant death."

"When Shem returns, he will deliver us from you."

"If Shem survives his meeting with Phut, he will not be allowed back in our land. Your only hope lies in denying your God and worshiping me."

"We cannot deny the only living God. He can deliver us from you if He wills, but if He does not then we are prepared to die."

"Then die you shall! Cast them into the river."

The guards grabbed the man, his wife, and two sons. A moment later all four were cast into the river Ar. Nearby a crocodile lay sunning along the shore. Seeing the thrashing humans, he slid into the water.

As Scorpion watched the family struggling in the water, he leaned over to his captain.

"Set a watch for Shem. It is possible he may escape my father's hand. If he returns and my brother allows him to turn south, you stop them and force them to leave our land."

"Yes, your lordship."

Just then there was a scream as the crocodile suddenly appeared near the wife. It opened its large mouth showing both large and small teeth. This particular crocodile appeared to be about 16 feet long although Scorpion had seen one as large as 20 feet.

He smiled as the crocodile's mouth slammed shut amid the woman's screams. The sudden action accompanied with blood soon attracted others crocodiles. He watched with pleasure as they dined on the helpless family.

&&&

As their wagon neared the lower (northern) kingdom of Egypt, Shem noticed the small force to his south.

"We are not going to be allowed back into the kingdom," he remarked to his wife.

"But how do we get down to the upper kingdom? We have converts there."

"I am afraid that they are on their own. With tensions between the brothers mounting, it is only a matter of time before war breaks out. And that will enable Mizraim to move in and take over."

"Take over?"

"Yes. Mizraim will not rest until he or his son rules all of Egypt. A war will weaken both brothers and he will be able to unite them under his rule. That means we will receive no help from him. We must turn north. Our mission here is done."

"And the believers?"

"It breaks my heart, but I would not be surprised if Aden has them murdered. It may have already happened."

Achsah bowed her head and soundlessly prayed for the believers.

# THIRTY SEVEN

## WORSHIP OF ISHTAR

2200BC (pop. 3648)

"You want to do what?"

Apphia flinched at Peleg's raised voice. An incredulous look was stamped upon his face. But she was adamant.

"I want to take Rue to the temple of Ishtar in Nineveh. He is eighteen and well past the age when young men dedicate themselves. It is time."

Peleg sighed.

"Apphia, father was extremely unhappy when we didn't have a Coming of Age rite for Rue. That was six years ago and he still reminds me of it!"

"Perhaps, but Eber will not use force. What is the worse he could do?"

"He could disown me. I am the first-born, but he could take that away."

"True, but Ishtar would reward you greatly. You don't really worship God; you don't even pray to Him. So why should you care if Reu worships Ishtar?

"I care because I know that it will hurt father greatly."

"What about MY father? He is a worshiper of Ishtar. Don't you think he would be hurt if Reu was not allowed to worship her as he does? We have tried to please your father for many years, and he still will not acknowledge our god. Well, it is time we took a stand. Besides, your father will not disown you, even though he disapproves."

"Fine, Apphia," he responded in defeat. "I'll endure father's wrath, but why Nineveh? It is so far away and we have a temple to Ishtar here in Erech."

"That is true. But a new temple is being dedicated to Ishtar in Nineveh. This would give Reu the opportunity to decide if he wants to worship her or not. I promise you that if Reu chooses your God over Ishtar, I will not fight it."

Peleg's resistance collapsed.

&&&

As anticipated, the news came as a shock to Eber. Normally a peaceful man, this was too much.

"My grandson a worshiper of Ishtar! Reu an idolater! I forbid it!"

Peleg squared his shoulders.

"Father, he is your grandson, but he is my son. Apphia and I have raised Reu with a knowledge of your God and of Ishtar. It is his choice to make. He may choose God or he may choose Ishtar. We have decided to honor whichever god he chooses."

"My God? He is also your God. Do you not remember your dedication?"

"That was years ago, father. It was just a rite. I never really believed; at least, not like you do. I have observed my wife and her family and found that the belief in Ishtar is very rewarding. I may never worship Ishtar myself, but I believe in giving him the choice."

Eber stared at his son in shock and disbelief before turning and storming out of the house. His heart filled with fury as he marched up to his house. Just before he was about to enter the door, his eye caught sight of his altar. He came to an abrupt halt.

It was like a bolt of lightning that the truth hit him! *When I dedicated Peleg to the Lord, I stopped to soon! I never challenged him to trust and serve God, nor did I direct him to look for the Redeemer. I just assumed he loved the Lord.*

Changing direction, he walked over to the altar and fell upon his face before it.

"O God," he whispered hoarsely, "I have failed You! My own son Peleg, whom I dedicated to You, has turned from You and now his son may become an Ishtarite. I failed to challenge him and to make certain of his walk with You. If only I had made the challenge.

"What do I do now? Do I take away his inheritance? Do I deny him as my son?"

Bitter tears coursed down his cheeks as he awaited God's answer. His knees grew sore and his back stiff with pain as it seemed like hours before he heard a still, small voice speak to him. Immediately alert, he concentrated on listening.

"Thou shalt not take away your son's inheritance nor shalt thou deny him as your son. It is true that you erred in the presentation of your son. But he is responsible for the choices he makes.

"He, his sons and his grandsons shall serve other gods. But one shall be born who shalt turn to Me. He shall serve Me."

"Then I should accept this?"

"Thy son has made his choice. He was never mine. Be thou faithful and I shall bless you."

In the silence that followed, Eber felt a great peace come upon him.

&&&

The trip to Niniveh took several days and they arrived during a summer storm. Entering the large city they passed through the gates. Peleg looked around, impressed with the city's ongoing construction.

As they moved down the street, he noted a small sign hanging outside a door. His eyes quickly noted the word "Inn." Peleg pulled up and jumped out, hurrying up to the inn's door and knocked.

A moment later a voice from the other side spoke.

"You want a room?"

"Yes. A room for my wife and myself, and a room for our son."

"I have only one room."

"We'll take it."

The innkeeper opened the door, filling the door frame with his presence.

Peleg signaled to Apphia and turned to discuss price. As the two men haggled over the room's rent, his wife and son hurriedly entered. A few minutes later they were all in a small room.

"This will do," Apphia said. "We can stay here tonight, the dedication is tomorrow, and we can be on our way home by nightfall, if you wish.

&&&

Reu followed his parents away from the temple. He had been very impressed by all that had transpired. While the offering of babies had made him a little queasy, it had still been very impressive. He smiled as he remembered the priestess taking him to a back room. It was the first time he had ever lain with a woman and it made him feel like a man!

As they mounted the wagon, Apphia glanced back at her son.

"What do you think, Reu? Did you enjoy worshiping?"

"Yes, mother. Wasn't she beautiful? I would like to see her again."

Peleg turned and faced Reu.

"The priestess' are there as part of the worship. They do not date."

Reu settled into the back of the wagon.

"Well, if that is the worship of Ishtar. I am a believer!"

Apphia glanced at Peleg and smiled.

# THIRTY EIGHT

## BIRTH OF ABRAM

2058BC (pop. 933,888)

About 151 years later, Reu's great grandson, Terah, held his first born son in his arms.

"He shall be called Abram, for he shall be a father of height. He shall rise above all around him."

He carried his son over to the statue of Ishtar that dominated the room. Holding his son aloft, he cried: "I dedicate my son to thee, O Ishtar. Make of him a mighty man, grant him great prosperity, and may his loins father many children."

The family looked on approvingly. Eber and Chloe had not shown up for the celebration as they strongly disapproved of Ishtar worship. It had been many years since they had visited the family, though they lived in the same city.

Terah had invited them and had said they could say a prayer to God for Abram.

"After all, we can't have too many prayers."

But they had sadly declined. Instead they remained at home and tearfully prayed to God on Abram's behalf.

"O God," Eber began. "We come to You once again acknowledging our failure. Our children and childrens' children have departed from Thy ways. They have turned to this Ishtar and become beguiled by her charms.

"We sought to teach them Thy Words and to raise them in Thy wisdom, but we have failed! O God, we pray that they will turn back to worshiping You. As for the new born baby, we pray that he might be the one You promised. O that You might use us to influence him, but if not us then somehow You will draw him unto Thyself."

He paused, wiping a tear from his eye. Chloe, kneeling beside him, reached over and held his hand. Eber took a breath and continued.

"O God, Thou Who art merciful and full of grace, we don't know the name chosen for this new born, but You do. This world is filling up with wickedness. Therefore, we pray that You will early put in the child's heart a desire for Thee. Perhaps this is the child you told me of so many years ago. Draw him to Thyself and cause him to seek Thee. Put a hedge about him and -"

He was interrupted by a firm knock on the door. He stopped and listened. Again there was knocking. Rising, he went to the door and opened it.

Surprise filled his face as he recognized Job, the son of Gether. Eber looked upon his great, great, great grandson and smiled with joy. *One of the few that still worships God. Thank You, Lord, for bringing him here tonight.*

"Job!" he exclaimed as they embraced.

"Hello, grandfather Eber. I hope I have not disturbed anything."

"O no, but rather you are an answer."

"An answer?"

"Yes, we were praying for the new baby. That God would raise him up to follow Him. And in the midst of the prayer, you arrived."

"O I am sorry."

"Nothing to be sorry for. God brought you to our door to encourage us. Now embrace your grandmother and tell us your news."

Job dutifully obeyed, fondly embracing Chloe. Then they all took seats and Job explained his visit.

"Yesterday I celebrated my 26th birthday and -"

"Twenty six!" Chloe exclaimed. "Why, it seems like only days ago you were crawling around the floor."

They all laughed at the memory and then Job resumed.

"Yes, I am twenty six. I received many fine gifts, but I also received a rather mysterious letter from Shem."

"What does our patriarch have to say?" Eber inquired.

"Only that he has a special surprise for me when he arrives in a few days. I have no idea what that surprise is going to be. He gave no hint whatsoever. But he did include another letter addressed to you. He did not explain why he sent it to me, but he clearly intended for me to deliver it to you."

"Because you are one of the few, Job, who still worship God and can be trusted with his letters. Do you have it with you?"

"Yes," Job replied as he reached inside his shirt and withdrew a small scroll. He smiled as he noted Eber and Chloe's raised eyebrows.

"This must be a very important letter and I wasn't taking any chances. Here," he said as he handed the letter over.

Eber opened the scroll and started reading. As he finished, he smiled as a fresh set of tears coursed down his cheeks.

"God is amazing. He answers prayers even before they are asked. Listen to this:

"Eber, I know how thy heart breaks over your childrens' idolatry. I have experienced the same tragedy in my family. But I have good news. God has told me in a night vision that the new child to be born shall be raised up to serve Him and he shall be a blessing to a multitude. Thou shalt see him prosper in thy old age."

For several moments, Eber and Chloe were so happy that only their crying could be heard. Job's own rejoicing brought tears to his eyes as well. Finally, Eber got control of himself.

"The date of this letter is before the child was ever born. That means God answered my prayers before I even knew what to pray. Praise the Lord! But what does he mean that I shall see him prosper in my old age?"

&&&

The next day, Job returned home after enjoying one of Chloe's fine breakfasts. Eber and Chloe then made their way to Terah's house to see the new child. A short time later they arrived and Eber knocked on the door.

The door was opened by Terah, who immediately ushered them inside. Walking over to his wife, he gently took from her his newborn son and turned to Eber. Smiling, Terah handed little Abram to Eber, who held the baby at eye level and looked into the happy face of his grandson.

"Abram, what a fitting name you have. For God Himself shall cause you to be a blessing to a multitude of people."

The smile on Terah's face vanished, replaced by a frown.

"I chose that name because he shall father a multitude. He shall be raised to worship Ishtar."

"Are you so afraid of God that you will forbid me from sharing the truth about Him with my grandson?"

"I will not stop you, but he shall be brought up to worship Ishtar."

"That is fine, Terah. You are the father and it is your responsibility to raise him for God, but we are more than willing to take it upon ourselves. Don't forget that we pray for you daily.'

"Grandfather, I respect your right to worship God as you please and I hope you respect my right to worship Ishtar. Your God is old, His ways are passed by. We have Ishtar and the host of heaven. But I do not deny your right to worship Him."

"Thank you, Terah. I don't agree with you at all, but thanks for letting your son have the opportunity to choose for himself."

&&&

They stayed for the rest of the morning and enjoyed the noon meal. Visiting with Terah and his wife was pleasant enough, but the disagreement over the worship of Ishtar hung in the air. But shortly after the meal was finished, the tension was such that Eber and Chloe politely excused themselves and left.

As they walked back to their house, Chloe stopped and looked at Eber.

"What will we do, Eber?"

"There is only one thing we can do, Chloe, other than pray. We will try to teach Abram about God whenever possible. Terah may not like it, but privilege comes with age. He has agreed not to deny us the right to influence his son."

"But we are the only ones left in our family who believe in the Elohim," Chloe sobbed.

"Except for Job," he agreed. "But as long as we live, we will worship God and tell others of His wonders!"

As Chloe leaned her head on his shoulder, he placed his hand upon her head and caressed her hair. *Dear God, what is happening to our world. Our children and grandchildren down to Terah have turned their backs on you. O, I pray Abram will grow up to worship You as You have said!*

&&&

The following day Shem and Achsah arrived, being warmly greeted by the Eber household. But instead of meeting all the families, Shem requested that they be allowed to spend the remainder of the day just with Eber and Chloe. It had been a long, hard trip and the couple were tired.

The next day, Shem approached Job's father and spent the morning in deep conversation. Shortly after the noon meal, Job was sent for and he arrived, anxious to know what was happening.

"Son," began Gether, "Shem has something he wants to discuss with you. If you two will excuse me, I have errands to do."

Job watched his father walk away. It was obvious from the tone of voice and the stiff back that his father wasn't pleased about whatever was going to happen. Turning to Shem, he found the great man smiling at him.

"Well Job, are you wondering what my surprise is?"

"Yes," Job replied. "I have seen nothing in your hands, so I assume you haven't brought whatever it is with you."

"Actually I have, in a manner of speaking. Job, how would you like to travel with me to Uz?"

"Uz?" Job asked in surprise. "I have heard of that land. Isn't that where my grandfather Joktan and his family live?"

"Yes. But we will be traveling there to visit someone other than Joktan. We plan on visiting Berechiah, a wealthy rancher in the area. More importantly, God has burdened my heart to take you with me."

"Why?"

"I don't know. But His voice is unmistakable. Has He spoken to you recently?"

Job thought a moment.

"Wait. I almost forgot. The other night I had a strange dream that I was going to ask you about. In the dream, an angel appeared unto me and said his name was Gabriel. He said that you were coming here and that I was to obey your wishes. But he didn't say anything more. I thought it was just a dream. I put it out of my mind and totally forgot it until you asked just now."

"God sent Gabriel, one of His highest, to tell you about my coming. That is because God must have plans for you in Uz."

"If it is God's will for me to go, then I will go with you. But I would like to say goodbye to my parents first. They obviously don't approve, but I want them to know that I do and always will love them."

"I will not be leaving for another day or two," Shem replied. "What is it to me if you use your time in such fashion. But, I warn you, your father does not want you to leave with me. I fear his faith in God is not as it should be. But he has agreed to abide by your wishes and not interfere."

"I know my father does disapprove of my devotion to the Elohim. He does business with the merchants of Ur and wishes to please them though they despise us for living in tents."

Shem nodded in understanding. In the past two hundred years, many of his line had moved out of Ur, taking up a nomadic life raising sheep and cattle. He had even noticed that Terah, while maintaining a house in Ur, now owned a small herd of cattle.

"Yes, I am aware of that and of his displeasure with you. I suspect that is why he didn't resist harder. His other sons are much more pleasing to him. But you are twenty six, old enough to serve the God Who has called you. Go, say your farewells."

# THIRTY NINE

## THE SURPRISE

2058BC (*continued*)
Jehoshabeath sat still watching as her son nursed upon her breast. She gently caressed his head and smiled. *Drink up my son. Drink and grow.*

She looked up as Terah entered the room.

"He's still nursing?"

She laughed softly, "He's almost done. Then you can take your son. O, I think he just finished."

She gently removed Abram from her breast and handed him to his father.

Terah took his son and looked him over.

"He will grow up to be a strong man," he said proudly.

"Like his father," she agreed. "He looks just like you."

Terah looked the boy over again. But he couldn't see any similarities.

"Are you sure?"

"Trust me. He's you. But if you doubt, ask your mother."

"I will. But what of you? How are you doing?"

"I'm fine. I'll be on my feet tomorrow. If need be, I could get up now."

"No, no. Rest. Tomorrow is soon enough."

He left her bedside and entered the common room. His friend and cousin Gether was there.

"Gether, it is good of you to come. How is it with my good friend?"

"All goes well, I suppose. Shem has arrived and will be leaving with my son."

"With your son? Why?"

"Shem says that his God has called Job to sojourn in a land I have never heard of."

"That doesn't sound good. What does Job say?"

"He is excited. I suppose I should be as well. Shem says it is always good when God wants to use your son."

Terah squirmed inside. *I would not think that good! The God of Noah and Shem demands too much. I much prefer the gods of Nimrod.*

"Where is he going?"

"He calls it Edom of the land of Uz. He says it is southwest of here, but he will have to travel north before turning south. He prayed about it last night and he is committed on going."

"I'm sorry! When do they leave?"

"He thinks it will be in about five or six days. He'll be traveling with Shem."

"Well, at least he will get a chance to meet my son Abram."

"Yes, he will be coming over tomorrow."

"Good."

&&&

Eber watched as the small caravan came to a stop before his home. He was surprised that Shem had returned so quickly. Earlier at dawn he and Achsah had left. It had been a tearful goodbye. Yet here he was, back.

*That looks like young Job sitting behind him! Is Shem taking him along?*

Shem dismounted from the wagon and approached Eber.

"Shem, greetings! Welcome back. Did you forget something? Is Job traveling with you?"

Shem smiled and waited as Chloe stepped out.

"Yes, I am taking Job with me. To the land of Uz. God has told me to take him with me. Seems the Lord has something for him to do there.

"As for why I came back. The Lord has spoken to me and told me to come and get you."

"Me? You want me to go to Uz?"

"No. God wants you to travel a bit further to a land called Canaan. He will guide you. I am to take you north with me, but you will turn west while we turn south."

"But my family."

"You are to take your wife, of course. And any other God-fearing people you want."

"All my servants worship God, which is more than I can say of my sons and grandsons. But my grandson Abram. If I leave, how shall he be raised to worship God?"

"God shall provide for Abram. Obey His call and leave that to Him."

"How long do I have?"

"We are going to continue on until evening before making camp. Loaded as we are, we will be traveling slower than normal. So if you hurry and don't delay, you can catch us by nightfall."

"I will do as you command, Shem."

"Not I, but the Lord."

The two men embraced before Shem returned to the wagon and took his seat beside Achsah, with Job sitting behind them. Eber watched them slowly pull away, then turned and entered his house. *God is calling me to serve Him! What a joy!*

&&&

That evening Eber, Chloe, and their servants arrived at the camp after a hard, dusty ride. Everyone was excited and talked until late. Finally Shem took Eber by the arm and led him aside.

"You have not asked about God's calling."

"I knew you would tell me when you were ready."

"Then I am ready to tell what I know," Shem smiled. "God has not shared a great deal with me about your mission. He will speak to you Himself later, when we separate. But I do know that our futures are tied together somehow. So when you do head west to this land of Canaan, it will not be the last we see of each other."

"He told you nothing of my mission?"

"Only that he has a place for you to go and settle. There you shall settle your family. There you shall await your destiny."

"It is so mysterious. But I shall wait on the Lord for His bidding."

&&&

Five months later the sun shone brightly upon a mountainous terrain. In the midst of the mountains was a dusty, well-traveled road leading to the south. Slowly moving upon it was a single wagon pulled by two mules.

The lone wagon followed the trail that would become known as the Kings Highway, which in turn would become a major route for merchants and armies. Day after dusty day they traveled south, going through the land of Ammon and Moab until they arrived at the Zered River.

As Shem expertly drove the wagon across the river, Achsah turned and looked back at Job.

"We are about to enter Edom of the land of Uz."

Job, who'd been half-asleep in the back of the wagon, sat up. Blinking his eyes so that he could focus better, he saw the mountains to the west. But little had changed except it appeared they were on another plateau. *A man could raise a lot of cattle here.*

His eyes drank in the stark beauty of the land. Unlike the Plains of Shiner, this land was dotted with rocky terrain suitable for livestock. From his vantage point, it looked like the mountains had the trees and other foliage necessary for cattle or sheep. But the desert was not far away.

"You can't see it from here," she continued, "but Bosrah is only about three hours ahead. So it won't be much longer before we can finally rest. And west of here is the Jordan River and the Salt Sea."

"Jordan River. I think I have heard of it before. But what is the Salt Sea?"

"The Jordan River empties into it, but my talkative husband says that it is dead. Nothing lives in it. It is called the Salt Sea because it has a lot of salt in it. Some people claim it has healing powers, but my talkative husband has neither said yea or nay."

Job grinned. For most of the trip Achsah had done the talking. Not that he minded. She was intelligent and obviously knew her facts. Plus her lively chatter had kept the trip from being boring.

Three hours later they arrived in the city of Bosrah, an unimpressive settlement that Job found hard to equate with a city. It was actually smaller than his own city of Ur. But his first impressions were modified somewhat when they pulled up to a two-story house built of rocks, brick, and wood. *Whoever lives here must be important!*

As they got out of their wagon, a husky gray-bearded man approached. Job was immediately impressed with the man's erect posture, sturdy appearance and long beard.

"Shem! Achsah! Does an old man's eyes deceive him?"

"No, Berechiah," laughed Shem as the two men embraced. "I've also brought Job, a friend, with me. God called him and directed me to bring him to you."

"God called him, eh? We need God fearing men here. Perhaps he is the answer to my wife's prayers."

Job glanced at Achsah, who leaned toward him and whispered, "Before her death, his wife prayed for a son. But they only have a daughter, Sitidos."

Berechiah beamed at Job and embraced him in a warm welcome.

"Welcome to Bosrah, Job. You will find the land of Uz a hospitable place for anyone willing to work, but not so good for the idle. Of course, you will live with us until you find a place of your own."

Job was about to protest such generosity, but a warning glance from Shem stilled his mouth.

Berechiah led them into his house where Job saw several servants going about their duties. An extremely attractive maiden approached with a tray of fruits, which she offered to him first. Long black hair and a modest yet revealing dress caused him to simply stare rather than take of the fruit.

"Job," laughed Berechiah, "our fruits are fresh and tasty, but if you stare at my daughter much longer, they will grow stale."

Both Sitidos and Job blushed.

Watching the scene unfold, Achsah nudged Shem, who merely smiled.

# FORTY

## JOURNEY WEST

2058BC (continued)

Eber ordered the caravan to stop.

"I'm climbing that hill. Do you want to go with me?"

"No. I'll wait."

Eber stood, climbed off the cart and promptly headed for the nearby hill. Chloe watched from her seat on the cart as he made his way through the brush and started climbing the hill. After awhile she saw him reach the top and continue down the other side, whereupon he disappeared from her view.

As the minutes slipped by she became fidgety until she could stand no more. Her curiosity had won out. Getting down from the cart, she climbed the hill following the trail he had left. When she reached the top he was nowhere to be seen at first. Looking around, she spied him to her left amongst some trees. She hurried over to him.

Aside from the beautiful land that lay before him, she saw nothing of interest.

"What is it, my lord?"

"Look," he said pointing southward. "What you see is the land of Canaan where we are going."

Excitement building, she looked back at the land she had so easily dismissed. But this time she looked with expectation. She nodded in pleasure as she realized how fertile the land had to be to support such vibrant foliage.

"Has God told you where we are to live?"

He shook his head.

"Every night before I close my eyes, I ask for His direction. And every morning when I first awake, I ask for His direction. But nothing."

"But you are certain this is the route He wants us to follow?"

"Yes, Chloe. Based on all that Shem told me, we are to turn south and enter this land."

Turning her attention southward again, she saw no roads. It suddenly became obvious to her that God wanted them to make their own trail.

"If God wants us to enter this land, then it must be good for us. Let us go back to the wagon and enter it immediately!"

Eber smiled at her enthusiasm. Taking her hands in his own, he squeezed them.

"It is too late in the day. We shall camp here for the night, and enter the land tomorrow."

The two of them returned to the caravan where he signaled the men to set up camp. Chloe took the servant girls and began preparing the evening meal. Gathering dried dung from previous travelers and small sticks, they placed them in the small, stone-lined hole they had prepared. Next, they rubbed the sticks together until they erupted into flames.

Soon the aroma of baking bread was in the air mixed with the equally pleasing aroma of lentils. By the time the meal was ready, everyone's appetite was ready as well!

After a very satisfying meal, they all stretched out on the solid ground and were soon asleep. All, that is, but Eber. Restless, he kept shifting his position. But nothing availed. Sighing, he got up and squatted before the smoldering fire. Placing more wood on it caused it to erupt into a steady flame once again.

Still restless, he looked at the hill where he had stood earlier and thought he saw something move. Quietly he stood and climbed the hill. But once there, he found nothing. Instead he felt an overwhelming urge to pray.

Kneeling, he stretched himself upon the ground and began praying.

"O Lord God, your servant is here. Tomorrow we turn south into a land we do not know. Search my heart, O Lord, and know that I will obey Thee. Only, I pray Thee, show me Thy will. For I know not where You want me to go."

Almost immediately he sensed someone's presence. Opening his eyes, he beheld an angel standing before him. A feeling of dread afflicted his soul.

"Fear not," the angel said, "for I am Gabriel, who standeth before the Lord your God. He has sent me to encourage you and direct thy steps. You are to travel south until you come to a mountain that He shall tell you of. There you shall settle."

In a moment, a twinkling of the eye, the angel disappeared. Eber rose and looked south. Then he smiled.

"I shall do as You command, my Lord."

He returned to the camp, settled upon the ground and was soon dreaming of a new land.

&&&

In the morning, the tiny caravan resumed its journey south. Since there were no roads, they had to travel slower. Sometimes they would have to stop and clear the way. This involved various techniques, depending upon the obstruction. Sometimes it involved cutting down brush, another time removing boulders, and yet another time crossing a stream.

With each passing mile, Eber felt a rising sense of danger. He could feel his hair almost tingling. Several times he stood in the cart and looked around, but there was no sight or sound of humans or animals.

At one point, he stopped, got out of the wagon, and mounted a horse. Chloe slid over, took the reins and soon they were moving again. Eber felt better about this arrangement and they continued southward.

About an hour later, a band of ill-kept men emerged from the hills and surrounded the caravan. Eber looked around until he spotted the leader and rode up to him. As he did so, he noticed that the man's eyes widened in fear. At first surprised that such a rough looking man would fear him, he quickly realized it wasn't him the man feared, but the horse!

Ordinarily he would have dismounted and met the man face to face. But realizing he had an advantage, he stayed mounted.

"What is this?" he demanded, trying to sound harsh. "We are peaceable people traveling through this land. Why do you impede our way?"

"This is our land. You cannot have it."

Eber was surprised that he understood the strange man's tongue. It wasn't exactly the same as his, but close enough.

"We do not want it. We are traveling south and will certainly pass out of your land into another. Let us pass."

The man stood there plainly intimidated by the horse, but also resolved to protect his land. It seemed like an eternity before the man made his decision.

"If you leave our land, you may pass through. If you turn to the right or the left, we shall attack and destroy you."

"Thou shalt not destroy us. Our God shall guide us and protect us. We shall follow wherever He leads. If you oppose us, He shall smite you."

As he finished speaking, Eber's horse suddenly snorted and pawed the ground. The alarmed man stepped back. For a moment everything became still. Eber watched, alert to any sign of aggression. But the man suddenly turned and led his men back into the forest.

Eber immediately ordered the caravan forward as he moved to the front.

&&&

A week later the caravan came to a stop as they emerged from a forest. There before them lay two mountains. Eber sensed that one of these mounts was to be his home, but he had no idea which one. At that moment, a small voice spoke in his mind.

*Here thou shalt settle on the southern mount and thou shalt name your city Salem for it shall be a city of peace.*

Signaling the caravan to follow him, he made a trail to the mountain and began ascending. He didn't stop until he reached the summit. Reining in his horse, he just sat drinking the beauty into his soul. He instantly knew this was not only the home of his body but of his soul.

As the horse labored to bring the wagon upon the summit, Chloe's voice rang out:

"O Eber, it is beautiful!"

Soon all the wagons arrived and unloading began. Eber went from wagon to wagon supervising the unloading. He directed each man where to put up his tent. By nightfall, a small village of tents had been erected, forming a small, protective circle.

Gathering everyone together in the middle around a campfire, he spoke.

"Listen to me all of you. Children, settle down.

"The Lord has guided us here. This is our new home, which He has named Salem. In the spirit of the moment, I have decided that henceforth this is your city as well as ours. Each family shall receive a plot of land that shall be yours to keep and to pass on to your descendants. Furthermore, though you are my servants, you shall be free. Free to stay and begin your own trades, free to enjoy the protection of the city, and free to worship God.

"There shall be no worship of Ishtar or other pagan gods."

All began cheering. Someone hollered, "Praise the God of King Eber!"

At first embarrassed, Eber finally raised his hands to quiet them.

"Your king I shall be. But not like Nimrod, nor as Asshur. God raised me up to found this city. I do not know why. But we shall hold it in trust for Him until He reveals His purpose."

# FORTY ONE

## AN UNFORGETABLE TOUR!

2040BC (pop. 3,735,552)

"It's Shem!"

Abram chuckled at his friend's outburst.

"Yes, it is," he replied.

"What do you think he is doing here?"

"Visiting like always. Perhaps he is on his way north to see Noah."

Helon thought that over for a moment.

"How old is Noah now?"

"He's over nine hundred. I think he's nine hundred and ten. Why?"

"Just curious. I wonder if we will grow that old."

"I don't think so. My grandfather says that people born on this side of the Flood are dying at earlier ages. Few in Shem's line have died that I know of, but there have been others."

The two boys stopped talking as Shem seemed to be heading straight for them. They watched as the wagon rolled up and stopped. A moment later the great man stepped down. Achsah remained in the wagon, smiling at them.

"Father Shem, it is good to see you again," Abram greeted him.

"Just Shem, please. Only God deserves that title. Are you pleased enough to travel north with us?"

"North?"

"Yes, Achsah and I are heading home to Noah's. We would like to take you two lads with us."

The boys were momentarily speechless, then words tumbled out of their mouths so fast that Shem held up his hand for them to cease.

"Well, I guess all of that unintelligible noise meant yes. I will talk to your fathers about it. If they agree, then we leave in two days."

R. Frederick Riddle

&&&

That night both fathers gave reluctant approval. They didn't like the idea at all, but Shem was adamant. Both men had learned not to argue with Shem, so approval was given and the boys told.

Eagerly the boys gathered what they would need and, on the second morning after Shem's arrival, they boarded the wagon and sat behind Achsah. Shem tied his horse to the back of the wagon, walked to the front, and got in. Taking the reins, he spoke to the mule and was soon on the way.

The horse represented Shem's begrudging acceptance of progress. He had loved his old mule, but the horse was already claiming a part of his heart. His most recent trip south had resulted in the death of the mule and the purchase of a replacement plus the mare, which he called Zebudah, since she was a gift.

The trip north led through the fabled streets of Babel. Shem didn't want to stay there long, but he drove the wagon through the broad main street, crossed the bridge, and drove up to the temple. Both boys looked up at the towering structure in amazement.

"This is where man chose to defy God," Shem began his narration. "Nimrod thought he could build this tower unto the heavens. You can't see it from here, but at the very top there is an altar that was going to be dedicated to the false goddess Ishtar."

"It is beautiful," remarked Abram.

"Yes it is. And it shows the tremendous capability of man. But it also demonstrates man's futility. You cannot build a temple high enough to reach God. It is impossible! Moreover, this tower represents man's turn to idolatry. And it required God's judgment!"

"I know," spoke up Helon, "this is where the Confusion of Tongues began."

"That is correct. God doesn't always judge in such great catastrophes, but He always judges sin."

"Can we stay here tonight?"

"No, Abram. During the day it is safe to pass through, but at night the streets are filled with men of Belial, men who are lovers of men as well as murderers and thieves. They have all denied God and are far too dangerous for us to risk meeting."

"Besides, Shem likes the open spaces," smiled Achsah.

Soon the little group was back in the wagon and heading north. Leaving through the east gate, they continued their journey northeasterly until they reached the Tigris. At that point they turned north and followed the river.

As darkness began settling upon the land, they looked for a likely place to halt. A short time later, Shem spotted an ideal spot and stopped there. Quickly they all got out of the wagon and set up camp.

It had been an exciting day and the boys quickly drifted off to sleep. Achsah quietly covered them with blankets and then joined her husband by the fire.

"I wonder if we are doing the right thing," Shem commented.

"We are. I am sure of it. Abram is eighteen and Helon is seventeen. We call them boys, but they are grown men. It is time for them to learn the truth about the Elohim."

Abram smiled to himself.

"Shouldn't that be me saying such words?"

"Yes, but I knew you needed to hear it for yourself."

The two of them sat staring into the fire. Achsah snuggled closer to her husband, enjoying both his warmth and the warmth of the fire. Already tired from the long trip, she relaxed and allowed sleep to overtake her. It took Shem a little longer, but he too fell asleep.

&&&

During the days that followed, Shem went to great effort to avoid the cities of Assur and Nineveh. The boys protested.

"But they are great cities, Shem. Why not visit them? Can't you teach us about them?"

"Both are cities of idolatry and immorality. Such things you don't need to see."

While he could avoid those two cities, he found that he couldn't protect the young men entirely. So it was on the road between Asshur and Nineveh that they came upon a slave camp.

Slavery was not unknown to either Abram or Helon, but both were unfamiliar with slave camps. The camps had been set up first by Asshur, then maintained by Nimrod. Their sole purpose was to break individual pride. Many of the new slaves had previously been free and owned land. But debt had landed them into this horrible situation. Part of the process was to split families up, thus taking away family support. Another thing was to strip them of all personal belongings. In the end, even the clothes they wore, were owned by their masters.

Shem made sure that they only stayed one night. The next morning, as the sun rose in the east, they were on the road again. They continued traveling far to the north until they reached the mountains. With a sure hand, Shem guided the wagon along a well-worn trail that took them deeper and deeper, higher and higher into the mountains.

Eventually they came upon a lake with a small grove next to it. Abram turned and looked back. Behind them lay a great forest they had already emerged from, while in front was a land forbidding and almost barren. Abram couldn't believe how barren it all was. *Shem says that when they first landed they had to use wood stored on the ship for building. Except for this small lake, they could have died of thirst! Yet, father Noah prefers this place to any other!*

Yet, both Abram and Helon were amazed at the sheer grandeur of it all. Plus, near the lake lay a small village consisting of only a few homes, all wooden structures. Both of the young men were disappointed as they had expected to see the Ark.

Achsah laughed.

"Shem, I think our young friends here are not impressed with your father's village."

Shem turned and looked back at their faces.

"That village may be small and insignificant, but the greatest man alive lives there!"

"That's where Noah lives?" the two asked incredulously.

"Yes."

With that, Shem flicked the reins and the two mules moved forward pulling the wagon along. A few minutes later they pulled up outside of Noah's door.

"Stay here, I'll see if he is home."

Shem got out and walked up to the door. He knocked sharply, but there was no reply. After several attempts with no response, he opened the door and went in.

He chuckled as he saw that Noah had left his home in disarray.

A few moments later he came out and got back in the wagon.

"Well, it looks like you're going to see the Ark."

&&&

Noah finished his prayers and stood. Looking down the trail he could see a wagon coming his way. *Must be Shem and Achsah. Maybe I should prepare a meal. Nope. Achsah makes a stew as good as Naamah did. I'll just wait.*

He retreated to his cave and started a fire.

&&&

The wagon pulled to a stop. Noah got up and walked out of the cave and was surprised when he saw the two young men in the back.

"Shem! Achsah! Welcome. And who are these?"

"Abram is the tall one and Helon is the short one. God, and my wife, laid it upon my heart to bring them to you. They know little about the Elohim, the Flood and the Ark."

"Well, we will have to correct that. Since the Ark already has captured their attention, let us take a tour."

He led the way to the giant structure.

"To begin with, the Ark is 450 feet long, 75 feet wide, and 45 feet tall. It is made of Gopher wood."

The young men listened to Noah, but kept their eyes upon the famous structure.

"We have never seen anything like that!" exclaimed Abram.

"True enough," agreed Noah. "I've heard that Nimrod is building ships, but haven't heard much detail. It's coming, but it will be a long time before anything this big is built.

"I'm sure you've heard how God told me to build the Ark. But let me rehearse it before you. You may hear details you have never heard before.

"My dear wife Naamah and I lived outside a city by the name of Uruk, which lay several miles from the towering Majestic Mountains. Our vineyard was north of the city and about the same distance from the mountains.

"In any case, God began pressing upon me to go to the mountains and meet Him there. Finally I did. When I met with Him on a secluded plateau, He gave me the command to build this Ark. I knew nothing of shipbuilding. I was a tiller of land, a farmer. Grapes were my only crops and I was good at it. But God told me to build this ship and obviously I did. The important thing to remember is that God knows all about ships. He gave the instructions and later provided the skilled men to build it.

"Now, take a look at the ship itself. You already know its size, but have you noticed the ship's stern? That is not only the rear of the ship, but the odd looking structure attached to it. You might think it was placed there to steer the ship, but that is not the case. It was placed there to resist sway that might have been caused by severe wave action. Hiram, my shipbuilder, told me that without it too much pressure would arise and the ship would break in two.

"When you go inside, pay attention to the beams of gopher wood placed throughout. Hiram was very careful where the beams were positioned. Again it was to provide stability and strength to the ship. If you look closely you'll notice we used bronze straps and spikes at the joints. That was also for the purpose of handling the extreme pressure and tension the ship would endure. He explained it more technically than that, but I never really understood. All I know is that it worked!"

"How come Hiram didn't come over on the Ark?" asked Helon.

"Because He did not understand that the Elohim were about to judge the earth and had the right to determine how man must be saved. He believed a flood was coming because he listened to me preach about it every day. But he thought it would only be local and that he would be safe in the mountains. A lot of people thought the same.

"But God spoke through me to warn man. It was always His plan to build the Ark for both animals and humans. You might be surprised to know that although we had quite a number of animals on board, they only took up a little more than half the space. But because Hiram and the rest of the world did not believe Him, there were only eight of us on board."

"Some day," interrupted Shem, "maybe father will share the story of his nephew Jareb and his magnificent city in the Majestic

Mountains. Plus, the role Hiram played in both the building of the Ark and Majestic City."

"Will you?" asked Abram and Helon almost in unison.

Noah laughed.

"Tonight, I shall share that story. But come, let's go inside."

He led the way up the ramp and into the ship. For him the ship was home. In recent years he hadn't been able to make the trip as often as he wanted, but every time it was like returning home.

For Shem and Achsah, it was going back to the days of the Flood. Many memories, good and bad, visited their minds.

But for Abram and Helon, it was the most exciting thing they had ever experienced. Entering the ship, they were immediately enthralled with its size. Outside the ship had appeared very large, but inside it was huge! They eagerly descended another ramp to the first floor where they saw large cages that Noah explained once held large animals.

"You see that cage over there? That's where we kept the Elephants. Right next to that is the cage for the tigers."

"And they didn't fight?" asked Helon.

"Nope. Slept right through the Flood. For over a year. God calls it hibernating."

"And they hibernate every year now," added Shem.

Noah motioned to Shem and Achsah to step back and let the boys explore. The minutes slipped by until they had visited all the cages on the floor. But while they explored, Noah had Achsah tell of the ladies role.

"First, let me explain what you are seeing," she began. "Both this deck and the second deck have thirty rooms. As you will see, each room is filled with cages of varying sizes. On average, there were probably six cages per room on this deck, while the second deck had closer to ten cages per room. That is because we kept the larger animals down here and the smaller ones on the second deck.

"Before the animals ever appeared, we prepared each cage with straw and provender so that they would be comfortable and well fed. We were going to be alone and on the sea for a long time, so it was important to keep the animals happy, comfortable and safe.

"If you will look up you can see what Hiram called water tanks, but are really ceramic urns. Naamah, Hagaba, Bithiah and myself had the responsibility to keep those urns filled with fresh water. Now, it sounds more difficult than it was. We had plenty of rainwater that we collected during the flood itself. But after the forty days of rain had stopped, we had periodic rain throughout the year. Enough to replenish the urns.

"We would make sure that the water tanks on the first and second decks received water from the main urn on the third deck. Most people wouldn't have thought of such things, but God used Hiram to make this provision."

"Let me interrupt," said Noah. "She is referring to the hoses you see coming from above the urns. Those were hand-sewn by the women during construction. And they worked extremely well. In addition, look down at the bottom of the cages. You will notice the floor is slotted. That was to dispose of their waste."

"And it made our jobs a whole lot easier," agreed Achsah. "In fact, Hiram so constructed the ship that our job was not nearly as hard as you might imagine, especially since we had so many animals. Those urns above and the slots below simply made our chores easier. But it was a miracle that really made it possible."

"A miracle? What kind of miracle?" asked Abram.

"Well, Noah already alluded to it a few moments ago. Remember when he said the animals slept through the whole time at sea? God calls it hibernating. We women simply called it sleeping. And let me tell you, caring for a sleeping tiger is a lot easier than one that is awake.

"But you should have seen them when they first arrived. It was like a grand parade as they approached the Ark in pairs in a line that stretched back toward the city. I had never seen anything like it before and I don't believe anyone else had either. They came right up to the ship and would have stopped, but Noah and his sons guided them up the ramp and into their respective cages. It was almost as if we had put a sign in front of each cage, they each went to the cage meant for them without any real help from us. I think the men might have tapped them with a pole, but not much more than that.

"Noah says they were led by the Spirit of God. In any case, the biggest animals stayed down here and the smaller ones went up to the second deck."

Abram, who had been examining a cell, stopped where he was and looked back at Achsah.

"I heard there were lots of people around the Ark. What did they do when they saw the animals coming? Did they believe?"

Achsah laughed.

"You should have seen the people scatter. The sight of all those animals heading straight at them scared the daylights out of everyone. But once they realized they weren't in any danger, they began wandering back. Of course, they continued to mock us and, in case you were wondering, they did not help us at all.

"But that's a good question. You would have thought that seeing the animals come that way and enter the ship; well, you would have thought they'd been more open to Noah's invitation. But they weren't. If anything, they became even more hostile."

Noah stepped forward.

"Let's go up to the second deck."

He turned and trudged back up the long ramp they had earlier descended. Abram couldn't help but notice that it was still in excellent shape after hundreds of years. Once they reached the next level, the boys began exploring and Achsah resumed her narration.

"On this floor all the smaller animals were kept. But not just the animals. In the stern was kept all our supplies needed to care for the animals, such as hay and provender. It was on these two decks where we women spent most of our time at the beginning. But once they all started sleeping, I mean hibernating, it was much easier.

"We had initially worried about how to care for so many animals. But all our fears of cleaning up after them and feeding them became naught. God had worked another miracle. And we were thus able to care for our men."

When the boys were finished exploring, Noah led the way up to the third deck. Abram's jaw dropped. While this floor was also divided into rooms, it was far more spacious than the lower even though actual size was smaller.

Noah took up the narration.

"This is the living quarters. Originally Hiram had planned to build as many rooms as on the previous decks. But they never got built, because of the lack of people responding to my preaching. His idea was that we could easily build new rooms as the need arose. Unfortunately there were only eight of us and the need never arose!

"So, all the wood meant to build as many rooms as needed was never used until after we landed here. The village down below is built with some of that wood, as was the altar here and outside my home.

"Follow me."

He led them to where he and Naamah had lived. Abram stared. He had always thought it had been a cramped space, but the rooms were big enough for full sized beds!

"Sorry for the barren look. But after we landed, we needed all our possessions to begin a new life. So everything was removed. Still, you can see that we had plenty of room.

"Now look up. See the window circling the ship. Just below the window is a platform. That was Hiram's idea. Although I suspect God put it in his mind. It enabled us to look out the window and see what was happening. Plus, it provided a way for us to get out into the fresh air.

"And those windows provided our only ventilation. The shutters were closed from the inside, but even with the shutters closed there was a gap running along the top that provided for air. Occasionally, during the first forty days, rain would come in through the gap and later through the hoses coming from outside. But a small trough was built into the platform and the water would drain into it and be taken to the urns. You can see two, one on the port, that means left, and one on the starboard, the right. It was all very ingenious."

After they had finished the tour, they left the ship and headed for his cave. It was now getting dark, so Noah laid wood on the fire and it was soon spreading warmth around.

Achsah quickly prepared a meal for everyone and the cave grew quiet as the boys stopped their questions and devoured the stew. Once the meal was finished, all attention was back on Noah.

There in the flickering light of the campfire, Noah related the story of God's call upon him in the midst of the Majestic Mountains. Then he moved on and told of the stories of Jareb and Hiram, and of their fatal trust in the mountain to protect them. He ended with the story of the Flood and their experiences afloat. Abram and Helon listened intently.

Abram couldn't help thinking, *This has been the greatest day of my life! I will never forget the Ark!*

Helon was tired and was soon fast asleep, but Abram remained wide-awake.

There in the midst of the cave while everyone else slept a soft voice whispered his name. Startled, Abram bolted upright. It was then that he saw the fire take on a different color and the voice seemed to come from it!

"I am the God of Adam, Enoch, Methuselah, and Noah. I am the Creator, Life-Giver, and the Judge. Worship ye Me."

As the Voice ceased, the fire returned to normal. Looking around, he saw all asleep.

*God spoke to me! Should I tell the others? No, but this one thing I shall do. From this day on I will worship Him.*

*Wait, what good is worshiping God if I don't tell others? Besides, Noah and Shem will be able to tell me what next to do. In the morning I shall tell them.*

He closed his eyes and was soon fast asleep.

&&&

The next morning Abram told everyone of the Voice. While Helon giggled, the others looked at him seriously.

"Son, it is an important thing that happened to you," commented Noah. "God visited you in the night. He must have something important for you to do."

"But what should I do?"

Noah was about to answer, but noticed Shem watching. As the oldest man alive, it was natural for everyone to defer to Noah, but he decided to change that at least this once.

"Shem, why don't you answer the lad's question."

Shem looked at his father in surprise, but when he realized Noah meant it, he spoke up.

"Abram, God uses whom He chooses. And he chooses for a variety of purposes. I won't pretend to know what God has for you, but I do know how you should respond.

"You must trust God. He is your Creator and will some day send your Redeemer. If you believe and trust God, the first thing to do is make it your daily habit to pray to God. Don't be afraid. Prayer is just you talking to God and then listening."

"Listening?"

"Yes. He may speak to you again. But God speaks to us through the Writings, and through people such as Noah and myself. But listening also includes obeying. If God tells you to do something, do it. Even though you don't understand the reasons."

"It's kind of scary," Abram said.

"Nothing to be scared of son," responded Noah.

"That's right," Shem added. "God loves you and wants you to love and worship him."

Achsah came over and placed a hand upon Abram's shoulder.

"Would you be interested in a woman's point of view?"

Abram nodded.

"I have found that the mere Presence of God brings joy and peace into my heart. When I am troubled, I have found it a special joy to read His Word."

"You can read?" asked a stunned Abram.

All three adults laughed.

"The idea of women not being taught to read and write did not start until after the Confusion of Tongues at Babel," Shem said. "Everyone on the Ark could read and write. While it is true only men were taught the Scriptures, women learned to read. Unfortunately, when man once again rebelled against God, they departed from His will in many directions."

"Even the way we treat women?"

"Yes. I hope and pray Abram, that when you find a good woman, you will love her even as yourself. My Achsah is the joy of my life after God. We share adventures. I find her to be a person of great wisdom."

"I hope I find someone like you, Achsah."

Achsah smiled as she blinked away a tear.

&&&

"That reminds me," Noah spoke up. "I have never told the story of how I met Naamah, not even to the boys. Guess we were too busy building the Ark to spend story telling."

"I would like to hear that," Achsah responded.

"Well, I think you know she was the younger sister of Tubal-cain. Well, that was a tough family to belong to for her. It would have been for anyone. Seems like her brothers wanted to run her life. They wanted to control everything about her, including who she married. Believe me, that was never going to work.

"Naamah was fiercely independent. As loving and loyal a woman as any, she was not the type to let them treat her that way. She could be quite independent in her ways.

"As she grew older, she resented their overbearing manner. When they decided she was going to marry someone that she absolutely detested, she fled to Abel. I never got the full story, but she left the city of Lamech and traveled north to Enoch before crossing the Gihon River.

"Although she had some close calls, she managed to remain undetected. Mostly due to the fact that she dressed as a common servant."

"Mother dressed as a servant?" Shem asked in a surprised voice.

"Yes, not her normal manner of dress, by any means. Naamah was on the run. She had quickly decided that to escape she would have to hide her identity. So she dressed in servant's clothes and made a conscientious effort to appear shy. Of course, she couldn't speak because it would have identified her as an important person.

"But that lasted only until she reached the city of Abel where I met her. At first, I thought she was just another servant girl. At that time I still lived in Abel in the home of my father Lamech. We kept a small structure in the back of the property where we stored supplies. One day I entered it to gather some supplies for the house, as was my daily chore, when I stumbled upon her hiding place.

"She thought I was trailing her and leaped out, attacking me with a hoe. Few men have fought as hard as she did. As you know, she was as tall as I am and wiry. Plus, she did not fight like a submissive servant. I, of course, fought back. Once I disarmed her it was pretty much over. Or so I thought.

"I no sooner got the hoe out of her hands and she picked up a shovel. I was forced to throw her to the ground.

"Father!" exclaimed Achsah.

"I told you I didn't know I was fighting a royalty. But that all stopped when I realized my mistake."

For a moment, everyone was quiet as they considered all that had occurred.

"What happened?" Shem asked, breaking the silence.

"You can imagine her reaction," Noah resumed. "Laying there on the ground, her face uncovered and her blouse torn. She didn't know whether to cover herself or flee, but before she could do either, I pinned her to the floor. Once she calmed down and realized I was not the enemy, I let her up. I was shocked that a poor servant girl would show so much spunk and she apparently was surprised that I had not killed her. But once we got properly acquainted with one another, we talked."

"Is that when you got married?" asked Abram.

"Not right away. But I fell in love that day and soon afterward I introduced her to Methuselah, who took her into his home. He treated her like a daughter and she lived there until we got married."

"I can see why you never told us before," Achsah chuckled. "And why she never told us. In a way it was romantic, but to her it must have been very embarrassing."

"Yes, if I even came close to mentioning it, I would get a stare that could kill."

Everyone had a good laugh as they got ready to retire for the night.

# FORTY TWO

## SHEM'S VISION

2037BC (pop. 4,652,321)

Three years had passed since the grand tour of the Ark. Afterward, Achsah and Shem returned the boys to their home. During those three years they had remained in the Plains of Shiner, recording news, and mapping the area. After delivering their latest news to Noah they proceeded on their new journey which took them to the Euphrates River. Eventually they reached the fork in the road where they had last seen Eber and his family.

Shem studied the land. Not far away he could see tents of traveling merchants.

"We shall stay here until God tells me where to go next."

"It would be nice to visit Job and his family," Achsah suggested.

"Perhaps that is what God wants, but I do not know. Let us camp here. Perhaps the Lord will give direction before the morning.

Soon they had unpacked and set up a small tent that was a recent gift. After eating, they entered the tent and lay down. Achsah was tired and fell asleep immediately, but Shem felt pressed in the spirit. Getting up and slipping out, he went to a nearby tree where he knelt and prayed. As he prayed, his eyes became heavy and he fell asleep.

Suddenly he sat up, aware that he was not alone. Turning and looking about, he was stunned to see his body upon the ground.

*Am I dead?*

"Shem."

The voice was so soft that he almost missed it. Turning, his eyes lit upon a heavenly being that looked like a man shrouded in light. Immediately he fell prostrate upon the ground.

"Speak my Lord."

260 R. Frederick Riddle

"Rise. Only the Holy One deserves your worship. I am Gabriel, who stands before the Lord."

Shem stood and glanced back at his prone body before once again looking at the angel.

"Thou art not dead, but thou sleepeth only. I have come in thy dreams to show thee a great and glorious future. Watch."

The angel moved his hands and Shem found himself on a mountain slope. Before him lay a small city, little larger than a village. Intrigued, he looked closer.

"That is Eber," he said as he pointed to a man who walked along the city's main street.

"Yes," Gabriel replied. "This is the city of Salem and Eber is its king. Here thou shalt visit and strengthen his hand even as the Lord God directs. But watch more."

The scene changed and yet seemed to be the same. The small city had grown and Eber seemed to have aged. Shem looked quizzically at Gabriel.

"This is also Salem's future. Here you shalt build a home and settle thy wife. Here thou shalt become the Priest of the Most High God. But thou shalt not settle yet. Watch again."

Again the angel moved his hands and Shem found himself perched upon a mount looking at the land below. An army was moving through the land. A vast army that Shem could not count. In the distance he saw cities, none of them Salem. He turned to Gabriel.

"What does this mean?"

"This is the army of Chedorlaomer, king of Elam. They shalt sweep through this land and take captives. Look behind the mountain, what do you see?"

"I see herds of cattle, sheep, and a large encampment. Who are these?"

"That is the encampment of Abram, whom thou knowest. He shall rescue the captives and defeat the army of Chedorlaomer, king of Elam. You shall be a priest unto Abram and shall receives tithes and offerings from him."

Suddenly he found himself standing on the ground again, standing near his sleeping body. Gabriel smiled at him before continuing.

"Thou shalt be a priest of the Most High God and shall serve as both priest and king of Salem. Eber has been called to prepare this city for you and shalt give you the kingship for a time. Upon thy death, he shall rule again. Thou shalt be a blessing to him and to his household."

"When shall all these things be?"

"The first vision is Salem now and that shalt be your destination. The second and third visions are yet to be."

Suddenly the angel was gone and Shem lay back down. A few minutes later he awoke and sat up. Remembering the dream, he stretched out upon the ground and worshiped God. When finished, he arose and returned to camp. Lying down, he slept peacefully under the twinkling stars.

&&&

Hearing a commotion outside, Eber opened his door, stepped out and noticed that the people of Salem had stopped all their activities and were staring to the north. The noise, he realized, was their shouting one to another. He turned his attention to the north and watched as a wagon slowly made its way upward toward the city.

He glanced around and was immediately assured that his men were ready for any trouble. Yet how much trouble could one man and woman cause? *One man and woman?*

He looked back at the wagon and could make out that indeed it was a man and woman. *Traveling alone! There is only one man who would still travel without the protection of a caravan. It must be Shem! And the woman must be Achsah, his wife.*

He remained where he was, stunned, as though rooted to the ground. Then a still, small voice spoke in his mind: *This is Shem. Listen to him.*

The wagon entered the city and rode up to Eber's door with Shem leaping out before it was completely stopped. He grabbed and embraced Eber.

"Shem, I thought we had seen the last of you. These old eyes are blessed with thy presence."

"As are mine with thee, Eber. Where is thy wife, Chloe?"

"She is at the market place. I must send a runner to her, for tonight we shall have a feast in thy honor!"

He turned, gave a servant directions and sent him on his way. As the servant left, Eber turned back to Shem.

"I knew it was you. Only you would still travel without a caravan in these dark and dangerous times when wicked men like Nimrod are in control. I have even heard of a new king rising, a Chedorlaomer, who is worse than Nimrod if that is possible. But enough of that, God told me that I am to listen to you."

"In time, my good friend. First, tell me of thy family and thy city."

Enthusiastically, Eber began relating his and Chloe's adventures since settling on the mount twenty one years ago. He led Shem into his home, which was large yet comfortable. Achsah, following behind, listened intently to Eber's news.

As they approached the house, Achsah noted how simple but beautiful it was. *Eber may have built this house, but Chloe gave it the woman's touch.*

The home was two stories tall, making it higher than some, but definitely smaller than others. She smiled. *Eber does not seek to glorify himself. He lets others build the tallest buildings, yet this house is built for a king!*

The building lacked the ostentatious appearance of the king's palaces back in the land of Shiner. Yet in some ways it was more kingly. She couldn't quite put her finger on what made the difference, finally deciding that it was Eber and Chloe's humbleness before God. *He isn't dressed like a king nor does he act like most kings. Yet there is about him a kingly stature that Nimrod could never muster.*

The walk up to the main door was paved with flowering bushes on either side. The two men walked past them with hardly a glance, but Achsah drank in the beauty and the flowering aroma. She paused momentarily to study the flowers, then had to rush to catch up with them.

When they reached the door, Shem stopped.

"Did you construct this house, Eber? The craftsmanship is the best I have seen away from the cities."

"Wish I could say yes. But my son-in-law built the house for us. Took him two years, but it was worth it."

Appraising the house again, Shem said, "I would like to meet your son-in-law."

"You shall, my friend. You shall."

Stepping inside was like stepping into an altogether different world. The interior was well lit with a carpet on the floor, and a table in the middle. The walls were decorated with tapestries that came from as far away as Nineveh and Ur. The lone window looked out over the beautiful Kidron valley.

Though the home was kingly, Achsah instantly relaxed.

Several minutes later Chloe burst in on the three and immediately embraced Achsah. Tears in her eyes, she turned to Shem and embraced him as well.

&&&

Later that night, after the ladies had retired, Shem spoke quietly to Eber.

"You mentioned earlier, Eber, that you have heard rumors of Chedorlaomer, king of Elam. Those are not rumors, my friend; they are fact. He has risen to power and is almost as great as Nimrod, but worse than Asshur. In time I fear he will be the greatest of the rulers. I must admit that the kingdom he rules is free of marauders that increasingly infects the land and makes travel so dangerous, but that is small comfort.

"God has shown me that this same king shall rule over this land as well. I am not free to share much more than that, except thou need not fear. God shalt protect you and this place."

Eber sat still as he pondered the things that Shem had told him. Minutes slipped by while both men remained quiet.

"Thank you, my friend, for sharing these thoughts with me. Chloe and I have trusted the Lord for a long time without the knowledge of His protection, yet fully experiencing it on many occasions. Hearing now of His promise is a comfort to my ears. But God spoke in my mind to listen to you. Is there more?"

"Yes. You and I have a future together here in Salem. We shall leave in a few days, but we shall return again. I can tell you this: Salem will be the home of mine and Achsah's in the future."

"That is wonderful! You will be an honored and welcome citizen of this city. When shall this be?"

"I do not know the time, but it shall come to pass."

The two men stood, stretched, yawned, and headed for bed.

&&&

The wagon bearing Abram, Nahor, and Haran stopped on a hill overlooking Nineveh. Sent by their father to purchase tools and other merchandise, they were full of excitement at visiting the famous city for the first time.

Abram turned and studied his two younger brothers. Nahor was seven years younger, while Haran, at eleven, had not yet reached manhood. Abram turned his attention back to the city. Although only 21 himself, as the oldest of the three he would be expected to be in charge of the entire enterprise.

Flicking the reins he watched with satisfaction as the oxen moved forward. As the wagon neared the great city, all three were in awe of the high walls and the huge gate that they entered through. Remembering his father's instructions, he followed the main street for a couple of blocks before turning right. A few moments later the cart pulled up in front of a simple inn that was exactly as Terah had described.

The three got out and stretched their legs before entering the inn. The owner met them at the door.

"You are looking for a room?"

"Yes, sir. My father, Terah of Ur, has arranged for a room for the three of us."

"I have been expecting you. You might want to stow your cart and goods behind in my covered yard. It will be safe there."

"Let's do that later, Abram," spoke up Nahor. "Haran is tired and we are all hungry."

"I would not advise that," the innkeeper said. "You could lose everything."

"Please, Abram," cried Haran. "I am so tired."

Abram had heard stories from his father about the thievery that seemed to dominate the streets of Nineveh. From his father's stories and the innkeeper's warnings, he knew what he should do.

"The innkeeper's right. We'll take it to the back first."

"Well I'm not!" Haran said, stomping his foot. "You may be big brother and all, but you can't make me do anything. I'm tired and need sleep."

"Come on, Abram," spoke up Nahor. "It'll only be a few minutes."

Abram looked to the innkeeper for support, but it was obvious he had no intention of saying any more. Abram sighed.

"OK, we'll check out a room. But then we come back here and put the wagon in the back."

Grabbing bundles of clothing, the three young men followed the innkeeper inside. As they entered, they saw a room off to the left that had a small cafe. But the innkeeper continued on until he came to some stairs. The boys followed him up to a small room having only one window.

Abram stopped and looked around. *It's small. It's a good thing that Haran is small or we'd have a hard time fitting into it.*

Unloading his bundle upon the floor, he turned to the innkeeper and paid him for a night's stay.

As he turned back, he saw that Haran had already lain down and was fast asleep.

"Well Nahor, it's you and me. Let's go take care of the wagon."

They left the room and descended the stairs, heading out the door. As they stepped outside, Abram had a bad feeling. The wagon and oxen were still there, but something was wrong!

Hurrying over to the wagon, he hardly needed to look inside to know what was wrong. With a sinking feeling in his gut, he saw that all the goods they'd brought from Ur were gone – stolen!

&&&

On the day after Shem's arrival, Eber took him on a tour of the city. Although Eber was obviously very proud, Shem couldn't help but compare it with the larger cities of Babel, Asshur, and Nineveh.

Here in Salem, the streets lacked the straight lines of those bigger cities. Instead, they meandered along between homes with an occasional tree growing on either side. *Still I like it. What it lacks in design, it makes up in a certain naturalness. It is comfortable and the people are relaxed and enjoying themselves.*

Stopping beside a fig tree growing beside the door to one of the many shops that dotted the city, Eber and Shem plucked figs and began enjoying them.

"I know it doesn't compare to the big cities," Eber said as if reading Shem's mind, "but the people are happy, prosperous, and they love God. This is the place God called me to, and apparently you as well."

"I feel right at home here, Eber. But have you considered building a wall around the city. Right now, you are defenseless? You can't depend on the mountain to protect you."

"You're right, of course. We have lived in peace here for so long, that we have forgotten how violent this world has become. While you are here, perhaps you could help plan a wall. For example, should it be wood or stone?"

"Some would argue for wood, as it is cheaper, but I favor mortared stone. It is much stronger and will resist decay better than wood. We'll be staying a few days, so let me pray about it and then I will make my suggestions."

Resuming their walk, they continued along the street, stopping often to talk to the merchants whose shops were all along the way. At one point, Shem stopped and pointed to the rooftops.

"The buildings are so close, it looks like a person could leap from building to building."

"Yes, a fact our children have gleefully discovered."

&&&

"O Achsah, I do hope the two of you will stay."

Achsah sat down beside Chloe and watched as the younger woman expertly mended a piece of clothing.

"Shem says that we will stay a short time, but that we will return. I hope it won't be long, as I already love Salem."

"I believe it is the people that makes it so special. Eber says it is the people's love for God that makes it special. He thinks Salem will play a big role under God."

"That is strange."

"Why do you say that?" asked Chloe.

"Because I have heard Shem say the same thing."

&&&

When Abram went inside and told the innkeeper what had happened, the old man simply shrugged his shoulders as though to say, I warned you. Abram turned to his brother.

"We need to track down those goods while it is still light. You head up that street and I'll take this one. We'll meet back here in an hour."

Nahor nodded and took off at an easy trot. Abram turned to the right, following the street. Any other time, he would have slowed down to admire the buildings, some six stories tall. But not this time.

Following the street, he would periodically stop and ask people if they had seen anyone carrying large bundles. The answer was always no. Finally, dejected, he returned to the inn dreading the return home. His father would be furious.

As he rounded the last corner, he saw his brother leaning against the cart. *He looks like he didn't find anything either.*

"Nahor," he yelled as he hurried toward his brother. "Did you find anything?"

"As a matter of fact, I did," Nahor responded with a grin.

"Where? Can we get it back?"

Haran turned and pointed at the cart. Abram stepped up to the wagon and looked inside. There, lying by itself, were the bundles of linens and other goods they had brought from Ur.

"But how did you manage to get them back?"

"Met some men who took pity on me. Especially when they saw me crying. They seemed to know who the thieves were. In any case, they got the bundles back and brought me back in their own wagon."

Abram sighed heavily.

"This could have been disastrous and father would have been quite angry."

"Only with you. You made the decision to leave it alone, not us."

Abram looked sharply at his brother and was about to retort when he realized that his father would look at it the same way. *I should never have compromised!*

&&&

Eber spotted his son-in-law Jaaziah, husband of his daughter Abigail, who was the town's only Master Carpenter and Bricklayer other than Eber. The only ones of his family who had come with him to this land.

"Jaaziah, could I speak with you a moment?"

"Yes, father," he responded, setting down his tools and walking over to his father-in-law.

"Jaaziah, Shem likes our small city. But he pointed out something that I agree we need. It's a wall that encircles the city, yet allows the city to grow. Could you build something like that?"

"Yes, father I could. Give me enough men and we could begin within days. I have been thinking of such a need as well, and I have a few ideas. If you have time, I could show you."

"Time to visit my youngest girl and her husband is one thing I always have. Will she make bread that I might eat?"

Jaaziah chuckled.

"I am certain that she would do that for you, father. Come and I will show you my thoughts."

"First let me get Shem. The two of you can exchange ideas."

&&&

Shem halted the wagon on a hill overlooking the city. After spending two weeks at Salem, they had finally left the day before. Looking at the city he was glad they wouldn't stay long.

"That is Sodom, Achsah. God wants me to deliver a message there. I am to enter, preach, and leave. We won't stay the night."

"Is it that bad?"

"Yes, and getting worse. It is filled with men working with men that which is unseemly. God calls it an abomination. It is because of such sin that you must remain in the wagon at all times. If anything happens to me, you take the wagon and flee."

"Shem, you are my lord. I will follow you anywhere and obey you in all things, except this. I will not leave you!"

He looked into her eyes and saw the fiery determination. Sighing, he turned back and, with a flick of the wrist, they were moving forward again. Within the hour they reached the city gate and drove into the city. Achsah felt a rare feeling of fear as she noticed small groups of men turn and stare at them.

Shem drove the cart to the city's center, dismounted, and immediately opened his mouth to preach.

"Ye people of Sodom, hear ye what the Lord God says.

"You have departed from My ways. You say, How have we departed? By acts that are an abomination to My eyes. You are filled with vile affection having left the natural use of women, burning with lust one toward another, men with men working that which is unseemly.

"Unless ye repent of your evil acts, judgment shall come."

The crowd of angry men had grown. Watching from the wagon seat, Achsah sensed their mounting anger. Suddenly she saw a man pull a knife from under his cloak.

*Dear God*, she whispered, *protect Shem from these men of Belial.*

She opened her eyes just as Shem turned to the would-be attacker and focused his attention upon the man.

"You think to stop me from speaking the truth of God? The very knife you suppose to slay me with, that very knife shall bring you down. Thou shalt not see another day."

The man's face was by now beat-red. He raised the knife above his head and rushed at Shem. As he moved forward, he stepped on something slippery, and fell forward. His friends rushed to help him back up, but when they lifted him they saw the knife protruding from his chest. They hastily dropped the body and moved backward, their faces filled with shock and fear!

Turning back, Shem stepped up into the wagon and sat beside his wife.

"Shem, you look so sad. Is it because the man who was going to kill you is dead?"

"Yes, for he has now gone to his just reward. The grave is his home until he is judged. Then shall come eternal damnation!"

She nodded. Noticing that the crowd of men was once again getting agitated, she touched her husband's arm.

"Perhaps, my lord, it is time to leave."

He glanced over at the men, nodded, and turned the wagon around. A few minutes later, they left the city and headed away. Achsah looked back and could see that a mob was forming at the gate. Both of them could hear the angry shouts directed their way.

# FORTY THREE

## BETROTHED!

2032BC (pop. 5,645,976)

Sarai was in love! Her heart sang a joyful song as she approached the tent and saw Abram talking to a neighbor.

Looking at her oldest brother, she smiled to herself. *He loves me also, but he won't say it. I will talk to father. After all, he promised me to Abram when I was born!*

Her mind made up, she turned to enter their home and almost ran into her twin brother, Haran.

"Where you going in such a hurry, Sarai?" he asked as he grasped her arm.

"I must speak to father."

"What about?"

"It is private," she said as she gaily escaped his grasp.

Their home was one of the largest tents in the whole community. Towering above her head to a height of sixteen feet, it consisted of a main room and several smaller rooms along the sides.

She found Terah sitting at his table writing.

"Father, may I speak?"

"Yes, my daughter. What do you require?"

"I am sixteen father. When I was born you said I would be the bride of my brother Abram when I turned sixteen. You have repeated that promise for many years, but now I am sixteen yet nothing has happened."

He smiled fondly at his daughter. *Ever since she was a little girl, her world has centered upon Abram. I did promise. It seems like only yesterday that I held her in my arms.*

"You are right, Sarai. I have been neglectful, my daughter. I promise I will speak with Abram tonight."

"Thank you, father. I know it is not my place to remind you, but neither you or Abram has done anything."

Terah nodded knowingly. *My daughter is certainly blunt.*

"Yes, my son has strong convictions and feelings, but rarely speaks them. It is good that he will have a wife who is not afraid to speak."

"Father! You make me sound terrible."

"No, my daughter. I speak but the truth. You have never been shy about expressing yourself. That is a trait you may need throughout your marriage. Now begone, while I contemplate what I must say to Abram."

Sarai almost floated out of the tent. As she emerged, she saw Abram coming toward her.

"Abram, how timely. Father is wanting to talk with you."

"Now?"

"Yes."

"But the sun is still young and work is to be done."

She shrugged and raced away.

Abram watched as the slim body of his half-sister seemed to glide over the ground as she disappeared behind a row of tents. Increasingly of late he had found her beauty to be disturbing. *I love her, but I don't always understand her. My heart desires her, but my mouth refuses to cooperate.*

Shaking his head, he entered the tent to see what his father wanted.

&&&

Normally the father of the young man to be wed would select himself a 'friend of the groom' to act as a deputy to bargain with the girl's father. However, Terah had the unique position of being the father to both.

He studied his son quietly.

"Abram, the time has come for you to take Sarai as your wife. When your mother died I promised her that I would select the right maiden for you. When your half-sister was born I kept that promise.

"Sarai is now sixteen and ready to be wed. We can forget the normal procedures of bargaining. I will provide both your marriage dowry and another dowry as the bride's father."

"But I should provide her a dowry, father."

"Then what shall you give?"

"I have thought upon this much. To give to you what is already yours would not be appropriate. So I shall give unto you a talent of gold, a bracelet of fine gold, and a coat of fine linen. Sarai's portion shall be a necklace of ten silver coins."

"Very well, my son. I shall, as the bride's father, give her a saddle both new and made of the finest materials."

"Then it is agreed. Do we wait the customary year?"

"Yes. Many relatives will want to come to your wedding as they did for mine. Plus, you will want to prepare your tent. However, the betrothal can take place immediately. Would this evening be agreeable for you?"

"Yes, father, it would."

"Then go and prepare."

&&&

That evening, all the family, servants, and a few invited guests were gathered together.

Abram stood as two young servant girls escorted Sarai into the chamber. She lifted the veil and stood still.

Abram felt a lump in his throat as he looked upon her. *She is beautiful!* For a moment he seemed paralyzed, unable to get up. Suddenly realizing that everyone was looking at him and waiting for him to do something, he shook off the paralysis.

Rising and approaching her, he placed a gold ring upon her finger saying loudly, "I swear unto thee, my sister Sarai, and covenant with thee that thou shalt be my wife. See, by this ring thou art set apart for me."

With that simple, yet profound statement, Abram and Sarai were properly betrothed. Immediately, everyone surrounded the couple.

In a matter of moments, Sarai was whisked away by the older women to another tent where she was soon receiving words of wisdom. Listening to the women, Sarai felt herself transported to another world. As she listened, she discovered that they were truly happy for her. That meant more than all the advice given!

In like manner, Abram was taken by the older men and congratulated with solid thumps on his back and general joviality. Quickly a man mentioned building a family and all the men joined in talking about the importance of getting a first-born son.

# FORTY FOUR

## SHIPS OF NIMROD

2031BC (pop. 6,145,900)

The best laid plans of men often are thwarted by means they have no control over. Back in 2238, Nimrod had decided immediately after defeating Asshur that it was time to build a navy. His idea was to use the Ark as his model along with diagrams from stolen tablets to guide his boat building.

However, this was thwarted by two unrelated events: 1) Noah's refusal to allow Nimrod access to the Ark for studying purposes and 2) the destruction of the tablet in a fire that destroyed parts of Erech in 2234.

That fire also caused further delay because all resources had to be turned toward rebuilding Erech. During this reconstruction, many new homes were built using materials both locally produced and acquired by trade with an increasing number of new kingdoms. Plus, new building concepts affected both the building trades and the construction trade.

He decided to experiment with one such new concept involving homes facing an open courtyard. Eventually he wanted to include this concept in his palace or, as some people called it, the Big House.

But Semiramis didn't want him to experiment on the palace. She encouraged him to begin a building project for the common people and erect homes for them, using earth plaster for sealing and finishing the interiors.

"If successful, they will adore you and think you did it for them," she said.

"You are right," he agreed.

So began the great building project. But it was not just a home with a courtyard. Other ideas were tried as well, such as one idea concerning the flooring. It was to be constructed of burnt lime and clay, then colored with ocher, and finally polished. The embedded crushed limestone gave it a slightly mottled appearance. The thickness was between 5 and 6 inches.

But below all that was a foundation built upon rammed earth. Not only the foundation, but the walls themselves used this concept. Basically the soil, usually subsoil where the house was to be located, would be removed, mixed with sand, clay, and lime, and compressed.

In addition, the homes were built using giant reeds for roofing and date palm for the ceiling lintels. But the central feature was the open courtyard that allowed residents to enjoy the sunlight and to work at tasks requiring light. This proved very popular with the people and raised their appreciation of their ruler.

Nimrod and Semiramis were so pleased that the Big House was torn down and rebuilt using this new technology.

&&&

Now, almost two hundred years later after deciding to build a navy, the first real ship since the Flood had been built using new technology. During this interval, small vessels were built, but none that was big enough to be considered a ship.

This new ship bore little resemblance to the Ark in size, shape, or construction materials. His shipbuilders had to invent an entirely new concept, which we now know as shell-of-planks. Even so, the methods of shipbuilding contained in the tablets were vitally important. Without them, the ship could not have been built.

This technique consisted of "sewing" the planks together with rope. No nails were used. The shell or "skin" of the plank was shaped and fastened together in a watertight manner so as to produce the hull. The planks were positioned edge to edge by tenons in mortices within the plank thickness, and fastened together transversely by ropes of grass or reeds.

This particular ship was about 70 feet in length, 12 feet beam to beam (width), and 6 feet high at each end. It's interior included quarters for the crew beneath the deck where they could sleep and eat.

The method of propulsion was the use of oars spaced about three feet apart, which allowed just enough room for an oarsman to sit. Each oarsman worked together with those in front and those sitting behind. This ship had a bank of 20 oars on each side for a total of forty oars, providing both propulsion and braking of the ship.

Nimrod ordered the entire city out to watch as the new ship was launched. He had a special platform from which he could watch. But first he spoke to the people.

"Citizens of Erech. Today we watch as a new era begins. Large Ships! This ship is the first of many that will be built and launched from our city. They shall be bigger, stronger, and better ships than the one before you. Erech is and shall be the shipping center of the world.

"I, Nimrod, foresaw the need for ships for both commerce and war. I gathered the men that would build it and the materials needed. I oversaw the construction. Also, I trained the men that shall be its crew."

He paused as the citizens obeyed the signals from Jamin and roared their approval.

"Henceforth, Erech shall be known for her prowess on land and sea. Nations shall fear us.

"But that is not all. Mankind is spreading out all over this planet in every direction. These ships will allow us to travel to distant lands and bring back the treasures of those lands that we might benefit. Erech shall reap where she has not planted and shall be the greatest city ever built!"

He smiled broadly as the citizens cheered. It mattered little that the cheers were prompted by Jamin and reinforced with the point of the sword.

&&&

Once the ship was launched, it took its maiden voyage down the Tigris and out into the The Gulf, as they named that great body of water. As it traveled south on the Tigris, they discovered that the river was much shallower the further south they went. But fortunately, the ship had a shallow draft, enabling it to work that portion without interruption. However, to be on the safe side, the captain ordered the ship to slow down.

Unknown to Nimrod or the captain was the fact that the southern Tigris would build up over the centuries and eventually doom major shipping. But at this time, the cruise was completely successful and marked Erech as a naval power. It would be years before commerce benefited from this development, but the military aspects were immediate.

# FORTY FIVE

## MARRIED

2031BC (continued)

"How do I look?"

Nahor and Haran looked him over. Although the family was considered rich, they had not yet attained to the comparable wealth of some townspeople. Still, Abram had managed to add to his traditional nomadic clothing a silken girdle that was brilliantly colored. His feet were adorned with carefully laced sandals, while upon his head was a garland of flowers. To top it all off, his clothes were scented with frankincense and myrrh.

"You look like a king!" Nahor pronounced.

"Then I best go get my bride," Abram smiled.

He stepped out of his tent, which was about half the size of his father's, and into the dark night. It only took him a few moments to reach the larger tent and enter. There he found his father and stepmother along with friends and relatives.

His brothers followed him inside and quickly joined Terah. At that moment, Sarai emerged from a side room attired in a very costly and beautiful dress that was decked with all the precious stones and jewels of the family inheritance. It was obvious that her mother had opened her own private collection for her daughter.

But what caught Abram's attention was her face and hair. Her complexion was glossy and shining with a luster like unto marble, while her dark locks of hair were braided with gold and pearls. Upon her head rested a beautiful wreath.

Abram's heart swelled with pride and approval.

As the second oldest, Nahor stepped forward and took her hands into his.

"Thou art our sister, Sarai. Be thou the mother of thousands of millions, and let thy seed possess the gate of those which hate them."

She smiled and lowered her eyes as her mother had instructed.

Terah stepped forward and placed his hands upon her shoulders. His mouth suddenly felt dry and rough.

"My dear Sarai. From the day you were born I have looked forward to this day. I often dreamed of you and Abram starting your own family. And now that it is here, I find myself reluctant to let you go."

"I'm not really going far, father," she interrupted.

*Still the outspoken daughter!*

"I know that what you say is true, but thou shalt be in another tent. No longer will you be under my roof and my authority. You shall belong to Abram and shall be under his authority.

"Your mother and I will miss your happy face of an evening. But you are our daughter and it is our heart's desire that you be happy and as your brother said to be the mother of thousands of millions."

Turning, he signaled to Abram that the procession should start.

Taking her hand, Abram led the way out of the tent with the final destination being his tent, now their home. He could take the most direct route to the tent, but he had already decided that such a short trip would not work out. Instead, he headed in the opposite direction with everyone falling in line behind.

The procession headed out of the camp then turned left and followed the outside perimeter. As was now common, everyone in the procession carried a lamp to light the way. As they continued around the camp more people joined the procession, each with their own lamp. It was an unwritten rule that if you wished to join a wedding procession, you must carry your own lamp.

Meanwhile, Sarai had loosed her hair and it was flowing behind while her face was now veiled. Many of her relatives had hurried ahead and were scattering ears of parched grain to the children along the way.

The entire route was marked with men playing drums or other musical instruments while the women and young girls danced. These and other demonstrations of joy preceded and followed them until they reached Abram's tent.

It was at this precise and most important moment that the older women converged upon Sarai and began rearranging her hair. Her glowing locks were now hidden beneath a thick veil. They checked her facial veil, as her face would henceforth be veiled when in public.

Satisfied with their work, the women guided her to a place under a canopy, which had been erected just outside the tent she would call home. Standing at the door was her husband, who was patiently waiting for her.

At this moment, surprise guests appeared. As they stepped out of a nearby tent Abram and Sarai recognized Shem and Achsah. Smiling broadly, they approached the new couple.

"Abram. Sarai," Shem said as he embraced the newlyweds. "Your father has graciously agreed that I would have the privilege to pronounce your benediction. Your father and brothers wanted this to be a surprise so we have kept ourselves hidden for just this moment."

Sarai looked over at her brothers with a look of disapproval, but all she got in return were innocent grins. Even her father and mother could hardly refrain from laughing at her expression.

Abram looked at his father with gratitude. Even though Terah did not share Abram's faith in God, he was willing to allow Shem, the spokesman for God, to perform the marriage. This meant a lot to him.

"Sarai," Shem continued. "You were selected at birth to be Abram's wife. For seventeen years you have been trained for that special relationship. I have talked to your family and friends and have been assured that you love God and desire His best for you. You are a woman of great faith and strength. Your husband will trust you with his heart. And your children shall be taught at your knees. I charge you to love and obey your husband. Seek to please him in every way. But mostly I charge you to worship God, our Creator and Provider."

He paused. Out of the corner of his eye he noticed Terah squirming and a look of discomfort on his face. Ignoring him, he turned his attention to the groom.

"Abram, God seeks to use you in ways that I do not yet know. But He has made it clear that you are special to Him. His love for you is great. And this day, He has given you a bride for you to love and nourish. Yes, she is beautiful to behold. But outward beauty must be matched by inward beauty. And Sarai fulfills that requirement.

"In the days ahead, God may call on the two of you to make great sacrifices. Don't ask questions for I know not the answer," he said laughing as the two had shown every inclination to shower him with questions.

"But if He does require of you sacrifices, I believe He will also reward thee greatly. Whether He blesses or not, I charge you Abram to first love Him, then your wife. You are to care for her as though caring for your own flesh remembering what Adam said: 'Therefore shall a man leave his father and his mother, and shall cleave unto his wife: and they shall be one flesh.'

"Now in the name of our great God and Creator, I pronounce God's blessing upon this couple and upon their house. Let no man come between you. May your seed be thousands of millions!"

Almost immediately the crowd of spectators erupted into glee and the wedding feast began in earnest. Nahor, acting as the ruler of the feast, soon had all the festivities going smoothly. He moved about making sure that every guest was wearing a wedding garment and that they were enjoying themselves. He couldn't help but smile to himself, as he heard different men stand forth and ask a riddle sometimes of the groom, mostly of the other guests.

Meanwhile, Shem and Achsah stayed long enough to greet Terah and the rest of the family before entering their wagon to continue their journey. As they left the happy celebrants, Achsah turned to Shem.

"I pray that they have a long and happy life together."

"That depends on Abram's obedience to God. Sometimes he shows a faithfulness that puts me to shame, but other times he seems weak, indecisive, and willing to compromise. It is a trait that can bring him great harm."

The two grew silent as they continued on their way. Back at Ur, the feast continued for 30 days.

# FORTY SIX

## JEZREEL

2031BC (*continued*)

The little wagon, carrying Shem and Achsah, left Ur and traveled north following the Euphrates. After a full day's travel, they reached a well worn and familiar caravan trail heading west.

Turning upon this road, they followed it for several days until they reached a large encampment where many other travelers were already lodging. Exhausted from the long trip, they decided to camp there for awhile.

They quickly set about unloading the tent from the wagon and getting it set up. Shortly after they had erected the tent, they were visited by Onam, an old and dear friend.

Achsah was outside cleaning dishes when he arrived.

"Onam, so good to see you. Shem's inside."

Onam ducked under the flap and found Shem sitting in the middle of the room.

"Am I interrupting anything?" Onam asked.

"No, my friend, you are not," Shem replied, standing and embracing his friend.

"What brings you to our humble tent?"

The two men sat opposite each other before Onam answered.

"I am traveling to the land they call Canaan. It is a profitable land of grapes, honey, cattle, and much more. I am traveling with others and we are heading for a small town called Salem."

"Achsah and I are heading for the same area. We want to stop at Salem, but many other cities as well," replied Shem. "Do you know the ruler of Salem? His name is Eber."

"Yes, yes! It is said that he truly loves the Lord our God. Is this true?"

"Yes," replied Shem. "I wish to see him and his wife again and to know how God is using them."

"Why not join up with us? Afterward, you can travel to wherever you want."

"That sounds good. We will do that."

"Good. And how is God treating Shem these days?"

"Excellent, my dear friend. God continues to watch over us and overshadows us with His presence. I suspect He is watching over you, as well, Onam. I hear you are doing quite well."

Onam smiled and nodded while stroking his beard.

"He has given me a head for trading and has blessed me with a wife and several sons. They are a blessing to these old eyes.

"By the way, last year I was in Uz and met a man named Job who is very wealthy and appears to be the ruler. He said to tell you hello."

"Job is a great believer. How is he doing?"

"Near as I can tell he is not only quite wealthy, but is well respected. You should visit him someday."

"That I would like, but God has not opened that door. Haven't seen him since we took him to Uz."

"You took him to Uz?" asked Onam in surprise.

"Yes. Seems God wanted him there. I don't know why or for what. But God has His purposes, it is not necessary for me to know what they are."

The two men continued to talk for some time, although to Achsah it seemed like they sat in silence, which was only occasionally broken by a brief conversation. Later, Onam arose and left.

&&&

Three days later, at the first light of day, Achsah was already busy packing the wagon while Shem was taking down the tent. Once he completed that task, the two of them folded and stored it in the wagon. After helping her get settled on the wagon seat, he walked around and got in.

"Whew! I wish there was an easier way," Achsah sighed.

Shem laughed as he gently urged the mules forward.

"Yes, I can see it now. A tent on wheels with all the modern conveniences," he said, as the wagon moved forward and headed west.

"You laugh," she replied. "But stranger things have happened."

"Like what?"

"Well, the Ark for one thing. No one would have ever thought that such a huge ship could be built. But it was."

Shem smiled and nodded. In spite of herself, Achsah soon was laughing with Abram as they contemplated such a contraption.

&&&

Their small caravan followed an inland route from the north that went south to the Sea of Chinnereth, then to Shechem, Salem, and further south where it intersected with southern roads leading to Egypt. Shem had traveled this route several times previously, so it was both familiar and more relaxing.

The two of them would often break out into song, rejoicing in the goodness of God! Sometimes others in the caravan would join in and the music could be heard for miles around.

Traveling southwest, the caravan arrived in the Jezreel Valley. When the caravan stopped at a small creek to water the animals, Shem got out of the wagon with a "could you water them?" He then walked a short distance away.

Achsah watched as her husband fell to his knees and pressed his face to the ground. *Is God talking to him?*

She unhitched the mules and led them to the creek. While they busied themselves drinking, Achsah joined other women who were gathered in a circle discussing the day's events. Nearby was a another circle of men, whom she presumed were also talking of the day's events.

Occasionally she would glance in the direction of Abram, who was still praying.

After awhile, he arose and walked back. She immediately noticed that his face was pale and his lips trembling. She hurried over to him.

"Is something wrong?" she asked in a concerned voice.

Shem slowly collected himself before answering.

"We have traveled this road many times, Achsah, but this is the first time that God has shown me the future of this valley. It is such a dire future. There shall be many battles fought here and and one great battle that He didn't explain."

"Why would He tell you that?"

"I'm not sure. Sometimes God tells me things I don't understand right away. Later, understanding comes. But there is a sense of death about this place and I don't want us to spend much time here. I'll talk to Onam and suggest we stop at Megiddo overnight, then continue in the morning. Then we will continue south to Salem."

Everyone got back into their wagons and resumed their journey, arriving at Megiddo that afternoon. For Achsah's sake, Shem left the caravan and entered the city, stopping at the first inn they came upon. Shem got out and went inside, while Achsah stayed in the wagon and observed the city. She took a deep breath, inhaling the aromas rising from nearby shops. Aside from stirring hunger pains, it also caused her mind to drift back to when they lived in Ararat. For a moment, she longed for such a life again.

Shem stepped out and came to her.

"Got us a room," he said as he helped her out.

"You take our things up to the room and I'll stow the wagon and feed the animals."

Nodding, she picked up her bag and entered the inn. The innkeeper greeted her and pointed out where her room was located. Pushing back the heavy curtain, she stepped inside and looked around. Although small with only a bed, a small table, and two chairs, it brought a smile of joy to her face. *I could stay here for weeks!*

# FORTY SEVEN

## CALLED

2005BC (pop. 14,942,208)

Haran felt extremely tired. *I don't understand this constant tiredness. I even came down from home to visit mother and father, but I still feel so tired.*

He first felt the sapping of his strength while still in Haran, the town he had founded only a few years ago. When discussing it with his wife, she urged him to take a break and visit his father. At first reluctant, he finally agreed that he needed rest. The next day he had traveled back to Ur, arriving yesterday.

But instead of feeling better, he actually felt worse. Some people had noted his paleness and lack of energy. Rumors spread throughout the campsite and the city.

Early the next morning, he approached his father.

"Father, I don't know what is wrong, but I need to lie down for awhile. I will take a short nap and then join you later. Is that all right with you?"

"Of course. Will you join us for the noon meal?"

"Yes."

Terah watched as his son retreated into the tent. *I have never seen him so tired before. I think I will make sure nobody disturbs him. Maybe a good sleep is all he needs.*

&&&

"Abram."

Abram, kneeling beside a tree where he regularly prayed, looked up. But no one was in sight.

"Abram."

Suddenly appearing before him was a shiny being clothed in white linen. Abram immediately fell prostrate before him.

"Arise. Be of good cheer. I am Gabriel, the messenger of God."

Abram stood, trembling.

"Be not afraid. The Lord God has sent me with a message for you. Thou art to take thy wife, Sarai, and get thee out of thy country and from thy kindred."

"Where are we to go?"

"The Lord Himself shall lead you."

"What of my parents, brothers and sisters? They are all kindred."

"The message I gave thee is the message from God and it is plain. He shall direct thy paths and lead thee in the way thou shalt go."

"But?"

As quickly as the angel had appeared, he was gone.

Thoughtfully, Abram headed for his father's house.

&&&

Terah turned to his wife Jehoshabeath.

"Haran is sleeping in his chamber. Perhaps I should go wake him."

"Yes, my lord. The meal will be ready by the time he comes."

Terah arose and crossed the main chamber to Haran's. Entering, he saw that his son was still sleeping. Shaking his head, he smiled. *I know he is tired, but he needs food. I'd better wake him.*

Walking over to the bed, he leaned over and gently shook his son's shoulders. But nothing happened. Suddenly he froze, the blood draining from his face.

"He's dead!" he blurted out.

Fear and uncertainty gripping his heart, he grabbed his son's shoulders and shook them violently, still with no response. He let go and Haran fell back on the bed. Terah sank to his knees beside the bed as tears freely flowed. It was several minutes before he rose and slowly left the room. When he saw his wife, he straightened and walked firmly over to her. Placing his hands upon her shoulders, he spoke the fateful words:

"Our son is dead."

Jehoshabeath was shocked. Though Haran was not the son of her flesh, she had loved him as though he were. The sudden announcement, so typical of Terah, left her speechless.

"I go to the altar," he added.

She watched as her husband left. Though he was trying to be tough, she could see the rigid back and stiff legs of a man in grief. She looked up at the statuette sitting upon the mantel.

*O, ye gods. Comfort my husband in this his hour of need.*

&&&

Abram left Nahor in the field and headed for the camp. He was already anticipating his wife's meal of bread and vegetables. *She will have them ready for me even as I enter the tent. The bread will be hot and the vegetables ripe. I will kiss her on the cheek and return to the field. But first I must go tell father of Gabriel's visit.*

Abram found his father at the altar of Ishtar, which was near his father's tent door. Terah didn't appear to be praying, so Abram approached him.

"Father, may I speak with you?"

"Yes, my son. What is it?"

"I had a visit from an angel. It was Gabriel."

"And what did he tell you?" Terah asked.

"I am to take Sarai and leave this land."

"Your God at least knows how to take advantage of situations."

"What do you mean?"

"We must take your brother Haran to his home. Your God must have known this."

As his father's face contorted into grief, Abram sensed that something bad had happened.

"What is it father?"

"It is your brother. He is dead."

Abram's eyes opened wide in shock.

"Dead? But how? When?"

"I don't know how. He is in on the bed where I found him. I have been praying to Ishtar. Your appearance indicates that I am to move the family to Haran. Perhaps to continue his legacy."

With that Terah turned back to the altar. Abram sadly gazed upon his father. *It was not Ishtar that commanded me to go to Haran. It was God.* Abram quietly left and entered the tent.

&&&

"Abram!"

Kneeling beside his brother's body in quiet contemplation, Abram recognized Helon's voice. Slowly he got up. Wiping tears from his eyes, he left the room. He found his friend just outside the tent door. Looking past him, Abram could see that his father was still at his altar.

"You look sad, Abram."

"I am sad, Helon," Abram responded quietly. "My brother Haran has died and I mourn for him. What brings you here?"

"Maybe I should come back later."

"No. My brother has departed this life and resides in Hades. There is nothing I can do to change that. Something important must be on your mind, I can sense it."

"I just wanted to see you. I have this feeling that you're leaving."

"That is amazing! The angel Gabriel just visited me and has told me to leave Ur."

"Where will you be going?

"He didn't say, but father thinks we are to move to Haran, where we will be taking my brother for burial."

"When do you leave?"

"Probably tomorrow or the day after. It is a long trip and he will begin to stink before we ever get there."

"Then it appears that we shall never see one another again."

Abram thought about that and slowly nodded his head.

"It does appear so. But you shall never be forgotten."

"Nor you," responded his friend. "I know you are still grieving and have plans to make, but could we spend some time together before you leave."

"Yes. We have much to talk about and so little time. Let's take a walk outside the camp and talk about what God is doing."

The two men walked side by side, quietly conversing with Abram relating Gabriel's visit and God's command. Although Helon was still not a believer, he had shown increasing interest in Abram's faith, which he found intriguing from an intellectual viewpoint. But as always, his intellectual curiosity never led him to faith.

But the sudden impending departure of Abram changed all that.

"Abram, what must I do to know God like you do?"

Abram's heavy heart jumped for joy.

"Believe that there is only one God, that He loves you, and has provided a Redeemer for you."

"Isn't there some great deed I must do?"

"Obey Him. If you truly love Him, you will obey Him. And He shall guide you along the path you are to take."

The two men stopped. Abram placed his hand upon Helon's shoulder.

"Do you believe in God, Helon?"

"Yes. I believe that He will send His Redeemer and that when I die I shall be taken to Paradise. Is that where Haran is now?"

Sadly Abram shook his head.

"My brother, indeed my whole family, has rejected God. Only Sarai and I believe."

&&&

The following day, Terah gathered his sons and their wives together, then headed for Haran. Because of Haran's death, Terah felt a degree of urgency.

"Only bring a change of clothes and food," he ordered. "We'll get the rest after my son is buried."

By mid-morning, everyone was ready and they boarded the wagons pulled by mules. Terah mounted a camel, which was gaining popularity as a means of travel.

A very sorrowful group of people made their way northward. It would take several days of travel, burdened as they were with women and children. Unlike most such trips, there was no laughter, not even of the children. All were in mourning.

Abram was greatly relieved that he had not had to break with his father. *I don't have to leave all my kindred. I can obey God and stay with them at the same time.*

The fact that God had directed a complete break seemed lost on his consciousness. Satisfied with his decision, he calmly settled down for the night.

# FORTY EIGHT

## DEATH OF NOAH

2000BC (pop. 15,009,876)

Noah sat in his favorite chair just outside his home. As always, he was facing the mountain. While he couldn't see the Ark from there, he knew where it was located.

"I should go up there soon," he mused aloud. "Maybe next month."

He leaned back enjoying the view. Looking up toward the top of Mt. Ararat, he could see the stars twinkling behind, while off to the left was the moon. He chuckled as he recalled little children asking him if there was a 'man in the moon.' The question had been asked him many times and every time he had given the same answer, "Never been there, but God would have told me if there was. Just an illusion boys. Just an illusion."

"I don't think I'll be going up to the Ark after all," he said to the night. "Heaven seems closer than ever tonight."

As darkness settled around the tiny town of Ararat, he stood and made his way inside. Blowing out the lone candle, he quietly undressed and lay down on his bed.

&&&

Only days after his 950th birthday Noah passed away in the night. Shem, who was making his annual visit, discovered him in the morning stretched upon his bed. He knew immediately that his father was dead. Quietly he picked up the blanket and covered his father.

Kneeling down beside his father's body, Shem bowed his head. *O my father, I know that you have now found the peace you so desired. As you explore Paradise, I pray that you might be reunited with Naamah and with the saints that have gone before.*

Rising, he left and soon gathered his family. Later, with the help of several of the townsmen, he tenderly bathed and wrapped the body in linen. Using spices and other burial ointments they prepared Noah's body for his final resting place.

Meanwhile, Shem sent several servants abroad with the news of Noah's death. They rode with orders to speedily deliver their messages without stopping for sleep. With the news also went an invitation to as many as would choose to do so, to come to Noah's funeral in three weeks. But to his brethren he wrote more detail and requested they arrive within seven days for the actual burial.

(It so happened that at that time his brothers were in Nineveh on business. Though they spoke in different languages, they were able to use local interpreters to conduct business. Neither had been interested in seeing the other, but the news of Noah's death brought them together. With several servants in tow, they quickly rode north toward Ararat.)

Considering the short notice and the distances involved, Shem was pleased and surprised that both Japheth and Ham arrived on the fifth day. Although the body was beginning to smell, each had an opportunity to spend some time alone with their father. Once finished, Shem ordered the procession to proceed.

The small village of Ararat emptied as all the citizens followed the wagon making its way up the narrow trail. The route was so long that they had to stop along the way and spend the night. The next morning the journey continued and they arrived at the Ark late that afternoon.

Nearby was Noah's favorite cave where he had spent many a night on his frequent visits to the Ark. Opening the walled up cave where Naamah slept, they entered in and carefully moved the skeletal remains of their mother. Then they placed his body where hers' had lain and rebuilt the wall.

But the sons decided that the entire cave should be closed. Therefore, they rolled boulders in place to seal off the cave forever as well as to protect against the elements and wild beasts. Once completed, the small crowd drew near and waited as Shem stepped forward.

"As you know, this place has been dear to our father's heart ever since the day we landed here on this hallowed mountain some 350 years ago. The cave we have buried him in was like a second home to him. He loved to come here and worship at the altar. This is also where our families lived for a short time and later where he buried his beloved Naamah.

"Father often mentioned that he wanted to be buried here. This is where the Ark is," he paused as he directed their attention to the weathered Ark. "And it is where he felt closest to God.

"Our world has changed much since the day we landed here in the Ark. We have grown from a mere 8 people to what I believe is over fifteen million souls! That would have pleased father immensely, except that the majority of the people have turned from God to idols. And in a few weeks, these same people will be coming to pay their respects.

"Among the visitors I hope to see is Nimrod and, perhaps, Chedorlaomer of Elam. I see the fear in your eyes, but even they won't cause any problems here. In spite of his rebellion, Nimrod has always honored Noah and, if he comes, he will be respectful. As for Chedorlaomer, I expect he will be respectful as well.

"Of course, there is the language problem. Since the day God confused our tongues, many languages have come about, necessitating interpreters. While I can communicate in every tongue, it will still be difficult. And I will be preaching in one tongue only without the use of interpreters.

"Still, I believe that God will make a way. All you who pray to God, I urge you to ask Him to intervene and make it possible for all to hear my sermon.

"That is all I have to say for now. Let us bow our heads and remember this great man and what he did for us."

As the words drifted away in the mountain breeze, everyone bowed their heads in silent prayer. As Shem looked them over, his heart warmed that his brothers were there in peace. But he was particularly pleased that the villagers had come in such great number. It showed how much they all loved Noah. Bowing his own head, he prayed, *Dear Lord give me, I pray, the wisdom to say the right thing.*

&&&

"Are you going?" asked Jamin, the high priest of Ishtar, goddess of love and war.

Nimrod looked at the priest and nodded.

"Noah was a great man. People all over the world admired him. Our own people still revere him. Semiramis and I must show our respect and honor for the man, else the people may revolt."

"I imagine Shem will preach."

"Probably, but never fear my dear priest. Aside from the language differences, his preaching will not sway me. I long ago left behind his God. Besides, I shall pay special homage to Ishtar before leaving."

"What of the danger. You are not popular there. If Chedorlaomer is there with his people, he may want revenge upon you for slaying Elam's twin brother Asshur."

"That won't happen for several reasons. One, it was 240 years ago when I slew Asshur. Secondly, Chedorlaomer will not cause trouble for the same reason I won't – out of respect for Noah. And lastly, I shall have Ishtar's protection plus a few soldiers."

Jamin nodded.

&&&

Meanwhile, the news had reached Haran. Gathering his sons together, Terah announced that he had decided to travel to Ararat for the funeral. The two young men, Abram the eldest at 58, looked forward to the trip.

"You thought a lot of Noah, Abram," spoke up Nahor. "How are you going to handle it?"

"I'll be all right. He is in Paradise now with his beloved wife and his Lord. I picture him watching me with a twinkle in his eye while cheering me on as he did when I was a child racing the other boys of Ur. I shall use the opportunity to revisit the Ark. It's been years since I last saw it."

"You forget your duty, Abram," remonstrated Nahor. "Father will not want us going about. He will insist we stay with him."

"Father is afraid of offending those he does business with every day. He does not have faith in God and he gets upset with me because

I fear God with my whole heart. But he will not object to my going to the Ark. Besides, Shem will be there and father will do nothing to offend the great man."

The two men continued to talk, even as they worked to prepare for the journey.

&&&

Chedorlaomer was eating grapes and drinking wine when the news of Noah's death arrived. Instinctively he knew that Nimrod would be going to the funeral. *I cannot let him go and I stay behind. It will look weak and disrespectful.* Reaching over, he pulled on the silken rope, ringing the bell.

A few moments later a servant entered and bowed before the king.

"You rang, your Highness?

"Yes. Tell my generals to prepare for a long trip. Noah has died and I, along with family and advisers, will attend his funeral. Tell them to prepare for a long trip and to be armed."

"Are we going to war, your Majesty?"

"No. But I want Nimrod and the rest of the world to know of our strength."

"Yes, your Majesty. I will notify them at once."

The servant backed out and the king was alone with his thoughts. *This should be interesting. Nimrod and I will meet on neutral land. My army is now more powerful than his. I have no desire to fight with him, so maybe the time is ripe for a treaty. Yes, that will work. We shall join forces, but the day will come when his kingdom shall fall to me and I will rule the world.*

&&&

The mourners arrived three weeks after the death of Noah, most arriving on the last day. Forming a long line, they made their way up Ararat to the plateau where the Ark rested. Most had never seen the Ark and their faces reflected their awe.

Therefore, a line of visitors would head for the Ark and pass by it before turning toward the cave. Upon reaching the closed cave, the line would pause as each person would stop and stand in silent contemplation, considering the great things their ancestor had accomplished.

When Abram's turn came, he stood staring at the walled up cavern. *Dear God, thank You for allowing me the honor and privilege of knowing Noah. What a man he was. I remember how well he treated me as I toured the Ark. When I trusted in You, his joy was true and complete.*

*Now he is with You, O God. He treasured You more than his beloved Naamah. Truly he was a man who walked with You and found grace in Thy sight.*

Finishing his prayer, he turned and moved past as someone else took his place. Leaving the cave tomb, he turned to look back at the towering Ark. He felt a hand upon his shoulder and looked back. Shem smiled at him.

"Remembering the tour?"

"Yes. But more than that, I remember that night within the cave with all of you. It was there that God visited me in the night and told me to worship Him. My life has never been the same since. And Noah, you and Achsah played a big role in that."

"And have you followed our advice since then?"

"You mean obeying God?"

"Yes."

"Well, He did call me out of Ur and I now live in Haran."

"Is that all He said?"

"No. He also said to leave my kindred and except for my father and brother, I have done that."

"Be careful Abram. Partial obedience is disobedience."

The statement stunned Abram. Watching Shem leave to talk to others, he wondered what the man meant.

&&&

The people divided into three camps, with each camp divided into clans, depending on the spoken language. Looking over the crowd, Shem estimated that there were several hundred men and women crowded on the small plateau.

He noted that Ham's camp appeared to be the largest with large militaristic clans headed by Nimrod, Mizraim, and others. *Mizraim talks of the land across the River where some of Phut's descendants dwell. They are called the 'Hawk' people. Nimrod's eyes light up when he hears such things. I imagine he dreams of conquering the Hawk people and adding them to his empire. Such a conquest would extend Nimrod's empire to the ends of the world. But then there is Chedorlaomer and his people. They would have something to say about that. As for that, Mizraim now rules Egypt and is strong enough to resist any move by Nimrod.*

He sighed as he looked over the multitude. *O Lord God, such a people. So many who are warlike. This is not what father envisioned or You wanted. How do I speak to so many different tongues? How do I convey Your love when only a few know my tongue?*

Stepping forward, he signaled for silence.

"Friends, you have come a long way to honor a great man."

As his first words drifted over the assembly, he could see understanding upon their faces. *God is giving them the ability to understand!* He continued on.

"It does not require a recital of Noah's entire life. You all know how God called him to build an Ark, though he was a farmer. You know how he preached for one hundred twenty years. I remember, as a young man, listening to him preach. He was strong of voice and passionate of heart. He moved people.

"But only a few people followed him and believed on the Lord. When the Flood came only eight people were saved. They were all that was left of those that had responded and believed before the Flood. One hundred and twenty years of preaching without great numbers believing. But he never got discouraged or stopped. He trusted God.

"The Ark was huge and could have provided refuge for a great many, but when the door closed there were only eight of us on board. It broke Noah's heart that so many, including friends and relatives, rejected his message and God's offer. They chose death rather than God. After the Flood, it broke Noah's heart again when so many of you turned aside to idols and worshiped gods of your own making.

"Because of your sins, God visited you and changed your tongues so that you could no longer be united in your sin. Today, God has lifted that curse so that you hear my words; the very words that God has laid upon my heart.

"Sadly, you have continued in your sin. Do not think that God does not see your wickedness nor that He will allow your sins to go unpunished.

"Today we are here to honor Noah, our ancestor. But let us gather together and honor him as our example in faith and in practice. Let us turn from our wicked ways and humbly turn to God. Let us yield our hearts to Him and worship only the God of creation. Such an act on our part would surely please Noah, but it is of greater importance to please our God. Our God is our Creator and the One who will send us the Redeemer.

"Friends, I invite you to enter into fellowship with our Creator and to live for Him. Join me at the Ark!"

Stopping, he looked around before walking briskly to the Ark and kneeling. Soon others were joining and kneeling beside him. But when he looked around, they were few in number and primarily his family. Everyone else remained aloof.

&&&

That night, as he lay on the ground, Shem thought over the day. While happy that some of his family had chosen to follow him, it grieved him that the great majority had rejected his plea.

"Shem."

He bolted upright, looking around.

"Shem."

As understanding flooded his soul, he stretched himself upon the ground.

"Speak Lord, for Thy servant listens."

"Do not be grieved for the people. They have not rejected thee, but they have rejected Me. Therefore shall I deal with them as a father with a disobedient child. I shall withdraw My protection and they shall know war and pestilence. Mothers shall lose their babies and fathers their first born."

"Shall God the Righteous One destroy His people?"

"I shall always have a remnant. Even as you serve Me, others shall I call and they shall serve Me. Thus I have spoken; thus shall it be."

Silence settled over him signifying that the Lord had departed.

# FORTY NINE

## SALEM

1999BC (pop. 15, 067,775)

Achsah sat down with a thud. Shem looked over at her with concern.

"What is it?"

"I am so tired of all this travel," she responded. "I know the Lord God called you to travel, but it is just too much for me.

"I suppose I am getting old," she added with a weak smile.

He came over and knelt beside her.

"I have noticed you have not been yourself. But I cannot stop until God tells me to stop."

"I would never ask you to do that," Achsah replied. "But perhaps you could travel more if I wasn't such a burden."

He sat back on his haunches.

"You would stay behind?"

"Yes. But only if your travels bring you home at least once a year."

"And where would this home be?"

She responded by pointing. Turning, he looked in that direction and saw a small village resting upon a plateau.

"That is Salem," he commented. "You would be amongst strangers."

"They are not complete strangers. We have friends there, like Eber and Chloe. I recall they have asked you to rule over them both as priest and king."

"True, but I have no desire to be a king."

"I know that my lord. But you have said that God will one day make you a king, right there. You could accept their offer and appoint someone to rule in your name. Eber rules now and would be willing to rule in your place. You would only need to be concerned with matters upon your return. And besides, as priest you would be able lead the people in the worship of God."

Shem grinned. His wife knew him well. Being able to preach the Word of God to such a large group of people appealed to him.

"Yes, you are right. OK, tomorrow I shall take you to Salem and I shall talk to Eber. Perhaps he will help us find a house where you can live. I will miss you on the trail, but it would be much safer for you. As for the kingship, we shall leave that in God's hands."

"Thank you, my lord."

&&&

The following morning as the sun peaked over Salem, Shem and Achsah arose and prepared breakfast. While Shem thoroughly enjoyed the meal, Achsah was not hungry. She was too excited to think about food. Moreover, she felt impatient as he took his time eating. She failed to notice the sly smile on his face as he busied himself around the wagon. It was late in the morning with the sun rising toward its peak when he was finally ready.

They got into the wagon and soon were heading toward the mountain village. When they reached the trail that led up to the village, the already slow progress got even slower. Achsah, sitting beside Shem, stared ahead as though she could 'will' their arrival in the next few minutes. Actually it took better than an hour to climb the mountain trail. When they finally arrived at the gate, she was so excited that she barely noticed the mules heavy breathing.

Driving through the gate, Shem pulled on the reins and they came to a stop. He sat there looking about the village. *It has grown since our last visit. I will have to stop calling it a village for it is now a small city.* He noticed a crowd heading toward them. *Achsah is right! Over the years we have made many friends here including Eber. They all have expressed a desire for me to be king.* He sighed. *The angel did warn me this day would come.*

Taking a deep breath, he shook the reins and the mules continued on to Eber's house. There they were warmly greeted by Eber and Chloe. After a refreshing meal, the two men went for a walk through the city. Eber was overjoyed. The great Shem, son of Noah, was going to make Salem his home!

&&&

Three nights later an angel appeared unto Shem in a dream.

"Shem."

Looking up from his bed, Shem beheld and recognized the angel. Glancing over at his sleeping wife, he sat up.

"You are Gabriel."

"Yes. The time has come."

This strange statement puzzled Shem. He sat there mulling over it until he remembered the last time the angel had appeared. Feeling he now knew the meaning, he decided to make sure.

"Time for what?"

"Time for you to become the king of Salem. You shall be king unto the people of Salem and thou shalt be the priest to the Most High God, Possessor of Heaven and Earth. Thou shalt be known as Melchizedek, without father or beginning."

"I don't understand."

"Thou shalt take the name Melchizedek. You shall no longer be known as Shem."

"But what of Eber and his family? They know me."

"You are known of your people, but future generations shalt not know that the son of Noah was the mysterious Melchizedek, priest-king of Salem."

"Am I to no longer travel?"

"Eber shalt rule in your stead until thy travels end. Lo, the Lord your God shall direct thy paths and shall return you to Salem to take up thy kingship."

"This is a growing city. How shall I rule?"

"Eber has ruled and shall rule. He shall teach you to be king. But the Spirit of God shall come upon you as the priest-king. Thou shalt make a name for thyself and forever be known as Melchizedek, priest-king of Salem."

As the angel finished, Shem considered this shocking news. For several moments he considered the words that the angel had spoken. Finally, he looked at the angel with acceptance.

"How shall this come to pass?"

"Thy Lord God shall bring these things to pass. Only be thou faithful unto the end."

As his last words faded away, the angel disappeared. Shem lay back upon his bed, closing his eyes in contemplation.

&&&

In the morning, Shem visited Eber and told him of the angelic visit.

"That is an answer to prayer!"

"You have been praying for this?"

"Yes. It is a struggle for me to rule. When Salem was but a village, I ruled effectively. But now the people grow in number and I find it increasingly difficult to exercise real authority. I will be glad to turn the rule of this people over to you."

"But as I have told you, Eber, I still must travel. You will continue to rule, only as my Regent until my Lord requires me to stop."

"True," Eber admitted. "But you shall be King Melchizedek. Most of the people don't know you as Shem, the son of Noah. But as Melchizedek, they shall know you as their king and because they already have great respect for you, they shall be willing to obey thy rule."

Shem smiled at him.

"I see. By being my Regent instead of king, you can rule using me as your authority."

Eber looked sheepishly at the ground.

"Like I told you, King Melchizedek, it has been increasingly hard to rule. People know I have a soft side and they play it; rather well I might add. But as Regent, I can say that you have decreed a certain thing and they will accept it."

"Then, in the interest of keeping you honest, let me state this: 'Every decree that you issue will be in my name and shall have my authority. You as my Regent are to rule this people with authority and power.' Will that do?"

"Yes. Thank you."

"Good. God has a purpose in all of this that I do not know. But I shall obey His will as I am sure you will also."

"Yes I will. Where will you travel to next?"

"God has at least one more mission for me. I shall visit many cities before returning. Then, unless He directs otherwise, I shall rule this great city with thy help."

&&&

Two weeks after Shem left, Achsah realized she was out of certain items. Instead of waiting for the morning, she visited the city's market place as the sun was sinking in the west. Carrying a basket, she stopped at a booth, looking at the appetizing fruit.

"Look at this. An old woman all by herself."

She turned and saw five rough looking men standing behind her. *Sons of Belial!*

"Pardon?"

"I'll bet a woman of your age knows how to please a man," said the leader, who was leering at her.

Nearby, a merchant witnessed the confrontation. Calling his son over, he whispered instructions.

"Go. Tell Eber what is happening. Make sure he knows it is Melchizedek's wife. Now run!"

As the lad ran off on the errand, the merchant looked back in time to see the worthless fellows surround the woman. He knew he should go to her assistance, but his feet wouldn't move.

"You would attack a defenseless woman?" Achsah said, forcing contempt into her voice. "How brave!"

"Mock us if you want woman. When we are done with you, your pretty face will lose its contempt. I see no man to protect you."

He stepped forward and reached for her. She tensed, closing her eyes and praying. *O Lord God, protect me from these men of Belial.*

When nothing happened, she opened her eyes and was startled to see all five men lying on the ground. *What happened? Who did this?*

Looking around, she saw no hero. Only startled merchants, one of which came over to her.

"Are you all right?"

"Yes, but what happened?"

"You don't know?"

"My eyes were closed and I was busy praying."

"You must be close to God's heart."

"What do you mean?"

"While you were praying, this one here," he said as he pointed to one of the fallen, "was about to grab you. They would have taken you and done evil unto you. But suddenly, they were lifted off their feet and slammed to the ground so hard, they are still unconscious."

"But surely you and the others would have rescued me."

He lowered his eyes in shame.

"I am sorry, but we are afraid of these men and their friends. It took all my courage just to send my son for help. Please forgive us."

Achsah stood there looking at the merchants, one by one. They had gathered around and were showing the same fear and shame. She looked down at her would-be assailants, who were beginning to regain consciousness.

"I forgive you," she said, looking at the merchants and smiling.

Just then Eber and his troops arrived. As his men seized the assailants, he turned to Achsah.

"Is your Highness well?"

"I am fine, Eber."

"You should never be in the streets at night," he rebuked her. "It is unsafe. These men of Belial have the courage that only darkness brings."

"I am sorry, Eber. I am so used to freely moving about, I gave no consideration to possible dangers."

"That is OK. These men shall not harm you any more. For attacking you, they shall be taken out of the city and slain."

Achsah was amused by the sudden fear showing in the would-be attackers' eyes. But as quickly as it came, she felt remorse. *Forgive me, Father.*

"Eber, do I have the power to forgive?"

"Yes, your Highness. But you would be wasting it on these worthless ones."

She stepped forward, looking the leader in the eyes.

"According to the law of Salem, you and your friends should die for attacking me. But my God could have slain you moments ago and did not. I, the wife of Melchizedek the servant of the most high God, cannot do what He would not do. I forgive you. You are free to go."

As the soldiers released them, the men fell to their knees before the queen. The leader looked up at her and spoke loudly.

"You have spared your humble servant. From this day forward, we shall be your guardians. No man shall touch thee nor mistreat thee."

Eber moved closer to the queen and whispered in her ear.

"I would not have forgiven them, but this is Amittai. A rough man of the streets, but he is also a truthful man. If he says he will protect thee, he means it."

"Rise Amittai. I accept your protection. But that means that you must never again assault any woman nor cause harm to anyone else except in my defense."

"Yes, your Highness."

"Forget the highness. I am your queen, but I do not want titles. Just call me Achsah."

From that day on, Amittai and his friends became her constant companions. Welcoming the protection, Achsah saw the opportunity and began sharing the message of the Redeemer with them. By the time Shem would next appear, these ungodly heathen would have become worshipers of the One God and His Redeemer.

But it went much further then that. The news of the queen's gracious forgiveness spread quickly throughout Salem. Many hearts were turned toward God.

# FIFTY

## JOB

1990BC (pop. 15,978,332)

It had been sixty-eight years since Job first arrived in Uz. A fact that gave Job a great sense of gratitude toward God. The reason was easy to discern.

In those sixty-eight years he had been richly blessed. On the same day of arriving, he met the beautiful Sitidos, who lived up to her name by being an excellent cook. Her father, Berechiah, provided a rich dowry for his daughter when they married a year later. But Job inherited all of Berechiah's wealth when the great man died five years later. When combined with his own wealth, this inheritance meant that he now owned large herds of sheep and oxen, along with many servants to care for them. He had become the wealthiest man in Uz!

As he stepped out of his house, he thought about his nine children. His seven sons were good, strong men that he counted upon to manage their lands and cattle. He often wondered what he would do without such faithful sons. His two daughters were in the house with their mother, who was pregnant again.

Looking down the street he noticed a man walking toward him with a familiar stride. Joy quickly filled his heart. *It is Eliphaz! But why on foot?*

He watched with apprehension as his friend approached with head down. *Something is wrong.*

Eliphaz stopped in front of him.

"Hello, Eliphaz. Here on business?"

"Actually, I need a favor Job."

Job was taken aback by the somber tone. For the past sixty years they had been friends and business associates. It had always been a friendly, trusting relationship in which they had overcome both great trials and adversity. But Job had never seen his friend so downcast.

"Have a seat," he replied waving his friend toward a bench overlooking the city. As the two took a seat, Eliphaz continued staring at his feet.

"I need your help, Job," he finally spoke. "I foolishly invested all my money in what I thought was a sure thing. But now I am about to lose everything."

"How much do you owe?"

"One hundred talents of silver."

Job sat stunned! *One hundred talents?* He took a deep breath.

"That's what friends are for Eliphaz. Let me ask you a question. Do you still have that herd of camels near Teman?"

"Yes, but no one will buy them. Last I heard you weren't interested. Said you had more than you could handle."

"True, but like I said, that is what friends are for. I will pay a hundred talents for your camels. Would that help?"

"Yes! But are you sure you can pay that much?"

"Yes. My wife will object since we are expecting another child. But you are worth a little nagging."

Eliphaz smiled and wiped away a tear.

"Thank you, Job. You were my last hope."

Job quietly placed his hand upon his friend's knee.

"Don't thank me, my friend. Thank the Lord. He put me in position to help you. I was not really your last hope. God loves you. He is your real hope."

"For you, not for me. God has not blessed me like He has you. I don't know how you live such a righteous life Job, but I envy you."

"It's not me, Eliphaz. Any righteousness I have comes from God."

"But look at you," Eliphaz objected. "You are a teacher of righteousness. You have strengthened weak hands and feeble knees. You are young, yet old men look to you for guidance. With hardly a thought, you help me and encourage me. Surely God is pleased with you."

"I pray that you are correct," Job responded. "But none of those things of which you have spoken are of me alone. It is not my works that God is pleased with, but His works that He worketh in me. He desires to work in you also Eliphaz. You're a good and generous man. But God wants your heart more than your body. Trust in the Redeemer, Who shall take away all our sins."

"I know, I know. That is why I like being your friend, Job. You are close to God and I'm not."

Job smiled and shook his head.

"Hanging around me won't make you any closer to God. If that worked, I would send you to my friend Abram. Now there's a man that loves God. The Lord is going to use him in a mighty way. But the only way to draw closer to God is to trust and obey Him.

"Some day He will send His Redeemer into this wicked world and He will redeem us of our sins. If you want to give thanks, thank God for His great love!"

"Easy to say, Job. But I'm not sure that will work for me."

&&&

A few days later, the transaction completed, Job found himself owning a herd of camels that were grazing east of Uz. The purchase temporarily dried up his funds, but God continued to bless.

Already king and powerful, this herd of camels played an important part in increasing his wealth over the next seven years. But none of this affected him. Through it all he remained a humble man worshiping God and raising his children to also worship God.

His fame as a godly and wise man spread throughout Uz. People sought him out for advice and help. And whenever possible he extended a helping hand.

His reputation was such that he attracted Satan's attention. Not satisfied with his successful corruption of Mizraim and Phut, Satan turned his attention upon this godly man. He called his princes into his presence.

"I have heard of this Job. He worships God and is known as a just man. He stands as a beacon to the people. If he is not brought down, people will be attracted to his God. I will not allow that to happen."

All the princes remained quiet, waiting for his decision. After what seemed a long time, he looked them over with a savage smile creasing his face.

"Destroy his cattle. Cause him to lose all that he has."

With that simple command, the wicked angels sprang into action. Their goal: cause Job major disasters. Their strategy was simple: stir up the hearts of the people round about so that they would attack Job and destroy his possessions. But all their efforts failed!

They tried to stir up the Sabeans, but they failed. They turned to the Chaldeans, Job's relatives moving into the area, and failed. Every attempt failed miserably. The people, even those that hated Job, remained aloof. There simply wasn't any interest.

As each report of failure came to him, Satan angrily realized that God had placed a hedge about Job and Job's possessions. They couldn't touch him!

Satan clutched his fist. *Someday I will find a way to attack this Job. I don't know how, but I will!*

# FIFTY ONE

## LOT

1985BC (pop. 21,478,256)

Lot found his uncle checking on his shepherds, who were tending his flocks.

"Uncle Abram, I need to speak with you about something important."

Abram nodded and gave some last instructions.

"I know that each of you know how to fight. But you need to know more. From now on, I want you to train as an army. You are only few in number, but a small well-trained force can defeat a larger force. Remember that Nimrod still rules, while Chedorlaomer is rising in the east."

Finished, he turned to his nephew.

"What is it, Lot?"

"I have noticed that you walk close to God."

"I try."

"Well, I have observed you. I want to know this God of yours."

Abram studied Lot and quietly nodded.

"Let's go over to yonder tree and I will share with you about the Almighty God."

The two men walked over to the tree and sat under its spreading shadow.

"Lot, God is our Creator. He created this earth and all that is therein out of nothing. He created man and woman. Moreover, when Adam and Eve sinned and were cast out of the Garden of Eden, He promised them a Redeemer."

"I have heard of this tale before, but I thought that was all it was, just a tale," Lot remarked.

"It is more than that, Lot. I have been privileged to see the written Words of God that tell of this event. It really happened.

"But the promised Redeemer is also real! We are all born sinners and our sins need to be redeemed just as you would redeem a slave."

"A slave? I am not a slave."

"Not in the literal sense, but you are spiritually. We all are slaves to our human nature, which is full of hypocrisy, anger, and jealousy. Worst of all, we tend to worship idols, which bring us into even greater slavery. The Redeemer will some day change all that."

"You know Him?"

"In a matter of speaking, yes," Abram replied, smiling.

Lot was quiet as he thought over what had been said.

"What great work must I do to get to know this Redeemer like you know Him?" he finally asked.

Abram smiled.

"It is not great works that God wants, but an obedient servant. He has rules He wants us to follow, but it is our heart He really wants."

"What rules?"

"First, He wants us to worship Him and not idols. Second, He wants us to be honest. He wants us to treat one another with respect, to separate ourselves from the ungodly, and to trust Him for our daily needs."

"How does one trust a God you cannot see?"

"It is both easy and hard. Hard, because we want to see and touch. Easy, because it is with the heart we believe."

"I would like to believe in this God," Lot stated.

"Then simply believe and obey. Worship Him and not the idols of your kindred. Trust and obey, Lot. There is no other way. Place your trust in Him and He will take care of you."

Lot closed his eyes and prayed quietly. *O God, I believe You are the God of Adam, the God of Noah, and the God of Abram. I trust You now with all my heart.*

&&&

On the eastern shore of the Tigris, Chedorlaomer stood. Beside him was his top general.

"What do you see, general?"

"The Tigris, your highness."

"What do you see on the other side?"

"The land of Shiner."

"Mark my words, general, the day will come when I shall rule all of the land of Shiner. I shall rule to the Great Sea, that I am told lies to the west."

"Your men shall follow you wherever you go, my lord. But what about Nimrod?"

"We have an understanding. He still rules and the people think he is the greatest man alive. But he knows that his army and navy are no match for us. Our own forces are superior to anything he can send against us. But it is convenient for me to allow him to continue to rule.

"Still, the day will come when I tire of such generosity. Then I shall seize his kingdom!"

&&&

"Hey, Lot!"

Lot turned and smiled warmly as he spotted his friend Almodad heading his way. A few moments later the two friends embraced.

"Almodad, my friend, it has been awhile. Are you moving here from Ur?"

"Yes, it has been awhile," agreed his friend. "But I still live in Ur. Business is thriving and father has sent me here to see Coz the Merchant."

"Coz?" Lot raised his eyebrows. "Almodad, there is a reason he is called Coz. It is not that he is physically nimble, but that his honesty is suspect. When it comes to truth, he is very nimble."

"Perhaps, but he is also the most successful merchant here in Haran. He deals with all the caravans coming through. One has to be careful, but dealing with him can also be very profitable. Why don't you come with me and find out for yourself?"

Lot frowned. The reputation of Coz among the citizens of Haran was not high. *Yes, he is successful. But he is a liar and a dishonest businessman. He is also a seller of slaves and of wine. Ha, from what I hear, his wine is cheap and mixed with strange herbs that can rob a man of his wits. He is certainly not the type of man I should do business with! But Almodad is my friend. Surely, I shall be safe with him.*

"Sounds good to me," he replied.

&&&

Lot and Almodad arrived at Coz' tent where the merchant welcomed them.

"And what can I do for you, my friends?"

"My name is Almodad and I believe my father has already communicated to you our needs."

"Yes, that he has. But before we settle up, let me introduce you to a new drink called beer."

"Beer? What is that?"

"It is a new invention. Have you ever heard the Hymn to Ninkasi? No? I thought not. In any case, it has the recipe for making beer. Seems it comes from bread. I have it on good authority that barley is used. Seems they discovered this when the barley set too long."

He produced a flask and poured some beer into three cups. As Lot tasted the beer, he thought, *I could get to like this.*

"Come and let us settle on the price."

Lot stayed outside while the two men entered the tent. He smiled as he heard them already bickering over price. He knew it could take quite awhile for the two men to come to agreement, but he also knew that both men already knew the final price. It was just a matter of intense haggling. He took another drink.

Wandering outside the tent, Lot looked over the merchandise that lay on the ground. *It is believed that Coz deals with bandits and other sons of Belial to get his merchandise. But I must admit, he has some good merchandise. This beer is excellent!*

Two hours later, the men exited the tent having come to a final agreement. Lot approached Coz and began negotiating for the merchandise, among which was a golden image of Ishtar.

&&&

"What's the meaning of this?" Sarai shouted at Lot.

Lot looked at her with guilt all over his face. It had been weeks since his purchase of the idol and he had kept it hidden among his garments. But today it had fallen out when Sarai moved the pile, as she was looking for a missing jewel.

Lot lowered his head in shame.

"It was beautiful. It means nothing to me."

"Beautiful! You call this gross image beautiful? Lot, if Abram were to see this he would banish you from our home. You must destroy it!"

Lot paled. But he knew she was right. Taking the idol from her hands, he left. But with each step, he found it harder to destroy the golden image. He finally decided to take the image to a trader, who bought the idol for less than a third of what he had paid. *At least I made some money back*, he thought.

But later that night his conscience assailed him and he went to the altar to ask God for forgiveness. It soon became apparent to Lot that Abram knew of his failure although Abram never spoke to him about it. But a certain degree of coolness affected their relationship from that day onward.

# FIFTY TWO

## SECOND CHANCE

1983BC (pop. 23,651,978)

A servant came and presented a leather scroll to Abram. He took it, broke the seal, and noted with pleasure that it was from Job.

"Sarai! Job has written us."

"What's he up to now?" she asked.

He looked down, reading the letter.

"It says that they now have seven children! Can you believe that?"

"Yes. But I wish God would open my womb so that I could bare you children."

"It will come. I am sure of it.

"Hey, listen to this," he added, his voice rising. "He is the wealthiest man in all of Uz. Wealthy and respected. And all his children worship God!"

"That is wonderful. He has always been a man who loved God."

"Yes, that is true," he sighed.

"You miss him, don't you?"

"Yes. Job and I, though separated by years and distance, have always had a connection with each other. Did you know I was born just before he left for Uz?

"Yes, my lord, you have told me before."

Abram smiled sheepishly.

"I wish I had known him as a child. Our hearts would have been knit right from the beginning."

He sighed again. *It is good to know that Job still follows God and that God's hand of blessing is upon him.*

&&&

"Abram."

Abram shielded his eyes. Having just stepped out of his father's house where he and his family were quietly celebrating his 75th year, his eyes were momentarily blinded by the bright sun. Focusing his eyes, he became aware that standing before him was a Being he knew immediately was God Himself. He stretched out upon the ground.

"Remove thy sandals for thou art on holy ground."

Quickly removing his sandals, he resumed his position.

"Get thee out of thy country, and from thy kindred, and from thy father's house, unto a land that I will shew thee: And I will make of thee a great nation, and I will bless thee, and make thy name great; and thou shalt be a blessing:

"And I will bless them that bless thee, and curse him that curseth thee: and in thee shall all families of the earth be blessed."

Abram listened in shock. God had specifically mentioned his father.

"But my father is old and his days are short. Perchance he shall die."

"Let the dead bury the dead. Thou art to leave thy father's house and I will make of thee a great nation."

Then He was gone.

&&&

Sarai was excited. She embraced Abram, who blushed at such a public expression of love.

"I am so tired of this town," she said. "We can all move right away as far I am concerned."

"All? Sarai, He only indicated the two of us. No one else."

"Surely, we can't leave your father. He is old and frail. He needs us. He could die at any time. Not only that, but what about Lot? He worships the ground you walk on. Are you going to leave him?"

Abram sighed. Arguing with her was going to be difficult. *Just the same, God said to leave my kindred and my father.*

"Abram, you didn't answer me."

"Sarai, God was very specific. He said to leave my kindred."

"OK. That means your father. Lot can still go."

"Lot is my nephew."

"Precisely, but God probably meant your family. That means your father."

"Woman, you give me a headache! God said leave, and I must leave."

"Then it will be without me! Lot is like a son to us, or at least a close brother. If God wants you to leave your father and all his house - that is one thing. But not Lot!"

"OK. OK," he said, giving into her. "But I will expect him to worship with us on a regular basis. No more absences!"

Sarai rejoiced triumphantly.

As Abram watched his wife hurry off to tell Lot, a disturbing thought crossed his mind. *I have given into my wife's demands rather than God's command. This will mean trouble!*

Then he remembered Shem's warning: "Partial obedience is disobedience."

# FIFTY THREE

## MELCHIZEDEK

1983BC (*continued*)

Shem emerged from the forest and beheld the town of Ararat for the first time in seventeen years. With the sunlight bearing down from straight overhead it seemed the same sleepy town he had known when Noah had lived there. The thought of Noah gave him pause. *What a man! He gave so much to the world and yet he chose this town to live and die in above all others. He loved everyone here and was loved in return.*

The town had grown since his last visit, although only in a small way. As he sat on his horse studying it, he could see small homes and shops. Peering intently, he spotted his own home and Noah's. They were too far away to see detail, but he could still picture them in his mind.

Resuming his ride, he rode into town and watched with a smile as the townspeople moved about in the same slow, easy manner he remembered so well. Riding up to the first cross street, he turned right and continued until he was outside the house where he and Achsah had lived. As he approached, he noticed little girls sitting on what was a new porch to him. He didn't see any boys, but then remembered that they were probably in school. A woman stepped out to call the girls inside. Pausing, she gave the man a head to toe appraisal before re-entering the house. *I guess I am a stranger now. She didn't recognize me although I remember her. Back then she was only about thirteen, but who could forget those eyes!*

He shook the reins and the horse continued moving forward. Shem guided it to his father's old house. Even from the outside, the house looked in bad shape. Weeds were all around the house and some seemed to grow from within the house itself.

*Abandoned*! Dismounting, he approached the house and saw that the door was ajar. Stepping inside, he immediately noticed the cobwebs and other signs of decay. He shook his head in dismay. He had anticipated that the town would maintain the house, if for no other reason than to honor and remember Noah.

*I wonder if I should clean it up?* He stood there, looking around. *Broken furniture, dust, cobwebs, and general decay. If I was going to stay here, I could fix it up. But it seems no one cares.*

He stepped out and met a man coming up to the house.

"Hello. Are you looking for someone?" the man asked in a friendly voice.

"No, I was just checking out this house. Who lived here before?"

"Well, now that you mention it I don't know. It's been empty a long time."

Shem stared in disbelief.

"I see," Shem responded. "You lived here long?"

"Yep, my whole life. Oh, I'm sorry, I'm the mayor of Ararat. Welcome to our small town? Are you staying in town tonight?"

"Thank you. No. I plan on riding up the mountain trail and visiting the Ark."

"The Ark? Wait, that's it. Old man Noah lived in this very house. I'd forgotten.

"As for the Ark, I was not quite twelve yet when he died. Mother wouldn't let me go to the funeral. So I've never seen it myself, but I hear it's pretty impressive. We occasionally get people who want to visit it. Be careful going up the trail, I hear it can be dangerous."

Shem forced a smile, nodding his head as he mounted his horse and rode toward the trail. *How sad. The greatest man that has ever lived this side of the Flood and they hardly remember him! Yet all of them are from his loins! Worse than that, the Ark that preserved mankind during the world-wide Flood and they are not even interested in visiting it.* He shook his head again.

Continuing on, he reached the trail. While the trail was now overgrown with grass and weeds, he was still able to make good time and was able to reach the caves where he, his brothers and their wives had spent that stormy night so many years ago.

Spending a quiet night there, he awoke early the next morning and rode the rest of the way to the plateau, reaching it before noon. As he rode onto the plateau, he halted and stared at the magnificent ship.

*It is as impressive now as it was then!*

He turned and rode to the blocked up cave.

Dismounting, he paused. *Here lies the grave of the greatest man since the Flood and the altar he once worshiped now stands in ruins, a silent testimony to neglect.*

Entering an adjoining cave that he and his brothers had not closed up, he lighted a candle and set it in a craggy place. The whole cave was immediately illuminated.

Retreating outside, he went over to the broken down altar and set about rebuilding it. It was late afternoon by the time he finished. Setting his tools aside, he knelt before the altar.

"O God, it breaks my heart how the people have forgotten the man who You used to bring us to this new world. He lived among them, he loved them and took care of them. While all others left, he remained behind like a silent guard. Both for them and this Ark. But the people have forgotten him and the Ark. I suppose that is to be expected since they have also forgotten You."

He paused, wiping the tears from his eyes. Taking a deep breath, he continued.

"Dear God. It has been three hundred and sixty seven years since the Ark landed on this mountain. So much has taken place. I pray that You are pleased with Your servant. I have tried to be faithful in the recording of history. I have preached Your Word and been a witness to many of Your faithfulness, love, care, and judgment. But, instead of responding with their own love toward You, most have turned from You and now worship a host of gods. They deny you, refuse to hear Your good news of the Redeemer. They laugh and scorn those who believe in You."

He paused again as the tears flowed unchecked.

"This is probably my last visit to this wonderful spot. I understand why Adam always remembered Eden, even to the building of a little Eden in his home. I cannot build a new Ark or construct a mountain such as Ararat, but they reside in my mind forever!

"Now I come to Thee seeking Thy blessing and direction even as my father did before me."

His heart breaking, Shem stopped speaking and waited. Years of praying and waiting on God had taught him that it could be hours before hearing an answer. Patiently he waited.

Thus, he was surprised when God spoke as his last words were drifting away.

"Shem, My faithful and loyal servant, I am well pleased with thee. You have been faithful in all that I have directed you. The people have not rejected you, but Me. So comfort yourself in this knowledge: you have served me well and the words of your records will be a blessing to multitudes. But I am not done with thee.

"Arise, return thou unto Salem and take up the mantel as the priest of the Most High God and the king of Salem. Henceforth, thou art Melchizedek. Eber shall be with you and shall teach you to be king. Indeed, he shall outlive you and take back the kingship when you die. But thou art my priest and thy priesthood shall continue forever."

Shem listened in shock. *A priesthood forever?*

"O my God, I shall do all as Thou sayest, but what shall happen to the Ark? It stands as a testimony to Thy faithfulness and Thy judgment. Will thou use it to restore the people's faith?"

"The Ark is holy, but if I choose to hide the Ark or reveal it anew, what is that to you? Leave it in My care. Only be thou faithful!"

As silence once again settled over the plateau, Melchizedek realized that God had departed. Rising, he walked back to his campsite and prepared a meal. As the sun dipped behind the mountain peak and darkness settled over the land, he lay down for the night. *Tomorrow I shall return to Salem and to my Achsah. There I shall be priest and king. God must still have a role for me that He has not yet revealed. Dear God, I shall await Your revelation with an eager heart.*

## THE END

# Would you like to see your manuscript become a book?

If you are interested in becoming a PublishAmerica author, please submit your manuscript for possible publication to us at:

**acquisitions@publishamerica.com**

You may also mail in your manuscript to:

**PublishAmerica
PO Box 151
Frederick, MD 21705**

---

# We also offer free graphics for Children's Picture Books!

---

# www.publishamerica.com

CPSIA information can be obtained at www.ICGtesting.com
Printed in the USA
LVOW110848010612

284147LV00001B/48/P